CW00516081

Henry A. Bee

Brief History of English and American Literature

Henry A. Beers

Brief History of English and American Literature

1st Edition | ISBN: 978-3-75231-379-6

Place of Publication: Frankfurt am Main, Germany

Year of Publication: 2020

Outlook Verlag GmbH, Germany.

Reproduction of the original.

BRIEF HISTORY OF ENGLISH AND AMERICAN LITERATURE

by
HENRY A. BEERS

In so brief a history of so rich a literature, the problem is how to get room enough to give, not an adequate impression—that is impossible—but any impression at all of the subject. To do this I have crowded out everything but *belles-lettres*. Books in philosophy, history, science, etc., however important in the history of English thought, receive the merest incidental mention, or even no mention at all. Again, I have omitted the literature of the Anglo-Saxon period, which is written in a language nearly as hard for a modern Englishman to read as German is, or Dutch. Caedmon and Cynewulf are no more a part of English literature than Vergil and Horace are of Italian. I have also left out {8} the vernacular literature of the Scotch before the time of Burns. Up to the date of the union Scotland was a separate kingdom, and its literature had a development independent of the English, though parallel with it.

In dividing the history into periods, I have followed, with some modifications, the divisions made by Mr. Stopford Brooke in his excellent little *Primer of English Literature*. A short reading course is appended to each chapter.

CHAPTER I.

FROM THE CONQUEST TO CHAUCER.

1066-1400.

The Norman conquest of England, in the 11th century, made a break in the natural growth of the English language and literature. The old English or Anglo-Saxon had been a purely Germanic speech, with a complicated grammar and a full set of inflections. For three hundred years following the battle of Hastings this native tongue was driven from the king's court and the courts of law, from parliament, school, and university. During all this time there were two languages spoken in England. Norman French was the birth-tongue of the upper classes and English of the lower. When the latter finally got the better in the struggle, and became, about the middle of the 14th century, the national speech of all England, it was no longer the English of King Alfred. It was a new language, a grammarless tongue, almost wholly {12} stripped of its inflections. It had lost a half of its old words, and had filled their places with French equivalents. The Norman lawyers had

2

introduced legal terms; the ladies and courtiers, words of dress and courtesy. The knight had imported the vocabulary of war and of the chase. The master-builders of the Norman castles and cathedrals contributed technical expressions proper to the architect and the mason. The art of cooking was French. The naming of the living animals, *ox, swine, sheep, deer,* was left to the Saxon churl who had the herding of them, while the dressed meats, *beef, pork, mutton, venison,* received their baptism from the table-talk of his Norman master. The four orders of begging friars, and especially the Franciscans or Gray Friars, introduced into England in 1224, became intermediaries between the high and the low. They went about preaching to the poor, and in their sermons they intermingled French with English. In their hands, too, was almost all the science of the day; their *medicine, botany,* and *astronomy* displaced the old nomenclature of *leechdom, wort-cunning,* and *star-craft.* And, finally, the translators of French poems often found it easier to transfer a foreign word bodily than to seek out a native synonym, particularly when the former supplied them with a rhyme. But the innovation reached even to the commonest words in every-day use, so that *voice* drove out *steven, poor* drove out *earm,* and *color, use,* and *place* made good their footing beside *hue,* {13} *wont,* and *stead.* A great part of the English words that were left were so changed in spelling and pronunciation as to be practically new. Chaucer stands, in date, midway between King Alfred and Alfred Tennyson, but his English differs vastly more from the former's than from the latter's. To Chaucer Anglo-Saxon was as much a dead language as it is to us.

The classical Anglo-Saxon, moreover, had been the Wessex dialect, spoken and written at Alfred's capital, Winchester. When the French had displaced this as the language of culture, there was no longer a "king's English" or any literary standard. The sources of modern standard English are to be found in the East Midland, spoken in Lincoln, Norfolk, Suffolk, Cambridge, and neighboring shires. Here the old Anglian had been corrupted by the Danish settlers, and rapidly threw off its inflections when it became a spoken and no longer a written language, after the Conquest. The West Saxon, clinging more tenaciously to ancient forms, sunk into the position of a local dialect; while the East Midland, spreading to London, Oxford, and Cambridge, became the literary English in which Chaucer wrote.

The Normans brought in also new intellectual influences and new forms of literature. They were a cosmopolitan people, and they connected England with the continent. Lanfranc and Anselm, the first two Norman archbishops of Canterbury, were learned and splendid prelates of a {14} type quite unknown to the Anglo-Saxons. They introduced the scholastic philosophy taught at the University of Paris, and the reformed discipline of the Norman abbeys. They bound the English Church more closely to Rome, and officered it with Normans. English bishops were deprived of their sees for illiteracy, and French abbots were set over monasteries of Saxon monks. Down to the middle of the 14th century the learned literature of England was mostly in Latin, and the polite literature in French. English did not at any time altogether cease to be a written language, but the extant remains of the period from 1066 to 1200 are few and, with one exception, unimportant. After 1200 English came more and more into written use, but mainly in translations, paraphrases, and imitations of French works. The native genius was at school, and followed awkwardly the copy set by its master.

The Anglo-Saxon poetry, for example, had been rhythmical and alliterative. It was commonly written in lines containing four rhythmical accents and with three of the accented syllables alliterating.

_R_este hine thâ _r_úm-heort; _r_éced hlifade
_G_eáp and _g_óld-fâh, gäst inne swäf.

Rested him then the great-hearted; the hall towered
Roomy and gold-bright, the guest slept within.

This rude energetic verse the Saxon *scôp* had sung to his harp or *glee-beam*, dwelling on the {15} emphatic syllables, passing swiftly over the others which were of undetermined number and position in the line. It was now displaced by the smooth metrical verse with rhymed endings, which the French introduced and which our modern poets use, a verse fitted to be recited rather than sung. The old English alliterative verse continued, indeed, in occasional use to the 16th century. But it was linked to a forgotten literature and an obsolete dialect, and was doomed to give way. Chaucer lent his great authority to the more modern verse system, and his own literary models and inspirers were all foreign, French or Italian. Literature in England began to be once more English and truly national in the hands of Chaucer and his contemporaries, but it was the literature of a nation cut off from its own past by three centuries of foreign rule.

The most noteworthy English document of the 11th and 12th centuries was the continuation of the Anglo-Saxon chronicle. Copies of these annals, differing somewhat among themselves, had been kept at the monasteries in Winchester, Abingdon, Worcester, and elsewhere. The yearly entries were mostly brief, dry records of passing events, though occasionally they become full and animated. The fen country of Cambridge and Lincolnshire was a region of monasteries. Here were the great abbeys of Peterborough and Croyland and Ely minster. One of the earliest English songs tells how the savage heart of the Danish {16} king Cnut was softened by the singing of the monks in Ely.

4

Merie sungen muneches binnen Ely
Tha Cnut chyning reu ther by;
Roweth, cnihtes, noer the land,
And here we thes muneches sang.

It was among the dikes and marshes of this fen country that the bold outlaw Hereward, "the last of the English," held out for some years against the conqueror. And it was here, in the rich abbey of Burch or Peterborough, the ancient Medeshamstede (meadow-homestead) that the chronicle was continued for nearly a century after the Conquest, breaking off abruptly in 1154, the date of King Stephen's death. Peterborough had received a new Norman abbot, Turold, "a very stern man," and the entry in the chronicle for 1170 tells how Hereward and his gang, with his Danish backers, thereupon plundered the abbey of its treasures, which were first removed to Ely, and then carried off by the Danish fleet and sunk, lost, or squandered. The English in the later portions of this Peterborough chronicle becomes gradually more modern, and falls away more and more from the strict grammatical standards of the classical Anglo-Saxon. It is a most valuable historical monument, and some passages of it are written with great vividness, notably the sketch of William the Conqueror put down in the year of his death (1086) by one who had "looked upon him and at another time dwelt in his court." {17} "He who was before a rich king, and lord of many a land, he had not then of all his land but a piece of seven feet.... . Likewise he was a very stark man and a terrible, so that one durst do nothing against his will.... . Among other things is not to be forgotten the good peace that he made in this land, so that a man might fare over his kingdom with his bosom full of gold unhurt. He set up a great deer preserve, and he laid laws therewith that whoso should slay hart or hind, he should be blinded. As greatly did he love the tall deer as if he were their father."

With the discontinuance of the Peterborough annals, English history written in English prose ceased for three hundred years. The thread of the nation's story was kept up in Latin chronicles, compiled by writers partly of English and partly of Norman descent. The earliest of these, such as Ordericus Vitalis, Simeon of Durham, Henry of Huntingdon, and William of Malmesbury, were contemporary with the later entries of the Saxon chronicle. The last of them, Matthew of Westminster, finished his work in 1273. About 1300 Robert, a monk of Gloucester, composed a chronicle in English verse, following in the main the authority of the Latin chronicles, and he was succeeded by other rhyming chroniclers in the 14th century. In the hands of these the true history of the Saxon times was overlaid with an ever-increasing mass of fable and legend. All real knowledge of the period {18} dwindled away until in Capgrave's *Chronicle of England*, written in prose in 1463-64, hardly any thing of it is left. In history as in literature the English had forgotten their past, and had turned to foreign sources. It is noteworthy that Shakspere, who borrowed his subjects and his heroes sometimes from authentic English history, sometimes from the legendary history of ancient Britain, Denmark, and Scotland, as in Lear, Hamlet, and Macbeth, ignores the Saxon period altogether. And Spenser, who gives in his second book of the *Faerie Queene*, a *resumé* of the reigns of fabulous British kings—the supposed ancestors of Queen Elizabeth, his royal patron—has nothing to say of the real kings of early England. So completely had the true record faded away that it made no appeal to the imaginations of our most patriotic poets. The Saxon Alfred had been dethroned by the British Arthur, and the conquered Welsh had imposed their fictitious genealogies upon the dynasty of the conquerors. In the *Roman de Rou*, a verse chronicle of the dukes of Normandy, written by the Norman Wace, it is related that at the battle of Hastings the French *jongleur*, Taillefer, spurred out before the van of William's army, tossing his lance in the air and chanting of "Charlemagne and of Roland, of Oliver and the peers who died at Roncesvals." This incident is prophetic of the victory which Norman song, no less than Norman arms, was to win over England. The lines which Taillefer {19} sang were from the *Chanson de Roland*, the oldest and best of the French hero sagas. The heathen Northmen, who had ravaged the coasts of France in the 10th century, had become in the course of one hundred and fifty years, completely identified with the French. They had accepted Christianity, intermarried with the native women, and forgotten their own Norse tongue. The race thus formed was the most brilliant in Europe. The warlike, adventurous spirit of the vikings mingled in its blood with the French nimbleness of wit and fondness for display. The Normans were a nation of knights-errant, with a passion for prowess and for courtesy. Their architecture was at once strong and graceful. Their women were skilled in embroidery, a splendid sample of which is preserved in the famous Bayeux tapestry, in which the conqueror's wife, Matilda, and the ladies of her court wrought the history of the Conquest.

This national taste for decoration expressed itself not only in the ceremonious pomp of feast and chase and tourney, but likewise in literature. The most characteristic contribution of the Normans to English poetry were the metrical romances or chivalry tales. These were sung or recited by the minstrels, who were among the retainers of every great feudal baron, or by the *jongleurs*, who wandered from court to castle. There is a whole literature of these *romans d' aventure* in the Anglo-Norman dialect of French. Many of them are {20} very long—often thirty, forty, or fifty thousand lines—written sometimes in a strophic form, sometimes in long Alexandrines, but commonly in the short, eight-syllabled rhyming couplet. Numbers of them were turned into English verse in the 13th, 14th, and 15th centuries. The translations were usually inferior to the originals. The French *trouvere* (finder or poet) told his story in a straight-forward, prosaic fashion, omitting no details in the action and unrolling endless descriptions of dresses, trappings, gardens, etc. He invented plots and situations full of fine possibilities by which later poets have profited, but his own handling of them was feeble and prolix. Yet there was a simplicity about the old French language and a certain elegance and delicacy in the diction of the *trouveres* which the rude, unformed English failed to catch.

The heroes of these romances were of various climes: Guy of Warwick, and Richard the Lion Heart of England, Havelok the Dane, Sir Troilus of Troy, Charlemagne, and Alexander. But, strangely enough, the favorite hero of English romance was that mythical Arthur of Britain, whom Welsh legend had celebrated as the most formidable enemy of the Sassenach invaders and their victor in twelve great battles. The language and literature of the ancient Cymry or Welsh had made no impression on their Anglo-Saxon conquerors. There are a few Welsh borrowings in the English speech, such as *bard* and *druid*; but in the old Anglo-Saxon literature there are {21} no more traces of British song and story than if the two races had been sundered by the ocean instead of being borderers for over six hundred years. But the Welsh had their own national traditions, and after the Norman Conquest these were set free from the isolation of their Celtic tongue and, in an indirect form, entered into the general literature of Europe. The French came into contact with the old British literature in two places: in the Welsh marches in England and in the province of Brittany in France, where the population is of Cymric race and spoke, and still to some extent speaks, a Cymric dialect akin to the Welsh.

About 1140 Geoffrey of Monmouth, a Benedictine monk, seemingly of Welsh descent, who lived at the court of Henry the First and became afterward bishop of St. Asaph, produced in Latin a so-called *Historia Britonum* in which it was told how Brutus, the great grandson of Aeneas, came to Britain, and founded there his kingdom called after him, and his city of New Troy (Troynovant) on the site of the later London. An air of historic gravity was given to this tissue of Welsh legends by an exact chronology and the genealogy of the British kings, and the author referred, as his authority, to an imaginary Welsh book given him, as he said, by a certain Walter, archdeacon of Oxford. Here appeared that line of fabulous British princes which has become so familiar to modern readers in the plays of Shakspere and the poems of Tennyson: Lear and his {22} three daughters; Cymbeline, Gorboduc, the subject of the earliest regular English tragedy, composed by Sackville and acted in 1562; Locrine and his Queen Gwendolen, and his daughter Sabrina, who gave her name to the river Severn, was made immortal by an exquisite song in Milton's *Comus*, and became the heroine of the tragedy of *Locrine*, once attributed to Shakspere; and above all, Arthur, the son of Uther Pendragon, and the founder of the Table Round. In 1155 Wace, the author of the *Roman de Rou*, turned Geoffrey's work into a French poem entitled *Brut d' Angleterre*, "brut" being a Welsh word meaning chronicle. About the year 1200 Wace's poem was Englished by Layamon, a priest of Arley Regis, on the border stream of Severn. Layamon's *Brut* is in thirty thousand lines, partly alliterative and partly rhymed, but written in pure Saxon English with hardly any French words. The style is rude but vigorous, and, at times, highly imaginative. Wace had amplified Geoffrey's chronicle somewhat, but Layamon made much larger additions, derived, no doubt, from legends current on the Welsh border. In particular the story of Arthur grew in his hands into something like fullness. He tells of the enchantments of Merlin, the wizard; of the unfaithfulness of Arthur's queen, Guenever; and the treachery of his nephew, Modred. His narration of the last great battle between Arthur and Modred; of the wounding of the king—"fifteen fiendly wounds he had, one might in the least {23} three gloves thrust—"; and of the little boat with "two women therein, wonderly dight," which came to bear him away to Avalun and the Queen Argante, "sheenest of all elves," whence he shall come again, according to Merlin's prophecy, to rule the Britons; all this left little, in essentials, for Tennyson to add in his *Death of Arthur*. This new material for fiction was eagerly seized upon by the Norman romancers. The story of Arthur drew to itself other stories which were afloat. Walter Map, a gentleman of the Court of Henry II., in two French prose romances, connected with it the church legend of the Sangreal, or holy cup, from which Christ had drunk at his last supper, and which Joseph of Arimathea had afterward brought to England. Then it miraculously disappeared and became thenceforth the occasion of knightly quest, the mystic symbol of the object of the soul's desire, an adventure only to be achieved by the maiden knight, Galahad, the son of the great Launcelot, who in the romances had taken the place of Modred in Geoffrey's history, as the paramour of Queen Guenever. In like manner the love-story of Tristan and Isolde was joined by other romancers to the Arthur-Saga. This came probably from Brittany or Cornwall. Thus there grew up a great epic cycle of Arthurian romance, with a fixed shape and a unity and vitality which have prolonged it to our own day and rendered it capable of a deeper and more spiritual treatment and a more artistic {24} handling by such modern English poets as Tennyson in his *Idyls of the King*, by Matthew Arnold, Swinburne, and many others. There were innumerable Arthur romances in prose and verse, in Anglo-Norman and continental French dialects, in English, in German, and in other tongues. But the final form which the Saga took in mediaeval England was the prose *Morte Dartur* of Sir Thomas Malory, composed at the close of the 15th century. This was a digest of the earlier romances and is Tennyson's main authority.

Beside the literature of the knight was the literature of the cloister. There is a considerable body of religious writing in early English, consisting of homilies in prose and verse, books of devotion, like the *Ancren Riwle* (Rule of Anchoresses), 1225; the *Ayenbite of Inwyt* (Remorse of Conscience), 1340, both in prose; the *Handlyng Sinne*, 1303; the *Cursor Mundi*, 1320; and the *Pricke of Conscience*, 1340, in verse; metrical renderings of the Psalter, the Pater Noster, the Creed, and the Ten Commandments, the Gospels for the Day, such as the *Ormulum*, or Book of Orm, 1205; legends and miracles of saints; poems in praise of virginity, on the contempt of the world, on the five joys of the Virgin, the five wounds of Christ, the eleven pains of hell, the seven deadly sins, the fifteen tokens of the coming judgment, and dialogues between the soul and the body. These were the work not only of the monks, but also of the begging friars, and in {25} smaller part of the secular or parish clergy. They are full of the ascetic piety and superstition of the Middle Age, the childish belief in the marvelous, the allegorical interpretation of Scripture texts, the grotesque material horrors of hell with its grisly fiends, the vileness of the human body and the loathsome details of its corruption after death. Now and then a single poem rises above the tedious and hideous barbarism of the general level of this monkish literature, either from a more intensely personal feeling in the poet, or from an occasional grace or beauty in his verse. A poem so distinguished is, for example, *A Luve Ron* (A Love Counsel) by the Minorite friar, Thomas de Hales, one stanza of which recalls the French poet Villon's *Balade of Dead Ladies*, with its refrain.

> "Mais ou sont les neiges d'antan?"
> "Where are the snows of yester year?
> Where is Paris and Heleyne
>   That weren so bright and fair ofblee[1]
> Amadas, Tristan, and Idéyne
>   Yseudë and allë the,[2]
> Hector with his sharpë main,
>   And Caesar rich in worldës fee?
> They beth ygliden out of the reign[3]
>   As the shaft is of the dee." [4]

A few early English poems on secular subjects are also worthy of mention, among others, *The Owl and the Nightingale*, generally assigned to the reign of Henry III. (1216-1272), an *Estrif*, {26} or dispute, in which the owl represents the ascetic and the nightingale the aesthetic view of life. The debate is conducted with much animation and a spirited use of proverbial wisdom. *The Land of Cokaygne* is an amusing little poem of some two hundred lines, belonging to the class of *fabliaux*, short humorous tales or satirical pieces in verse. It describes a lubber-land, or fool's paradise, where the geese fly down all roasted on the spit, bringing garlic in the bills for their dressing, and where there is a nunnery upon a river of sweet milk, and an abbey of white monks and gray, whose walls, like the hall of little King Pepin, are "of pie-crust and pastry crust," with flouren cakes for the shingles and fat puddings for the pins.

There are a few songs dating from about 1300, and mostly found in a single collection (Harl, MS., 2253), which are almost the only English verse before Chaucer that has any sweetness to a modern ear. They are written in French strophic forms in the southern dialect, and sometimes have an intermixture of French and Latin lines. They are musical, fresh, simple, and many of them very pretty. They celebrate the gladness of spring with its cuckoos and throstle-cocks, its daisies and woodruff.

"When the nightingalë sings the woodës waxen green
Leaf and grass and blossom spring in Averil, I ween,
And love is to my hertë gone with a spear so keen,
Night and day my blood it drinks my hertë doth me tene."[5]

{27} Others are love plaints to "Alysoun" or some other lady whose "name is in a note of the nightingale;" whose eyes are as gray as glass, and her skin as "red as rose on ris." [6] Some employ a burden or refrain.

"Blow, northern wind,
Blow thou me, my sweeting.
Blow, northern wind, blow, blow, blow!"

Others are touched with a light melancholy at the coming of winter.

"Winter wakeneth all my care
Now these leavës waxeth bare.
Oft I sigh and mournë sare
When it cometh in my thought
Of this worldes joy, how it goeth all to nought"

Some of these poems are love songs to Christ or the Virgin, composed in the warm language of earthly passion. The sentiment of chivalry united with the ecstatic reveries of the cloister had produced Mariolatry and the imagery of the Song of Solomon, in which Christ wooes the soul, had made this feeling of divine love familiar. Toward the end of the 13th century a collection of lives of saints, a sort of English *Golden Legend*, was prepared at the great abbey of Gloucester for use on saints' days. The legends were chosen partly from the hagiology of the Church Catholic, as the lives of Margaret, Christopher, and Michael; partly from the calendar of the English Church, as the {28} lives of St. Thomas of Canterbury, of the Anglo-Saxons, Dunstan,

Swithin—who is mentioned by Shakspere—and Kenelm, whose life is quoted by Chaucer in the *Nonne Presto's Tale.* The verse was clumsy and the style monotonous, but an imaginative touch here and there has furnished a hint to later poets. Thus the legend of St. Brandan's search for the earthly paradise has been treated by Matthew Arnold and William Morris.

About the middle of the 14th century there was a revival of the Old English alliterative verse in romances like *William and the Werewolf,* and *Sir Gawayne,* and in religious pieces such as *Clannesse* (purity), *Patience* and *The Perle,* the last named a mystical poem of much beauty, in which a bereaved father sees a vision of his daughter among the glorified. Some of these employed rhyme as well as alliteration. They are in the West Midland dialect, although Chaucer implies that alliteration was most common in the north. "I am a sotherne man," says the parson in the *Canterbury Tales.* "I cannot geste rom, ram, ruf, by my letter." But the most important of the alliterative poems was the *Vision of William concerning Piers the Plowman.* In the second half of the 14th century French had ceased to be the mother-tongue of any considerable part of the population of England. By a statute of Edward III., in 1362, it was displaced from the law courts. By 1386 English had taken its place in the schools. The {29} Anglo-Norman dialect had grown corrupt, and Chaucer contrasts the French of Paris with the provincial French spoken by his prioress, "after the scole of Stratford-atte-Bowe." The native English genius was also beginning to assert itself, roused in part, perhaps, by the English victories in the wars of Edward III. against the French. It was the bows of the English yeomanry that won the fight at Crecy, fully as much as the prowess of the Norman baronage. But at home the times were bad. Heavy taxes and the repeated visitations of the pestilence, or Black Death, pressed upon the poor and wasted the land. The Church was corrupt; the mendicant orders had grown enormously wealthy, and the country was eaten up by a swarm of begging friars, pardoners, and apparitors. The social discontent was fermenting among the lower classes, which finally issued in the communistic uprising of the peasantry, under Wat Tyler and Jack Straw. This state of things is reflected in the *Vision of Piers Plowman,* written as early as 1362, by William Langland, a tonsured clerk of the west country. It is in form an allegory, and bears some resemblance to the later and more famous allegory of the *Pilgrim's Progress.* The poet falls asleep on the Malvern Hills, in Worcestershire, and has a vision of a "fair field full of folk," representing the world with its various conditions of men. There were pilgrims and palmers; hermits with hooked staves, who went to Walsingham—and {30} their wenches after them—great lubbers and long that were loth to work: friars glossing the Gospel for their own profit; pardoners cheating the people with relics and indulgences; parish priests who forsook their parishes—that had

11

been poor since the pestilence time—and went to London to sing there for simony; bishops, archbishops, and deacons, who got themselves fat clerkships in the Exchequer, or King's Bench; in short, all manner of lazy and corrupt ecclesiastics. A lady, who represents holy Church, then appears to the dreamer, explains to him the meaning of his vision, and reads him a sermon the text of which is, "When all treasure is tried, truth is the best." A number of other allegorical figures are next introduced, Conscience, Reason, Meed, Simony, Falsehood, etc., and after a series of speeches and adventures, a second vision begins in which the seven deadly sins pass before the poet in a succession of graphic impersonations, and finally all the characters set out on a pilgrimage in search of St. Truth, finding no guide to direct them save Piers the Plowman, who stands for the simple, pious laboring man, the sound heart of the English common folk. The poem was originally in eight divisions or "passus," to which was added a continuation in three parts, *Vita Do Wel, Do Bet,* and *Do Best.* About 1377 the whole was greatly enlarged by the author.

Piers Plowman was the first extended literary work after the Conquest which was purely English in character. It owed nothing to France but the {31} allegorical cast which the *Roman de la Rose* had made fashionable in both countries. But even here such personified abstractions as Langland's Fair-speech and Work-when-time-is, remind us less of the Fraunchise, Bel-amour, and Fals-semblaunt of the French courtly allegories than of Bunyan's Mr. Worldly Wiseman, and even of such Puritan names as Praise-God Barebones, and Zeal-of-the-land Busy. The poem is full of English moral seriousness, of shrewd humor, the hatred of a lie, the homely English love for reality. It has little unity of plan, but is rather a series of episodes, discourses, parables, and scenes. It is all astir with the actual life of the time. We see the gossips gathered in the ale-house of Betun the brewster, and the pastry cooks in the London streets crying "Hote pies, hote! Good gees and grys. Go we dine, go we!" Had Langland not linked his literary fortunes with an uncouth and obsolescent verse, and had he possessed a finer artistic sense and a higher poetic imagination, his book might have been, like Chaucer's, among the lasting glories of our tongue. As it is, it is forgotten by all but professional students of literature and history. Its popularity in its own day is shown by the number of MSS. which are extant, and by imitations, such as *Piers the Plowman's Crede* (1394), and the *Plowman's Tale,* for a long time wrongly inserted in the *Canterbury Tales.* Piers became a kind of typical figure, like the French peasant, *Jacques Bonhomme,* and was {32} appealed to as such by the Protestant reformers of the 16th century.

The attack upon the growing corruptions of the Church was made more systematically, and from the stand-point of a theologian rather than of a popular moralist and satirist, by John Wyclif, the rector of Lutterworth and professor of Divinity in Baliol College, Oxford. In a series of Latin and English tracts he made war against indulgences, pilgrimages, images, oblations, the friars, the pope, and the doctrine of transubstantiation. But his greatest service to England was his translation of the Bible, the first complete version in the mother tongue. This he made about 1380, with the help of Nicholas Hereford, and a revision of it was made by another disciple, Purvey, some ten years later. There was no knowledge of Hebrew or Greek in England at that time, and the Wiclifite versions were made not from the original tongues, but from the Latin Vulgate. In his anxiety to make his rendering close, and mindful, perhaps, of the warning in the Apocalypse, "If any man shall take away from the words of the book of this prophecy, God shall take away his part out of the book of life," Wiclif followed the Latin order of construction so literally as to make rather awkward English, translating, for example, *Quid sibi vult hoc somnium?* by *What to itself wole this sweven?* Purvey's revision was somewhat freer and more idiomatic. In the reigns of Henry IV. and V. it was forbidden to read or to have any {33} of Wiclif's writings. Such of them as could be seized were publicly burned. In spite of this, copies of his Bible circulated secretly in great numbers. Forshall and Madden, in their great edition (1850), enumerate one hundred and fifty MSS. which had been consulted by them. Later translators, like Tyndale and the makers of the Authorized Version, or "King James' Bible" (1611), followed Wiclif's language in many instances; so that he was, in truth, the first author of our biblical dialect and the founder of that great monument of noble English which has been the main conservative influence in the mother-tongue, holding it fast to many strong, pithy words and idioms that would else have been lost. In 1415; some thirty years after Wiclif's death, by decree of the Council of Constance, his bones were dug up from the soil of Lutterworth chancel and burned, and the ashes cast into the Swift. "The brook," says Thomas Fuller, in his *Church History*, "did convey his ashes into Avon; Avon into Severn; Severn into the narrow seas; they into the main ocean. And thus the ashes of Wiclif are the emblem of his doctrine, which now is dispersed all the world over."

Although the writings thus far mentioned are of very high interest to the student of the English language, and the historian of English manners and culture, they cannot be said to have much importance as mere literature. But in Geoffrey Chaucer (died 1400) we meet with a poet of the first rank, whose works are increasingly read and {34} will always continue to be a source of delight and refreshment to the general reader as well as a "well of English undefiled" to the professional man of letters. With the exception of Dante, Chaucer was the greatest of the poets of mediaeval Europe, and he remains one of the greatest of English poets, and certainly the foremost of English story-tellers in verse. He was the son of a London vintner, and was in his youth in the service of Lionel, Duke of Clarence, one of the sons of Edward III. He made a campaign in France in 1359-60, when he was taken prisoner. Afterward he was attached to the court and received numerous favors and appointments. He was sent on several diplomatic missions by the king, three of them to Italy, where, in all probability, he made the acquaintance of the new Italian literature, the writings of Dante, Petrarch, and Boccaccio. He was appointed at different times Comptroller of the Wool Customs, Comptroller of Petty Customs, and Clerk of the Works. He sat for Kent in Parliament, and he received pensions from three successive kings. He was a man of business as well as books, and he loved men and nature no less than study. He knew his world; he "saw life steadily and saw it whole." Living at the center of English social and political life, and resorting to the court of Edward III., then the most brilliant in Europe, Chaucer was an eye-witness of those feudal pomps which fill the high-colored pages of his contemporary, the French chronicler, {35} Froissart. His description of a tournament in the *Knight's Tale* is unexcelled for spirit and detail. He was familiar with dances, feasts, and state ceremonies, and all the life of the baronial castle, in bower and hall, the "trompes with the loude minstralcie," the heralds, the ladies, and the squires,

> "What hawkës sitten on the perch above,
> What houndës liggen on the floor adown."

But his sympathy reached no less the life of the lowly, the poor widow in her narrow cottage, and that "trewe swynkere and a good," the plowman whom Langland had made the hero of his vision. He is, more than all English poets, the poet of the lusty spring, of "Aprille with her showres sweet" and the "foulës song," of "May with all her floures and her greenë," of the new leaves in the wood, and the meadows new powdered with the daisy, the mystic Marguerite of his *Legend of Good Women*. A fresh vernal air blows through all his pages.

In Chaucer's earlier works, such as the translation of the *Romaunt of the Rose* (if that be his), the *Boke of the Duchesse*, the *Parlament of Foules*, the *Hous of Fame*, as well as in the *Legend of Good Women*, which was later, the inspiration of the French court poetry of the 13th and 14th centuries is manifest. He retains in them the mediaeval machinery of allegories and dreams, the elaborate descriptions of palaces, {36} temples, portraitures, etc., which had been made fashionable in France by such poems as Guillaume de Lorris's *Roman de la Rose*, and Jean Machault's *La Fontaine Amoureuse*. In some of these the influence of Italian poetry is also perceptible. There are suggestions from Dante, for example, in the *Parlament of Foules* and the *Hous of Fame*, and *Troilus and Cresseide* is a free handling rather than a translation of Boccaccio's *Filostrato*. In all of these there are passages of great beauty and force. Had Chaucer written nothing else, he would still have been remembered as the most accomplished English poet of his time, but he would not have risen to the rank which he now occupies, as one of the greatest English poets of all time. This position he owes to his masterpiece, the *Canterbury Tales*. Here he abandoned the imitation of foreign models and the artificial literary fashions of his age, and wrote of real life from his own ripe knowledge of men and things.

The *Canterbury Tales* are a collection of stories written at different times, but put together, probably, toward the close of his life. The frame-work into which they are fitted is one of the happiest ever devised. A number of pilgrims who are going on horseback to the shrine of St. Thomas à Becket, at Canterbury, meet at the Tabard Inn, in Southwark, a suburb of London. The jolly host of the Tabard, Harry Bailey, proposes that on their way to Canterbury, each of the company shall tell two tales, and two more on their way back, and {37} that the one who tells the best shall have a supper at the cost of the rest when they return to the inn. He himself accompanies them as judge and "reporter." In the setting of the stories there is thus a constant feeling of movement and the air of all outdoors. The little "head-links" and "end-links" which bind them together, give incidents of the journey and glimpses of the talk of the pilgrims, sometimes amounting, as in the prologue of the *Wife of Bath*, to full and almost dramatic character-sketches. The stories, too, are dramatically suited to the narrators. The general prologue is a series of such character-sketches, the most perfect in English poetry. The portraits of the pilgrims are illuminated with the soft brilliancy and the minute loving fidelity of the miniatures in the old missals, and with the same quaint precision in traits of expression and in costume. The pilgrims are not all such as one would meet nowadays at an English inn. The presence of a knight, a squire, a yeoman archer, and especially of so many kinds of ecclesiastics, a nun, a friar, a monk, a pardoner, and a sompnour or apparitor, reminds us that the England of that day must have been less like Protestant England, as we know it, than like the Italy of some thirty years ago. But however the outward face of society may have changed, the Canterbury pilgrims remain, in Chaucer's description, living and universal types of human nature. The *Canterbury Tales* are twenty-four in number. There were {38} thirty-two pilgrims, so that if finished as designed the whole collection would have numbered one hundred and twenty-eight stories.

Chaucer is the bright consummate flower of the English Middle Age. Like many another great poet, he put the final touch to the various literary forms that he found in cultivation. Thus his *Knight's Tale*, based upon Boccaccio's *Teseide*, is the best of English mediaeval romances. And yet the *Rime of Sir*

Thopas, who goes seeking an elf queen for his mate, and is encountered by the giant Sir Olifaunt, burlesques these same romances with their impossible adventures and their tedious rambling descriptions. The tales of the prioress and the second nun are saints' legends. The *Monk's Tale* is a set of dry, moral apologues in the manner of his contemporary, the "moral Gower." The stories told by the reeve, miller, friar, sompnour, shipman, and merchant, belong to the class of *fabliaux*, a few of which existed in English, such as *Dame Siriz*, the *Lay of the Ash*, and the *Land of Cokaygne*, already mentioned. The *Nonne Preste's Tale*, likewise, which Dryden modernized with admirable humor, was of the class of *fabliaux*, and was suggested by a little poem in forty lines, *Dou Coc et Werpil*, by Marie de France, a Norman poetess of the 13th century. It belonged, like the early English poem of *The Fox and the Wolf*, to the popular animal-saga of *Reynard the Fox*. The *Franklin's Tale*, whose scene is Brittany, and the *Wife of Baths' {39} Tale*, which is laid in the time of the British Arthur, belong to the class of French *lais*, serious metrical tales shorter than the romance and of Breton origin, the best representatives of which are the elegant and graceful *lais* of Marie de France.

Chaucer was our first great master of laughter and of tears. His serious poetry is full of the tenderest pathos. His loosest tales are delightfully humorous and life-like. He is the kindliest of satirists. The knavery, greed, and hypocrisy of the begging friars and the sellers of indulgences are exposed by him as pitilessly as by Langland and Wiclif, though his mood is not like theirs, one of stern, moral indignation, but rather the good-natured scorn of a man of the world. His charity is broad enough to cover even the corrupt sompnour of whom he says,

"And yet in sooth he was a good felawe."

Whether he shared Wiclif's opinions is unknown, but John of Gaunt, the Duke of Lancaster and father of Henry IV., who was Chaucer's life-long patron, was likewise Wiclif's great upholder against the persecution of the bishops. It is, perhaps, not without significance that the poor parson in the *Canterbury Tales*, the only one of his ecclesiastical pilgrims whom Chaucer treats with respect, is suspected by the host of the Tabard to be a "loller," that is, a Lollard, or disciple of Wiclif, and that because he objects to the jovial inn-keeper's swearing "by Goddes bones."

{40} Chaucer's English is nearly as easy for a modern reader as Shakspere's, and few of his words have become obsolete. His verse, when rightly read, is correct and melodious. The early English was, in some respects, more "sweet upon the tongue" than the modern language. The vowels had their broad Italian sounds, and the speech was full of soft gutturals and vocalic syllables, like the endings ën, ës, and ë, which made feminine rhymes and kept the consonants from coming harshly together.

Great poet as Chaucer was, he was not quite free from the literary weakness of his time. He relapses sometimes into the babbling style of the old chroniclers and legend writers; cites "auctours" and gives long catalogues of names and objects with a *naïve* display of learning; and introduces vulgar details in his most exquisite passages. There is something childish about almost all the thought and art of the Middle Ages—at least outside of Italy, where classical models and traditions never quite lost their hold. But Chaucer's artlessness is half the secret of his wonderful ease in story-telling, and is so engaging that, like a child's sweet unconsciousness, one would not wish it otherwise.

The *Canterbury Tales* had shown of what high uses the English language was capable, but the curiously trilingual condition of literature still continued. French was spoken in the proceedings of Parliament as late as the reign of Henry {41} VI. (1422-1471). Chaucer's contemporary, John Gower, wrote his *Vox Clamantis* in Latin, his *Speculum Meditantis* (a lost poem), and a number of *ballades* in Parisian French, and his *Confessio Amantis* (1393) in English. The last named is a dreary, pedantic work, in some 15,000 smooth, monotonous, eight-syllabled couplets, in which Grande Amour instructs the lover how to get the love of Bel Pucell.

1. Early English Literature. By Bernhard ten Brink. Translated from the German by H. M. Kennedy. New York: Henry Holt & Co., 1883.

2. Morris and Skeat's Specimens of Early English. (Clarendon Press Series.) Oxford.

3. Langland's Vision of William concerning Piers the Plowman. Wright's Edition; or Skeat's, in Early English Text Society publications.

4. Chaucer: Canterbury Tales. Tyrwhitt's Edition; or Wright's, in Percy Society publications.

5. Complete Writings. Morris's Edition. 6 vols. (In Aldine Series.)

[1] Hue.

[2] Those.

[3] Realm.

[4] Bowstring.

[5] Pain.

[6] Branch.

{42}

CHAPTER II

FROM CHAUCER TO SPENSER.

1400-1599.

The 15th century was a barren period in English literary history. It was nearly two hundred years after Chaucer's death before any poet came, whose name can be written in the same line with his. He was followed at once by a number of imitators who caught the trick of his language and verse, but lacked the genius to make any fine use of them. The manner of a true poet may be learned, but his style, in the high sense of the word, remains his own secret. Some of the poems which have been attributed to Chaucer and printed in editions of his works, as the *Court of Love*, the *Flower and the Leaf*, the *Cuckow and the Nightingale*, are now regarded by many scholars as the work of later writers. If not Chaucer's, they are of Chaucer's school, and the first two, at least, are very pretty poems after the fashion of his minor pieces, such as the *Boke of the Duchesse* and the *Parlament of Foules*.

Among his professed disciples was Thomas Occleve, a dull rhymer, who, in his *Governail of Princes*, a didactic poem translated from the Latin {43} about 1413, drew, or caused to be drawn, on the margin of his MS. a colored portrait of his "maister dere and fader reverent,"

>   "This londes verray tresour andrichesse,
>   Dethe by thy dethe hath harm irreparable
>   Unto us done; hir vengeable duresse
>   Dispoiled hath this londe of the swetnesse
>   Of Rhetoryk."

Another versifier of this same generation was John Lydgate, a Benedictine monk, of the Abbey of Bury St. Edmunds, in Suffolk, a very prolix writer, who composed, among other things, the *Story of Thebes*, as an addition to the *Canterbury Tales*. His ballad of *London Lyckpenny*, recounting the adventures of a countryman who goes to the law courts at Westminster in search of justice,

"But for lack of mony I could not speede,"

is of interest for the glimpse that it gives us of London street life.

Chaucer's influence wrought more fruitfully in Scotland, whither it was carried by James I., who had been captured by the English when a boy of eleven, and brought up at Windsor as a prisoner of State. There he wrote during the reign of Henry V. (1413-1422) a poem in six cantos, entitled the *King's Quhair* (King's Book), in Chaucer's seven lined stanza which had been employed by Lydgate in his *Falls of Princes* (from Boccaccio), and which was afterward called {44} the "rime royal," from its use by King James, The *King's Quhair* tells how the poet, on a May morning, looks from the window of his prison chamber into the castle garden full of alleys, hawthorn hedges, and fair arbors set with

"The sharpë, greenë, sweetë juniper."

He was listening to "the little sweetë nightingale," when suddenly casting down his eyes he saw a lady walking in the garden, and at once his "heart became her thrall." The incident is precisely like Palamon's first sight of Emily in Chaucer's *Knight's Tale*, and almost in the very words of Palamon, the poet addresses his lady:

"Ah, sweet, are ye a worldly crëature
Or heavenly thing in likeness of natúre?
Or are ye very Nature, the goddéss,
That have depainted with your heavenly hand
This garden full of flowrës as they stand?"

Then, after a vision in the taste of the age, in which the royal prisoner is transported in turn to the courts of *Venus, Minerva*, and *Fortune*, and receives their instruction in the duties belonging to Love's service, he wakes from sleep and a white turtle-dove brings to his window a spray of red gillyflowers, whose leaves are inscribed, in golden letters, with a message of encouragement.

James I. may be reckoned among the English poets. He mentions Chaucer, Gower, and Lydgate as his masters. His education was English, and so was the dialect of his poem, although the {45} unique MS. of it is in the Scotch spelling. The *King's Quhair* is somewhat overladen with ornament and with the fashionable allegorical devices, but it is, upon the whole, a rich and tender love song, the best specimen of court poetry between the time of Chaucer and the time of Spenser. The lady who walked in the garden on that May morning was Jane Beaufort, niece to Henry IV. She was married to her poet after his release from captivity and became Queen of Scotland in 1424. Twelve years later James was murdered by Sir Robert Graham and his Highlanders, and his wife, who strove to defend him, was wounded by the assassins. The story of the murder has been told of late by D. G. Rossetti, in his ballad, *The King's Tragedy*.

The whole life of this princely singer was, like his poem, in the very spirit of romance.

The effect of all this imitation of Chaucer was to fix a standard of literary style, and to confirm the authority of the East-Midland English in which he had written. Though the poets of the 15th century were not overburdened with genius, they had, at least, a definite model to follow. As in the 14th century, metrical romances continued to be translated from the French, homilies and saints' legends and rhyming chronicles were still manufactured. But the poems of Occleve and Lydgate and James I. had helped to polish and refine the tongue and to prolong the Chaucerian tradition. The literary English never again slipped {46} back into the chaos of dialects which had prevailed before Chaucer.

In the history of every literature the development of prose is later than that of verse. The latter being, by its very form, artificial, is cultivated as a fine art, and its records preserved in an early stage of society, when prose is simply the talk of men, and not thought worthy of being written and kept. English prose labored under the added disadvantage of competing with Latin, which was the cosmopolitan tongue and the medium of communication between scholars of all countries. Latin was the language of the Church, and in the Middle Ages churchman and scholar were convertible terms. The word *clerk* meant either priest or scholar. Two of the *Canterbury Tales* are in prose, as is also the *Testament of Love*, formerly ascribed to Chaucer, and the style of all these is so feeble, wandering, and unformed that it is hard to believe that they were written by the same man who wrote the *Knight's Tale* and the story of *Griselda*. *The Voiage and Travaile of Sir John Maundeville*—the forerunner of that great library of Oriental travel which has enriched our modern literature—was written, according to its author, first in Latin, then in French, and, lastly, in the year 1356, translated into English for the behoof of "lordes and knyghtes and othere noble and worthi men, that conne not Latyn but litylle." The author professed to have spent over thirty years in Eastern travel, to have penetrated as far {47} as Farther India and the "iles that ben abouten Indi," to have been in the service of the Sultan of Babylon in his wars against the Bedouins, and, at another time, in the employ of the Great Khan of Tartary. But there is no copy of the Latin version of his travels extant; the French seems to be much later than 1356, and the English MS. to belong to the early years of the fifteenth century, and to have been made by another hand. Recent investigations make it probable that Maundeville borrowed his descriptions of the remoter East from many sources, and particularly from the narrative of Odoric, a Minorite friar of Lombardy, who wrote about 1330. Some doubt is even cast upon the existence of any such person as Maundeville. Whoever wrote the book that passes under his name, however, would seem to have visited the Holy Land, and the part of the "voiage" that describes Palestine and the Levant is fairly close to the truth. The rest of the work, so far as it is not taken from the tales of other travelers, is a diverting tissue of fables about gryfouns that fly away with yokes of oxen, tribes of one-legged Ethiopians who shelter themselves from the sun by using their monstrous feet as umbrellas, etc.

During the 15th century English prose was gradually being brought into a shape fitting it for more serious uses. In the controversy between the Church and the Lollards Latin was still mainly employed, but Wiclif had written some of his tracts in English, and, in 1449, Reginald Peacock, Bishop of {48} St. Asaph, contributed, in English, to the same controversy, *The Represser of Overmuch Blaming of the Clergy.* Sir John Fortescue, who was chief-justice of the king's bench from 1442-1460, wrote during the reign of Edward IV. a book on the *Difference between Absolute and Limited Monarchy*, which may be regarded as the first treatise on political philosophy and constitutional law in the language. But these works hardly belong to pure literature, and are remarkable only as early, though not very good, examples of English prose in a barren time. The 15th century was an era of decay and change. The Middle Age was dying, Church and State were slowly disintegrating under the new intellectual influences that were working secretly under ground. In England the civil wars of the Red and White Roses were breaking up the old feudal society by decimating and impoverishing the baronage, thus preparing the way for the centralized monarchy of the Tudors. Toward the close of that century, and early in the next, happened the four great events, or series of events, which freed and widened men's minds, and, in a succession of shocks, overthrew the mediaeval system of life and thought. These were the invention of printing, the Renascence, or revival of classical learning, the discovery of America, and the Protestant Reformation.

William Caxton, the first English printer, learned the art in Cologne. In 1476 he set up his press and sign, a red pole, in the Almonry at Westminster. Just before the introduction of printing the demand {49} for MS. copies had grown very active, stimulated, perhaps, by the coming into general use of linen paper instead of the more costly parchment. The scriptoria of the monasteries were the places where the transcribing and illuminating of MSS. went on, professional copyists resorting to Westminster Abbey, for example, to make their copies of books belonging to the monastic library. Caxton's choice of a spot was, therefore, significant. His new art for multiplying copies began to supersede the old method of transcription at the very head-quarters of the MS. makers. The first book that bears his Westminster imprint was the *Dictes and Sayings of the Philosophers*, translated from the French by Anthony Woodville, Lord Rivers, a brother-in-law of Edward IV. The list of books printed by Caxton is interesting, as showing the taste of the time, as he naturally selected what was most in demand. The list shows that manuals of devotion and chivalry were still in chief request, books like the *Order of Chivalry*, *Faits of Arms*, and the *Golden Legend*, which last Caxton translated

21

himself, as well as *Reynard the Fox*, and a French version of the *Aeneid*. He also printed, with continuations of his own, revisions of several early chronicles, and editions of Chaucer, Gower, and Lydgate. A translation of *Cicero on Friendship*, made directly from the Latin, by Thomas Tiptoft, Earl of Worcester, was printed by Caxton, but no edition of a classical author in the original. The new learning of the Renascence had not, as {50} yet, taken much hold in England. Upon the whole, the productions of Caxton's press were mostly of a kind that may be described as mediaeval, and the most important of them, if we except his edition of Chaucer, was that "noble and joyous book," as Caxton called it, *Le Morte Darthur*, written by Sir Thomas Malory in 1469, and printed by Caxton in 1485. This was a compilation from French Arthur romances, and was by far the best English prose that had yet been written. It may be doubted, indeed, whether, for purposes of simple story telling, the picturesque charm of Malory's style has been improved upon. The episode which lends its name to the whole romance, the death of Arthur, is most impressively told, and Tennyson has followed Malory's narrative closely, even to such details of the scene as the little chapel by the sea, the moonlight, and the answer which Sir Bedwere made the wounded king, when bidden to throw Excalibur into the water, "'What saw thou there?' said the king. 'Sir,' he said, 'I saw nothing but the waters wap and the waves wan.'"

"I heard the ripple washing in the reeds
And the wild water lapping on the crag."

And very touching and beautiful is the oft-quoted lament of Sir Ector over Launcelot, in Malory's final chapter: "'Ah, Launcelot,' he said, 'thou were head of all Christian knights; and now I dare say,' said Sir Ector, 'thou, Sir Launcelot, there thou liest, that thou were never matched of earthly {51} knight's hand; and thou were the courtiest knight that ever bare shield; and thou were the truest friend to thy lover that ever bestrode horse; and thou were the truest lover of a sinful man that ever loved woman; and thou were the kindest man that ever strake with sword; and thou were the goodliest person ever came among press of knights; and thou were the meekest man and the gentlest that ever ate in hall among ladies; and thou were the sternest knight to thy mortal foe that ever put spear in the rest.'"

Equally good, as an example of English prose narrative, was the translation made by John Bourchier, Lord Berners, of that most brilliant of the French chroniclers, Chaucer's contemporary, Sir John Froissart. Lord Berners was the English governor of Calais, and his version of Froissart's *Chronicles* was made in 1523-25, at the request of Henry VIII. In these two books English chivalry spoke its last genuine word. In Sir Philip Sidney the character of the knight was merged into that of the modern gentleman. And although

tournaments were still held in the reign of Elizabeth, and Spenser cast his
Faery Queene into the form of a chivalry romance, these were but a
ceremonial survival and literary tradition from an order of things that had
passed away. How antagonistic the new classical culture was to the vanished
ideal of the Middle Age may be read in *Toxophilus*, a treatise on archery
published in 1545, by Roger Ascham, a Greek lecturer in Cambridge, and the
{52} tutor of the Princess Elizabeth and of Lady Jane Grey. "In our
forefathers' time, when Papistry as a standing pool covered and overflowed
all England, few books were read in our tongue saving certain books of
chivalry, as they said, for pastime and pleasure, which, as some say, were
made in monasteries by idle monks or wanton canons: as one, for example,
Morte Arthure, the whole pleasure of which book standeth in two special
points, in open manslaughter and bold bawdry. This is good stuff for wise
men to laugh at or honest men to take pleasure at. Yet I know when God's
Bible was banished the Court, and *Morte Arthure* received into the prince's
chamber."

The fashionable school of courtly allegory, first introduced into England by
the translation of the *Romaunt of the Rose*, reached its extremity in Stephen
Hawes's *Passetyme of Pleasure*, printed by Caxton's successor, Wynkyn de
Worde, in 1517. This was a dreary and pedantic poem, in which it is told how
Graunde Amoure, after a long series of adventures and instructions among
such shadowy personages as Verite, Observaunce, Falshed, and Good
Operacion, finally won the love of La Belle Pucel. Hawes was the last English
poet of note whose culture was exclusively mediaeval. His contemporary,
John Skelton, mingled the old fashions with the new classical learning. In his
Bowge of Courte (Court Entertainment or Dole), and in others of his earlier
pieces, he used, like Hawes, Chaucer's seven-lined stanza. But his later {53}
poems were mostly written in a verse of his own invention, called after him
Skeltonical. This was a sort of glorified doggerel, in short, swift, ragged lines,
with occasional intermixture of French and Latin.

"Her beautye to augment.
Dame Nature hath her lent
A warte upon her cheke,
Who so lyst to seke
In her vyságe a skar,
That semyth from afar
Lyke to the radyant star,
All with favour fret,
So properly it is set.
She is the vyolet,
The daysy delectáble,

The columbine commendáble,
The jelofer amyáble;
For this most goodly floure,
This blossom of fressh colóur,
So Jupiter me succoúr,
She florysheth new and new
In beaute and vertew;
Hac claritate gemina,
O gloriosa femina, etc."

Skelton was a rude railing rhymer, a singular mixture of a true and original poet with a buffoon; coarse as Rabelais, whimsical, obscure, but always vivacious. He was the rector of Diss, in Norfolk, but his profane and scurrilous wit seems rather out of keeping with his clerical character. His *Tunnyng of Elynoure Rummyng* is a study of very low life, reminding one slightly of Burns's *Jolly {54} Beggars.* His *Phyllyp Sparowe* is a sportive, pretty, fantastic elegy on the death of a pet bird belonging to Mistress Joanna Scroupe, of Carowe, and has been compared to the Latin poet Catullus's elegy on Lesbia's sparrow. In *Speke, Parrot,* and *Why Come ye not to Courte?* he assailed the powerful Cardinal Wolsey with the most ferocious satire, and was, in consequence, obliged to take sanctuary at Westminster, where he died in 1529. Skelton was a classical scholar, and at one time tutor to Henry VIII. The great humanist, Erasmus, spoke of him as the "one light and ornament of British letters." Caxton asserts that he had read Virgil, Ovid, and Tully, and quaintly adds, "I suppose he hath dronken of Elycon's well."

In refreshing contrast with the artificial court poetry of the 15th and first three quarters of the 16th century, was the folk-poetry, the popular ballad literature which was handed down by oral tradition. The English and Scotch ballads were narrative songs, written in a variety of meters, but chiefly in what is known as the ballad stanza.

"In somer, when the shawes[1] be sheyne,[2]
And leves be large and longe,
Hit is full merry in feyre forést
To here the foulys song.

"To se the dere draw to the dale,
And leve the hilles hee,[3]
And shadow them in the leves grene,
Under the grene-wode tree."

[55]

It is not possible to assign a definite date to these ballads. They lived on the lips of the people, and were seldom reduced to writing till many years after they were first composed and sung. Meanwhile they underwent repeated changes, so that we have numerous versions of the same story. They belonged to no particular author, but, like all folk-lore, were handled freely by the unknown poets, minstrels, and ballad reciters, who modernized their language, added to them, or corrupted them, and passed them along. Coming out of an uncertain past, based on some dark legend of heart-break or bloodshed, they bear no poet's name, but are *ferae naturae*, and have the flavor of wild game. In the forms in which they are preserved few of them are older than the 17th century, or the latter part of the 16th century, though many, in their original shape, are, doubtless, much older. A very few of the Robin Hood ballads go back to the 15th century, and to the same period is assigned the charming ballad of the *Nut Brown Maid* and the famous border ballad of *Chevy Chase*, which describes a battle between the retainers of the two great houses of Douglas and Percy. It was this song of which Sir Philip Sidney wrote, "I never heard the old song of Percy and Douglas but I found myself more moved than by a trumpet; and yet it is sung but by some blind crouder, [4] with no rougher voice than rude style." But the style of the ballads was not always rude. {56} In their compressed energy of expression, in the impassioned abrupt, yet indirect way in which they tell their tale of grief and horror, there reside often a tragic power and art superior to any English poetry that had been written since Chaucer, superior even to Chaucer in the quality of intensity. The true home of the ballad literature was "the north country," and especially the Scotch border, where the constant forays of moss-troopers and the raids and private warfare of the lords of the marches supplied many traditions of heroism, like those celebrated in the old poem of the *Battle of Otterbourne*, and in the *Hunting of the Cheviot*, or *Chevy Chase*, already mentioned. Some of these are Scotch and others English; the dialect of Lowland Scotland did not, in effect, differ much from that of Northumberland and Yorkshire, both descended alike from the old Northumbrian of Anglo-

25

Saxon times. Other ballads were shortened, popular versions of the chivalry romances which were passing out of fashion among educated readers in the 16th century, and now fell into the hands of the ballad makers. Others preserved the memory of local countryside tales, family feuds, and tragic incidents, partly historical and partly legendary, associated often with particular spots. Such are, for example, *The Dowie Dens of Yarrow*, *Fair Helen of Kirkconnell*, *The Forsaken Bride*, and *The Twa Corbies*. Others, again, have a coloring of popular superstition, like the beautiful ballad concerning {57} *Thomas of Ersyldoune*, who goes in at Eldon Hill with an Elf queen and spends seven years in fairy land.

But the most popular of all the ballads were those which cluster about the name of that good outlaw, Robin Hood, who, with his merry men, hunted the forest of merry Sherwood, where he killed the king's deer and waylaid rich travelers, but was kind to poor knights and honest workmen. Robin Hood is the true ballad hero, the darling of the common people, as Arthur was of the nobles. The names of his Confessor, Friar Tuck; his mistress, Maid Marian; his companions, Little John, Scathelock, and Much, the Miller's son, were as familiar as household words. Langland, in the 14th century, mentions "rimes of Robin Hood," and efforts have been made to identify him with some actual personage, as with one of the dispossessed barons who had been adherents of Simon de Montfort in his war against Henry III. But there seems to be nothing historical about Robin Hood. He was a creation of the popular fancy. The game laws under the Norman kings were very oppressive, and there were, doubtless, dim memories still cherished among the Saxon masses of Hereward and Edric the Wild, who had defied the power of the Conqueror, as well as of later freebooters, who had taken to the woods and lived by plunder. Robin Hood was a thoroughly national character. He had the English love of fair-play, the English readiness to shake hands and {58} make up, and keep no malice when worsted in a square fight. He beat and plundered the rich bishops and abbots, who had more than their share of wealth, but he was generous and hospitable to the distressed, and lived a free and careless life in the good green wood. He was a mighty archer, with those national weapons, the long-bow and the cloth-yard-shaft. He tricked and baffled legal authority in the person of the proud sheriff of Nottingham, thereby appealing to that secret sympathy with lawlessness and adventure which marked the free-born, vigorous yeomanry of England. And finally the scenery of the forest gives a poetic background and a never-failing charm to the exploits of "the old Robin Hood of England" and his merry men.

The ballads came, in time, to have certain tricks of style, such as are apt to characterize a body of anonymous folk-poetry. Such is their use of conventional epithets; "the red, red gold," "the good, green wood," "the gray goose wing." Such are certain recurring terms of phrase like,

"But out and spak their stepmother."

Such is, finally, a kind of sing-song repetition, which doubtless helped the ballad singer to memorize his stock, as, for example,

"She had'na pu'd a double rose,
A rose but only twae."

{59}

Or again,

"And mony ane sings o' grass, o' grass,
And mony ane sings o' corn;
An mony ane sings o' Robin Hood,
Kens little whare he was born.

It was na in the ha', the ha',
Nor in the painted bower;
But it was in the gude green wood,
Amang the lily flower."

Copies of some of these old ballads were hawked about in the 16th century, printed in black letter, "broad sides," or single sheets. Wynkyn de Worde printed, in 1489, *A Lytell Geste of Robin Hood*, which is a sort of digest of earlier ballads on the subject. In the 17th century a few of the English popular ballads were collected in miscellanies, called *Garlands*. Early in the 18th century the Scotch poet, Allan Ramsay, published a number of Scotch ballads in the *Evergreen* and *Tea-Table Miscellany*. But no large and important collection was put forth until Percy's *Reliques*, 1765, a book which had a powerful influence upon Wordsworth and Walter Scott. In Scotland some excellent ballads in the ancient manner were written in the 18th century, such as Jane Elliott's *Lament for Flodden*, and the fine ballad of Sir Patrick Spence. Walter Scott's *Proud Maisie is in the Wood*, is a perfect reproduction of the pregnant, indirect method of the old ballad makers.

In 1453 Constantinople was taken by the Turks, {60} and many Greek scholars, with their MSS., fled into Italy, where they began teaching their language and literature, and especially the philosophy of Plato. There had been little or no knowledge of Greek in western Europe during the Middle Ages, and only a very imperfect knowledge of the Latin classics. Ovid and Statius were widely read, and so was the late Latin poet, Boethius, whose *De Consolatione Philosophiae* had been translated into English by King Alfred and by Chaucer. Little was known of Vergil at first hand, and he was popularly supposed to have been a mighty wizard, who made sundry works of

27

enchantment at Rome, such as a magic mirror and statue. Caxton's so-called translation of the *Aeneid* was in reality nothing but a version of a French romance based on Vergil's epic. Of the Roman historians, orators, and moralists, such as Livy, Tacitus, Caesar, Cicero, and Seneca, there was an almost entire ignorance, as also of poets like Horace, Lucretius, Juvenal, and Catullus. The gradual rediscovery of the remains of ancient art and literature which took place in the 15th century, and largely in Italy, worked an immense revolution in the mind of Europe. MSS. were brought out of their hiding places, edited by scholars and spread abroad by means of the printing-press. Statues were dug up and placed in museums, and men became acquainted with a civilization far more mature than that of the Middle Age, and with models of perfect {61} workmanship in letters and the fine arts. In the latter years of the 15th century a number of Englishmen learned Greek in Italy and brought it back with them to England. William Grocyn and Thomas Linacre, who had studied at Florence under the refugee, Demetrius Chalcondylas, began teaching Greek, at Oxford, the former as early as 1491. A little later John Colet, Dean of St. Paul's and the founder of St. Paul's School, and his friend, William Lily, the grammarian and first master of St. Paul's (1500), also studied Greek abroad, Colet in Italy, and Lily at Rhodes and in the city of Rome. Thomas More, afterward the famous chancellor of Henry VIII., was among the pupils of Grocyn and Linacre at Oxford. Thither also, in 1497, came in search of the new knowledge, the Dutchman, Erasmus, who became the foremost scholar of his time. From Oxford the study spread to the sister university, where the first English Grecian of his day, Sir Jno. Cheke, who "taught Cambridge and King Edward Greek," became the incumbent of the new professorship founded about 1540. Among his pupils was Roger Ascham, already mentioned, in whose time St. John's College, Cambridge, was the chief seat of the new learning, of which Thomas Nash testifies that it "was as an universitie within itself; having more candles light in it, every winter morning before four of the clock, than the four of clock bell gave strokes." Greek was not introduced at the universities without violent {62} opposition from the conservative element, who were nicknamed Trojans. The opposition came in part from the priests, who feared that the new study would sow seeds of heresy. Yet many of the most devout churchmen were friends of a more liberal culture, among them Thomas More, whose Catholicism was undoubted and who went to the block for his religion. Cardinal Wolsey, whom More succeeded as chancellor, was also a munificent patron of learning and founded Christ Church College, at Oxford. Popular education at once felt the impulse of the new studies, and over twenty endowed grammar schools were established in England in the first twenty years of the 16th century. Greek became a passion even with English ladies. Ascham in his *Schoolmaster*, a treatise on education, published in 1570, says, that Queen Elisabeth "readeth here now at Windsor more Greek every day, than some prebendarie of this Church doth read Latin in a whole week." And in the same book he tells how calling once upon Lady Jane Grey, at Brodegate, in Leicestershire, he "found her in her chamber reading *Phaedon Platonis* in Greek, and that with as much delite as some gentlemen would read a merry tale in *Bocase*," and when he asked her why she had not gone hunting with the rest, she answered, "I wisse, all their sport in the park is but a shadow to that pleasure that I find in Plato." Ascham's *Schoolmaster*, as well as his earlier book, *Toxophilus*, a Platonic dialogue on archery, bristles with quotations from the Greek and Latin {63} classics, and with that perpetual reference to the authority of antiquity on every topic that he touches, which remained the fashion in all serious prose down to the time of Dryden.

One speedy result of the new learning was fresh translations of the Scriptures into English, out of the original tongues. In 1525 William Tyndal printed at Cologne and Worms his version of the New Testament from the Greek. Ten years later Miles Coverdale made, at Zurich, a translation of the whole Bible from the German and the Latin. These were the basis of numerous later translations, and the strong beautiful English of Tyndal's *Testament* is preserved for the most part in our Authorized Version (1611). At first it was not safe to make or distribute these early translations in England. Numbers of copies were brought into the country, however, and did much to promote the cause of the Reformation. After Henry VIII. had broken with the Pope the new English Bible circulated freely among the people. Tyndal and Sir Thomas More carried on a vigorous controversy in English upon some of the questions at issue between the Church and the Protestants. Other important contributions to the literature of the Reformation were the homely sermons preached at Westminster and at Paul's Cross by Bishop Hugh Latimer, who was burned at Oxford in the reign of Bloody Mary. The English Book of Common Prayer was compiled in 1549-52. More was, perhaps, the best {64} representative of a group of scholars who wished to enlighten and reform the Church from inside, but who refused to follow Henry VIII. in his breach with Rome. Dean Colet and John Fisher, Bishop of Rochester, belonged to the same company, and Fisher was beheaded in the same year (1535) with More, and for the same offense, namely, refusing to take the oath to maintain the act confirming the king's divorce from Catherine of Arragon and his marriage with Anne Boleyn. More's philosophy is best reflected in his *Utopia*, the description of an ideal commonwealth, modeled on Plato's Republic, and printed in 1516. The name signifies "no place" (*Outopos*), and has furnished an adjective to the language. The *Utopia* was in Latin, but More's *History of Edward V. and Richard III.*, written in 1513, though not printed till 1557, was in English. It is the first example in the tongue of a history as distinguished from a chronicle; that is, it is a reasoned and artistic presentation of an historic period, and not a mere chronological narrative of events.

The first three quarters of the 16th century produced no great original work of literature in England. It was a season of preparation, of education. The storms of the Reformation interrupted and delayed the literary renascence through the reigns of Henry VIII., Edward VI., and Queen Mary. When Elizabeth came to the throne, in 1558, a more settled order of things began, and a period of great national prosperity and {65} glory. Meanwhile the English mind had been slowly assimilating the new classical culture, which was extended to all classes of readers by the numerous translations of Greek and Latin authors. A fresh poetic impulse came from Italy. In 1557 appeared *Tottel's Miscellany*, containing songs and sonnets by a "new company of courtly makers." Most of the pieces in the volume had been written years before, by gentlemen of Henry VIII.'s court, and circulated in MS. The two chief contributors were Sir Thomas Wiat, at one time English embassador to Spain, and that brilliant noble, Henry Howard, the Earl of Surrey, who was beheaded in 1547 for quartering the king's arms with his own. Both of them were dead long before their work was printed. The pieces in *Tottel's Miscellany* show very clearly the influence of Italian poetry. We have seen that Chaucer took subjects and something more from Boccaccio and Petrarch. But the sonnet, which Petrarch had brought to great perfection, was first introduced into England by Wiat. There was a great revival of sonneteering in Italy in the 16th century, and a number of Wiat's poems were adaptations of the sonnets and *canzoni* of Petrarch and later poets. Others were imitations of Horace's satires and epistles. Surrey introduced the Italian blank verse into English in his translation of two books of the *Aeneid*. The love poetry of *Tottel's Miscellany* is polished and artificial, like the models which it followed. Dante's {66} Beatrice was a child, and so was Petrarch's Laura. Following their example, Surrey addressed his love complaints, by way of compliment, to a little girl of the noble Irish family of Geraldine. The Amourists, or love sonneters, dwelt on the metaphysics of the passion with a tedious minuteness, and the conventional nature of their sighs and complaints may often be guessed by an experienced reader from the titles of their poems: "Description of the restless state of a lover, with suit to his lady to rue on his dying heart;" "Hell tormenteth not the damned ghosts so sore as unkindness the lover;" "The lover prayeth not to be disdained, refused, mistrusted, nor forsaken," etc. The most genuine utterance of Surrey was his poem written while imprisoned in Windsor—a cage where so many a song-bird has grown vocal. And Wiat's little piece of eight lines, "Of his Return from Spain," is worth reams of his amatory affections. Nevertheless the writers in *Tottel's Miscellany* were real reformers of English poetry. They introduced new models of style and new metrical forms, and they broke away from the mediaeval traditions which had hitherto obtained. The language had undergone some changes since Chaucer's time, which made his scansion obsolete. The accent of many words of French origin, like *natúre, couráge, virtúe, matére,* had shifted to the first syllable, and the *e* of the final syllables *ës, ën, ëd,* and *ë,* had largely disappeared. But the language of poetry tends {67} to keep up archaisms of this kind, and in Stephen Hawes, who wrote a century after Chaucer, we still find such lines as these:

"But he my strokës might right well endure,
   He was so great and huge of puissánce." [5]

Hawes's practice is variable in this respect, and so is his contemporary, Skelton's. But in Wiat and Surrey, who wrote only a few years later, the reader first feels sure that he is reading verse pronounced quite in the modern fashion.

But Chaucer's example still continued potent. Spenser revived many of his obsolete words, both in his pastorals and in his *Faery Queene,* thereby imparting an antique remoteness to his diction, but incurring Ben Jonson's censure, that he "writ no language." A poem that stands midway between Spenser and late mediaeval work of Chaucer's school—such as Hawes's *Passetyme of Pleasure*—was the *Induction* contributed by Thomas Sackville, Lord Buckhurst, in 1563 to a collection of narrative poems called the *Mirrour for Magistrates.* The whole series was the work of many hands, modeled upon Lydgate's *Falls of Princes* (taken from Boccaccio), and was designed as a warning to great men of the fickleness of fortune. The *Induction* is the only noteworthy part of it. It was an allegory, written in Chaucer's seven-lined stanza and described with a somber imaginative power, the figure of Sorrow, her abode {68} in the "griesly lake" of Avernus and her attendants, Remorse, Dread, Old Age, etc. Sackville was the author of the first regular English tragedy, *Gorboduc,* and it was at his request that Ascham wrote the *Schoolmaster.*

Italian poetry also fed the genius of Edmund Spenser (1552-99). While a student at Pembroke Hall, Cambridge, he had translated some of the *Visions of Petrarch,* and the *Visions of Bellay,* a French poet, but it was only in 1579 that the publication of his *Shepheard's Calendar* announced the coming of a great original poet, the first since Chaucer. The *Shepheard's Calendar* was a pastoral in twelve eclogues—one for each month in the year. There had been a great revival of pastoral poetry in Italy and France, but, with one or two insignificant exceptions, Spenser's were the first bucolics in English. Two of his eclogues were paraphrases from Clement Marot, a French Protestant poet, whose psalms were greatly in fashion at the court of Francis I. The pastoral machinery had been used by Vergil and by his modern imitators, not merely to portray the loves of Strephon and Chloe, or the idyllic charms of rustic life; but also as a vehicle of compliment, elegy, satire, and personal allusion of many kinds. Spenser, accordingly, alluded to his friends, Sidney and Harvey, as the shepherds, Astrophel and Hobbinol, paid court to Queen Elizabeth as Cynthia, and introduced, in the form of anagrams, names of the High-Church Bishop of London, Aylmer, {69} and the Low-Church Archbishop Grindal. The conventional pastoral is a somewhat delicate exotic in English poetry, and represents a very unreal Arcadia. Before the end of the 17th century the squeak of the oaten pipe had become a burden, and the only piece of the kind which it is easy to read without some impatience is Milton's wonderful *Lycidas*. The *Shepheard's Calendar*, however, though it belonged to an artificial order of literature, had the unmistakable stamp of genius in its style. There was a broad, easy mastery of the resources of language, a grace, fluency, and music which were new to English poetry. It was written while Spenser was in service with the Earl of Leicester, and enjoying the friendship of his nephew, the all-accomplished Sidney, and was, perhaps, composed at the latter's country seat of Penshurst. In the following year Spenser went to Ireland as private secretary to Arthur Lord Grey of Wilton, who had just been appointed Lord Deputy of that kingdom. After filling several clerkships in the Irish government, Spenser received a grant of the castle and estate of Kilcolman, a part of the forfeited lands of the rebel Earl of Desmond. Here, among landscapes richly wooded, like the scenery of his own fairy land, "under the cooly shades of the green alders by the Mulla's shore," Sir Walter Raleigh found him, in 1589, busy upon his *Faery Queene*. In his poem, *Colin Clouts Come Home Again*, Spenser tells, in pastoral language, how "the shepherd of the {70} ocean" persuaded him to go to London, where he presented him to the Queen, under whose patronage the first three books of his great poem were printed, in 1590. A volume of minor poems, entitled *Complaints*, followed in 1591, and the three remaining books of the *Faery Queene* in 1596. In 1595-96 he published also his *Daphnaida, Prothalamion*, and the four hymns *On Love* and *Beauty*, and *On Heavenly Love* and *Heavenly Beauty*. In 1598, in Tyrone's rebellion, Kilcolman Castle was sacked and burned, and Spenser, with his family, fled to London, where he died in January, 1599.

The *Faery Queene* reflects, perhaps, more fully than any other English work, the many-sided literary influences of the renascence. It was the blossom of a richly composite culture. Its immediate models were Ariosto's *Orlando Furioso*, the first forty cantos of which were published in 1515, and Tasso's *Gerusalemme Liberata*, printed in 1581. Both of these were, in subject, romances of chivalry, the first based upon the old Charlemagne epos—

Orlando being identical with the hero of the French *Chanson de Roland*—the second upon the history of the first Crusade, and the recovery of the Holy City from the Saracen. But in both of them there was a splendor of diction and a wealth of coloring quite unknown to the rude mediaeval romances. Ariosto and Tasso wrote with the great epics of Homer and Vergil constantly in mind, and all about them was the brilliant light of Italian art, in its early freshness {71} and power. The *Faery Queene*, too, was a tale of knight-errantry. Its hero was King Arthur, and its pages swarm with the familiar adventures and figures of Gothic romance; distressed ladies and their champions, combats with dragons and giants, enchanted castles, magic rings, charmed wells, forest hermitages, etc. But side by side with these appear the fictions of Greek mythology and the personified abstractions of fashionable allegory. Knights, squires, wizards, hamadryads, satyrs, and river gods, Idleness, Gluttony, and Superstition jostle each other in Spenser's fairy land. Descents to the infernal shades, in the manner of Homer and Vergil, alternate with descriptions of the Palace of Pride in the manner of the *Romaunt of the Rose*. But Spenser's imagination was a powerful spirit, and held all these diverse elements in solution. He removed them to an ideal sphere "apart from place, withholding time," where they seem all alike equally real, the dateless conceptions of the poet's dream.

The poem was to have been "a continued allegory or dark conceit," in twelve books, the hero of each book representing one of the twelve moral virtues. Only six books and the fragment of a seventh were written. By way of complimenting his patrons and securing contemporary interest, Spenser undertook to make his allegory a double one, personal and historical, as well as moral or abstract. Thus Gloriana, the Queen of Faery, stands not only for Glory but for Elizabeth, {72} to whom the poem was dedicated. Prince Arthur is Leicester, as well as Magnificence. Duessa is Falsehood, but also Mary Queen of Scots. Grantorto is Philip II. of Spain. Sir Artegal is Justice, but likewise he is Arthur Grey de Wilton. Other characters shadow forth Sir Walter Raleigh, Sir Philip Sidney, Henry IV. of France, etc.; and such public events as the revolt of the Spanish Netherlands, the Irish rebellion, the execution of Mary Stuart, and the rising of the northern Catholic houses against Elizabeth are told in parable. In this way the poem reflects the spiritual struggle of the time, the warfare of young England against Popery and Spain.

The allegory is not always easy to follow. It is kept up most carefully in the first two books, but it sat rather lightly on Spenser's conscience, and is not of the essence of the poem. It is an ornament put on from the outside and detachable at pleasure. The "Spenserian stanza," in which the *Faery Queene* was written, was adapted from the *ottava riwa* of Ariosto. Spenser changed somewhat the order of the rimes in the first eight lines and added a ninth line of twelve syllables, thus affording more space to the copious luxuriance of his style and the long-drawn sweetness of his verse. It was his instinct to dilate and elaborate every image to the utmost, and his similes, especially—each of which usually fills a whole stanza—have the pictorial amplitude of Homer's. Spenser was, in fact, a great painter. His poetry {73} is almost purely sensuous. The personages in the *Faery Queene* are not characters, but richly colored figures, moving to the accompaniment of delicious music, in an atmosphere of serene remoteness from the earth. Charles Lamb said that he was the poet's poet, that is, he appealed wholly to the artistic sense and to the love of beauty. Not until Keats did another English poet appear so filled with the passion for all outward shapes of beauty, so exquisitely alive to all impressions of the senses. Spenser was, in some respects, more an Italian than an English poet. It is said that the Venetian gondoliers still sing the stanzas of Tasso's *Gerusalemme Liberata*. It is not easy to imagine the Thames bargees chanting passages from the *Faery Queene*. Those English poets who have taken strongest hold upon their public have done so by their profound interpretation of our common life. But Spenser escaped altogether from reality into a region of pure imagination. His aerial creations resemble the blossoms of the epiphytic orchids, which have no root in the soil, but draw their nourishment from the moisture of the air.

"*Their* birth was of the womb of morning dew, And *their* conception of the glorious prime."

Among the minor poems of Spenser the most delightful were his *Prothalamion* and *Epithalamion*. The first was a "spousal verse," made for the double wedding of the Ladies Catherine and {74} Elizabeth Somerset, whom the poet figures as two white swans that come swimming down the Thames, whose surface the nymphs strew with lilies, till it appears "like a bride's chamber-floor."

"Sweet Thames, run softly till I end my song,"

is the burden of each stanza. The *Epithalamion* was Spenser's own marriage song, written to crown his series of *Amoretti*, or love sonnets, and is the most splendid hymn of triumphant love in the language. Hardly less beautiful than these was *Muiopotmos; or, the Fate of the Butterfly*, an addition to the classical myth of Arachne, the spider. The four hymns in praise of *Love* and *Beauty*, *Heavenly Love* and *Heavenly Beauty*, are also stately and noble poems, but by reason of their abstractness and the Platonic mysticism which they express, are less generally pleasing than the others mentioned. Allegory and mysticism had no natural affiliation with Spenser's genius. He was a seer of visions, of *images* full, brilliant, and distinct, and not like Bunyan, Dante, or Hawthorne, a projector into bodily shapes of *ideas*, typical and emblematic, the shadows which haunt the conscience and the mind.

1. A First Sketch of English Literature. By Henry Morley.

2. English Writers. By the same. Vol. iii. From Chaucer to Dunbar.

{75}

3. Skeat's Specimens of English Literature, 1594-1579. Clarendon Press Series.

4. Morte Darthur. Globe Edition.

5. Child's English and Scottish Ballads. 8 vols.

6. Hale's edition of Spenser. Globe.

7. "A Royal Poet." Irving's Sketch-Book.

[1] Woods.

[2] Bright.

[3] High.

[4] Fiddler.

[5] Trisyllable—like *creature*, *neighebour*, etc, in Chaucer.

{76}

CHAPTER III.

THE AGE OF SHAKSPERE.

1564-1616.

The great age of English poetry opened with the publication of Spenser's *Shepheard's Calendar*, in 1579, and closed with the printing of Milton's *Samson Agonistes*, in 1671. Within this period of little less than a century English thought passed through many changes, and there were several successive phases of style in our imaginative literature. Milton, who acknowledged Spenser as his master, and who was a boy of eight years at Shakspere's death, lived long enough to witness the establishment of an entirely new school of poets, in the persons of Dryden and his contemporaries. But, roughly speaking, the dates above given mark the limits of one literary epoch, which may not improperly be called the Elisabethan. In strictness the Elisabethan age ended with the queen's death, in 1603. But the poets of the succeeding reigns inherited much of the glow and splendor which marked the diction of their forerunners; and "the spacious times of great Elisabeth" have been, by courtesy, prolonged to the year of the Restoration (1660). There is a certain likeness {77} in the intellectual products of the whole period, a largeness of utterance, and a high imaginative cast of thought which stamp them all alike with the queen's seal.

Nor is it by any undue stretch of the royal prerogative that the name of the monarch has attached itself to the literature of her reign and of the reigns succeeding hers. The expression "Victorian poetry" has a rather absurd sound when one considers how little Victoria counts for in the literature of her time. But in Elisabethan poetry the maiden queen is really the central figure. She is Cynthia, she is Thetis, great queen of shepherds and of the sea; she is Spenser's Gloriana, and even Shakspere, the most impersonal of poets, paid tribute to her in *Henry VIII.*, and, in a more delicate and indirect way, in the little allegory introduced into *Midsummer Night's Dream.*

> "That very time I marked—but thou could'st not—
> Flying between the cold moon and the earth,
> Cupid all armed. A certain aim he took
> At a fair vestal throned by the west,
> And loosed his love-shaft smartly from his bow
> As he would pierce a hundred thousand hearts.
> But I might see young Cupid's fiery dart
> Quenched in the chaste beams of the watery moon,
> And the imperial votaress passed on
> In maiden meditation, fancy free"—

an allusion to Leicester's unsuccessful suit for Elisabeth's hand.

The praises of the queen, which sound through {78} all the poetry of her time, seem somewhat overdone to a modern reader. But they were not merely the insipid language of courtly compliment. England had never before had a female sovereign, except in the instance of the gloomy and bigoted Mary. When she was succeeded by her more brilliant sister, the gallantry of a gallant and fantastic age was poured at the latter's feet, the sentiment of chivalry mingling itself with loyalty to the crown. The poets idealized Elisabeth. She was to Spenser, to Sidney, and to Raleigh, not merely a woman and a virgin queen, but the champion of Protestantism, the lady of young England, the heroine of the conflict against popery and Spain. Moreover Elisabeth was a great woman. In spite of the vanity, caprice, and ingratitude which disfigured her character, and the vacillating, tortuous policy which often distinguished her government, she was at bottom a sovereign of large views, strong will, and dauntless courage. Like her father, she "loved a *man*," and she had the magnificent tastes of the Tudors. She was a patron of the arts, passionately fond of shows and spectacles, and sensible to poetic flattery. In her royal progresses through the kingdom, the universities and the nobles and the cities vied with one another in receiving her with plays, revels, masques, and triumphs, in the mythological taste of the day. "When the queen paraded through a country town," says Warton, the historian of English poetry, "almost every {79} pageant was a pantheon. When she paid a visit at the house of any of her nobility, at entering the hall she was saluted by the Penates. In the afternoon, when she condescended to walk in the garden, the lake was covered with tritons and nereids; the pages of the family were converted into wood-nymphs, who peeped from every bower; and the footmen gamboled over the lawns in the figure of satyrs. When her majesty hunted in the park she was met by Diana who, pronouncing our royal prude to be the brightest paragon of unspotted chastity, invited her to groves free from the intrusions of Acteon." The most elaborate of these entertainments of which we have any notice, were, perhaps, the games celebrated in her honor by the Earl of Leicester, when she visited him at Kenilworth, in 1575. An account of these was published by a contemporary poet, George Gascoigne, *The Princely Pleasures at the Court of Kenilworth*, and Walter Scott has made them familiar to modern readers in his novel of *Kenilworth*. Sidney was present on this occasion, and, perhaps, Shakspere, then a boy of eleven, and living at Stratford, not far off, may have been taken to see the spectacle, may have seen Neptune, riding on the back of a huge dolphin in the castle lake, speak the copy of verses in which he offered his trident to the empress of the sea, and may have

> "heard a mermaid on a dolphin's back, Utter such dulcet and harmonious breath, That the rude sea grew civil at the sound."

{80} But in considering the literature of Elisabeth's reign it will be convenient to speak first of the prose. While following up Spenser's career to its close (1599), we have, for the sake of unity of treatment, anticipated somewhat the literary history of the twenty years preceding. In 1579 appeared a book which had a remarkable influence on English prose. This was John Lyly's *Euphues, the Anatomy of Wit*. It was in form a romance, the history of a young Athenian who went to Naples to see the world and get an education; but it is in substance nothing but a series of dialogues on love, friendship, religion, etc., written in language which, from the title of the book, has received the name of *Euphuism*. This new English became very fashionable among the ladies, and "that beauty in court which could not parley Euphuism," says a writer of 1632, "was as little regarded as she which now there speaks not French."

Walter Scott introduced a Euphuist into his novel the *Monastery*, but the peculiar jargon which Sir Piercie Shafton is made to talk is not at all like the real Euphuism. That consisted of antithesis, alliteration, and the profuse illustration of every thought by metaphors borrowed from a kind of fabulous natural history. "Descend into thine own conscience and consider with thyself the great difference between staring and stark-blind, wit and wisdom, love and lust; be merry, but with modesty; be sober, but not too sullen; {81} be valiant, but not too venturous." "I see now that, as the fish *Scolopidus* in the flood *Araxes* at the waxing of the moon is as white as the driven snow, and at the waning as black as the burnt coal; so Euphues, which at the first increasing of our familiarity was very zealous, is now at the last cast become most faithless." Besides the fish *Scolopidus*, the favorite animals of Lyly's menagerie are such as the chameleon, which, "though he have most guts draweth least breath;" the bird *Piralis*, "which sitting upon white cloth is white, upon green, green;" and the serpent *Porphirius*, which, "though he be full of poison, yet having no teeth, hurteth none but himself."

Lyly's style was pithy and sententious, and his sentences have the air of proverbs or epigrams. The vice of Euphuism was its monotony. On every page of the book there was something pungent, something quotable; but many pages of such writing became tiresome. Yet it did much to form the hitherto loose structure of English prose, by lending it point and polish. His carefully balanced periods were valuable lessons in rhetoric, and his book became a manual of polite conversation and introduced that fashion of witty repartee, which is evident enough in Shakspere's comic dialogue. In 1580 appeared the second part, *Euphues and his England*, and six editions of the whole work were printed before 1598. Lyly had many imitators. In Stephen Gosson's *School {82} of Abuse*, a tract directed against the stage and published about four months later than the first part of Euphues, the language is distinctly Euphuistic. The dramatist, Robert Greene, published, in 1587, his *Menaphon; Camilla's Alarum to Slumbering Euphues*, and his *Euphues's Censure to Philautus*. His brother dramatist, Thomas Lodge, published; in 1590, *Rosalynde: Euphues's Golden Legacy*, from which Shakspere took the plot of *As You Like It*. Shakspere and Ben Jonson both quote from *Euphues* in their plays, and Shakspere was really writing Euphuism, when he wrote such a sentence as "Tis true, 'tis pity; pity 'tis 'tis true."

That knightly gentleman, Philip Sidney, was a true type of the lofty aspiration and manifold activity of Elizabethan England. He was scholar, poet, courtier, diplomatist, statesman, soldier, all in one. Educated at Oxford and then introduced at court by his uncle, the Earl of Leicester, he had been sent to France when a lad of eighteen, with the embassy which went to treat of the queen's proposed marriage to the Duke of Alencon, and was in Paris at the time of the Massacre of St. Bartholomew, in 1572. Afterward he had traveled through Germany, Italy, and the Netherlands, had gone as embassador to the Emperor's Court, and every-where won golden opinions. In 1580, while visiting his sister Mary, Countess of Pembroke, at Wilton, he wrote, for her pleasure, the *Countess of Pembroke's Arcadia*, which {83} remained in MS. till 1590. This was a pastoral romance, after the manner of the Italian *Arcadia* of Sanazzaro, and the *Diana Enamorada* of Montemayor, a Portuguese author. It was in prose, but intermixed with songs and sonnets, and Sidney finished only two books and a portion of a third. It describes the adventures of two cousins, Musidorus and Pyrocles, who are wrecked on the coast of Sparta. The plot is very involved and is full of the stock episodes of romance: disguises, surprises, love intrigues, battles, jousts and single combats. Although the insurrection of the Helots against the Spartans forms a part of the story, the Arcadia is not the real Arcadia of the Hellenic Peloponnesus, but the fanciful country of pastoral romance, an unreal clime, like the Faery Land of Spenser.

Sidney was our first writer of poetic prose. The poet Drayton says that he

"did first reduce
Our tongue from Lyly's writing, then in use,
Talking of stones, stars, plants, of fishes, flies,
Playing with words and idle similes."

Sidney was certainly no Euphuist, but his style was as "Italianated" as Lyly's, though in a different way. His English was too pretty for prose. His "Sidneian showers of sweet discourse" sowed every page of the *Arcadia* with those flowers of conceit, those sugared fancies which his contemporaries loved, but which the taste of a severer {84} age finds insipid. This splendid vice of the Elisabethan writers appears in Sidney, chiefly in the form of an excessive personification. If he describes a field full of roses, he makes "the roses add such a ruddy show unto it, as though the field were bashful at his own beauty." If he describes ladies bathing in a stream, he makes the water break into twenty bubbles, as "not content to have the picture of their face in large upon him, but he would in each of those bubbles set forth the miniature of them." And even a passage which should be tragic, such as the death of his heroine, Parthenia, he embroiders with conceits like these: "For her exceeding fair eyes having with continued weeping got a little redness about them, her round sweetly swelling lips a little trembling, as though they kissed their neighbor Death; in her cheeks the whiteness striving by little and little to get upon the rosiness of them; her neck, a neck indeed of alabaster, displaying the wound which with most dainty blood labored to drown his own beauties; so as here was a river of purest red, there an island of perfectest white," etc.

The *Arcadia*, like *Euphues*, was a lady's book. It was the favorite court romance of its day, but it surfeits a modern reader with its sweetness, and confuses him with its tangle of adventures. The lady for whom it was written was the mother of that William Herbert, Earl of Pembroke, to whom Shakspere's sonnets are thought to have been {85} dedicated. And she was the subject of Ben Jonson's famous epitaph.

"Underneath this sable herse
Lies the subject of all verse,
Sidney's sister, Pembroke's mother;
Death, ere thou hast slain another
Learn'd and fair and good as she,
Time shall throw a dart at thee."

Sidney's *Defense of Poesy*, composed in 1581, but not printed till 1595, was written in manlier English than the *Arcadia*, and is one of the very few books of criticism belonging to a creative and uncritical time. He was also the author of a series of love sonnets, *Astrophel and Stella*, in which he paid Platonic court to the Lady Penelope Rich (with whom he was not at all in love), according to the conventional usage of the amourists.

Sidney died in 1586, from a wound received in a cavalry charge at Zutphen, where he was an officer in the English contingent, sent to help the Dutch against Spain. The story has often been told of his giving his cup of water to a wounded soldier with the words, "Thy necessity is yet greater than mine." Sidney was England's darling, and there was hardly a poet in the land from whom his death did not obtain "the meed of some melodious tear." Spenser's *Ruins of Time* were among the number of these funeral songs; but the best of them all was by one Matthew Royden, concerning whom little is known.

{86} Another typical Englishman of Elisabeth's reign was Walter Raleigh, who was even more versatile than Sidney, and more representative of the restless spirit of romantic adventure, mixed with cool, practical enterprise that marked the times. He fought against the Queen's enemies by land and sea in many quarters of the globe; in the Netherlands and in Ireland against Spain, with the Huguenot Army against the League in France. Raleigh was from Devonshire, the great nursery of English seamen. He was half-brother to the famous navigator, Sir Humphrey Gilbert, and cousin to another great captain, Sir Richard Grenville. He sailed with Gilbert on one of his voyages against the Spanish treasure fleet, and in 1591 he published a report of the fight, near the Azores, between Grenville's ship, the Revenue, and fifteen great ships of Spain, an action, said Francis Bacon, "memorable even beyond credit, and to the height of some heroical fable." Raleigh was active in raising a fleet against the Spanish Armada of 1588. He was present in 1596 at the brilliant action in which the Earl of Essex "singed the Spanish king's beard," in the harbor of Cadiz. The year before he had sailed to Guiana, in search of the fabled El Dorado, destroying on the way the Spanish town of San José, in the West Indies; and on his return he published his *Discovery of the Empire of Guiana*. In 1597 he captured the town of Fayal, in the Azores. He took a prominent part in colonizing {87} Virginia, and he introduced tobacco and the potato plant into Europe.

America was still a land of wonder and romance, full of rumors, nightmares, and enchantments. In 1580, when Francis Drake, "the Devonshire Skipper," had dropped anchor in Plymouth harbor, after his voyage around the world, the enthusiasm of England had been mightily stirred. These narratives of Raleigh, and the similar accounts of the exploits of the bold sailors, Davis, Hawkins, Frobisher, Gilbert, and Drake; but especially the great cyclopedia of nautical travel, published by Richard Hakluyt, in 1589, *The Principal Navigations, Voyages, and Discoveries made by the English Nation*, worked powerfully on the imaginations of the poets. We see the influence of this literature of travel in the *Tempest*, written undoubtedly after Shakspere had been reading the narrative of Sir George Somers's shipwreck on the Bermudas or "Isles of Devils."

Raleigh was not in favor with Elizabeth's successor, James I. He was sentenced to death on a trumped-up charge of high treason. The sentence hung over him until 1618, when it was revived against him and he was beheaded. Meanwhile, during his twelve years' imprisonment in the Tower, he had written his *magnum opus*, the *History of the World*. This is not a history, in the modern sense, but a series of learned dissertations on law, government, theology, magic, war, etc. A chapter with such a caption as the following {88} would hardly be found in a universal history nowadays: "Of their opinion which make Paradise as high as the moon; and of others which make it higher than the middle region of the air." The preface and conclusion are noble examples of Elisabethan prose, and the book ends with an oft-quoted apostrophe to Death. "O eloquent, just: and mighty Death! Whom none could advise, thou has persuaded; what none hath dared, thou hast done; and whom all the world hath flattered, thou only hast cast out of the world and despised; thou hast drawn together all the far-fetched greatness, all the pride, cruelty, and ambition of man, and covered it all over with these two narrow words, *hic jacet*."

Although so busy a man, Raleigh found time to be a poet. Spenser calls him "the summer's nightingale," and George Puttenham, in his *Art of English Poesy* (1589), finds his "vein most lofty, insolent, and passionate." Puttenham used *insolent* in its old sense, *uncommon*; but this description is hardly less true, if we accept the word in its modern meaning. Raleigh's most notable verses, *The Lie*, are a challenge to the world, inspired by indignant pride and the weariness of life—the *saeva indignatio* of Swift. The same grave and caustic melancholy, the same disillusion marks his quaint poem, *The Pilgrimage*. It is remarkable how many of the verses among his few poetical remains are asserted in the MSS. or by tradition to have been "made by Sir Walter {89} Raleigh the night before he was beheaded." Of one such poem the assertion is probably true, namely, the lines "found in his Bible in the gate-house at Westminster."

> "Even such is Time, that takes in trust,
> Our youth, our joys, our all we have,
> And pays as but with earth and dust;
> Who in the dark and silent grave,
> When we have wandered all our ways,
> Shuts up the story of our days;
> But from this earth, this grave, this dust,
> My God shall raise me up, I trust!"

The strictly *literary* prose of the Elisabethan period bore a small proportion to the verse. Many entire departments of prose literature were as yet undeveloped. Fiction was represented—outside of the *Arcadia* and *Euphues* already mentioned—chiefly by tales translated or imitated from Italian *novelle*. George Turberville's *Tragical Tales* (1566) was a collection of such stories, and William Paynter's *Palace of Pleasure* (1576-1577) a similar collection from Boccaccio's *Decameron* and the novels of Bandello. These translations are mainly of interest, as having furnished plots to the English dramatists. Lodge's *Rosalind* and Robert Greene's *Pandosto*, the sources respectively of Shakspere's *As You Like It* and *Winter's Tale*, are short pastoral romances, not without prettiness in their artificial way. The satirical pamphlets of Thomas Nash and his fellows, against "Martin Marprelate," an anonymous writer, or {90} company of writers, who attacked the bishops, are not wanting in wit, but are so cumbered with fantastic whimsicalities, and so bound up with personal quarrels, that oblivion has covered them. The most noteworthy of them were Nash's *Piers Penniless's Supplication to the Devil*, Lyly's *Pap with a Hatchet*, and Greene's *Groat's Worth of Wit*. Of books which were not so much literature as the material of literature, mention may be made of the *Chronicle of England*, compiled by Ralph Holinshed in 1577. This was Shakspere's English history, and its strong Lancastrian bias influenced Shakspere in his representation of Richard III. and other characters in his historical plays. In his Roman tragedies Shakspere followed closely Sir Thomas North's translation of Plutarch's *Lives*, made in 1579 from the French version of Jacques Amyot.

Of books belonging to other departments than pure literature, the most important was Richard Hooker's *Ecclesiastical Polity*, the first four books of which appeared in 1594. This was a work on the philosophy of law and a defense, as against the Presbyterians, of the government of the English Church by bishops. No work of equal dignity and scope had yet been published in English prose. It was written in sonorous, stately and somewhat involved periods, in a Latin rather than an English idiom, and it influenced strongly the diction of later writers, such as Milton and Sir Thomas Browne. Had the *Ecclesiastical Polity* been written one hundred, or perhaps even fifty, {91} years earlier, it would doubtless have been written in Latin.

The life of Francis Bacon, "the father of inductive philosophy," as he has been called—better, the founder of inductive logic—belongs to English history, and the bulk of his writings, in Latin and English, to the history of English philosophy. But his volume of *Essays* was a contribution to general literature. In their completed form they belong to the year 1625, but the first edition was printed in 1597 and contained only ten short essays, each of them rather a string of pregnant maxims—the text for an essay—than that developed treatment of a subject which we now understand by the word essay. They were, said their author, "as grains of salt that will rather give you an appetite than offend you with satiety." They were the first essays so-called in the language. "The word," said Bacon, "is late, but the thing is ancient." The word he took from the French *essais* of Montaigne, the first two books of which had been published in 1592. Bacon testified that his essays were the most popular of his writings because they "came home to men's business and bosoms." Their alternate title explains their character: *Counsels Civil and Moral*, that is, pieces of advice touching the conduct of life, "of a nature whereof men shall find much in experience, little in books." The essays contain the quintessence of Bacon's practical wisdom, his wide knowledge of the world of {92} men. The truth and depth of his sayings, and the extent of ground which they cover, as well as the weighty compactness of his style, have given many of them the currency of proverbs. "Revenge is a kind of wild justice." "He that hath wife and children hath given hostages to fortune." "There is no excellent beauty that hath not some strangeness in the proportion." Bacon's reason was illuminated by a powerful imagination, and his noble English rises now and then, as in his essay *On Death*, into eloquence—the eloquence of pure thought, touched gravely and afar off by emotion. In general, the atmosphere of his intellect is that *lumen siccum* which he loved to commend, "not drenched or bloodied by the affections." Dr. Johnson said that the wine of Bacon's writings was a dry wine.

A popular class of books in the 17th century were "characters" or "witty descriptions of the properties of sundry persons," such as theGood

Schoolmaster, the Clown, the Country Magistrate; much as in some modern *Heads of the People* where Douglas Jerrold or Leigh Hunt sketches the Medical Student, the Monthly Nurse, etc. A still more modern instance of the kind is George Eliot's *Impressions of Theophrastus Such*, which derives its title from the Greek philosopher, Theophrastus, whose character-sketches were the original models of this kind of literature. The most popular character-book in Europe in the 17th century was La Bruyère's *Caractères*. But {93} this was not published till 1588. In England the fashion had been set in 1614, by the *Characters* of Sir Thomas Overbury, who died by poison the year before his book was printed. One of Overbury's sketches—the *Fair and Happy Milkmaid*—is justly celebrated for its old-world sweetness and quaintness. "Her breath is her own, which scents all the year long of June, like a new-made hay-cock. She makes her hand hard with labor, and her heart soft with pity; and when winter evenings fall early, sitting at her merry wheel, she sings defiance to the giddy wheel of fortune. She bestows her year's wages at next fair, and, in choosing her garments, counts no bravery in the world like decency. The garden and bee-hive are all her physic and surgery, and she lives the longer for it. She dares go alone and unfold sheep in the night, and fears no manner of ill, because she means none; yet to say truth, she is never alone, but is still accompanied with old songs, honest thoughts and prayers, but short ones. Thus lives she, and all her care is she may die in the spring-time, to have store of flowers stuck upon her winding-sheet."

England was still merry England in the times of good Queen Bess, and rang with old songs, such as kept this milkmaid company; songs, said Bishop Joseph Hall, which were "sung to the wheel and sung unto the pail." Shakspere loved their simple minstrelsy; he put some of them into the mouth of Ophelia, and scattered snatches of {94} them through his plays, and wrote others like them himself:

"Now, good Cesario, but that piece of song,
That old and antique song we heard last night,
Methinks it did relieve my passion much,
More than light airs and recollected terms
Of these most brisk and giddy-paced times.
Mark it, Cesario, it is old and plain.
The knitters and the spinners in the sun
And the free maids that weave their threads with bones
Do use to chant it; it is silly sooth
And dallies with the innocence of love
Like the old age."

Many of these songs, so natural, fresh, and spontaneous, together with sonnets and other more elaborate forms of lyrical verse, were printed in miscellanies, such as the *Passionate Pilgrim*, *England's Helicon*, and Davison's *Poetical Rhapsody*. Some were anonymous, or were by poets of whom little more is known than their names. Others were by well-known writers, and others, again, were strewn through the plays of Lyly, Shakspere, Jonson, Beaumont, Fletcher, and other dramatists. Series of love sonnets, like Spenser's *Amoretti* and Sidney's *Astrophel and Stella*, were written by Shakspere, Daniel, Drayton, Drummond, Constable, Watson, and others, all dedicated to some mistress real or imaginary. Pastorals, too, were written in great number, such as William Browne's *Britannia's Pastorals* and *Shephera's Pipe* (1613-1616) and Marlowe's charmingly rococo little idyl, {95} *The Passionate Shepherd to his Love*, which Shakspere quoted in the *Merry Wives of Windsor*, and to which Sir Walter Raleigh wrote a reply. There were love stories in verse, like Arthur Brooke's *Romeo and Juliet* (the source of Shakspere's tragedy), Marlowe's fragment, *Hero and Leander*, and Shakspere's *Venus and Adonis*, and *Rape of Lucrece*, the first of these on an Italian and the other three on classical subjects, though handled in any thing but a classical manner. Wordsworth said finely of Shakspere, that he "could not have written an epic: he would have died of a plethora of thought." Shakspere's two narrative poems, indeed, are by no means models of their kind. The current of the story is choked at every turn, though it be with golden sand. It is significant of his dramatic habit of mind that dialogue and soliloquy usurp the place of narration, and that, in the *Rape of Lucrece* especially, the poet lingers over the analysis of motives and feelings, instead of hastening on with the action, as Chaucer, or any born story-teller, would have done.

In Marlowe's poem there is the same spendthrift fancy, although not the same subtlety. In the first two divisions of the poem the story does, in some sort, get forward; but in the continuation, by George Chapman (who wrote the last four "sestiads"), the path is utterly lost, "with woodbine and the gadding vine o'ergrown."

One is reminded that modern poetry, if it has {96} lost in richness, has gained in directness, when one compares any passage in Marlowe and Chapman's *Hero and Leander* with Byron's ringing lines:

"The wind is high on Helle's wave,
As on that night of stormy water,
When Love, who sent, forgot to save
The young, the beautiful, the brave,
The lonely hope of Sestos' daughter."

Marlowe's continuator, Chapman, wrote a number of plays, but he is best remembered by his royal translation of Homer, issued in parts from 1598-

1615. This was not so much a literal translation of the Greek, as a great Elisabethan poem, inspired by Homer. It has Homer's fire, but not his simplicity; the energy of Chapman's fancy kindling him to run beyond his text into all manner of figures and conceits. It was written, as has been said, as Homer would have written if he had been an Englishman of Chapman's time. Certainly all later versions—Pope's and Cowper's and Lord Derby's and Bryant's—seem pale against the glowing exuberance of Chapman's English. His verse was not the heroic line of ten syllables, chosen by most of the standard translators, but the long fourteen-syllabled measure, which degenerates easily into sing-song in the hands of a feeble metrist. In Chapman it is often harsh, but seldom tame, and in many passages it reproduces wonderfully the ocean-like roll of Homer's hexameters.

{97}

"From his bright helm and shield did burn a most unwearied fire,
Like rich Autumnus' golden lamp, whose brightness men admire,
Past all the other host of stars when, with his cheerful face,
Fresh washed in lofty ocean waves, he doth the sky enchase."

Keats's fine ode, *On First Looking into Chapman's Homer*, is well-known. Fairfax's version of Tasso's *Jerusalem Delivered* (1600) is one of the best metrical translations in the language.

The national pride in the achievements of Englishmen, by land and sea, found expression, not only in prose chronicles and in books, like Stow's *Survey of London*, and Harrison's *Description of England* (prefixed to Holinshed's *Chronicle*), but in long historical and descriptive poems, like William Warner's *Albion's England*, 1586; Samuel Daniel's *History of the Civil Wars*, 1595-1602; Michael Drayton's *Baron's Wars*, 1596, *England's Heroical Epistles*, 1598, and *Polyolbion*, 1613. The very plan of these works was fatal to their success. It is not easy to digest history and geography into poetry. Drayton was the most considerable poet of the three, but his *Polyolbion* was nothing more than "a gazeteer in rime," a topographical survey of England and Wales, with tedious personifications of rivers, mountains, and valleys, in thirty books and nearly one hundred thousand lines. It was Drayton who said of Marlowe, that he "had in him those brave translunary things that the first poets had;" and there are brave {98} things in Drayton, but they are only occasional passages, oases among dreary wastes of sand. His *Agincourt* is a spirited war-song, and his *Nymphidia; or, Court of Faery*, is not unworthy of comparison with Drake's *Culprit Fay*, and is interesting as bringing in Oberon and Robin Goodfellow, and the popular fairy lore of Shakspere's *Midsummer Night's Dream*.

The "well-languaged Daniel," of whom Ben Jonson said that he was "a good honest man, but no poet," wrote, however, one fine meditative piece, his *Epistle to the Countess of Cumberland*, a sermon apparently on the text of the Roman poet Lucretius's famous passage in praise of philosophy,

"Suave mari magno, turbantibus aequora ventis," etc.

But the Elisabethan genius found its fullest and truest expression in the drama. It is a common phenomenon in the history of literature that some old literary form or mold will run along for centuries without having any thing poured into it worth keeping, until the moment comes when the genius of the time seizes it and makes it the vehicle of immortal thought and passion. Such was in England the fortune of the stage play. At a time when Chaucer was writing character-sketches that were really dramatic, the formal drama consisted of rude miracle plays that had no literary quality whatever. These were taken from the Bible and acted at first by the priests as illustrations of Scripture history and additions to the {99} church service on feasts and saints' days. Afterward the town guilds, or incorporated trades, took hold of them and produced them annually on scaffolds in the open air. In some English cities, as Coventry and Chester, they continued to be performed almost to the close of the 16th century. And in the celebrated Passion Play, at Oberammergau, in Bavaria, we have an instance of a miracle play that has survived to our own day. These were followed by the moral plays, in which allegorical characters, such as Clergy, Lusty Juventus, Riches, Folly, and Good Demeanaunce, were the persons of the drama. The comic character in the miracle plays had been the Devil, and he was retained in some of the moralities side by side with the abstract vice, who became the clown or fool of Shaksperian comedy. The "formal Vice, Iniquity," as Shakspere calls him, had it for his business to belabor the roaring Devil with his wooden sword

. . "with his dagger of lath
In his rage and his wrath
Cries 'Aha!' to the Devil,
'Pare your nails, Goodman Evil!'"

He survives also in the harlequin of the pantomimes, and in Mr. Punch, of the puppet shows, who kills the Devil and carries him off on his back, when the latter is sent to fetch him to hell for his crimes.

Masques and interludes—the latter a species of {100} short farce—were popular at the Court of Henry VIII. Elisabeth was often entertained at the universities or at the inns of court with Latin plays, or with translations from Seneca, Euripides, and Ariosto. Original comedies and tragedies began to be written, modeled upon Terence, and Seneca, and chronicle histories founded on the annals of English kings. There was a Master of the Revels at court, whose duty it was to select plays to be performed before the queen, and these were acted by the children of the Royal Chapel, or by the choir boys of St. Paul's Cathedral. These early plays are of interest to students of the history of the drama, and throw much light upon the construction of later plays, like Shakspere's; but they are rude and inartistic, and without any literary quality.

There were also private companies of actors maintained by wealthy noblemen, like the Earl of Leicester, and bands of strolling players, who acted in inn-yards and bear-gardens. It was not until stationary theaters were built and stock companies of actors regularly licensed and established, that any plays were produced which deserve the name of literature. In 1576 the first play-house was built in London. This was the *Black Friars*, which was located within the liberties of the dissolved monastery of the Black Friars, in order to be outside of the jurisdiction of the Mayor and Corporation, who were Puritan, and determined in their opposition to the stage. For the same reason the {101} *Theater* and the *Curtain* were built in the same year, outside the city walls in Shoreditch. Later the *Rose*, the *Globe*, and the *Swan*, were erected on the Bankside, across the Thames, and play-goers resorting to them were accustomed to "take boat."

These early theaters were of the rudest construction. The six-penny spectators, or "groundlings," stood in the yard, or pit, which had neither floor nor roof. The shilling spectators sat on the stage, where they were accommodated with stools and tobacco pipes, and whence they chaffed the actors or the "opposed rascality" in the yard. There was no scenery, and the female parts were taken by boys. Plays were acted in the afternoon. A placard, with the letters "Venice," or "Rome," or whatever, indicated the place of the action. With such rude appliances must Shakspere bring before his audience the midnight battlements of Elsinore and the moonlit garden of the Capulets. The dramatists had to throw themselves upon the imagination of their public, and it says much for the imaginative temper of the public of that day, that it responded to the appeal. It suffered the poet to transport it over wide intervals of space and time, and "with aid of some few foot and half-foot words, fight over York and Lancaster's long jars." Pedantry undertook, even at the very beginnings of the Elisabethan drama, to shackle it with the so-called rules of Aristotle, or classical unities of time and place, {102} to make it keep violent action off the stage and comedy distinct from tragedy. But the playwrights appealed from the critics to the truer sympathies of the audience, and they decided for freedom and action, rather than restraint and recitation. Hence our national drama is of Shakspere, and not of Racine. By 1603 there were twelve play-houses in London in full blast, although the city then numbered only one hundred and fifty thousand inhabitants.

Fresh plays were produced every year. The theater was more to the

Englishman of that time than it has ever been before or since. It was his club, his novel, his newspaper all in one. No great drama has ever flourished apart from a living stage, and it was fortunate that the Elisabethan dramatists were, almost all of them, actors and familiar with stage effect. Even the few exceptions, like Beaumont and Fletcher, who were young men of good birth and fortune, and not dependent on their pens, were probably intimate with the actors, lived in a theatrical atmosphere, and knew practically how plays should be put on.

It had now become possible to earn a livelihood as an actor and playwright. Richard Burbage and Edward Alleyn, the leading actors of their generation, made large fortunes. Shakspere himself made enough from his share in the profits of the *Globe* to retire with a competence, some seven years before his death, and purchase a handsome {103} property in his native Stratford. Accordingly, shortly after 1580, a number of men of real talent began to write for the stage as a career. These were young graduates of the universities, Marlowe, Greene, Peele, Kyd, Lyly, Lodge, and others, who came up to town and led a Bohemian life as actors and playwrights. Most of them were wild and dissipated, and ended in wretchedness. Peele died of a disease brought on by his evil courses; Greene, in extreme destitution, from a surfeit of Rhenish wine and pickled herring; and Marlowe was stabbed in a tavern brawl.

The Euphuist Lyly produced eight plays from 1584 to 1601. They were written for court entertainments, in prose and mostly on mythological subjects. They have little dramatic power, but the dialogue is brisk and vivacious, and there are several pretty songs in them. All the characters talk Euphuism. The best of these was *Alexander and Campaspe*, the plot of which is briefly as follows. Alexander has fallen in love with his beautiful captive, Campaspe, and employs the artist Apelles to paint her portrait. During the sittings, Apelles becomes enamored of his subject and declares his passion, which is returned. Alexander discovers their secret, but magnanimously forgives the treason and joins the lovers' hands. The situation is a good one, and capable of strong treatment in the hands of a real dramatist. But Lyly slips smoothly over the crisis of the action and, in place of passionate scenes, gives {104} us clever discourses and soliloquies, or, at best, a light interchange of question and answer, full of conceits, repartees, and double meanings. For example:

"*Apel.* Whom do you love best in the world?

"*Camp.* He that made me last in the world.

"*Apel.* That was a God.

"*Camp.* I had thought it had been a man," etc.

49

Lyly's service to the drama consisted in his introduction of an easy and sparkling prose as the language of high comedy, and Shakspere's indebtedness to the fashion thus set is seen in such passages as the wit combats between Benedict and Beatrice in *Much Ado about Nothing*, greatly superior as they are to any thing of the kind in Lyly.

The most important of the dramatists, who were Shakspere's forerunners, or early contemporaries, was Christopher or—as he was familiarly called—Kit Marlowe. Born in the same year with Shakspere (1564), he died in 1593, at which date his great successor is thought to have written no original plays, except the *Comedy of Errors* and *Love's Labour's Lost*. Marlowe first popularized blank verse as the language of tragedy in his *Tamburlaine*, written before 1587, and in subsequent plays he brought it to a degree of strength and flexibility which left little for Shakspere to do but to take it as he found it. *Tamburlaine* was a crude, violent piece, full of exaggeration and bombast, but with passages here and there of splendid {105} declamation, justifying Ben Jonson's phrase, "Marlowe's mighty line." Jonson, however, ridiculed, in his *Discoveries*, the "scenical strutting and furious vociferation" of Marlowe's hero; and Shakspere put a quotation from Tamburlaine into the mouth of his ranting Pistol. Marlowe's *Edward II.* was the most regularly constructed and evenly written of his plays. It was the best historical drama on the stage before Shakspere, and not undeserving of the comparison which it has provoked with the latter's *Richard II.* But the most interesting of Marlowe's plays, to a modern reader, is the *Tragical History of Doctor Faustus*. The subject is the same as in Goethe's *Faust*, and Goethe, who knew the English play, spoke of it as greatly planned. The opening of Marlowe's *Faustus* is very similar to Goethe's. His hero, wearied with unprofitable studies, and filled with a mighty lust for knowledge and the enjoyment of life, sells his soul to the Devil in return for a few years of supernatural power. The tragic irony of the story might seem to lie in the frivolous use which Faustus makes of his dearly bought power, wasting it in practical jokes and feats of legerdemain; but of this Marlowe was probably unconscious. The love story of Margaret, which is the central point of Goethe's drama, is entirely wanting in Marlowe's, and so is the subtle conception of Goethe's Mephistophiles. Marlowe's handling of the supernatural is materialistic and downright, as befitted an age which believed in witchcraft. The {106} greatest part of the English *Faustus* is the last scene, in which the agony and terror of suspense with which the magician awaits the stroke of the clock that signals his doom are powerfully drawn.

"O lente, lente currile, noctis equi!
The stars move still, time runs, the clock will strike.
O soul, be changed into little water-drops,
And fall into the ocean, ne'er be found!"

Marlowe's genius was passionate and irregular. He had no humor, and the comic portions of *Faustus* are scenes of low buffoonery.

George Peele's masterpiece, *David and Bethsabe*, was also, in many respects, a fine play, though its beauties were poetic rather than dramatic, consisting not in the characterization—which is feeble—but in the eastern luxuriance of the imagery. There is one noble chorus—

"O proud revolt of a presumptuous man," etc.

which reminds one of passages in Milton's *Samson Agonistes*, and occasionally Peele rises to such high Aeschylean audacities as this:

"At him the thunder shall discharge his bolt,
And his fair spouse, with bright and fiery wings,
Sit ever burning on his hateful bones."

Robert Greene was a very unequal writer. His plays are slovenly and careless in construction, and he puts classical allusions into the mouths of milkmaids and serving boys, with the grotesque pedantry and want of keeping common among the {107} playwrights of the early stage. He has, notwithstanding, in his comedy parts, more natural lightness and grace than either Marlowe or Peele. In his *Friar Bacon and Friar Bungay*, and his *Pinner of Wakefield*, there is a fresh breath, as of the green English country, in such passages as the description of Oxford, the scene at Harleston Fair, and the picture of the dairy in the keeper's lodge at merry Fressingfield.

In all these ante-Shaksperian dramatists there was a defect of art proper to the first comers in a new literary departure. As compared not only with Shakspere, but with later writers, who had the inestimable advantage of his example, their work was full of imperfection, hesitation, experiment. Marlowe was probably, in native genius, the equal at least of Fletcher or Webster, but his plays, as a whole, are certainly not equal to theirs. They wrote in a more developed state of the art. But the work of this early school settled the shape which the English drama was to take. It fixed the practice and traditions of the national theater. It decided that the drama was to deal with the whole of life, the real and the ideal, tragedy and comedy, prose and verse, in the same play, without limitations of time, place, and action. It decided that the English play was to be an action, and not a dialogue, bringing boldly upon the mimic scene feasts, dances, processions, hangings, riots, plays within plays, drunken revels, beatings, battle, murder, and sudden death.

It established blank verse, {108} with occasional riming couplets at the close of a scene or of a long speech, as the language of the tragedy and high comedy parts, and prose as the language of the low comedy and "business" parts. And it introduced songs, a feature of which Shakspere made exquisite use. Shakspere, indeed, like all great poets, invented no new form of literature, but touched old forms to finer purposes, refining every thing, discarding nothing. Even the old chorus and dumb show he employed, though sparingly, as also the old jig, or comic song, which the clown used to give between the acts.

Of the life of William Shakspere, the greatest dramatic poet of the world, so little is known that it has been possible for ingenious persons to construct a theory—and support it with some show of reason—that the plays which pass under his name were really written by Bacon or some one else. There is no danger of this paradox ever making serious headway, for the historical evidence that Shakspere wrote Shakspere's plays, though not overwhelming, is sufficient. But it is startling to think that the greatest creative genius of his day, or perhaps of all time, was suffered to slip out of life so quietly that his title to his own works could even be questioned only two hundred and fifty years after the event. That the single authorship of the Homeric poems should be doubted is not so strange, for Homer is almost prehistoric. But Shakspere was a modern Englishman, and at the time of his death the first English colony in {109} America was already nine years old. The important known facts of his life can be told almost in a sentence. He was born at Stratford-on-Avon in 1564, married when he was eighteen, went to London probably in 1587, and became an actor, playwriter, and stockholder in the company which owned the Blackfriars and the Globe Theaters. He seemingly prospered in his calling and retired about 1609 to Stratford, where he lived in the house that he had bought some years before, and where he died in 1616. His *Venus and Adonis* was printed in 1593, the *Rape of Lucrece* in 1594, and his *Sonnets* in 1609. So far as is known, only eighteen of the thirty-seven plays generally attributed to Shakspere were printed during his life-time. These were printed singly, in quarto shape, and were little more than stage books, or librettos. The first collected edition of his works was the so-called "First Folio" of 1623, published by his fellow-actors, Heming and Condell. No contemporary of Shakspere thought it worth while to write a life of the stage-player. There are a number of references to him in the literature of the time; some generous, as in Ben Jonson's well-known verses; others singularly unappreciative, like Webster's mention of "the right happy and copious industry of Master Shakspere." But all these together do not begin to amount to the sum of what was said about Spenser, or Sidney, or Raleigh, or Ben Jonson. There is, indeed, nothing to show that his contemporaries understood what a man they had {110} among them in the person of "Our English Terence, Mr. Will Shakespeare!" The age, for the rest, was not a self-conscious one, nor greatly given to review writing and literary biography. Nor is there enough of self-revelation in Shakspere's plays to aid the reader in forming a notion of the man. He lost his identity completely in the characters of his plays, as it is the duty of a dramatic writer to do. His sonnets have been examined carefully in search of internal evidence as to his character and life, but the speculations founded upon them have been more ingenious than convincing.

Shakspere probably began by touching up old plays. *Henry VI.* and the bloody tragedy of *Titus Andronicus*, if Shakspere's at all, are doubtless only his revision of pieces already on the stage. The *Taming of the Shrew* seems to be an old play worked over by Shakspere and some other dramatist, and traces of another hand are thought to be visible in parts of *Henry VIII.*, *Pericles*, and *Timon of Athens*. Such partnerships were common among the Elisabethan dramatists, the most illustrious example being the long association of Beaumont and Fletcher. The plays in the First Folio were divided into histories, comedies, and tragedies, and it will be convenient to notice them briefly in that order.

It was a stirring time when the young adventurer came to London to try his fortune. Elisabeth had finally thrown down the gage of battle to Catholic Europe, by the execution of Mary Stuart, in 1587. {111} The following year saw the destruction of the colossal Armada, which Spain had sent to revenge Mary's death, and hard upon these events followed the gallant exploits of Grenville, Essex, and Raleigh.

That Shakspere shared the exultant patriotism of the times, and the sense of their aloofness from the continent of Europe, which was now born in the breasts of Englishmen, is evident from many a passage in his plays.

"This happy breed of men, this little world,
This precious stone set in a silver sea,
This blessed plot, this earth, this realm, this England,
This land of such dear souls, this dear, dear land,
England, bound in with the triumphant sea!"

His English histories are ten in number. Of these *King John* and *Henry VIII.* are isolated plays. The others form a consecutive series, in the following order: *Richard III.*, the two parts of *Henry IV.*, *Henry V.*, the three parts of *Henry VI.*, and *Richard III.* This series may be divided into two, each forming a tetralogy, or group of four plays. In the first the subject is the rise of the house of Lancaster. But the power of the Red Rose was founded in usurpation. In the second group, accordingly, comes the Nemesis, in the civil wars of the Roses, reaching their catastrophe in the downfall ofboth

53

Lancaster and York, and the tyranny of Gloucester. The happy conclusion is finally reached in the last play of the series, when this new usurper is overthrown in turn, and Henry {112} VII., the first Tudor sovereign, ascends the throne, and restores the Lancastrian inheritance, purified, by bloody atonement, from the stain of Richard II.'s murder. These eight plays are, as it were, the eight acts of one great drama; and if such a thing were possible, they should be represented on successive nights, like the parts of a Greek trilogy. In order of composition, the second group came first. *Henry VI.* is strikingly inferior to the others. *Richard III.* is a good acting play, and its popularity has been sustained by a series of great tragedians, who have taken the part of the king. But, in a literary sense, it is unequal to *Richard II.*, or the two parts of *Henry IV.* The latter is unquestionably Shakspere's greatest historical tragedy, and it contains his master-creation in the region of low comedy, the immortal Falstaff.

The constructive art with which Shakspere shaped history into drama is well seen in comparing his King John with the two plays on that subject, which were already on the stage. These, like all the other old "Chronicle histories," such as *Thomas Lord Cromwell* and the *Famous Victories of Henry V.*, follow a merely chronological, or biographical, order, giving events loosely, as they occurred, without any unity of effect, or any reference to their bearing on the catastrophe. Shakspere's order was logical. He compressed and selected, disregarding the fact of history oftentimes, in favor of the higher truth of fiction; bringing together a crime and its punishment, as cause and effect, even {113} though they had no such relation in the chronicle, and were separated, perhaps, by many years.

Shakspere's first two comedies were experiments. *Love's Labour's Lost* was a play of manners, with hardly any plot. It brought together a number of humors, that is, oddities and affectations of various sorts, and played them off on one another, as Ben Jonson afterward did in his comedies of humor. Shakspere never returned to this type of play, unless, perhaps, in the *Taming of the Shrew*. There the story turned on a single "humor," Katherine's bad temper, just as the story in Jonson's *Silent Woman* turned on Morose's hatred of noise. The *Taming of the Shrew* is, therefore, one of the least Shaksperian of Shakspere's plays; a *bourgeois*, domestic comedy, with a very narrow interest. It belongs to the school of French comedy, like Moliere's *Malade Imaginaire*, not to the romantic comedy of Shakspere and Fletcher.

The *Comedy of Errors* was an experiment of an exactly opposite kind. It was a play, purely of incident; a farce, in which the main improbability being granted, namely, that the twin Antipholi and twin Dromios are so alike that they cannot be distinguished, all the amusing complications follow naturally enough. There is little character-drawing in the play. Any two pairs of twins, in the same predicament, would be equally droll. The fun lies in the situation. This was a comedy of the Latin school, and resembled the *Menaechmi* of Plautus. Shakspere never returned to this type of {114} play, though there is an element of "errors" in *Midsummer Night's Dream*. In the *Two Gentlemen of Verona* he finally hit upon that species of romantic comedy which he may be said to have invented or created out of the scattered materials at hand in the works of his predecessors. In this play, as in the *Merchant of Venice, Midsummer Night's Dream, Much Ado about Nothing, As You Like It, Twelfth Night, Winters Tale, All's Well that Ends Well, Measure for Measure*, and the *Tempest*, the plan of construction is as follows. There is one main intrigue carried out by the high comedy characters, and a secondary intrigue, or underplot, by the low comedy characters. The former is by no means purely comic, but admits the presentation of the noblest motives, the strongest passions, and the most delicate graces of romantic poetry. In some of the plays it has a prevailing lightness and gayety, as in *As You Like It* and *Twelfth Night*. In others, like *Measure for Measure*, it is barely saved from becoming tragedy by the happy close. Shylock certainly remains a tragic figure, even to the end, and a play like *Winter's Tale*, in which the painful situation is prolonged for years, is only technically a comedy. Such dramas, indeed, were called, on many of the title-pages of the time, "tragi-comedies." The low comedy interlude, on the other hand, was broadly comic. It was cunningly interwoven with the texture of the play, sometimes loosely, and by way of variety or relief, as in the episode of {115} Touchstone and Audrey, in *As You Like It*; sometimes closely, as in the case of Dogberry and Verges, in *Much Ado about Nothing*, where the blundering of the watch is made to bring about the *denouement* of the main action. The *Merry Wives of Windsor* is an exception to this plan of construction. It is Shakspere's only play of contemporary, middle-class English life, and is written almost throughout in prose. It is his only pure comedy, except the *Taming of the Shrew*.

Shakspere did not abandon comedy when writing tragedy, though he turned it to a new account. The two species graded into one another. Thus *Cymbeline* is, in its fortunate ending, really as much of a comedy as *Winter's Tale*—to which its plot bears a resemblance—and is only technically a tragedy, because it contains a violent death. In some of the tragedies, as *Macbeth* and *Julius Caesar*, the comedy element is reduced to a minimum. But in others, as *Romeo and Juliet*, and *Hamlet*, it heightens the tragic feeling by the irony of contrast. Akin to this is the use to which Shakspere put the old Vice, or Clown, of the moralities. The Fool in *Lear*, Touchstone in *As You Like It*, and Thersites in *Troilus and Cressida*, are a sort of parody of the function of the Greek chorus, commenting the action of the drama with scraps of bitter, or half-crazy, philosophy, and wonderful gleams of insight into the depths of man's nature.

The earliest of Shakspere's tragedies, unless *Titus Andronicus* be his, was, doubtless, *Romeo and {1 6} Juliet*, which is full of the passion and poetry of youth and of first love. It contains a large proportion of riming lines, which is usually a sign in Shakspere of early work. He dropped rime more and more in his later plays, and his blank verse grew freer and more varied in its pauses and the number of its feet. *Romeo and Juliet* is also unique, among his tragedies, in this respect, that the catastrophe is brought about by a fatality, as in the Greek drama. It was Shakspere's habit to work out his tragic conclusions from within, through character, rather than through external chances. This is true of all the great tragedies of his middle life, *Hamlet, Othello, Lear, Macbeth*, in every one of which the catastrophe is involved in the character and actions of the hero. This is so, in a special sense, in *Hamlet*, the subtlest of all Shakspere's plays, and if not his masterpiece, at any rate the one which has most attracted and puzzled the greatest minds. It is observable that in Shakspere's comedies there is no one central figure, but that, in passing into tragedy, he intensified and concentrated the attention upon a single character. This difference is seen, even in the naming of the plays; the tragedies always take their titles from their heroes, the comedies never.

Somewhat later, probably, than the tragedies already mentioned, were the three Roman plays, *Julius Caesar, Coriolanus*, and *Antony and Cleopatra*. It is characteristic of Shakspere that he invented the plot of none of his plays, but took {117} material that he found at hand. In these Roman tragedies, he followed Plutarch closely, and yet, even in so doing, gave, if possible, a greater evidence of real creative power than when he borrowed a mere outline of a story from some Italian novelist. It is most instructive to compare *Julius Caesar* with Ben Jonson's *Catiline and Sejanus*. Jonson was careful not to go beyond his text. In *Catiline* he translates almost literally the whole of Cicero's first oration against Catiline. Sejanus is a mosaic of passages, from Tacitus and Suetonius. There is none of this dead learning in Shakspere's play. Having grasped the conception of the characters of Brutus, Cassius, and Mark Anthony, as Plutarch gave them, he pushed them out into their consequences in every word and act, so independently of his original, and yet so harmoniously with it, that the reader knows that he is reading history, and needs no further warrant for it than Shakspere's own. *Timon of Athens* is the least agreeable and most monotonous of Shakspere's undoubted tragedies, and *Troilus and Cressida*, said Coleridge, is the hardest to characterize. The figures of the old Homeric world fare but hardly under the glaring light of modern standards of morality which Shakspere turns upon them. Ajax becomes a stupid bully, Ulysses a crafty politician, and swift-footed Achilles a vain and sulky chief of faction. In losing their ideal remoteness, the heroes of the *Iliad* lose their poetic quality, and the lover of Homer experiences an unpleasant disenchantment.

{118}

It was customary in the 18th century to speak of Shakspere as a rude though prodigious genius. Even Milton could describe him as "warbling his native wood-notes wild." But a truer criticism, beginning in England with Coleridge, has shown that he was also a profound artist. It is true that he wrote for his audiences, and that his art is not every-where and at all points perfect. But a great artist will contrive, as Shakspere did, to reconcile practical exigencies, like those of the public stage, with the finer requirements of his art. Strained interpretations have been put upon this or that item in Shakspere's plays; and yet it is generally true that some deeper reason can be assigned for his method in a given case than that "the audience liked puns," or, "the audience liked ghosts." Compare, for example, his delicate management of the supernatural with Marlowe's procedure in *Faustus*. Shakspere's age believed in witches, elves, and apparitions; and yet there is always something shadowy or allegorical in his use of such machinery. The ghost in *Hamlet* is merely an embodied suspicion. Banquo's wraith, which is invisible to all but Macbeth, is the haunting of an evil conscience. The witches in the same play are but the promptings of ambition, thrown into a human shape, so as to become actors in the drama. In the same way, the fairies in *Midsummer Night's Dream* are the personified caprices of the lovers, and they are unseen by the human characters, whose likes and dislikes they control, save in the instance where {119} Bottom is "translated" (that is, becomes mad) and has sight of the invisible world. So in the *Tempest*, Ariel is the spirit of the air and Caliban of the earth, ministering, with more or less of unwillingness, to man's necessities.

Shakspere is the most universal of writers. He touches more men at more points than Homer, or Dante, or Goethe. The deepest wisdom, the sweetest poetry, the widest range of character, are combined in his plays. He made the English language an organ of expression unexcelled in the history of literature. Yet he is not an English poet simply, but a world-poet. Germany has made him her own, and the Latin races, though at first hindered in a true appreciation of him by the canons of classical taste, have at length learned to know him. An ever-growing mass of Shaksperian literature, in the way of comment and interpretation, critical, textual, historical, or illustrative, testifies to the durability and growth of his fame. Above all, his plays still keep, and probably always will keep, the stage. It is common to speak of Shakspere and the other Elisabethan dramatists as if they stood, in some sense, on a level.

But in truth there is an almost measureless distance between him and all his contemporaries. The rest shared with him in the mighty influences of the age. Their plays are touched here and there with the power and splendor of which they were all joint heirs. But, as a whole, they are obsolete. They live in books, but not in the hearts and on the tongues of men. The {120} most remarkable of the dramatists contemporary with Shakspere was Ben Jonson, whose robust figure is in striking contrast with the other's gracious impersonality. Jonson was nine years younger than Shakspere. He was educated at Westminster School, served as a soldier in the low countries, became an actor in Henslowe's company, and was twice imprisoned—once for killing a fellow-actor in a duel, and once for his part in the comedy of *Eastward Hoe*, which gave offense to King James. He lived down to the times of Charles I. (1635), and became the acknowledged arbiter of English letters and the center of convivial wit combats at the *Mermaid*, the *Devil*, and other famous London taverns.

"What things have we seen
Done at the Mermaid; heard words that have been
So nimble and so full of subtle flame,
As if that every one from whom they came
Had meant to put his whole wit in a jest,
And had resolved to live a fool the rest
Of his dull life." [1]

The inscription on his tomb, in Westminster Abbey, is simply

"O rare Ben Jonson!"

Jonson's comedies were modeled upon the *vetus comaedia* of Aristophanes, which was satirical in purpose, and they belonged to an entirely different school from Shakspere's. They were classical and not romantic, and were pure comedies, admitting {121} no admixture of tragic motives. There is hardly one lovely or beautiful character in the entire range of his dramatic creations. They were comedies not of character, in the high sense of the word, but of manners or humors. His design was to lash the follies and vices of the day, and his *dramatis persona* consisted for the most part of gulls, impostors, fops, cowards, swaggering braggarts, and "Pauls men." In his first play, *Every Man in his Humor* (acted in 1598), in *Every Man Out of his Humor*, *Bartholomew Fair*, and indeed, in all of his comedies, his subject was the "spongy humors of the time," that is, the fashionable affectations, the whims, oddities, and eccentric developments of London life. His procedure was to bring together a number of these fantastic humorists, to play them off upon each other, involve them in all manner of comical misadventures, and render them utterly ridiculous and contemptible. There was thus a perishable element

58

in his art, for manners change; and however effective this exposure of contemporary affectations may have been, before an audience of Jonson's day, it is as hard for a modern reader to detect his points as it will be for a reader two hundred years hence to understand the satire upon the aesthetic craze in such pieces of the present day, as *Patience* or the *Colonel.* Nevertheless, a patient reader, with the help of copious foot-notes, can gradually put together for himself an image of that world of obsolete humors in which Jonson's comedy dwells, and can admire the dramatist's solid good {122} sense, his great learning, his skill in construction, and the astonishing fertility of his invention. His characters are not revealed from within, like Shakspere's, but built up painfully from outside by a succession of minute, laborious particulars. The difference will be plainly manifest if such a character as Slender, in the *Merry Wives of Windsor*, be compared with any one of the inexhaustible variety of idiots in Jonson's plays; with Master Stephen, for example, in *Every Man in his Humor*; or, if Falstaff be put side by side with Captain Bobadil, in the same comedy, perhaps Jonson's masterpiece in the way of comic caricature. *Cynthia's Revels* was a satire on the courtiers and the *Poetaster* on Jonson's literary enemies. The *Alchemist* was an exposure of quackery, and is one of his best comedies, but somewhat overweighted with learning. *Volpone* is the most powerful of all his dramas, but is a harsh and disagreeable piece; and the state of society which it depicts is too revolting for comedy. The *Silent Woman* is, perhaps, the easiest of all Jonson's plays for a modern reader to follow and appreciate. There is a distinct plot to it, the situation is extremely ludicrous, and the emphasis is laid upon single humor or eccentricity, as in some of Moliere's lighter comedies, like *Le Malade Imaginaire*, or *Le Médecin malgrê lui.*

In spite of his heaviness in drama, Jonson had a light enough touch in lyric poetry. His songs have not the careless sweetness of Shakspere's, but they have a grace of their own. Such pieces as his {123} *Love's Triumph, Hymn to Diana, The Noble Mind*, and the adaptation from *Philostratus,*

"Drink to me only with thine eyes,"

and many others entitle their author to rank among the first English lyrists. Some of these occur in his two collections of miscellaneous verse, the *Forest* and *Underwoods*; others in the numerous masques which he composed. These were a species of entertainment, very popular at the court of James I., combining dialogue with music, intricate dances, and costly scenery. Jonson left an unfinished pastoral drama, the *Sad Shepherd*, which, though not equal to Fletcher's *Faithful Shepherdess*, contains passages of great beauty, one, especially, descriptive of the shepherdess

"Earine,

Who had her very being and her name
With the first buds and breathings of the spring,
Born with the primrose and the violet
And earliest roses blown."

1. Ward's History of English Dramatic Literature.

2. Palgrave's Golden Treasury of Songs and Lyrics.

3. The Courtly Poets from Raleigh to Montrose. Edited by J. Hannah.

4. Sir Philip Sidney's Arcadia. (First and Second Books.)

5. Bacon's Essays. Edited by W. Aldis Wright

{124}

6. The Cambridge Shakspere. [Clark & Wright.]

7. Charles Lamb's Specimens of English Dramatic Poets.

8. Ben Jonson's Volpone and Silent Woman. (Cunningham's or Gifford's Edition.)

[1] Francis Beaumont. *Letter to Ben Jonson.*

{125}

CHAPTER IV.

THE AGE OF MILTON.

1608-1674.

The Elisabethan age proper closed with the death of the queen, and the accession of James I., in 1603, but the literature of the fifty years following was quite as rich as that of the half-century that had passed since she came to the throne, in 1557. The same qualities of thought and style which had marked the writers of her reign, prolonged themselves in their successors, through the reigns of the first two Stuart kings and the Commonwealth. Yet there was a change in *spirit*. Literature is only one of the many forms in which the national mind expresses itself. In periods of political revolution, literature, leaving the serene air of fine art, partakes the violent agitation of the times. There were seeds of civil and religious discord in Elisabethan England. As between the two parties in the Church there was a compromise and a truce rather than a final settlement. The Anglican doctrine was partly Calvinistic and partly Arminian. The form of government was Episcopal, but there was a large body of Presbyterians in the Church who desired a change. In {126} the ritual and ceremonies many "rags of popery" had been retained, which the extreme reformers wished to tear away. But Elisabeth was a worldly-minded woman, impatient of theological disputes. Though circumstances had made her the champion of Protestantism in Europe, she kept many Catholic notions, disapproved, for example, of the marriage of priests, and hated sermons. She was jealous of her prerogative in the State, and in the Church she enforced uniformity. The authors of the *Martin Marprelate* pamphlets against the bishops, were punished by death or imprisonment. While the queen lived things were kept well together and England was at one in face of the common foe. Admiral Howard, who commanded the English naval forces against the Armada, was a Catholic.

But during the reigns of James I. (1603-1625) and Charles I. (1625-1649) Puritanism grew stronger through repression. "England," says the historian Green, "became the people of a book, and that book the Bible." The power of the king was used to impose the power of the bishops upon the English and Scotch Churches until religious discontent became also political discontent, and finally overthrew the throne. The writers of this period divided more and more into two hostile camps. On the side of Church and king was the bulk of the learning and genius of the time. But on the side of free religion and the Parliament were the stern conviction, the fiery zeal, the excited imagination of English Puritanism. The {127} spokesman of this movement was Milton, whose great figure dominates the literary history of his generation, as Shakspere's does of the generation preceding.

The drama went on in the course marked out for it by Shakspere's example, until the theaters were closed, by Parliament, in 1642. Of the Stuart dramatists, the most important were Beaumont and Fletcher, all of whose plays were produced during the reign of James I. These were fifty-three in number, but only thirteen of them were joint productions. Francis Beaumont was twenty years younger than Shakspere, and died a few years before him. He was the son of a judge of the Common Pleas. His collaborator, John Fletcher, a son of the bishop of London, was five years older than Beaumont, and survived him nine years. He was much the more prolific of the two and wrote alone some forty plays. Although the life of one of these partners was conterminous with Shakspere's, their works exhibit a later phase of the dramatic art. The Stuart dramatists followed the lead of Shakspere rather than of Ben Jonson. Their plays, like the former's, belong to the romantic drama. They present a poetic and idealized version of life, deal with the highest passions and the wildest buffoonery, and introduce a great variety of those daring situations and incidents which we agree to call romantic. But while Shakspere seldom or never overstepped the modesty of nature, his successors ran into every license. They {128} sought to stimulate the jaded appetite of their audience by exhibiting monstrosities of character, unnatural lusts,

61

subtleties of crime, virtues and vices both in excess.

Beaumont and Fletcher's plays are much easier and more agreeable reading than Ben Jonson's. Though often loose in their plots and without that consistency in the development of their characters which distinguished Jonson's more conscientious workmanship, they are full of graceful dialogue and beautiful poetry. Dryden said that after the Restoration two of their plays were acted for one of Shakspere's or Jonson's throughout the year, and he added, that they "understood and imitated the conversation of *gentlemen* much better, whose wild debaucheries and quickness of wit in repartees no poet can ever paint as they have done." Wild debauchery was certainly not the mark of a gentleman in Shakspere, nor was it altogether so in Beaumont and Fletcher. Their gentlemen are gallant and passionate lovers, gay cavaliers, generous, courageous, courteous—according to the fashion of their times— and sensitive on the point of honor. They are far superior to the cold-blooded rakes of Dryden and the Restoration comedy. Still the manners and language in Beaumont and Fletcher's plays are extremely licentious, and it is not hard to sympathize with the objections to the theater expressed by the Puritan writer, William Prynne, who, after denouncing the long hair of the cavaliers in his tract, *The {129} Unloveliness of Lovelocks*, attacked the stage, in 1633, with *Histrio-mastix: the Player's Scourge*; an offense for which he was fined, imprisoned, pilloried, and had his ears cropped. Coleridge said that Shakspere was coarse, but never gross. He had the healthy coarseness of nature herself. But Beaumont and Fletcher's pages are corrupt. Even their chaste women are immodest in language and thought. They use not merely that frankness of speech which was a fashion of the times, but a profusion of obscene imagery which could not proceed from a pure mind. Chastity with them is rather a bodily accident than a virtue of the heart, says Coleridge.

Among the best of their light comedies are *The Chances*, *The Scornful Lady*, *The Spanish Curate*, and *Rule a Wife and Have a Wife*. But far superior to these are their tragedies and tragi-comedies, *The Maia's Tragedy*, *Philaster*, *A King and No King*—all written jointly—and *Valentinian* and *Thierry and Theodoret*, written by Fletcher alone, but perhaps, in part, sketched out by Beaumont. The tragic masterpiece of Beaumont and Fletcher is *The Maid's Tragedy*, a powerful but repulsive play, which sheds a singular light not only upon its authors' dramatic methods, but also upon the attitude toward royalty favored by the doctrine of the divine right of kings, which grew up under the Stuarts. The heroine, Evadne, has been in secret a mistress of the king, who marries her to Amintor, a gentleman of his court, {130} because, as she explains to her bridegroom, on the wedding night,

"I must have one

To father children, and to bear the name
Of husband to me, that my sin may be
More honorable."

This scene is, perhaps, the most affecting and impressive in the whole range
of Beaumont and Fletcher's drama. Yet when Evadne names the king as her
paramour, Amintor exclaims:

"O thou hast named a word that wipes away
All thoughts revengeful. In that sacred name
'The king' there lies a terror. What frail man
Dares lift his hand against it? Let the gods
Speak to him when they please; till when, let us
Suffer and wait."

And the play ends with the words

"On lustful kings,
Unlooked-for sudden deaths from heaven are sent,
But cursed is he that is their instrument."

Aspatia, in this tragedy, is a good instance of Beaumont and Fletcher's
pathetic characters. She is troth-plight wife to Amintor, and after he, by the
king's command, has forsaken her for Evadne, she disguises herself as a man,
provokes her unfaithful lover to a duel, and dies under his sword, blessing the
hand that killed her. This is a common type in Beaumont and Fletcher, and
was drawn originally from Shakspere's *Ophelia*. All their good women have
the instinctive fidelity of a dog, and a superhuman patience and devotion,
{131} a "gentle forlornness" under wrongs, which is painted with an almost
feminine tenderness. In *Philaster, or Love Lies Bleeding*, Euphrasia,
conceiving a hopeless passion for Philaster—who is in love with Arethusa—
puts on the dress of a page and enters his service. He employs her to carry
messages to his lady-love, just as Viola, in *Twelfth Night*, is sent by the Duke
to Olivia. Philaster is persuaded by slanderers that his page and his lady have
been unfaithful to him, and in his jealous fury he wounds Euphrasia with his
sword. Afterward, convinced of the boy's fidelity, he asks forgiveness,
whereto Euphrasia replies,

"Alas, my lord, my life is not a thing
Worthy your noble thoughts. 'Tis not a life,
'Tis but a piece of childhood thrown away."

Beaumont and Fletcher's love-lorn maids wear the willow very sweetly, but in
all their piteous passages there is nothing equal to the natural pathos—the
pathos which arises from the deep springs of character—of that one brief
question and answer in *King Lear*.

"*Lear*. So young and so untender?

"*Cordelia*. So young, my lord, and true."

The disguise of a woman in man's apparel is a common incident in the
romantic drama; and the fact, that on the Elisabethan stage the female parts
were taken by boys, made the deception easier. Viola's situation in *Twelfth
Night* is precisely similar to Euphrasia's, but there is a {132} difference in the
handling of the device which is characteristic of a distinction between
Shakspere's art and that of his contemporaries. The audience in *Twelfth Night*
is taken into confidence and made aware of Viola's real nature from the start,
while Euphrasia's *incognito* is preserved till the fifth act, and then disclosed
by an accident. This kind of mystification and surprise was a trick below
Shakspere. In this instance, moreover, it involved a departure from dramatic
probability. Euphrasia could, at any moment, by revealing her identity, have
averted the greatest sufferings and dangers from Philaster, Arethusa, and
herself, and the only motive for her keeping silence is represented to have
been a feeling of maidenly shame at her position. Such strained and fantastic
motives are too often made the pivot of the action in Beaumont and Fletcher's
tragi-comedies. Their characters have not the depth and truth of Shakspere's,
nor are they drawn so sharply. One reads their plays with pleasure and
remembers here and there a passage of fine poetry, or a noble or lovely trait.
But their characters, as wholes, leave a fading impression. Who, even after a
single reading or representation, ever forgets Falstaff, or Shylock, or King
Lear?

The moral inferiority of Beaumont and Fletcher is well seen in such a play as
A King and No King. Here Arbaces falls in love with his sister, and, after a
furious conflict in his own mind, finally succumbs to his guilty passion. He is
rescued from {133} the consequences of his weakness by the discovery that
Panthea is not, in fact, his sister. But this is to cut the knot and not to untie it.
It leaves the *denouement* to chance, and not to those moral forces through
which Shakspere always wrought his conclusions. Arbaces has failed, and the
piece of luck which keeps his failure innocent is rejected by every right-
feeling spectator. In one of John Ford's tragedies, the situation which in *A
King and No King* is only apparent, becomes real, and incest is boldly made
the subject of the play. Ford pushed the morbid and unnatural in character and
passion into even wilder extremes than Beaumont and Fletcher. His best play,
the *Broken Heart*, is a prolonged and unrelieved torture of the feelings.

Fletcher's *Faithful Shepherdess* is the best English pastoral drama. Its choral
songs are richly and sweetly modulated, and the influence of the whole poem
upon Milton is very apparent in his *Comus*. *The Knight of the Burning Pestle*,
written by Beaumont and Fletcher jointly, was the first burlesque comedy in

the language, and is excellent fooling. Beaumont and Fletcher's blank verse is musical, but less masculine than Marlowe's or Shakspere's, by reason of their excessive use of extra syllables and feminine endings.

In John Webster the fondness for the abnormal and sensational themes, which beset the Stuart stage, showed itself in the exaggeration of the terrible into the horrible. Fear, in Shakspere—as in {134} the great murder scene in *Macbeth* —is a pure passion; but in Webster it is mingled with something physically repulsive. Thus his *Duchess of Malfi* is presented in the dark with a dead man's hand, and is told that it is the hand of her murdered husband. She is shown a dance of madmen and, "behind a traverse, the artificial figures of her children, appearing as if dead." Treated in this elaborate fashion, that "terror," which Aristotle said it was one of the objects of tragedy to move, loses half its dignity. Webster's images have the smell of the charnel house about them.

> "She would not after the report keep fresh
> As long as flowers on graves."
> "We are only like dead walls or vaulted graves,
> That, ruined, yield no echo.
>   O this gloomy world!
> In what a shadow or deep pit of darkness
> Doth womanish and fearful mankind live!"

Webster had an intense and somber genius. In diction he was the most Shaksperian of the Elisabethan dramatists, and there are sudden gleams of beauty among his dark horrors, which light up a whole scene with some abrupt touch of feeling.

"Cover her face; mine eyes dazzle; she died young,"

says the brother of the Duchess, when he has procured her murder and stands before the corpse. *Vittoria Corombona* is described in the old editions as "a night-piece," and it should, indeed, be {135} acted by the shuddering light of torches, and with the cry of the screech-owl to punctuate the speeches. The scene of Webster's two best tragedies was laid, like many of Ford's, Cyril Tourneur's, and Beaumont and Fletcher's, in Italy—the wicked and splendid Italy of the Renaissance, which had such a fascination for the Elisabethan imagination. It was to them the land of the Borgias and the Cenci; of families of proud nobles, luxurious, cultivated, but full of revenges and ferocious cunning; subtle poisoners, who killed with a perfumed glove or fan; parricides, atheists, committers of unnamable crimes, and inventors of strange and delicate varieties of sin.

But a very few have here been mentioned of the great host of dramatists who kept the theaters busy through the reigns of Elisabeth, James I., and Charles I.

The last of the race was James Shirley, who died in 1666, and whose thirty-eight plays were written during the reign of Charles I. and the Commonwealth.

In the miscellaneous prose and poetry of this period there is lacking the free, exulting, creative impulse of the elder generation, but there is a soberer feeling and a certain scholarly choiceness which commend themselves to readers of bookish tastes. Even that quaintness of thought, which is a mark of the Commonwealth writers, is not without its attraction for a nice literary palate. Prose became now of greater relative importance than ever before. Almost every distinguished writer of {136} the time lent his pen to one or the other party in the great theological and political controversy of the time. There were famous theologians, like Hales, Chillingworth, and Baxter; historians and antiquaries, like Selden, Knolles, and Cotton; philosophers, such as Hobbes, Lord Herbert of Cherbury, and More, the Platonist; and writers in rural science—which now entered upon its modern, experimental phase, under the stimulus of Bacon's writings—among whom may be mentioned Wallis, the mathematician; Boyle, the chemist, and Harvey, the discoverer of the circulation of the blood. These are outside of our subject, but in the strictly literary prose of the time, the same spirit of roused inquiry is manifest, and the same disposition to a thorough and exhaustive treatment of a subject which is proper to the scientific attitude of mind. The line between true and false science, however, had not yet been drawn. The age was pedantic, and appealed too much to the authority of antiquity. Hence we have such monuments of perverse and curious erudition as Robert Burton's *Anatomy of Melancholy*, 1621; and Sir Thomas Browne's *Pseudodoxia Epidemica*, or *Inquiries into Vulgar and Common Errors*, 1646. The former of these was the work of an Oxford scholar, an astrologer, who cast his own horoscope, and a victim himself of the atrabilious humor, from which he sought relief in listening to the ribaldry of barge-men, and in compiling this *Anatomy*, in which the causes, symptoms, prognostics, and cures of {137} melancholy are considered in numerous partitions, sections, members, and subsections. The work is a mosaic of quotations. All literature is ransacked for anecdotes and instances, and the book has thus become a mine of out-of-the-way learning, in which later writers have dug. Lawrence Sterne helped himself freely to Burton's treasures, and Dr. Johnson said that the *Anatomy* was the only book that ever took him out of bed two hours sooner than he wished to rise.

The vulgar and common errors which Sir Thomas Browne set himself to refute, were such as these: That dolphins are crooked, that Jews stink, that a man hath one rib less than a woman, that Xerxes's army drank up rivers, that cicades are bred out of cuckoo-spittle, that Hannibal split Alps with vinegar, together with many similar fallacies touching Pope Joan, the Wandering Jew, the decuman or tenth wave, the blackness of negroes, Friar Bacon's brazen head, etc. Another book in which great learning and ingenuity were applied to trifling ends, was the same author's *Garden of Cyrus; or, the Quincuncial Lozenge or Network Plantations of the Ancients,* in which a mystical meaning is sought in the occurrence throughout nature and art of the figure of the quincunx or lozenge. Browne was a physician of Norwich, where his library, museum, aviary, and botanic garden were thought worthy of a special visit by the Royal Society. He was an antiquary and a naturalist, and deeply read in the schoolmen and the Christian fathers. He was {138} a mystic, and a writer of a rich and peculiar imagination, whose thoughts have impressed themselves upon many kindred minds, like Coleridge, De Quincey, and Emerson. Two of his books belong to literature, *Religio Medici,* published in 1642, and *Hydriotaphia; or, Urn Burial,* 1658, a discourse upon rites of burial and incremation, suggested by some Roman funeral urns, dug up in Norfolk. Browne's style, though too highly Latinized, is a good example of Commonwealth prose, that stately, cumbrous, brocaded prose, which had something of the flow and measure of verse, rather than the quicker, colloquial movement of modern writing. Browne stood aloof from the disputes of his time, and in his very subjects there is a calm and meditative remoteness from the daily interests of men. His *Religio Medici* is full of a wise tolerance and a singular elevation of feeling. "At the sight of a cross, or crucifix, I can dispense with my hat, but scarce with the thought or memory of my Saviour." "They only had the advantage of a bold and noble faith, who lived before his coming." "They go the fairest way to heaven, that would serve God without a hell." "All things are artificial, for Nature is the art of God." The last chapter of the *Urn Burial* is an almost rithmical descant on mortality and oblivion. The style kindles slowly into a somber eloquence. It is the most impressive and extraordinary passage in the prose literature of the time. Browne, like Hamlet, loved to "consider too curiously." His subtlety {139} led him to "pose his apprehension with those involved enigmas and riddles of the Trinity—with incarnation and resurrection;" and to start odd inquiries; "what song the Syrens sang, or what name Achilles assumed when he hid himself among women;" or whether, after Lazarus was raised from the dead, "his heir might lawfully detain his inheritance." The quaintness of his phrase appears at every turn. "Charles the Fifth can never hope to live within two Methuselahs of Hector." "Generations pass, while some trees stand, and old families survive not three oaks." "Mummy is become merchandise; Mizraim cures wounds, and Pharaoh is sold for balsams."

One of the pleasantest of old English humorists is Thomas Fuller, who was a chaplain in the royal army during the civil war, and wrote, among other things, a *Church History of Britain*; a book of religious meditations, *Good Thoughts in Bad Times*, and a "character" book, *The Holy and Profane State*. His most important work, the *Worthies of England*, was published in 1662, the year after his death. This was a description of every English county; its natural commodities, manufactures, wonders, proverbs, etc., with brief biographies of its memorable persons. Fuller had a well-stored memory, sound piety, and excellent common sense. Wit was his leading intellectual trait, and the quaintness which he shared with his contemporaries appears in his writings in a fondness for puns, droll turns of expressions, and bits of eccentric {140} suggestion. His prose, unlike Browne's, Milton's, and Jeremy Taylor's, is brief, simple, and pithy. His dry vein of humor was imitated by the American Cotton Mather, in his *Magnalia*, and by many of the English and New England divines of the 17th century.

Jeremy Taylor was also a chaplain in the king's army, was several times imprisoned for his opinions, and was afterward made, by Charles II., Bishop of Down and Connor. He is a devotional rather than a theological writer, and his *Holy Living* and *Holy Dying* are religious classics. Taylor, like Sidney, was a "warbler of poetic prose." He has been called the prose Spenser, and his English has the opulence, the gentle elaboration, the "linked sweetness long drawn out" of the poet of the *Faery Queene*. In fullness and resonance, Taylor's diction resembles that of the great orators, though it lacks their nervous energy. His pathos is exquisitely tender, and his numerous similes have Spenser's pictorial amplitude. Some of them have become commonplaces for admiration, notably his description of the flight of the skylark, and the sentence in which he compares the gradual awakening of the human faculties to the sunrise, which "first opens a little eye of heaven, and sends away the spirits of darkness, and gives light to a cock, and calls up the lark to matins, and by and by gilds the fringes of a cloud, and peeps over the eastern hills." Perhaps the most impressive single passage of Taylor's is the concluding chapter in {141} *Holy Dying*. From the midst of the sickening paraphernalia of death which he there accumulates, rises that delicate image of the fading rose, one of the most perfect things in its wording, in all our prose literature: "But so have I seen a rose newly springing from the clefts of its hood, and at first it was as fair as the morning, and full with the dew of heaven as a lamb's fleece; but when a ruder breath had forced open its virgin modesty, and dismantled its too youthful and unripe retirements, it began to put on darkness and to decline to softness and the symptoms of a sickly age; it bowed the head and broke its stock; and at night, having lost some of its leaves and all its beauty, it fell into the portion of weeds and outworn faces."

With the progress of knowledge and discussion many kinds of prose literature, which were not absolutely new, now began to receive wider extension. Of this sort are the *Letters from Italy,* and other miscellanies included in the *Reliquiae Wottonianae,* or remains of Sir Henry Wotton, English embassador at Venice in the reign of James I., and subsequently Provost of Eton College. Also the *Table Talk*—full of incisive remarks—left by John Selden, whom Milton pronounced the first scholar of his age, and who was a distinguished authority in legal antiquities and international law, furnished notes to Drayton's *Polyolbion,* and wrote upon Eastern religions, and upon the Arundel marbles. Literary biography was represented by the charming little *Lives* of good old Izaak Walton, the first {142} edition of whose *Compleat Angler* was printed in 1653. The lives were five in number, of Hooker, Wotton, Donne, Herbert, and Sanderson. Several of these were personal friends of the author, and Sir Henry Wotton was a brother of the angle. The *Compleat Angler,* though not the first piece of sporting literature in English, is unquestionably the most popular, and still remains a favorite with "all that are lovers of virtue, and dare trust in providence, and be quiet, and go a-angling." As in Ascham's *Toxophilus,* the instruction is conveyed in dialogue form, but the technical part of the book is relieved by many delightful digressions. *Piscator* and his pupil *Venator* pursue their talk under a honeysuckle hedge or a sycamore tree during a passing shower. They repair, after the day's fishing, to some honest ale-house, with lavender in the window, and a score of ballads stuck about the wall, where they sing catches —"old-fashioned poetry but choicely good"—composed by the author or his friends, drink barley wine, and eat their trout or chub. They encounter milkmaids, who sing to them and give them a draft of the red cow's milk, and they never cease their praises of the angler's life, of rural contentment among the cowslip meadows, and the quiet streams of Thames, or Lea, or Shawford Brook.

The decay of a great literary school is usually signalized by the exaggeration of its characteristic traits. The manner of the Elisabethan poets was {143} pushed into mannerism by their successors. That manner, at its best, was hardly a simple one, but in the Stuart and Commonwealth writers it became mere extravagance. Thus Phineas Fletcher—a cousin of the dramatist— composed a long Spenserian allegory, the *Purple Island,* descriptive of the human body. George Herbert and others made anagrams and verses shaped like an altar, a cross, or a pair of Easter wings. This group of poets was named, by Dr. Johnson, in his life of Cowley, the metaphysical school. Other critics have preferred to call them the fantastic or conceited school, the later Euphuists, or the English Marinists and Gongorists, after the poets Marino and Gongora, who brought this fashion to its extreme in Italy and in Spain. The English *conceptistas* were mainly clergymen of the established Church, Donne, Herbert, Vaughan, Quarles, and Herrick. But Crashaw was a Roman

Catholic, and Cowley—the latest of them—a layman.

The one who set the fashion was Dr. John Donne. Dean of St. Paul's, whom Dryden pronounced a great wit, but not a great poet, and whom Ben Jonson esteemed the best poet in the world for some things, but likely to be forgotten for want of being understood. Besides satires and epistles in verse, he composed amatory poems in his youth, and divine poems in his age, both kinds distinguished by such subtle obscurity, and far-fetched ingenuities, that they read like a series of puzzles. When this poet has occasion to write a valediction {144} to his mistress upon going into France, he compares their temporary separation to that of a pair of compasses:

"Such wilt thou be to me, who must,
Like the other foot obliquely run;
Thy firmness makes my circle just,
And makes me end where I begun."

If he would persuade her to marriage he calls her attention to a flea—

"Me it sucked first and now sucks thee,
And in this flea our two bloods mingled be."

He says that the flea is their marriage-temple, and bids her forbear to kill it lest she thereby commit murder, suicide, and sacrilege all in one. Donne's figures are scholastic and smell of the lamp. He ransacked cosmography, astrology, alchemy, optics, the canon law, and the divinity of the schoolmen for ink-horn terms and similes. He was in verse what Browne was in prose. He loved to play with distinctions, hyperboles, paradoxes, the very casuistry and dialectics of love or devotion.

"Thou canst not every day give me thy heart:
If thou canst give it then thou never gav'st it;
Love's riddles are that though thy heart depart,
It stays at home and thou with losing sav'st it."

Donne's verse is usually as uncouth as his thought. But there is a real passion slumbering under these ashy heaps of conceit, and occasionally {145} a pure flame darts up, as in the justly admired lines:

"Her pure and eloquent blood
Spoke in her cheek and so divinely wrought
That one might almost say her body thought."

This description of Donne is true, with modifications, of all the metaphysical poets. They had the same forced and unnatural style. The ordinary laws of the association of ideas were reversed with them. It was not the nearest, but the remotest, association that was called up. "Their attempts," said Johnson, "were always analytic: they broke every image into fragments." The finest spirit among them was "holy George Herbert," whose *Temple* was published in 1631. The titles in this volume were such as the following: Christmas, Easter, Good Friday, Holy Baptism, The Cross, The Church Porch, Church Music, The Holy Scriptures, Redemption, Faith, Doomsday. Never since, except, perhaps, in Keble's *Christian Year*, have the ecclesiastic ideals of the Anglican Church—the "beauty of holiness"—found such sweet expression in poetry. The verses entitled *Virtue*—

"Sweet day so cool, so calm, so bright," etc.

are known to most readers, as well as the line,

"Who sweeps a room, as for thy laws, makes that and the action fine."

The quaintly named pieces, the *Elixir*, the *Collar*, the *Pulley*, are full of deep thought and spiritual {146} feeling. But Herbert's poetry is constantly disfigured by bad taste. Take this passage from *Whitsunday*,

"Listen, sweet dove, unto my song,
And spread thy golden wings on me,
Hatching my tender heart so long,
  Till it get wing and fly away with thee,"

which is almost as ludicrous as the epitaph, written by his contemporary, Carew, on the daughter of Sir Thomas Wentworth, whose soul

… "grew so fast within
It broke the outward shell of sin,
And so was hatched a cherubin."

Another of these Church poets was Henry Vaughan, "the Silurist," or Welshman, whose fine piece, the *Retreat*, has been often compared with Wordsworth's *Ode on the Intimations of Immortality*. Francis Quarles' *Divine Emblems* long remained a favorite book with religious readers, both in Old and New England. Emblem books, in which engravings of a figurative design were accompanied with explanatory letterpress in verse, were a popular class of literature in the 17th century. The most famous of them all were Jacob Catt's Dutch emblems.

One of the most delightful of English lyric poets is Robert Herrick, whose *Hesperides*, 1648 has lately received such sympathetic illustration from the pencil of an American artist, Mr. E. A. Abbey. Herrick was a clergyman of the English Church, {147} and was expelled by the Puritans from his living, the vicarage of Dean Prior, in Devonshire. The most quoted of his religious poems is, *How to Keep a True Lent*. But it may be doubted whether his tastes were prevailingly clerical; his poetry certainly was not. He was a disciple of

Ben Jonson and his boon companion at

> … "those lyric feasts
>   Made at the Sun,
> The Dog, the Triple Tun;
> Where we such clusters had
> As made us nobly wild, not mad.
> And yet each verse of thine
> Outdid the meat, outdid the frolic wine."

Herrick's *Noble Numbers* seldom rises above the expression of a cheerful gratitude and contentment. He had not the subtlety and elevation of Herbert, but he surpassed him in the grace, melody, sensuous beauty, and fresh lyrical impulse of his verse. The conceits of the metaphysical school appear in Herrick only in the form of an occasional pretty quaintness. He is the poet of English parish festivals and of English flowers, the primrose, the whitethorn, the daffodil. He sang the praises of the country life, love songs to "Julia," and hymns of thanksgiving for simple blessings. He has been called the English Catullus, but he strikes rather the Horatian note of *Carpe diem*, and regret at the shortness of life and youth in many of his best-known poems, such as {148} *Gather ye Rose-buds while ye may*, and *To Corinna, To Go a Maying*.

Abraham Cowley is now less remembered for his poetry than for his pleasant volume of Essays, published after the Restoration; but he was thought in his own time a better poet than Milton. His collection of love songs—the *Mistress*—is a mass of cold conceits, in the metaphysical manner; but his elegies on Crashaw and Harvey have much dignity and natural feeling. He introduced the Pindaric ode into English, and wrote an epic poem on a biblical subject—the *Davideis*—now quite unreadable. Cowley was a royalist and followed the exiled court to France. Side by side with the Church poets were the cavaliers—Carew, Waller, Lovelace, Suckling, L'Estrange, and others—gallant courtiers and officers in the royal army, who mingled love and loyalty in their strains. Colonel Richard Lovelace, who lost every thing in the king's service and was several times imprisoned, wrote two famous songs —*To Lucasta on going to the Wars*—in which occur the lines,

> "I could not love thee, dear, so much,
> Loved I not honor more."

and *To Althaea from Prison*, in which he sings "the sweetness, mercy, majesty, and glories of his king," and declares that "stone walls do not a prison make, nor iron bars a cage." Another of the cavaliers was sir John Suckling, who formed a plot to rescue the Earl of Stratford, raised a troop of horse {149} for Charles I., was impeached by the Parliament and fled to France. He was a man of wit and pleasure, who penned a number of gay

trifles, but has been saved from oblivion chiefly by his exquisite *Ballad upon a Wedding*. Thomas Carew and Edmund Waller were poets of the same stamp —graceful and easy, but shallow in feeling. Waller, who followed the court to Paris, was the author of two songs, which are still favorites, *Go, Lovely Rose,* and *On a Girdle*, and he first introduced the smooth correct manner of writing in couplets, which Dryden and Pope carried to perfection. Gallantry rather than love was the inspiration of these courtly singers. In such verses as Carew's *Encouragements to a Lover*, and George Wither's *The Manly Heart*
—

"If she be not so to me,
  What care I how fair she be?"

we see the revolt against the high, passionate, Sidneian love of the Elisabethan sonneteers, and the note of *persiflage* that was to mark the lyrical verse of the Restoration. But the poetry of the cavaliers reached its high-water mark in one fiery-hearted song by the noble and unfortunate James Graham, Marquis of Montrose, who invaded Scotland in the interest of Charles II., and was taken prisoner and put to death at Edinburgh in 1650.

"My dear and only love, I pray
  That little world of thee
Be governed by no other sway
  Than purest monarchy."

{150} In language borrowed from the politics of the time, he cautions his mistress against *synods* or *committees* in her heart; swears to make her glorious by his pen and famous by his sword; and with that fine recklessness which distinguished the dashing troopers of Prince Rupert, he adds, in words that have been often quoted,

"He either fears his fate too much,
  Or his deserts are small,
That dares not put it to the touch
  To gain or lose it all."

John Milton, the greatest English poet except Shakspere, was born in London in 1608. His father was a scrivener, an educated man, and a musical composer of some merit. At his home Milton was surrounded with all the influences of a refined and well ordered Puritan household of the better class. He inherited his father's musical tastes, and during the latter part of his life, he spent a part of every afternoon in playing the organ. No poet has written more beautifully of music than Milton. One of his sonnets was addressed to Henry Lawes, the composer, who wrote the airs to the songs in *Comus*. Milton's education was most careful and thorough. He spent seven years at Cambridge where, from his personal beauty and fastidious habits, he was called "The lady of Christ's." At Horton, in Buckinghamshire, where his father had a country seat, he passed five years more, perfecting himself in his studies, and then traveled for fifteen months, {151} mainly in Italy, visiting Naples and Rome, but residing at Florence. Here he saw Galileo, a prisoner of the Inquisition "for thinking otherwise in astronomy than his Dominican and Franciscan licensers thought." Milton is the most scholarly and the most truly classical of English poets. His Latin verse, for elegance and correctness, ranks with Addison's; and his Italian poems were the admiration of the Tuscan scholars. But his learning appears in his poetry only in the form of a fine and chastened result, and not in laborious allusion and pedantic citation, as too often in Ben Jonson, for instance. "My father," he wrote, "destined me, while yet a little child, for the study of humane letters." He was also destined for the ministry, but, "coming to some maturity of years and perceiving what tyranny had invaded the Church, … I thought it better to prefer a blameless silence, before the sacred office of speaking, bought and begun with servitude and forswearing." Other hands than a bishop's were laid upon his head. "He who would not be frustrate of his hope to write well hereafter," he says, "ought himself to be a true poem." And he adds that his "natural haughtiness" saved him from all impurity of living. Milton had a sublime self-respect. The dignity and earnestness of the Puritan gentleman blended in his training with the culture of the Renaissance. Born into an age of spiritual conflict, he dedicated his gift to the service of Heaven, and he became, like Heine, a valiant soldier in the war for {152} liberation. He was the poet of a cause, and his song was keyed to

"The Dorian mood
Of flutes and soft recorders such as raised
To heighth of noblest temper, heroes old
Arming to battle."

On comparing Milton with Shakspere, with his universal sympathies and receptive imagination, one perceives a loss in breadth, but a gain in intense personal conviction. He introduced a new note into English poetry, the passion for truth and the feeling of religious sublimity. Milton's was an heroic age, and its song must be lyric rather than dramatic; its singer must be in the fight and of it.

Of the verses which he wrote at Cambridge, the most important was his splendid ode *On the Morning of Christ's Nativity*. At Horton he wrote, among other things, the companion pieces, *L'Allegro* and *Il Penseroso*, of a kind quite new in English, giving to the landscape an expression in harmony with two contrasted moods. *Comus*, which belongs to the same period, was the perfection of the Elisabethan court masque, and was presented at Ludlow Castle in 1634, on the occasion of the installation of the Earl of Bridgewater as Lord President of Wales. Under the guise of a skillful addition to the Homeric allegory of Circe, with her cup of enchantment, it was a Puritan song in praise of chastity and temperance. *Lycidas*, in like manner, was the perfection of the Elisabethan {153} pastoral elegy. It was contributed to a volume of memorial verses on the death of Edward King, a Cambridge friend of Milton's, who was drowned in the Irish Channel in 1637. In one stern strain, which is put into the mouth of St. Peter, the author "foretells the ruin of our corrupted clergy, then at their height."

"But that two-handed engine at the door
Stands ready to smite once and smite no more."

This was Milton's last utterance in English verse before the outbreak of the civil war, and it sounds the alarm of the impending struggle. In technical quality *Lycidas* is the most wonderful of all Milton's poems. The cunningly intricate harmony of the verse, the pressed and packed language with its fullness of meaning and allusion make it worthy of the minutest study. In these early poems, Milton, merely as a poet, is at his best. Something of the Elisabethan style still clings to them; but their grave sweetness, their choice wording, their originality in epithet, name, and phrase, were novelties of Milton's own. His English masters were Spenser, Fletcher, and Sylvester, the translator of Du Bartas's *La Sepmaine*, but nothing of Spenser's prolixity, or Fletcher's effeminacy, or Sylvester's quaintness is found in Milton's pure, energetic diction. He inherited their beauties, but his taste had been tempered to a finer edge by his studies in Greek and Hebrew poetry. He was the last of the Elisabethans, and {154} his style was at once the crown of the old and a departure into the new. In masque, elegy, and sonnet, he set the seal to the Elisabethan poetry, said the last word, and closed one great literary era.

In 1639 the breach between Charles I. and his Parliament brought Milton back from Italy. "I thought it base to be traveling at my ease for amusement, while my fellow-countrymen at home were fighting for liberty." For the next twenty years he threw himself into the contest, and poured forth a succession of tracts, in English and Latin, upon the various public questions at issue. As a political thinker, Milton had what Bacon calls "the humor of a scholar." In a country of endowed grammar schools and universities hardly emerged from a mediaeval discipline and curriculum, he wanted to set up Greek gymnasia and philosophical schools, after the fashion of the Porch and the Academy. He would have imposed an Athenian democracy upon a people trained in the traditions of monarchy and episcopacy. At the very moment when England had grown tired of the Protectorate and was preparing to welcome back the

Stuarts, he was writing *An Easy and Ready Way to Establish a Free Commonwealth*. Milton acknowledged that in prose he had the use of his left hand only. There are passages of fervid eloquence, where the style swells into a kind of lofty chant, with a rithmical rise and fall to it, as in parts of the English Book of Common Prayer. But in {155} general his sentences are long and involved, full of inventions and latinized constructions. Controversy at that day was conducted on scholastic lines. Each disputant, instead of appealing at once to the arguments of expediency and common sense, began with a formidable display of learning, ransacking Greek and Latin authors and the fathers of the Church for opinions in support of his own position. These authorities he deployed at tedious length and followed them up with heavy scurrilities and "excusations," by way of attack and defense. The dispute between Milton and Salmasius over the execution of Charles I. was like a duel between two knights in full armor striking at each other with ponderous maces. The very titles of these pamphlets are enough to frighten off a modern reader: *A Confutation of the Animadversions upon a Defense of a Humble Remonstrance against a Treatise, entitled Of Reformation*. The most interesting of Milton's prose tracts is his *Areopagitica: A Speech for the Liberty of Unlicensed Printing*, 1644. The arguments in this are of permanent force; but if the reader will compare it, or Jeremy Taylor's *Liberty of Prophesying*, with Locke's *Letters on Toleration*, he will see how much clearer and more convincing is the modern method of discussion, introduced by writers like Hobbes and Locke and Dryden. Under the Protectorate Milton was appointed Latin Secretary to the Council of State. In the diplomatic correspondence which was his official duty, and in the composition of his tract, {156} *Defensio pro Populo Anglicano*, he overtasked his eyes, and in 1654 became totally blind. The only poetry of Milton's belonging to the years 1640-1660 are a few sonnets of the pure Italian form, mainly called forth by public occasions. By the Elisabethans the sonnet had been used mainly in love poetry. In Milton's hands, said Wordsworth, "the thing became a trumpet." Some of his were addressed to political leaders, like Fairfax, Cromwell, and Sir Henry Vane; and of these the best is, perhaps, the sonnet written on the massacre of the Vaudois Protestants—"a collect in verse," it has been called —which has the fire of a Hebrew prophet invoking the divine wrath upon the oppressors of Israel. Two were on his own blindness, and in these there is not one selfish repining, but only a regret that the value of his service is impaired

—

"Will God exact day labor, light denied?"

After the restoration of the Stuarts, in 1660, Milton was for a while in peril, by reason of the part that he had taken against the king. But

"On evil days though fallen, and evil tongues,
In darkness and with dangers compassed round
And solitude,"

he bated no jot of heart or hope. Henceforth he becomes the most heroic and affecting figure in English literary history. Years before he had planned an epic poem on the subject of King {157} Arthur, and again a sacred tragedy on man's fall and redemption. These experiments finally took shape in *Paradise Lost*, which was given to the world in 1667. This is the epic of English Puritanism and of Protestant Christianity. It was Milton's purpose to

"assert eternal Providence And justify the ways of God to men,"

or, in other words, to embody his theological system in verse. This gives a doctrinal rigidity and even dryness to parts of the *Paradise Lost*, which injure its effect as a poem. His "God the father turns a school divine:" his Christ, as has been wittily said, is "God's good boy:" the discourses of Raphael to Adam are scholastic lectures: Adam himself is too sophisticated for the state of innocence, and Eve is somewhat insipid. The real protagonist of the poem is Satan, upon whose mighty figure Milton unconsciously bestowed something of his own nature, and whose words of defiance might almost have come from some Republican leader when the Good Old Cause went down.

"What though the field be lost?
All is not lost, the unconquerable will
And study of revenge, immortal hate,
And courage never to submit or yield."

But when all has been said that can be said in disparagement or qualification, *Paradise Lost* remains the foremost of English poems and the {158} sublimest of all epics. Even in those parts where theology encroaches most upon poetry, the diction, though often heavy, is never languid. Milton's blank verse in itself is enough to bear up the most prosaic theme, and so is his epic English, a style more massive and splendid than Shakspere's, and comparable, like Tertullian's Latin, to a river of molten gold. Of the countless single beauties that sow his page

"Thick as autumnal leaves that strew the brooks
In Valombrosa,"

there is no room to speak, nor of the astonishing fullness of substance and multitude of thoughts which have caused the *Paradise Lost* to be called the book of universal knowledge. "The heat of Milton's mind," said Dr. Johnson, "might be said to sublimate his learning and throw off into his work the spirit of science, unmingled with its grosser parts." The truth of this remark is clearly seen upon a comparison of Milton's description of the creation, for example, with corresponding passages in Sylvester's *Divine Weeks and Works* (translated from the Huguenot poet, Du Bartas), which was, in some sense, his original. But the most heroic thing in Milton's heroic poem is Milton. There are no strains in *Paradise Lost* so absorbing as those in which the poet breaks the strict epic bounds and speaks directly of himself, as in the majestic lament over his own blindness, and in the invocation to Urania, which open the third and seventh {159} books. Every-where, too, one reads between the lines. We think of the dissolute cavaliers, as Milton himself undoubtedly was thinking of them, when we read of "the sons of Belial flown with insolence and wine," or when the Puritan turns among the sweet landscapes of Eden, to denounce

"court amours
Mixed dance, or wanton mask, or midnight ball,
Or serenade which the starved lover sings
To his proud fair, best quitted with disdain."

And we think of Milton among the triumphant royalists when we read of the Seraph Abdiel "faithful found among the faithless."

"Nor number nor example with him wrought
To swerve from truth or change his constant mind,
Though single. From amidst them forth he passed,
Long way through hostile scorn, which he sustained
Superior, nor of violence feared aught:
And with retorted scorn his back he turned
On those proud towers to swift destruction doomed."

Paradise Regained and *Samson Agonistes* were published in 1671. The first of these treated in four books Christ's temptation in the wilderness, a subject that had already been handled in the Spenserian allegorical manner by Giles Fletcher, a brother of the Purple Islander, in his *Christ's Victory and Triumph*, 1610. The superiority of *Paradise Lost* to its sequel is not without significance. The Puritans were Old Testament men. Their God was the Hebrew Jehovah, whose single divinity the Catholic mythology had overlaid with the {160} figures of the Son, the Virgin Mary, and the saints. They identified themselves in thought with his chosen people, with the militant theocracy of the Jews. Their sword was the sword of the Lord and of Gideon. "To your tents, O Israel," was the cry of the London mob when the bishops were committed to the Tower. And when the fog lifted, on the morning of the battle of Dunbar, Cromwell exclaimed, "Let God arise and let his enemies be scattered: like as the sun riseth, so shalt thou drive them away."

Samson Agonistes, though Hebrew in theme and in spirit, was in form a Greek tragedy. It had chorus and semi-chorus, and preserved the so-called dramatic unities; that is, the scene was unchanged, and there were no intervals of time between the acts. In accordance with the rules of the Greek theater, but two speakers appeared upon the stage at once, and there was no violent action. The death of Samson is related by a messenger. Milton's reason for the choice of this subject is obvious. He himself was Samson, shorn of his strength, blind, and alone among enemies; given over

> "to the unjust tribunals, under change of times, And
> condemnation of the ungrateful multitude."

As Milton grew older he discarded more and more the graces of poetry, and relied purely upon the structure and the thought. In *Paradise Lost*, although there is little resemblance to Elisabethan work—such as one notices in *Comus* and the {161} Christmas hymn—yet the style is rich, especially in the earlier books. But in *Paradise Regained* it is severe to bareness, and in *Samson*, even to ruggedness. Like Michelangelo, with whose genius he had much in common, Milton became impatient of finish or of mere beauty. He blocked out his work in masses, left rough places and surfaces not filled in, and inclined to express his meaning by a symbol, rather than work it out in detail. It was a part of his austerity, his increasing preference for structural over decorative methods, to give up rime for blank verse. His latest poem, *Samson Agonistes*, a metrical study of the highest interest.

Milton was not quite alone among the poets of his time in espousing the popular cause. Andrew Marvell, who was his assistant in the Latin secretaryship and sat in Parliament for Hull, after the Restoration, was a good Republican, and wrote a fine *Horatian Ode upon Cromwell's Return from Ireland*. There is also a rare imaginative quality in his *Song of the Exiles in Bermuda*, *Thoughts in a Garden*, and *The Girl Describes her Fawn*. George Wither, who was imprisoned for his satires, also took the side of the Parliament, but there is little that is distinctively Puritan in his poetry.

1. Milton's Poetical Works. Edited by David Masson. Macmillan.

2. Selections from Milton's Prose. Edited by F. D. Myers. (Parchment Series.)

{162}

3. England's Antiphon. By George Macdonald.

4. Robert Herrick's Hesperides.

5. Sir Thomas Browne's Religio Medici and Hydriotaphia. Edited by Willis Bund. Sampson Low & Co., 1873.

6. Thomas. Fuller's Good Thoughts in Bad Times.

7. Izaak Walton's Compleat Angler.

{163}

CHAPTER V.

FROM THE RESTORATION TO THE DEATH OF POPE.

1660-1744.

The Stuart Restoration was a period of descent from poetry to prose, from passion and imagination to wit and understanding. The serious, exalted mood of the Civil War and the Commonwealth had spent itself and issued in disillusion. There followed a generation of wits, logical, skeptical, and prosaic, without earnestness, as without principle. The characteristic literature of such a time is criticism, satire, and burlesque, and such, indeed, continued to be the course of English literary history for a century after the return of the Stuarts. The age was not a stupid one, but one of active inquiry. The Royal Society, for the cultivation of the natural sciences, was founded in 1662. There were able divines in the pulpit and at the universities—Barrow, Tillotson, Stillingfleet, South, and others: scholars, like Bentley; historians, like Clarendon and Burnet; scientists, like Boyle and Newton; philosophers, like Hobbes and Locke. But of poetry, in any high sense of the word, there was little between the time of Milton and the time of Goldsmith and Gray.

{164} The English writers of this period were strongly influenced by the contemporary literature of France, by the comedies of Molière, the tragedies of Corneille and Racine, and the satires, epistles, and versified essays of Boileau. Many of the Restoration writers—Waller, Cowley, Davenant, Wycherley, Villiers, and others—had been in France during the exile, and brought back with them French tastes. John Dryden (1631-1700), who is the great literary figure of his generation, has been called the first of the moderns. From the reign of Charles II., indeed, we may date the beginnings of modern English life. What we call "society" was forming, the town, the London world. "Coffee, which makes the politician wise," had just been introduced, and the ordinaries of Ben Jonson's time gave way to coffee-houses, like Will's and Button's, which became the head-quarters of literary and political gossip. The two great English parties, as we know them to-day, were organized: the words *Whig* and *Tory* date from this reign. French etiquette and fashions came in and French phrases of convenience—such as *coup de grace*, *bel esprit*, etc.

—began to appear in English prose. Literature became intensely urban and partisan. It reflected city life, the disputes of faction, and the personal quarrels of authors. The politics of the Great Rebellion had been of heroic proportions, and found fitting expression in song. Rut in the Revolution of 1688 the issues were constitutional and to be settled by the arguments of lawyers. Measures were in {165} question rather than principles, and there was little inspiration to the poet in Exclusion Bills and Acts of Settlement.

Court and society, in the reign of Charles II. and James II., were shockingly dissolute, and in literature, as in life, the reaction against Puritanism went to great extremes. The social life of the time is faithfully reflected in the diary of Samuel Pepys. He was a simple-minded man, the son of a London tailor, and became, himself, secretary to the admiralty. His diary was kept in cipher, and published only in 1825. Being written for his own eye, it is singularly outspoken; and its naïve, gossipy, confidential tone makes it a most diverting book, as it is, historically, a most valuable one.

Perhaps the most popular book of its time was Samuel Butler's *Hudibras* (1663-64), a burlesque romance in ridicule of the Puritans. The king carried a copy of it in his pocket, and Pepys testifies that it was quoted and praised on all sides. Ridicule of the Puritans was nothing new. Zeal-of-the-land Busy, in Ben Jonson's *Bartholomew Fair*, is an early instance of the kind. There was nothing laughable about the earnestness of men like Cromwell, Milton, Algernon Sidney, and Sir Henry Vane. But even the French Revolution had its humors; and as the English Puritan Revolution gathered head and the extremer sectaries pressed to the front—Quakers, New Lights, Fifth Monarchy Men, Ranters, etc.—its grotesque sides came uppermost. Butler's hero is a Presbyterian Justice of the Peace {166} who sallies forth with his secretary, Ralpho—an Independent and Anabaptist—like Don Quixote with Sancho Panza, to suppress May games and bear-baitings. (Macaulay, it will be remembered, said that the Puritans disapproved of bear-baiting, not because it gave pain to the bear, but because it gave pleasure to the spectators.) The humor of *Hudibras* is not of the finest. The knight and squire are discomfited in broadly comic adventures, hardly removed from the rough, physical drolleries of a pantomime or a circus. The deep heart-laughter of Cervantes, the pathos on which his humor rests, is, of course, not to be looked for in Butler. But he had wit of a sharp, logical kind, and his style surprises with all manner of verbal antics. He is almost as great a phrase-master as Pope, though in a coarser kind. His verse is a smart doggerel, and his poem has furnished many stock sayings, as, for example,

"'Tis strange what difference there can be
'Twixt tweedle-dum and tweedle-dee."

Hudibras has had many imitators, not the least successful of whom was the American John Trumbull, in his revolutionary satire *M'Fingal*, some couplets of which are generally quoted as Butler's, as, for example,

"No man e'er felt the halter draw
 With good opinion of the law."

The rebound against Puritanism is seen no less plainly in the drama of the Restoration, and the {167} stage now took vengeance for its enforced silence under the Protectorate. Two theaters were opened under the patronage, respectively, of the king and of his brother, the Duke of York. The manager of the latter, Sir William Davenant—who had fought on the king's side, been knighted for his services, escaped to France, and was afterward captured and imprisoned in England for two years—had managed to evade the law against stage plays as early as 1656, by presenting his *Siege of Rhodes* as an "opera," with instrumental music and dialogue in recitative, after a fashion newly sprung up in Italy. This he brought out again in 1661, with the dialogue recast into riming couplets in the French fashion. Movable painted scenery was now introduced from France, and actresses took the female parts formerly played by boys. This last innovation was said to be at the request of the king, one of whose mistresses, the famous Nell Gwynne, was the favorite actress at the King's Theater.

Upon the stage, thus reconstructed, the so-called "classical" rules of the French theater were followed, at least in theory. The Louis XIV. writers were not purely creative, like Shakspere and his contemporaries in England, but critical and self-conscious. The Academy had been formed in 1636, for the preservation of the purity of the French language, and discussion abounded on the principles and methods of literary art. Corneille not only wrote tragedies, but essays on tragedy, and {168} one in particular on the *Three Unities*. Dryden followed his example in his *Essay of Dramatic Poesie* (1667), in which he treated of the unities, and argued for the use of rime in tragedy in preference to blank verse. His own practice varied. Most of his tragedies were written in rime, but in the best of them, *All for Love*, 1678, founded on Shakspere's *Antony and Cleopatra*, he returned to blank verse. One of the principles of the classical school was to keep comedy and tragedy distinct. The tragic dramatists of the Restoration, Dryden, Howard, Settle, Crowne, Lee, and others, composed what they called "heroic plays," such as the *Indian Emperor*, the *Conquest of Granada*, the *Duke of Lerma*, the *Empress of Morocco*, the *Destruction of Jerusalem*, *Nero*, and the *Rival Queens*. The titles of these pieces indicate their character. Their heroes were great historic personages. Subject and treatment were alike remote from nature and real life. The diction was stilted and artificial, and pompous declamation took the place of action and genuine passion. The tragedies of Racine seem chill to an Englishman brought up on Shakspere, but to see how great an artist Racine was, in his own somewhat narrow way, one has but to compare his *Phedre*, or *Iphigenie*, with Dryden's ranting tragedy of *Tyrannic Love*. These bombastic heroic plays were made the subject of a capital burlesque, the *Rehearsal*, by George Villiers, Duke of Buckingham, acted in 1671 at the King's Theater. The indebtedness of {169} the English stage to the French did not stop with a general adoption of its dramatic methods, but extended to direct imitation and translation. Dryden's comedy, *An Evening's Love*, was adapted from Thomas Corneille's *Le Feint Astrologue*, and his *Sir Martin Mar-all*, from Molière's *L'Etourdi*. Shadwell borrowed his *Miser* from Molière, and Otway made versions of Racine's *Bérénice* and Molière's *Fourberies de Scapin*. Wycherley's *Country Wife* and *Plain Dealer*, although not translations, were based, in a sense, upon Molière's *Ecole des Femmes* and *Le Misanthrope*. The only one of the tragic dramatists of the Restoration who prolonged the traditions of the Elisabethan stage, was Otway, whose *Venice Preserved*, written in blank verse, still keeps the boards. There are fine passages in Dryden's heroic plays, passages weighty in thought and nobly sonorous in language. There is one great scene (between Antony and Ventidius) in his *All for Love*. And one, at least, of his comedies, the *Spanish Friar*, is skillfully constructed. But his nature was not pliable enough for the drama, and he acknowledged that, in writing for the stage, he "forced his genius."

In sharp contrast with these heroic plays was the comic drama of the Restoration, the plays of Wycherley, Killigrew, Etherege, Farquhar, Van Brugh, Congreve, and others; plays like the *Country Wife*, the *Parson's Wedding*, *She Would if She Could*, the *Beaux' Stratagem*, the *Relapse*, and the *Way of the World*. These were in prose, and represented {170} the gay world and the surface of fashionable life. Amorous intrigue was their constantly recurring theme. Some of them were written expressly in ridicule of the Puritans. Such was the *Committee* of Dryden's brother-in-law, Sir Robert Howard, the hero of which is a distressed gentleman, and the villain a London cit, and president of the committee appointed by Parliament to sit upon the sequestration of the estates of royalists. Such were also the *Roundheads* and the *Banished Cavaliers* of Mrs. Aphra Behn, who was a female spy in the service of Charles II., at Antwerp, and one of the coarsest of the Restoration comedians. The profession of piety had become so disagreeable that a shameless cynicism was now considered the mark of a gentleman. The ideal hero of Wycherley or Etherege was the witty young profligate, who had seen life, and learned to disbelieve in virtue. His highest qualities were a contempt for cant, physical courage, a sort of spendthrift generosity, and a good-natured readiness to back up a friend in a quarrel, or an amour. Virtue was *bourgeois*

—reserved for London trades-people. A man must be either a rake or a hypocrite. The gentlemen were rakes, the city people were hypocrites. Their wives, however, were all in love with the gentlemen, and it was the proper thing to seduce them, and to borrow their husbands' money. For the first and last time, perhaps, in the history of the English drama, the sympathy of the audience was deliberately sought for the seducer and the rogue, and the laugh {171} turned against the dishonored husband and the honest man. (Contrast this with Shakspere's *Merry Wives of Windsor*.) The women were represented as worse than the men—scheming, ignorant, and corrupt. The dialogue in the best of these plays was easy, lively, and witty; the situations in some of them audacious almost beyond belief. Under a thin varnish of good breeding, the sentiments and manners were really brutal. The loosest gallants of Beaumont and Fletcher's theater retain a fineness of feeling and that *politesse de coeur* —which marks the gentleman. They are poetic creatures, and own a capacity for romantic passion. But the Manlys and Homers of the Restoration comedy have a prosaic, cold-blooded profligacy that disgusts. Charles Lamb, in his ingenious essay on "The Artificial Comedy of the Last Century," apologized for the Restoration stage, on the ground that it represented a world of whim and unreality in which the ordinary laws of morality had no application.

But Macaulay answered truly, that at no time has the stage been closer in its imitation of real life. The theater of Wycherley and Etherege was but the counterpart of that social condition which we read of in Pepys's *Diary*, and in the *Memoirs* of the Chevalier de Grammont. This prose comedy of manners was not, indeed, "artificial" at all, in the sense in which the contemporary tragedy—the "heroic play"—was artificial. It was, on the contrary, far more natural, and, intellectually, of {172} much higher value. In 1698 Jeremy Collier, a non-juring Jacobite clergyman, published his *Short View of the Immorality and Profaneness of the English Stage*, which did much toward reforming the practice of the dramatists. The formal characteristics, without the immorality, of the Restoration comedy, re-appeared briefly in Goldsmith's *She Stoops to Conquer*, 1772, and Sheridan's *Rival, School for Scandal*, and *Critic*, 1775-9, our last strictly "classical" comedies. None of this school of English comedians approached their model, Molière. He excelled his imitators not only in his French urbanity—the polished wit and delicate grace of his style—but in the dexterous unfolding of his plot, and in the wisdom and truth of his criticism of life, and his insight into character. It is a symptom of the false taste of the age that Shakspere's plays were rewritten for the Restoration stage. Davenant made new versions of *Macbeth* and *Julius Caasar*, substituting rime for blank verse. In conjunction with Dryden, he altered the *Tempest*, complicating the intrigue by the introduction of a male counterpart to Miranda—a youth who had never seen a woman. Shadwell "improved" *Timon of Athens*, and Nahum Tate furnished a new fifth act to *King Lear*, which turned the play into a comedy! In the prologue to his doctored version of *Troilus and Cressida*, Dryden made the ghost of Shakspere speak of himself as

"Untaught, unpracticed in a barbarous age."

{172} Thomas Rymer, whom Pope pronounced a good critic, was very severe upon Shakspere in his *Remarks on the Tragedies of the Last Age*; and in his *Short View of Tragedy*, 1693, he said, "In the neighing of a horse or in the growling of a mastiff, there is more humanity than, many times, in the tragical flights of Shakspere." "To Deptford by water," writes Pepys, in his diary for August 20, 1666, "reading Othello, Moor of Venice; which I ever heretofore esteemed a mighty good play; but, having so lately read the *Adventures of Five Hours*, it seems a mean thing."

In undramatic poetry the new school, both in England and in France, took its point of departure in a reform against the extravagances of the Marinists, or conceited poets, specially represented in England by Donne and Cowley. The new poets, both in their theory and practice, insisted upon correctness, clearness, polish, moderation, and good sense. Boileau's *L'Art Poetique*, 1673, inspired by Horace's *Ars Poetica*, was a treatise in verse upon the rules of correct composition, and it gave the law in criticism for over a century, not only in France, but in Germany and England. It gave English poetry a didactic turn and started the fashion of writing critical essays in riming couplets. The Earl of Mulgrave published two "poems" of this kind, an *Essay on Satire*, and an *Essay on Poetry*. The Earl of Roscommon—who, said Addison, "makes even rules a noble poetry"—made a metrical version of Horace's *Ars Poetica*, {174} and wrote an original *Essay on Translated Verse*. Of the same kind were Addison's epistle to Sacheverel, entitled *An Account of the Greatest English Poets*, and Pope's *Essay on Criticism*, 1711, which was nothing more than versified maxims of rhetoric, put with Pope's usual point and brilliancy. The classicism of the 18th century, it has been said, was a classicism in red heels and a periwig. It was Latin rather than Greek; it turned to the least imaginative side of Latin literature and found its models, not in Vergil, Catullus, and Lucretius, but in the satires, epistles, and didactic pieces of Juvenal, Horace, and Persius.

The chosen medium of the new poetry was the heroic couplet. This had, of course, been used before by English poets as far back as Chaucer. The greater part of the *Canterbury Tales* was written in heroic couplets. But now a new strength and precision were given to the familiar measure by imprisoning the sense within the limit of the couplet, and by treating each line as also a unit in itself. Edmund Waller had written verse of this kind as early as the reign of

Charles I. He, said Dryden, "first showed us to conclude the sense most commonly in distichs, which, in the verse of those before him, runs on for so many lines together that the reader is out of breath to overtake it." Sir John Denham, also, in his *Cooper's Hill*, 1643, had written such verse as this:

"O, could I flow like thee, and make thy stream
My great example as it is my theme!
{175}
Though deep yet clear, though gentle yet not dull,
Strong without rage, without o'erflowing full."

Here we have the regular flow, and the nice balance between the first and second member of each couplet, and the first and second part of each line, which characterized the verse of Dryden and Pope.

"Waller was smooth, but Dryden taught to join
The varying verse, the full resounding line,
The long resounding march and energy divine."

Thus wrote Pope, using for the nonce the triplet and alexandrine by which Dryden frequently varied the couplet. Pope himself added a greater neatness and polish to Dryden's verse and brought the system to such monotonous perfection that he "made poetry a mere mechanic art."

The lyrical poetry of this generation was almost entirely worthless. The dissolute wits of Charles the Second's court, Sedley, Rochester, Sackville, and the "mob of gentlemen who wrote with ease" threw off a few amatory trifles; but the age was not spontaneous or sincere enough for genuine song. Cowley introduced the Pindaric ode, a highly artificial form of the lyric, in which the language was tortured into a kind of spurious grandeur, and the meter teased into a sound and fury, signifying nothing. Cowley's Pindarics were filled with something which passed for fire, but has now utterly gone out. Nevertheless, the fashion spread, and "he who could do nothing else," said Dr. Johnson, {176} "could write like Pindar." The best of these odes was Dryden's famous *Alexander's Feast*, written for a celebration of St. Cecilia's day by a musical club. To this same fashion, also, we owe Gray's two fine odes, the *Progress of Poesy* and the *Bard*, written a half-century later.

Dryden was not so much a great poet, as a solid thinker, with a splendid mastery of expression, who used his energetic verse as a vehicle for political argument and satire. His first noteworthy poem, *Annus Mirabilis*, 1667, was a narrative of the public events of the year 1666, namely: the Dutch war and the great fire of London. The subject of *Absalom and Ahitophel*—the first part of which appeared in 1681—was the alleged plot of the Whig leader, the Earl of Shaftesbury, to defeat the succession of the Duke of York, afterward James

86

II., by securing the throne to Monmouth, a natural son of Charles II. The parallel afforded by the story of Absalom's revolt against David was wrought out by Dryden with admirable ingenuity and keeping. He was at his best in satirical character-sketches, such as the brilliant portraits in this poem of Shaftesbury, as the false counselor, Ahitophel, and of the Duke of Buckingham as Zimri. The latter was Dryden's reply to the *Rehearsal*. *Absalom and Ahitophel* was followed by the *Medal*, a continuation of the same subject, and *Mac Flecknoe*, a personal onslaught on the "true blue Protestant poet," Thomas Shadwell, a political and literary foe of Dryden. Flecknoe, an {177} obscure Irish poetaster, being about to retire from the throne of duncedom, resolved to settle the succession upon his son, Shadwell, whose claims to the inheritance are vigorously asserted.

"The rest to some faint meaning make pretense,
But Shadwell never deviates into sense... .
The midwife laid her hand on his thick skull
With this prophetic blessing—Be thou dull."

Dryden is our first great satirist. The formal satire had been written in the reign of Elisabeth by Donne, and by Joseph Hall, Bishop of Exeter, and subsequently by Marston, the dramatist, by Wither, Marvell, and others; but all of these failed through an over violence of language, and a purpose too pronouncedly moral. They had no lightness of touch, no irony and mischief. They bore down too hard, imitated Juvenal, and lashed English society in terms befitting the corruption of Imperial Rome. They denounced, instructed, preached, did every thing but satirize. The satirist must raise a laugh. Donne and Hall abused men in classes: priests were worldly, lawyers greedy, courtiers obsequious, etc. But the easy scorn of Dryden and the delightful malice of Pope gave a pungent personal interest to their sarcasm, infinitely more effective than these commonplaces of satire. Dryden was as happy in controversy as in satire, and is unexcelled in the power to reason in verse. His *Religio Laici*, 1682, was a poem in defense of the {178} English Church. But when James II. came to the throne Dryden turned Catholic and wrote the *Hind and Panther*, 1687, to vindicate his new belief. Dryden had the misfortune to be dependent upon royal patronage and upon a corrupt stage. He sold his pen to the court, and in his comedies he was heavily and deliberately lewd, a sin which he afterward acknowledged and regretted. Milton's "soul was like a star and dwelt apart," but Dryden wrote for the trampling multitude. He had a coarseness of moral fiber, but was not malignant in his satire, being of a large, careless, and forgetting nature. He had that masculine, enduring cast of mind which gathers heat and clearness from motion, and grows better with age. His *Fables*—modernizations from Chaucer and translations from Boccaccio—written the year before he died, are among his best works.

Dryden is also our first critic of any importance. His critical essays were mostly written as prefaces or dedications to his poems and plays. But his *Essay on Dramatic Poesie*, which Dr. Johnson called our "first regular and valuable treatise on the art of writing," was in the shape of a Platonic dialogue. When not misled by the French classicism of his day, Dryden was an admirable critic, full of penetration and sound sense. He was the earliest writer, too, of modern literary prose. If the imitation of French models was an injury to poetry it was a benefit to prose. The best modern prose is French, and it was the essayists of the {179} Gallicised Restoration age—Cowley, Sir William Temple, and, above all, Dryden—who gave modern English prose that simplicity, directness, and colloquial air, which marks it off from the more artificial diction of Milton, Taylor, and Browne.

A few books whose shaping influences lay in the past belong by their date to this period. John Bunyan, a poor tinker, whose reading was almost wholly in the Bible and Fox's *Book of Martyrs*, imprisoned for twelve years in Bedford jail for preaching at conventicles, wrote and, in 1678, published his *Pilgrim's Progress*, the greatest of religious allegories. Bunyan's spiritual experiences were so real to him that they took visible concrete shape in his imagination as men, women, cities, landscapes. It is the simplest, the most transparent of allegories. Unlike the *Faery Queene*, the story of *Pilgrim's Progress* has no reason for existing apart from its inner meaning, and yet its reality is so vivid that children read of Vanity Fair and the Slough of Despond and Doubting Castle and the Valley of the Shadow of Death with the same belief with which they read of Crusoe's cave or Aladdin's palace.

It is a long step from the Bedford tinker to the cultivated poet of *Paradise Lost*. They represent the poles of the Puritan party. Yet it may admit of a doubt, whether the Puritan epic is, in essentials, as vital and original a work as the Puritan allegory. They both came out quietly and made little noise at first. But the *Pilgrim's Progress* got at once {180} into circulation, and not even a single copy of the first edition remains. Milton, too—who received 10 pounds for the copyright of *Paradise Lost*—seemingly found that "fit audience though few" for which he prayed, as his poem reached its second impression in five years (1672). Dryden visited him in his retirement and asked leave to turn it into rime and put it on the stage as an opera. "Ay," said Milton, good humoredly, "you may tag my verses." And accordingly they appeared, duly tagged, in Dryden's operatic masque, the *State of Innocence*. In this startling conjunction we have the two ages in a nut-shell: the Commonwealth was an epic, the Restoration an opera.

The literary period covered by the life of Pope, 1688-1744, is marked off by no distinct line from the generation before it. Taste continued to be governed by the precepts of Boileau and the French classical school. Poetry remained chiefly didactic and satirical, and satire in Pope's hands was more personal even than in Dryden's, and addressed itself less to public issues. The literature of the "Augustan age" of Queen Anne (1702-1714) was still more a literature of the town and of fashionable society than that of the Restoration had been. It was also closely involved with party struggles of Whig and Tory, and the ablest pens on either side were taken into alliance by the political leaders. Swift was in high favor with the Tory ministers, Oxford and Bolingbroke, and his pamphlets, the *Public Spirit of the Whigs* and the {181} *Conduct of the Allies*, were rewarded with the deanery of St. Patrick's, Dublin. Addison became Secretary of State under a Whig government. Prior was in the diplomatic service. Daniel De Foe, the author of *Robinson Crusoe*, 1719, was a prolific political writer, conducted his *Review* in the interest of the Whigs and was imprisoned and pilloried for his ironical pamphlet, *The Shortest Way with the Dissenters.* Steele, who was a violent writer on the Whig side, held various public offices, such as Commissioner of Stamps and Commissioner for Forfeited Estates, and sat in Parliament. After the Revolution of 1688 the manners and morals of English society were somewhat on the mend. The court of William and Mary, and of their successor, Queen Anne, set no such example of open profligacy as that of Charles II. But there was much hard drinking, gambling, dueling, and intrigue in London, and vice was fashionable till Addison partly preached and partly laughed it down in the *Spectator.* The women were mostly frivolous and uneducated, and not unfrequently fast. They are spoken of with systematic disrespect by nearly every writer of the time, except Steele. "Every woman," wrote Pope, "is at heart a rake." The reading public had now become large enough to make letters a profession. Dr. Johnson said that Pope was the first writer in whose case the book-seller took the place of the patron. His translation of Homer, published by subscription, brought him between eight and nine thousand {182} pounds and made him independent. But the activity of the press produced a swarm of poorly-paid hack-writers, penny-a-liners, who lived from hand to mouth and did small literary jobs to order. Many of these inhabited Grub Street, and their lampoons against Pope and others of their more successful rivals called out Pope's *Dunciad*, or epic of the dunces, by way of retaliation. The politics of the time were sordid and consisted mainly of an ignoble scramble for office. The Whigs were fighting to maintain the Act of Succession in favor of the House of Hanover, and the Tories were secretly intriguing with the exiled Stuarts. Many of the leaders, such as the great Whig champion, John Churchill, Duke of Marlborough, were without political principle or even personal honesty. The Church, too, was in a condition of spiritual deadness. Bishoprics and livings were sold and given to political favorites. Clergymen, like Swift and Lawrence Sterne, were worldly in their lives and immoral in their writings, and were practically unbelievers. The growing religious skepticism appeared in the Deist controversy. Numbers of men in high position were Deists; the Earl of Shaftesbury, for example, and Pope's brilliant friend, Henry St. John, Lord Bolingbroke, the head of the Tory ministry, whose political writings had much influence upon his young French acquaintance, Voltaire. Pope was a Roman Catholic, though there is little to show it in his writings, and the underlying thought of his famous *Essay {183} on Man* was furnished him by Bolingbroke. The letters of the cold-hearted Chesterfield to his son were accepted as a manual of conduct, and La Rochefoucauld's cynical maxims were quoted as authority on life and human nature. Said Swift:

"As Rochefoucauld his maxims drew
From nature, I believe them true.
They argue no corrupted mind
In him; the fault is in mankind."

The succession which Dryden had willed to Congreve was taken up by Alexander Pope. He was a man quite unlike Dryden, sickly, deformed, morbidly precocious, and spiteful; nevertheless he joined on to and continued Dryden. He was more careful in his literary workmanship than his great forerunner, and in his *Moral Essays* and *Satires* he brought the Horatian epistle in verse, the formal satire and that species of didactic poem of which Boileau had given the first example, to an exquisite perfection of finish and verbal art. Dryden had translated Vergil, and so Pope translated Homer. The throne of the dunces, which Dryden had conferred upon Shadwell, Pope, in his *Dunciad*, passed on to two of his own literary foes, Theobald and Colley Cibber. There is a great waste of strength in this elaborate squib, and most of the petty writers, whose names it has preserved, as has been said, like flies in amber, are now quite unknown. But, although we have to read it with notes, to get the point of its allusions, it is easy to {184} see what execution it must have done at the time, and it is impossible to withhold admiration from the wit, the wickedness, the triumphant mischief of the thing. The sketch of Addison—who had offended Pope by praising a rival translation of Homer—as "Atticus," is as brilliant as any thing of the kind in Dryden. Pope's very malignity made his sting sharper than Dryden's. He secreted venom, and worked out his revenges deliberately, bringing all the resources of his art to bear upon the question of how to give the most pain most cleverly.

Pope's masterpiece is, perhaps, the *Rape of the Lock*, a mock heroic poem, a "dwarf Iliad," recounting, in five cantos, a society quarrel, which arose from Lord Petre's cutting a lock of hair from the head of Mrs. Arabella Fermor. Boileau, in his *Lutrin*, had treated, with the same epic dignity, a dispute over the placing of the reading desk in a parish church. Pope was the Homer of the drawing-room, the boudoir, the tea-urn, the omber-party, the sedan-chair, the parrot cage, and the lap-dogs. This poem, in its sparkle and airy grace, is the topmost blossom of a highly artificial society, the quintessence of whatever poetry was possible in those

"Teacup times of hood and hoop,
And when the patch was worn,"

with whose decorative features, at least, the recent Queen Anne revival has made this generation familiar. It may be said of it, as Thackeray said of {185} Gay's pastorals: "It is to poetry what charming little Dresden china figures are to sculpture, graceful, minikin, fantastic, with a certain beauty always accompanying them." The *Rape of the Lock*, perhaps, stops short of beauty, but it attains elegance and prettiness in a supreme degree. In imitation of the gods and goddesses in the Iliad, who intermeddle for or against the human characters, Pope introduced the Sylphs of the Rosicrucian philosophy. We may measure the distance between imagination and fancy, if we will compare these little filagree creatures with Shakspere's elves, whose occupation it was

"To tread the ooze of the salt deep,
Or run upon the sharp wind of the north,...
Or on the beached margent of the sea,
To dance their ringlets to the whispering wind."

Very different were the offices of Pope's fays:

"Our humble province is to tend the fair;
Not a less pleasing, though less glorious, care;
To save the powder from too rude a gale,
Nor let the imprisoned essences exhale.... .
Nay oft in dreams invention we bestow
To change a flounce or add a furbelow."

Pope was not a great poet; it has been doubted whether he was a poet at all. He does not touch the heart, or stimulate the imagination, as the true poet always does. In the poetry of nature, and the poetry of passion, he was altogether impotent. {186} His *Windsor Forest* and his *Pastorals* are artificial and false, not written with "the eye upon the object." His epistle of *Eloisa to Abelard* is declamatory and academic, and leaves the reader cold. The only one of his poems which is at all possessed with feeling is his pathetic *Elegy to the Memory of an Unfortunate Lady*. But he was a great literary artist. Within the cramped and starched regularity of the heroic couplet, which the fashion of the time and his own habit of mind imposed upon him, he secured the largest variety of modulation and emphasis of which that verse was capable.

He used antithesis, periphrasis, and climax with great skill. His example dominated English poetry for nearly a century, and even now, when a poet like Dr. Holmes, for example, would write satire or humorous verse of a dignified kind, he turns instinctively to the measure and manner of Pope. He was not a consecutive thinker, like Dryden, and cared less about the truth of his thought than about the pointedness of its expression. His language was closer-grained than Dryden's. His great art was the art of putting things. He is more quoted than any other English poet, but Shakspere. He struck the average intelligence, the common sense of English readers, and furnished it with neat, portable formulas, so that it no longer needed to "vent its observation in mangled terms," but could pour itself out compactly, artistically, in little, ready-made molds. But his high-wrought brilliancy, this unceasing point, soon fatigue. His {187} poems read like a series of epigrams; and every line has a hit or an effect.

From the reign of Queen Anne date the beginnings of the periodical essay. Newspapers had been published since the time of the Civil War; at first irregularly, and then regularly. But no literature of permanent value appeared in periodical form until Richard Steele started the *Tatler*, in 1709. In this he was soon joined by his friend, Joseph Addison and in its successor the *Spectator*, the first number of which was issued March 1, 1711, Addison's contributions outnumbered Steele's. The *Tatler* was published on three, the *Spectator* on six, days of the week. The *Tatler* gave political news, but each number of the *Spectator* consisted of a single essay. The object of these periodicals was to reflect the passing humors of the time, and to satirize the follies and minor immoralities of the town. "I shall endeavor," wrote Addison, in the tenth paper of the *Spectator*, "to enliven morality with wit, and to temper wit with morality... . It was said of Socrates that he brought Philosophy down from Heaven to inhabit among men; and I shall be ambitious to have it said of me that I have brought Philosophy out of closets and libraries, schools and colleges, to dwell in clubs and assemblies, at tea-tables and in coffee-houses." Addison's satire was never personal. He was a moderate man, and did what he could to restrain Steele's intemperate party zeal. His character was dignified and pure, and his strongest emotion seems to have {188} been his religious feeling. One of his contemporaries called him "a parson in a tie wig," and he wrote several excellent hymns. His mission was that of censor of the public taste. Sometimes he lectures and sometimes he preaches, and in his Saturday papers, he brought his wide reading and nice scholarship into service for the instruction of his readers. Such was the series of essays, in which he gave an elaborate review of *Paradise Lost*. Such also was his famous paper, the *Vision of Mirza*, an oriental allegory of human life. The adoption of this slightly pedagogic tone was justified by the prevalent ignorance and frivolity of the age. But the lighter portions of the *Spectator* are those which have worn the best. Their style is at once correct and easy, and it is as a humorist, a sly observer of manners, and above all, a delightful talker, that Addison is best known to posterity. In the personal sketches of the members of the Spectator Club, of Will Honeycomb, Captain Sentry, Sir Andrew Freeport, and, above all, Sir Roger de Coverley, the quaint and honest country gentleman, may be found the nucleus of the modern prose fiction of character. Addison's humor is always a trifle grave. There is no whimsy, no frolic in it, as in Sterne or Lamb. "He thinks justly," said Dr. Johnson, "but he thinks faintly." The *Spectator* had a host of followers, from the somewhat heavy *Rambler* and *Idler* of Johnson, down to the *Salmagundi* papers of our own Irving, who was, perhaps, Addison's latest and {189} best literary descendant. In his own age Addison made some figure as a poet and dramatist. His *Campaign*, celebrating the victory of Blenheim, had one much-admired couplet, in which Marlborough was likened to the angel of tempest, who

"Pleased the Almighty's orders to perform,
Rides in the whirlwind and directs the storm."

His stately, classical tragedy, *Cato*, which was acted at Drury Lane Theater in 1712, with immense applause, was pronounced by Dr. Johnson "unquestionably the noblest production of Addison's genius." It is, notwithstanding, cold and tedious, as a whole, though it has some fine declamatory passages—in particular the soliloquy of Cato in the fifth act—

"It must be so: Plato, thou reasonest well," etc.

The greatest of the Queen Anne wits, and one of the most savage and powerful satirists that ever lived, was Jonathan Swift. As secretary in the family of Sir William Temple, and domestic chaplain to the Earl of Berkeley, he had known in youth the bitterness of poverty and dependence. Afterward he wrote himself into influence with the Tory ministry, and was promised a bishopric, but was put off with the deanery of St. Patrick's, and retired to Ireland to "die like a poisoned rat in a hole." His life was made tragical by the forecast of the madness which finally overtook him. "The stage darkened," said Scott, "ere the curtain fell." Insanity {190} deepened into idiocy and a hideous silence, and for three years before his death he spoke hardly ever a word. He had directed that his tombstone should bear the inscription, *Ubi saeva indignatio cor ulterius lacerare nequit.* "So great a man he seems to me," wrote Thackeray, "that thinking of him is like thinking of an empire falling." Swift's first noteworthy publication was his *Tale of a Tub*, 1704, a satire on religious differences. But his great work was *Gulliver's Travels*, 1726, the book in which his hate and scorn of mankind, and the long rage of mortified pride and thwarted ambition found their fullest expression. Children read the voyages to Lilliput and Brobdingnag, to the flying island of Laputa and the country of the Houyhnhnms, as they read *Robinson Crusoe*, as stories of wonderful adventure. Swift had all of De Foe's realism, his power of giving veri-similitude to his narrative by the invention of a vast number of small, exact, consistent details. But underneath its fairy tales, *Gulliver's Travels* is a satire, far more radical than any of Dryden's or Pope's, because directed, not against particular parties or persons, but against human nature. In his account of Lilliput and Brobdingnag, Swift tries to show—looking first through one end of the telescope and then through the other—that human greatness, goodness, beauty disappear if the scale be altered a little. If men were six inches high instead of six feet—such is the logic of his tale—their wars, governments, science, religion—all their institutions, {191} in fine, and all the courage, wisdom, and virtue by which these have been built up, would appear laughable. On the other hand, if they were sixty feet high instead of six, they would become disgusting. The complexion of the finest ladies would show blotches, hairs, excrescences, and an overpowering effluvium would breathe from the pores of the skin. Finally, in his loathsome caricature of mankind, as Yahoos, he contrasts them to their shame with the beasts, and sets instinct above reason.

The method of Swift's satire was grave irony. Among his minor writings in this kind are his *Argument against Abolishing Christianity*, his *Modest Proposal* for utilizing the surplus population of Ireland by eating the babies of the poor, and his *Predictions of Isaac Bickerstaff*. In the last he predicted the death of one Partridge, an almanac maker, at a certain day and hour. When the time set was past, he published a minute account of Partridge's last moments; and when the subject of this excellent fooling printed an indignant denial of his own death, Swift answered very temperately, proving that he was dead and remonstrating with him on the violence of his language. "To call a man a fool and villain, an impudent fellow, only for differing from him in a point merely speculative, is, in my humble opinion, a very improper style for a person of his education." Swift wrote verses as well as prose, but their motive was the reverse of poetical. His gross and cynical humor vulgarized whatever it touched. He leaves us no illusions, {192} and not only strips his subject, but flays it and shows the raw muscles beneath the skin. He delighted to dwell upon the lowest bodily functions of human nature. "He saw bloodshot," said Thackeray.

1. Macaulay's Essay, The Comic Dramatists of the Restoration.

2. The Poetical Works of John Dryden. Globe Edition. Macmillan & Co.

3. Thackeray's English Humorists of the Last Century.

4. Sir Roger de Coverley. New York: Harper, 1878.

5. Swift's Tale of a Tub, Gulliver's Travels, Directions to Servants, Polite Conversation, The Great Question Debated, Verses on the Death of Dean Swift.

6. The Poetical Works of Alexander Pope. Globe Edition. Macmillan & Co.

{193}

CHAPTER VI.

FROM THE DEATH OF POPE TO THE FRENCH REVOLUTION.

1744-1789.

Pope's example continued potent for fifty years after his death. Especially was this so in satiric and didactic poetry. Not only Dr. Johnson's adaptations from *Juvenal*, London, 1738, and the *Vanity of Human Wishes*, 1749, but Gifford's *Baviad*, 1791, and *Maeviad*, 1795, and Byron's *English Bards and Scotch Reviewers*, 1809, were in the verse and manner of Pope. In Johnson's *Lives of the Poets*, 1781, Dryden and Pope are treated as the two greatest English poets. But long before this a revolution in literary taste had begun, a movement which is variously described as The Return to Nature, or The Rise of the New Romantic School.

For nearly a hundred years poetry had dealt with manners and the life of towns, the gay, prosaic life of Congreve or of Pope. The sole concession to the life of nature was the old pastoral, which, in the hands of cockneys, like Pope and Ambrose Philips, who merely repeated stock descriptions at second or third hand, became even more artificial than a *Beggar's Opera* or a *Rape of the {194} Lock*. These, at least, were true to their environment, and were natural, just *because* they were artificial. But the *Seasons* of James Thomson, published in installments from 1726-30, had opened a new field. Their theme was the English landscape, as varied by the changes of the year, and they were written by a true lover and observer of nature. Mark Akenside's *Pleasures of Imagination*, 1744, published the year of Pope's death, was written like the *Seasons*, in blank verse; and although its language had much of the formal, didactic cast of the Queen Anne poets, it pointed unmistakably in the new direction. Thomson had painted the soft beauties of a highly cultivated land—lawns, gardens, forest-preserves, orchards, and sheep-walks. But now a fresh note was struck in the literature, not of England alone, but of Germany and France—romanticism, the chief element in which was a love of the wild. Poets turned from the lameness of modern existence to savage nature and the heroic simplicity of life among primitive tribes. In France,

Rousseau introduced the idea of the natural man, following his instincts in disregard of social conventions. In Germany Bodmer published, in 1753, the first edition of the old German epic, the *Nibelungen Lied*. Works of a similar tendency in England were the odes of William Collins and Thomas Gray, published between 1747-57, especially Collins's *Ode on the Superstitions of the Highlands*, and Gray's *Bard*, a pindaric, in which the last survivor of the Welsh bards invokes vengeance on {195} Edward I., the destroyer of his guild. Gray and Mason, his friend and editor, made translations from the ancient Welsh and Norse poetry. Thomas Percy's *Reliques of Ancient English Poetry*, 1765, aroused a taste for old ballads. Richard Hurd's *Letters on Chivalry and Romance*, Thomas Warton's *History of English Poetry*, 1774-78, Tyrwhitt's critical edition of Chaucer, and Horace Walpole's Gothic romance, the *Castle of Otranto*, 1765, stimulated this awakened interest in the picturesque aspects of feudal life, and contributed to the fondness for supernatural and mediaeval subjects. James Beattie's *Minstrel*, 1771, described the educating influence of Scottish mountain scenery upon the genius of a young poet. But the most remarkable instances of this passion for wild nature and the romantic past were the *Poems of Ossian* and Thomas Chatterton's literary forgeries.

In 1762 James Macpherson published the first installment of what professed to be a translation of the poems of Ossian, a Gaelic bard, whom tradition placed in the 3d century. Macpherson said that he made his version— including two complete epics, *Fingal* and *Temora*, from Gaelic MSS., which he had collected in the Scottish Highlands. A fierce controversy at once sprang up over the genuineness of these remains. Macpherson was challenged to produce his originals, and when, many years after, he published the Gaelic text, it was asserted that this was nothing but a translation of his own English into modern Gaelic. Of {196} the MSS. which he professed to have found not a scrap remained: the Gaelic text was printed from transcriptions in Macpherson's handwriting or in that of his secretaries.

But whether these poems were the work of Ossian or of Macpherson, they made a deep impression upon the time. Napoleon admired them greatly, and Goethe inserted passages from the "Songs of Selma" in his *Sorrows of Werther*. Macpherson composed—or translated—them in an abrupt, rhapsodical prose, resembling the English version of Job or of the prophecies of Isaiah. They filled the minds of their readers with images of vague sublimity and desolation; the mountain torrent, the mist on the hills, the ghosts of heroes half seen by the setting moon, the thistle in the ruined courts of chieftains, the grass whistling on the windy heath, the gray rock by the blue stream of Lutha, and the cliffs of sea-surrounded Gormal.

"A tale of the times of old!"

"Why, thou wanderer unseen! Thou bender of the thistle of Lora; why, thou breeze of the valley, hast thou left mine ear? I hear no distant roar of streams! No sound of the harp from the rock! Come, thou huntress of Lutha, Malvina, call back his soul to the bard. I look forward to Lochlin of lakes, to the dark billowy bay of U-thorno, where Fingal descends from Ocean, from the roar of winds. Few are the heroes of Morven in a land unknown."

Thomas Chatterton, who died by his own hand {197} in 1770, at the age of seventeen, is one of the most wonderful examples of precocity in the history of literature. His father had been sexton of the ancient Church of St. Mary Redcliff, in Bristol, and the boy's sensitive imagination took the stamp of his surroundings. He taught himself to read from a black-letter Bible. He drew charcoal sketches of churches, castles, knightly tombs, and heraldic blazonry. When only eleven years old, he began the fabrication of documents in prose and verse, which he ascribed to a fictitious Thomas Rowley, a secular priest at Bristol in the 15th century. Chatterton pretended to have found these among the contents of an old chest in the muniment room of St. Mary Redcliff's. The Rowley poems included two tragedies, *Aella* and *Goddwyn*, two cantos of a long poem on the *Battle of Hastings*, and a number of ballads and minor pieces. Chatterton had no precise knowledge of early English, or even of Chaucer. His method of working was as follows: He made himself a manuscript glossary of the words marked as archaic in Bailey's and Kersey's English dictionaries, composed his poems first in modern language, and then turned them into ancient spelling, and substituted here and there the old words in his glossary for their modern equivalents. Naturally he made many mistakes, and though Horace Walpole, to whom he sent some of his pieces, was unable to detect the forgery, his friends, Gray and Mason, to whom he submitted them, at once pronounced them {198} spurious. Nevertheless there was a controversy over Rowley, hardly less obstinate than that over Ossian, a controversy made possible only by the then almost universal ignorance of the forms, scansion, and vocabulary of early English poetry. Chatterton's poems are of little value in themselves, but they are the record of an industry and imitative quickness, marvelous in a mere child, and they show how, with the instinct of genius, he threw himself into the main literary current of his time. Discarding the couplet of Pope, the poets now went back for models to the Elisabethan writers. Thomas Warton published, in 1753, his *Observations on the Faerie Queene*. Beattie's *Minstrel*, Thomson's *Castle of Indolence*, William Shenstone's *Schoolmistress*, and John Dyer's *Fleece*, were all written in the Spenserian stanza. Shenstone gave a partly humorous effect to his poem by imitating Spenser's archaisms, and Thomson reproduced in many passages the copious harmony and luxuriant imagery of the *Faerie Queene*. The *Fleece* was a poem on English wool-growing, after the fashion of Vergil's *Georgics*. The subject was unfortunate, for, as Dr. Johnson said, it is impossible to make poetry out of serges and druggets. Dyer's *Grongar Hill*, which mingles reflection with natural description in the manner of Gray's *Elegy written in a Country Churchyard*, was composed in the octosyllabic verse of Milton's *L'Allegro* and *Il Penseroso*. Milton's minor poems, which had hitherto been neglected, {199} exercised a great influence on Collins and Gray. Collins's *Ode to Simplicity* was written in the stanza of Milton's *Nativity*, and his exquisite unrimed *Ode to Evening* was a study in versification, after Milton's translation of Horace's *Ode to Pyrrha*, in the original meters. Shakspere began to to be studied more reverently: numerous critical editions of his plays were issued, and Garrick restored his pure text to the stage. Collins was an enthusiastic student of Shakspere, and one of his sweetest poems, the *Dirge in Cymbeline*, was inspired by the tragedy of *Cymbeline*. The verse of Gray, Collins, and the Warton brothers, abounds in verbal reminiscences of Shakspere; but their genius was not allied to his, being exclusively lyrical, and not at all dramatic. The Muse of this romantic school was Fancy rather than Passion. A thoughtful melancholy, a gentle, scholarly pensiveness, the spirit of Milton's *Il Penseroso*, pervades their poetry. Gray was a fastidious scholar, who produced very little, but that little of the finest quality. His famous *Elegy*, expressing a meditative mood in language of the choicest perfection, is the representative poem of the second half of the 18th century, as the *Rape of the Lock* is of the first. The romanticists were quietists, and their scenery is characteristic. They loved solitude and evening, the twilight vale, the mossy hermitage, ruins, glens, and caves. Their style was elegant and academic, retaining a little of the stilted poetic diction of their classical {200} forerunners. Personification and periphrasis were their favorite mannerisms: Collins's Odes were largely addressed to abstractions, such as Fear, Pity, Liberty, Mercy, and Simplicity. A poet in their dialect was always a "bard;" a countryman was "the untutored swain," and a woman was a "nymph" or "the fair," just as in Dryden and Pope. Thomson is perpetually mindful of Vergil, and afraid to speak simply. He uses too many Latin epithets, like *amusive* and *precipitant*, and calls a fish-line

"The floating line snatched from the hoary steed."

They left much for Cowper and Wordsworth to do in the way of infusing the new blood of a strong, racy English into our exhausted poetic diction. Their poetry is impersonal, bookish, literary. It lacks emotional force, except now and then in Gray's immortal *Elegy*, in his *Ode on a Distant Prospect of Eton College*, in Collins's lines, *On the Death of Thomson*, and his little ode beginning, "How sleep the brave?"

The new school did not lack critical expounders of its principles and practice. Joseph Warton published, in 1756, the first volume of his *Essay on the Genius and Writings of Pope*, an elaborate review of Pope's writings *seriatim*, doing him certainly full justice, but ranking him below Shakspere, Spenser, and Milton. "Wit and satire," wrote Warton, "are transitory and perishable, but nature and passion are eternal.... . He stuck to {201} describing modern manners; but those manners, because they are familiar, artificial, and polished, are, in their very nature, unfit for any lofty effort of the Muse. Whatever poetical enthusiasm he actually possessed he withheld and stifled. Surely it is no narrow and niggardly encomium to say, he is the great Poet of Reason, the first of Ethical authors in verse." Warton illustrated his critical positions by quoting freely not only from Spenser and Milton, but from recent poets, like Thomson, Gray, Collins, and Dyer. He testified that the Seasons had "been very instrumental in diffusing a general taste for the beauties of nature and landscape." It was symptomatic of the change in literary taste that the natural or English school of landscape gardening now began to displace the French and Dutch fashion of clipped hedges, regular parterres, etc., and that Gothic architecture came into repute. Horace Walpole was a virtuoso in Gothic art, and in his castle, at Strawberry Hill, he made a collection of ancient armor, illuminated MSS., and bric-a-brac of all kinds. Gray had been Walpole's traveling companion in France and Italy, and the two had quarreled and separated, but were afterward reconciled. From Walpole's private printing-press, at Strawberry Hill, Gray's two "sister odes," the *Bard* and the *Progress of Poesy*, were first printed, in 1757. Both Gray and Walpole were good correspondents, and their printed letters are among the most delightful literature of the kind.

{202} The central figure among the English men of letters of that generation was Samuel Johnson (1709-84), whose memory has been preserved less by his own writings than by James Boswell's famous *Life of Johnson*, published in 1791. Boswell was a Scotch laird and advocate, who first met Johnson in London, when the latter was fifty-four years old. Boswell was not a very wise or witty person, but he reverenced the worth and intellect which shone through his subject's uncouth exterior. He followed him about, note-book in hand, bore all his snubbings patiently, and made the best biography ever written. It is related that the doctor once said that if he thought Boswell meant to write *his* life, he should prevent it by taking *Boswell's*. And yet Johnson's own writings and this biography of him have changed places in relative importance so completely, that Carlyle predicted that the former would soon be reduced to notes on the latter; and Macaulay said that the man who was known to his contemporaries as a great writer was known to posterity as an agreeable companion.

Johnson was one of those rugged, eccentric, self-developed characters, so common among the English. He was the son of a Lichfield book-seller, and after a course at Oxford, which was cut short by poverty, and an unsuccessful career as a school-master, he had come up to London, in 1737, where he supported himself for many years as a book-seller's hack. Gradually his great learning {203} and abilities, his ready social wit and powers as a talker, caused his company to be sought at the tables of those whom he called "the great." He was a clubbable man, and he drew about him at the tavern a group of the most distinguished intellects of the time, Edmund Burke, the orator and statesman, Oliver Goldsmith, Sir Joshua Reynolds, the portrait painter, and David Garrick, the great actor, who had been a pupil in Johnson's school, near Lichfield. Johnson was the typical John Bull of the last century. His oddities, virtues, and prejudices were thoroughly English. He hated Frenchmen, Scotchmen, and Americans, and had a cockneyish attachment to London. He was a high Tory, and an orthodox churchman; he loved a lord in the abstract, and yet he asserted a sturdy independence against any lord in particular. He was deeply religious, but had an abiding fear of death. He was burly in person, and slovenly in dress, his shirt-frill always covered with snuff. He was a great diner out, an inordinate tea-drinker, and a voracious and untidy feeder. An inherited scrofula, which often took the form of hypochondria and threatened to affect his brain, deprived him of control over the muscles of his face. Boswell describes how his features worked, how he snorted, grunted, whistled, and rolled about in his chair when getting ready to speak. He records his minutest traits, such as his habit of pocketing the orange peels at the club, and his superstitious way of {204} touching all the posts between his house and the Mitre Tavern, going back to do it, if he skipped one by chance. Though bearish in his manners and arrogant in dispute, especially when talking "for victory," Johnson had a large and tender heart. He loved his ugly, old wife—twenty-one years his senior—and he had his house full of unfortunates—a blind woman, an invalid surgeon, a destitute widow, a negro servant—whom he supported for many years, and bore with all their ill-humors patiently.

Among Johnson's numerous writings the ones best entitled to remembrance are, perhaps, his *Dictionary of the English Language*, 1755; his moral tale, *Rasselas*, 1759; the introduction to his *Edition of Shakspere*, 1765; and his *Lives of the Poets*, 1781. Johnson wrote a sonorous, cadenced prose, full of big Latin words and balanced clauses. Here is a sentence, for example, from his *Visit to the Hebrides*: "We were now treading that illustrious island which was once the luminary of the Caledonian regions, whence savage clans and roving barbarians derived the benefits of knowledge and the blessings of religion. To abstract the mind from all local emotion would be impossible, if it were endeavored, and would be foolish, if it were possible." The difference between his colloquial style and his book style is well illustrated in the instance cited by Macaulay. Speaking of Villier's *Rehearsal*, Johnson said, "It has not wit enough to keep it sweet;" then paused and {205} added—translating English into Johnsonese—"it has not vitality sufficient to preserve it from putrefaction." There is more of this in Johnson's *Rambler* and *Idler papers* than in his latest work, the *Lives of the Poets*. In this he showed himself a sound and judicious critic, though with decided limitations. His understanding was solid, but he was a thorough classicist, and his taste in poetry was formed on Pope. He was unjust to Milton and to his own contemporaries, Gray, Collins, Shenstone, and Dyer. He had no sense of the higher and subtler graces of romantic poetry, and he had a comical indifference to the "beauties of nature." When Boswell once ventured to remark that poor Scotland had, at least, some "noble, wild prospects," the doctor replied that the noblest prospect a Scotchman ever saw was the road that led to London.

The English novel of real life had its origin at this time. Books like De Foe's *Robinson Crusoe, Captain Singleton, Journal of the Plague*, etc., were tales of incident and adventure rather than novels. The novel deals primarily with character and with the interaction of characters upon one another, as developed by a regular plot. The first English novelist, in the modern sense of the word, was Samuel Richardson, a printer, who began authorship in his fiftieth year with his *Pamela*, the story of a young servant girl, who resisted the seductions of her master, and finally, as the reward of her virtue, became his wife. *Clarissa Harlowe*, {206} 1748, was the tragical history of a high spirited young lady, who being driven from home by her family, because she refused to marry the suitor selected for her, fell into the toils of Lovelace, an accomplished rake. After struggling heroically against every form of artifice and violence, she was at last drugged and ruined. She died of a broken heart, and Lovelace, borne down by remorse, was killed in a duel by a cousin of Clarissa. Sir *Charles Grandison*, 1753, was Richardson's portrait of an ideal fine gentleman, whose stately doings fill eight volumes, but who seems to the modern reader a bore and a prig. All of these novels were written in the form of letters passing between the characters, a method which fitted Richardson's subjective cast of mind. He knew little of life, but he identified himself intensely with his principal character and produced a strong effect by minute, accumulated touches. *Clarissa Harlowe* is his masterpiece, though even in that the situation is painfully prolonged, the heroine's virtue is self-conscious and rhetorical, and there is something almost ludicrously unnatural in the copiousness with which she pours herself out in gushing epistles to her female correspondent at the very moment when she is beset with dangers, persecuted, agonized, and driven nearly mad. In Richardson's novels appears, for the first time, that sentimentalism which now began to infect European literature. *Pamela* was translated into French and German, and fell in with that current {207} of popular feeling which found fullest expression in Rousseau's *Nouvelle Heloise*, 1759, and Goethe's *Leiden des Jungen Werther*, which set all the world a-weeping in 1774.

Coleridge said that to pass from Richardson's books to those of Henry Fielding was like going into the fresh air from a close room heated by stoves. Richardson, it has been affirmed, knew *man*, but Fielding knew *men*. The latter's first novel, *Joseph Andrews*, 1742, was begun as a travesty of *Pamela*. The hero, a brother of Pamela, was a young footman in the employ of Lady Booby, from whom his virtue suffered a like assault to that made upon Pamela's by her master. This reversal of the natural situation was in itself full of laughable possibilities, had the book gone on simply as a burlesque. But the exuberance of Fielding's genius led him beyond his original design. This hero, leaving Lady Booby's service, goes traveling with good Parson Adams, and is soon engaged in a series of comical and rather boisterous adventures.

Fielding had seen life, and his characters were painted from the life with a bold, free hand. He was a gentleman by birth, and had made acquaintance with society and the town in 1727, when he was a handsome, stalwart young fellow, with high animal spirits and a great appetite for pleasure. He soon ran himself into debt and began writing for the stage; married, and spent his wife's fortune, living for awhile in much splendor as a {208} country gentleman, and afterward in a reduced condition as a rural justice with a salary of 500 pounds of "the dirtiest money on earth." Fielding's masterpiece was *Tom Jones*, 1749, and it remains one of the best of English novels. Its hero is very much after Fielding's own heart, wild, spendthrift, warm-hearted, forgiving, and greatly in need of forgiveness. The same type of character, with the lines deepened, re-appears in Captain Booth, in *Amelia*, 1751, the heroine of which is a portrait of Fielding's wife. With Tom Jones is contrasted Blifil, the embodiment of meanness, hypocrisy, and cowardice. Sophia Western, the heroine, is one of Fielding's most admirable creations. For the regulated morality of Richardson, with its somewhat old-grannified air, Fielding substituted instinct. His virtuous characters are virtuous by impulse only, and his ideal of character is manliness. In *Jonathan Wild* the hero is a highwayman. This novel is ironical, a sort of prose mock-heroic, and is one of the strongest, though certainly the least pleasing, of Fielding's writings.

Tobias Smollett was an inferior Fielding with a difference. He was a Scotch ship-surgeon and had spent some time in the West Indies. He introduced into fiction the now familiar figure of the British tar, in the persons of Tom Bowling and Commodore Trunnion, as Fielding had introduced, in Squire Western, the equally national type of the hard-swearing, deep-drinking, fox-hunting Tory squire. Both Fielding and Smollett were of the {209} hearty British "beef-and-beer" school; their novels are downright, energetic, coarse, and high-blooded; low life, physical life, runs riot through their pages— tavern brawls, the breaking of pates, and the off-hand courtship of country wenches. Smollett's books, such as *Roderick Random*, 1748, *Peregrine Pickle*, 1751, and *Ferdinand Count Fathom*, 1752, were more purely stories of broadly comic adventure than Fielding's. The latter's view of life was by no means idyllic; but with Smollett this English realism ran into vulgarity and a hard Scotch literalness, and character was pushed to caricature. "The generous wine of Fielding," says Taine, "in Smollett's hands becomes brandy of the dram-shop." A partial exception to this is to be found in his last and best novel, *Humphrey Clinker*, 1770. The influence of Cervantes and of the French novelist, Le Sage, who finished his *Adventures of Gil Blas* in 1735, are very perceptible in Smollett.

A genius of much finer mold was Lawrence Sterne, the author of *Tristram Shandy*, 1759-67, and the *Sentimental Journey*, 1768. *Tristram Shandy* is hardly a novel: the story merely serves to hold together a number of characters, such as Uncle Toby and Corporal Trim, conceived with rare subtlety and originality. Sterne's chosen province was the whimsical, and his great model was Rabelais. His books are full of digressions, breaks, surprises, innuendoes, double meanings, mystifications, and all manner of odd turns. {210} Coleridge and Carlyle unite in pronouncing him a great humorist. Thackeray says that he was only a great jester. Humor is the laughter of the heart, and Sterne's pathos is closely interwoven with his humor. He was the foremost of English sentimentalists, and he had that taint of insincerity which distinguishes sentimentalism from genuine sentiment, like Goldsmith's, for example. Sterne, in life, was selfish, heartless, and untrue. A clergyman, his worldliness and vanity and the indecency of his writings were a scandal to the Church, though his sermons were both witty and affecting. He enjoyed the titilation of his own emotions, and he had practiced so long at detecting the latent pathos that lies in the expression of dumb things and of poor, patient animals, that he could summon the tear of sensibility at the thought of a discarded postchaise, a dead donkey, a starling in a cage, or of Uncle Toby putting a house fly out of the window, and saying, "There is room enough in the world for thee and me." It is a high proof of his cleverness that he generally succeeds in raising the desired feeling in his readers even from such trivial occasions. He was a minute philosopher, his philosophy was kindly, and he taught the delicate art of making much out of little. Less coarse than Fielding, he is far more corrupt. Fielding goes bluntly to the point; Sterne lingers among the temptations and suspends the expectation to tease and excite it. Forbidden fruit had a relish for him, and his pages {211} seduce. He is full of good sayings, both tender and witty. It was Sterne, for example, who wrote, "God tempers the wind to the shorn lamb."

A very different writer was Oliver Goldsmith, whose *Vicar of Wakefield*, 1766, was the earliest, and is still one of the best, novels of domestic and rural life. The book, like its author, was thoroughly Irish, full of bulls and inconsistencies. Very improbable things happened in it with a cheerful defiance of logic. But its characters are true to nature, drawn with an idyllic sweetness and purity, and with touches of a most loving humor. Its hero, Dr. Primrose, was painted after Goldsmith's father, a poor clergyman of the English Church in Ireland, and the original, likewise, of the country parson in Goldsmith's *Deserted Village*, 1770, who was "passing rich on forty pounds a year." This poem, though written in the fashionable couplet of Pope, and even containing a few verses contributed by Dr. Johnson—so that it was not at all in line with the work of the romanticists—did, perhaps, as much as any thing of Gray or of Collins to recall English poetry to the simplicity and freshness of country life.

Except for the comedies of Sheridan and Goldsmith, and, perhaps, a few other plays, the stage had now utterly declined. The novel, which is dramatic in essence, though not in form, began to take its place, and to represent life, though less intensely, yet more minutely, than the theater could do. In the novelists of the 18th century, the life {212} of the people, as distinguished from "society" or the upper classes, began to invade literature.

Richardson was distinctly a bourgeois writer, and his contemporaries— Fielding, Smollett, Sterne, and Goldsmith—ranged over a wide variety of ranks and conditions. This is one thing which distinguishes the literature of the second half of the 18th century from that of the first, as well as in some degree from that of all previous centuries. Among the authors of this generation whose writings belonged to other departments of thought than pure literature may be mentioned, in passing, the great historian, Edward Gibbon, whose *Decline and Fall of the Roman Empire* was published from 1776-88, and Edmund Burke, whose political speeches and pamphlets possess a true literary quality. The romantic poets had addressed the imagination rather than the heart. It was reserved for two men—a contrast to one another in almost every respect—to bring once more into British song a strong individual feeling, and with it a new warmth and directness of speech. These were William Cowper (1731-1800) and Robert Burns (1759-96). Cowper spoke out of his own life experience, his agony, his love, his worship and despair; and straightway the varnish that had glittered over all our poetry since the time of Dryden melted away. Cowper had scribbled verses when he was a young law student at the Middle Temple in London, and he had contributed to the *Olney Hymns*, published in 1779 by his friend and pastor, the Rev. John Newton; but {213} he only began to write poetry in earnest when he was nearly fifty years old. In 1782, the date of his first volume, he said, in a letter to a friend, that he had read but one English poet during the past twenty years. Perhaps, therefore, of all English poets of equal culture, Cowper owed the least impulse to books and the most to the need of uttering his inmost thoughts and feelings. Cowper had a most unhappy life. As a child, he was shy, sensitive, and sickly, and suffered much from bullying and fagging at a school whither he was sent after his mother's death. This happened when he was six years old; and in his affecting lines written *On Receipt of My Mother's Picture*, he speaks of himself as a

"Wretch even then, life's journey just begun."

In 1763 he became insane and was sent to an asylum, where he spent a year. Judicious treatment restored him to sanity, but he came out a broken man and remained for the rest of his life an invalid, unfitted for any active occupation. His disease took the form of religious melancholy. He had two recurrences of madness, and both times made attempts upon his life. At Huntingdon, and afterward at Olney, in Buckinghamshire, he found a home with the Unwin family, whose kindness did all which the most soothing and delicate care could do to heal his wounded spirit. His two poems *To Mary Unwin*, together with the lines on his mother's picture, were almost the first examples of deep {214} and tender sentiment in the lyrical poetry of the last century. Cowper found relief from the black thoughts that beset him only in an ordered round of quiet household occupations. He corresponded indefatigably, took long walks through the neighborhood, read, sang, and conversed with Mrs. Unwin and his friend, Lady Austin; and amused himself with carpentry, gardening, and raising pets, especially hares, of which gentle animals he grew very fond. All these simple tastes, in which he found for a time a refuge and a sheltered happiness, are reflected in his best poem, *The Task*, 1785. Cowper is the poet of the family affections, of domestic life, and rural retirement; the laureate of the fireside, the tea-table, the evening lamp, the garden, the green-house, and the rabbit-coop. He draws with elegance and precision a chair, a clock, a harpsichord, a barometer, a piece of needle-work. But Cowper was an out-door as well as an in-door man. The Olney landscape was tame, a fat, agricultural region, where the sluggish Ouse wound between plowed fields and the horizon was bounded by low hills. Nevertheless Cowper's natural descriptions are at once more distinct and more imaginative than Thomson's. *The Task* reflects, also, the new philanthropic spirit, the enthusiasm of humanity, the feeling of the brotherhood of men to which Rousseau had given expression in France and which issued in the French Revolution. In England this was the time of Wilberforce, the antislavery agitator; of Whitefield, the eloquent revival preacher; {215} of John and Charles Wesley, and of the Evangelical and Methodist movements which gave new life to the English Church. John Newton, the curate of Olney and the keeper of Cowper's conscience, was one of the leaders of the Evangelicals; and Cowper's first volume of *Table Talk* and other poems, 1782, written under Newton's inspiration, was a series of sermons in verse, somewhat intolerant of all worldly enjoyments, such as hunting, dancing, and theaters. "God made the country and man made the town," he wrote. He was a moralizing poet, and his morality was sometimes that of the invalid and the recluse. Byron called him a "coddled poet." And, indeed, there is a suspicion of gruel and dressing-gowns about him. He lived much among women, and his sufferings had refined him to a feminine delicacy. But there is no sickliness in his poetry, and he retained a charming playful humor—displayed in his excellent comic ballad, *John Gilpin*; and Mrs. Browning has sung of him,

"How when one by one sweet sounds and wandering lights departed
He bore no less a loving face, because so broken-hearted."

At the close of the year 1786 a young Scotchman, named Samuel Rose, called upon Cowper at Olney, and left with him a small volume, which had appeared at Edinburgh during the past summer, entitled *Poems chiefly in the Scottish Dialect, by Robert Burns*. Cowper read the book through {216} twice, and, though somewhat bothered by the dialect, pronounced it a "very extraordinary production." This momentary flash, as of an electric spark, marks the contact not only of the two chief British poets of their generation, but of two literatures. Scotch poets, like Thomson and Beattie, had written in Southern English, and, as Carlyle said, *in vacuo*, that is, with nothing specially national in their work. Burns's sweet though rugged Doric first secured the vernacular poetry of his country a hearing beyond the border. He had, to be sure, a whole literature of popular songs and ballads behind him, and his immediate models were Allan Ramsay and Robert Ferguson; but these remained provincial, while Burns became universal.

He was born in Ayrshire, on the banks of "bonny Doon," in a clay biggin not far from "Alloway's auld haunted kirk," the scene of the witch dance in *Tam O'Shanter*. His father was a hard-headed, God-fearing tenant farmer, whose life and that of his sons was a harsh struggle with poverty. The crops failed; the landlord pressed for his rent; for weeks at a time the family tasted no meat; yet this life of toil was lightened by love and homely pleasures. In the *Cotter's Saturday Night*, Burns has drawn a beautiful picture of his parents' household, the rest that came at the week's end, and the family worship about the "wee bit ingle, blinkin' bonnily." Robert was handsome, wild, and witty. He was universally susceptible, and his first songs, like his last, were of "the lasses." His head had been {217} stuffed, in boyhood, with "tales and songs concerning devils, ghosts, fairies, brownies, witches, warlocks, spunkies, kelpies, elf-candles, dead-lights," etc., told him by one Jenny Wilson, an old woman who lived in the family. His ear was full of ancient Scottish tunes, and as soon as he fell in love he began to make poetry as naturally as a bird sings. He composed his verses while following the plow or working in the stack-yard; or, at evening, balancing on two legs of his chair and watching the light of a peat fire play over the reeky walls of the cottage. Burns's love songs are in many keys, ranging from strains of the most pure and exalted passion, like *Ae Fond Kiss* and *To Mary in Heaven*, to such loose ditties as *When Januar' Winds* and *Green Grow the Rashes O*.

Burns liked a glass almost as well as a lass, and at Mauchline, where he carried on a farm with his brother Gilbert, after their father's death, he began to seek a questionable relief from the pressure of daily toil and unkind fates, in the convivialities of the tavern. There, among the wits of the Mauchline Club, farmers' sons, shepherds from the uplands, and the smugglers who swarmed over the west coast, he would discuss politics and farming, recite his verses, and join in the singing and ranting, while

> "Bousin o'er the nappy,
> And gettin' fou and unco happy."

To these experiences we owe not only those excellent drinking songs, *John Barleycorn* and *Willie {218} Brewed a Peck o' Maut*, but the headlong fun of *Tam O'Shanter*, and the visions, grotesquely terrible, of *Death and Dr. Hornbook*, and the dramatic humor of the *Jolly Beggars*. Cowper had celebrated "the cup which cheers but not inebriates." Burns sang the praises of *Scotch Drink*. Cowper was a stranger to Burns's high animal spirits, and his robust enjoyment of life. He had affections, but no passions. At Mauchline, Burns, whose irregularities did not escape the censure of the kirk, became involved, through his friendship with Gavin Hamilton, in the controversy between the Old Light and New Light clergy. His *Holy Fair, Holy Tulzie, Two Herds, Holy Willie's Prayer*, and *Address to the Unco Gude*, are satires against bigotry and hypocrisy. But in spite of the rollicking profanity of his language, and the violence of his rebound against the austere religion of Scotland, Burns was at bottom deeply impressible by religious ideas, as may be seen from his *Prayer under the Pressure of Violent Anguish*, and *Prayer in Prospect of Death*.

His farm turned out a failure, and he was on the eve of sailing for Jamaica, when the favor with which his volume of poems was received, stayed his departure, and turned his steps to Edinburgh. There the peasant poet was lionized for a winter season by the learned and polite society of the Scotch capital, with results in the end not altogether favorable to Burns's best interests. For when society finally turned the cold shoulder on {219} him, he had to go back to farming again, carrying with him a bitter sense of injustice and neglect. He leased a farm in Ellisland, in 1788, and some friends procured his appointment as exciseman for his district. But poverty, disappointment, irregular habits, and broken health clouded his last years, and brought him to an untimely death at the age of thirty-seven. He continued, however, to pour forth songs of unequaled sweetness and force. "The man sank," said Coleridge, "but the poet was bright to the last."

Burns is the best of British song-writers. His songs are singable; they are not merely lyrical poems. They were meant to be sung, and they are sung. They were mostly set to old Scottish airs, and sometimes they were built up from ancient fragments of anonymous, popular poetry, a chorus, or stanza, or even a single line. Such are, for example, *Auld Lang Syne, My Heart's in the Highlands*, and *Landlady, Count the Lawin*. Burns had a great, warm heart. His sins were sins of passion, and sprang from the same generous soil that nourished his impulsive virtues. His elementary qualities as a poet were sincerity, a healthy openness to all impressions of the beautiful, and a sympathy which embraced men, animals, and the dumb objects of nature. His tenderness toward flowers and the brute creation may be read in his lines *To a Mountain Daisy*, *To a Mouse*, and *The Auld Farmer's New Year's Morning Salutation to his Auld Mare Maggie*. Next after love and good {220} fellowship, patriotism is the most frequent motive of his song. Of his national anthem, *Scots wha hae wi' Wallace bled*, Carlyle said: "So long as there is warm blood in the heart of Scotchman, or man, it will move in fierce thrills under this war ode."

Burns's politics were a singular mixture of sentimental toryism with practical democracy. A romantic glamour was thrown over the fortunes of the exiled Stuarts, and to have been "out" in '45 with the Young Pretender was a popular thing in parts of Scotland. To this purely poetic loyalty may be attributed such Jacobite ballads of Burns as *Over the Water to Charlie*. But his sober convictions were on the side of liberty and human brotherhood, and are expressed in the *Twa Dogs*, the *First Epistle to Davie*, and *A Man's a Man for a' that*. His sympathy with the Revolution led him to send four pieces of ordnance, taken from a captured smuggler, as a present to the French Convention, a piece of bravado which got him into difficulties with his superiors in the excise. The poetry which Burns wrote, not in dialect, but in the classical English, is in the stilted manner of his century, and his prose correspondence betrays his lack of culture by his constant lapse into rhetorical affectation and fine writing.

1. T. S. Perry's English Literature in the Eighteenth Century.

2. James Thomson. The Castle of Indolence.

3. The Poems of Thomas Gray.

{221}

4. William Collins. Odes.

5. The Six Chief Lives from Johnson's Lives of the Poets. Edited by Matthew Arnold. Macmillan, 1878.

6. Boswell's Life of Johnson [abridged]. Henry Holt & Co., 1878.

7. Samuel Richardson. Clarissa Harlowe.

8. Henry Fielding. Tom Jones.

9. Tobias Smollett. Humphrey Clinker.

10. Lawrence Sterne. Tristram Shandy.

11. Oliver Goldsmith. Vicar of Wakefield and Deserted Village.

12. William Cowper. The Task and John Gilpin.

13. The Poems and Songs of Robert Burns.

{222}

CHAPTER VII

1789-1832.

The burst of creative activity at the opening of the 19th century has but one parallel in English literary history, namely, the somewhat similar flowering out of the national genius in the time of Elisabeth and the first two Stuart kings. The later age gave birth to no supreme poets, like Shakspere and Milton. It produced no *Hamlet* and no *Paradise Lost*; but it offers a greater number of important writers, a higher average of excellence, and a wider range and variety of literary work than any preceding era. Wordsworth, Coleridge, Scott, Byron, Shelley, and Keats are all great names; while Southey, Landor, Moore, Lamb, and De Quincey would be noteworthy figures at any period, and deserve a fuller mention than can be here accorded them. But in so crowded a generation, selection becomes increasingly needful, and in the present chapter, accordingly, the emphasis will be laid upon the first-named group as not only the most important, but the most representative of the various tendencies of their time.

{223}

The conditions of literary work in this century have been almost unduly stimulating. The rapid advance in population, wealth, education, and the means of communication has vastly increased the number of readers. Every one who has any thing to say can say it in print, and is sure of some sort of a hearing. A special feature of the time is the multiplication of periodicals. The great London dailies, like the *Times* and the *Morning Post*, which were started during the last quarter of the 18th century, were something quite new in journalism. The first of the modern reviews, the *Edinburgh*, was established in 1802, as the organ of the Whig party in Scotland. This was followed by the *London Quarterly*, in 1808, and by *Blackwood's Magazine*, in 1817, both in the Tory interest. The first editor of the *Edinburgh* was Francis Jeffrey, who assembled about him a distinguished corps of contributors, including the versatile Henry Brougham, afterward a great parliamentary orator and lord-chancellor of England, and the Rev. Sydney Smith, whose witty sayings are still current. The first editor of the *Quarterly* was William Gifford, a satirist, who wrote the *Baviad* and *Maeviad* in ridicule of literary affectations. He was succeeded in 1824 by James Gibson Lockhart, the son-in-law of Walter Scott, and the author of an excellent *Life of Scott*. *Blackwood's* was edited by John Wilson, Professor of Moral Philosophy in the University of Edinburgh, who, under the pen-name of "Christopher North," contributed to his magazine a series {224} of brilliant, imaginary dialogues between famous characters of the day, entitled *Noctes Ambrosianae*, because they were supposed to take place at Ambrose's tavern in Edinburgh. These papers were full of a profuse, headlong eloquence, of humor, literary criticism, and personalities interspersed with songs expressive of a roystering and convivial Toryism and an uproarious contempt for Whigs and cockneys. These reviews and magazines, and others which sprang up beside them, became the *nuclei* about which the wit and scholarship of both parties gathered. Political controversy under the Regency and the reign of George IV. was thus carried on more regularly by permanent organs, and no longer so largely by privateering, in the shape of pamphlets, like Swift's *Public Spirit of the Whigs*, Johnson's *Taxation No Tyranny*, and Burke's *Reflections on the Revolution in France*. Nor did politics by any means usurp the columns of the reviews. Literature, art, science, the whole circle of human effort and achievement passed under review. *Blackwood's*, *Fraser's*, and the other monthlies, published stories, poetry, criticism, and correspondence—every thing, in short, which enters into the make-up of our magazines to-day, except illustrations.

Two main influences, of foreign origin, have left their trace in the English writers of the first thirty years of the 19th century, the one communicated by contact with the new German literature of the latter half of the 18th century, and in particular {225} with the writings of Goethe, Schiller, and Kant; the other springing from the events of the French Revolution. The influence of German upon English literature in the 19th century was more intellectual and less formal than that of the Italian in the 16th and of the French in the 18th. In other words, the German writers furnished the English with ideas and ways of feeling rather than with models of style. Goethe and Schiller did not become subjects for literary imitation as Molière, Racine, and Boileau had become in Pope's time. It was reserved for a later generation and for Thomas Carlyle to domesticate the diction of German prose. But the nature and extent of this influence can, perhaps, best be noted when we come to take up the authors of the time one by one.

The excitement caused by the French Revolution was something more obvious and immediate. When the Bastile fell, in 1789, the enthusiasm among the friends of liberty and human progress in England was hardly less intense than in France. It was the dawn of a new day: the shackles were stricken from the slave; all men were free and all men were brothers, and radical young England sent up a shout that echoed the roar of the Paris mob. Wordsworth's lines on the *Fall of the Bastile*, Coleridge's *Fall of Robespierre* and *Ode to France*, and Southey's revolutionary drama, *Wat Tyler*, gave expression to the hopes and aspirations of the English democracy. In after life Wordsworth, looking back regretfully to those years of promise, {226} wrote his poem on the *French Revolution as it appeared to Enthusiasts at its Commencement.*

"Bliss was it in that dawn to be alive,
But to be young was very heaven. Ohtimes
In which the meager, stale, forbidding ways
Of custom, law, and statute took at once
The attraction of a country in romance."

Those were the days in which Wordsworth, then an under-graduate at Cambridge, spent a college vacation in tramping through France, landing at Calais on the eve of the very day (July 14, 1790) on which Louis XVI. signalized the anniversary of the fall of the Bastile by taking the oath of fidelity to the new Constitution. In the following year Wordsworth revisited France, where he spent thirteen months, forming an intimacy with the republican general, Beaupuis, at Orleans, and reaching Paris not long after the September massacres of 1792. Those were the days, too, in which young Southey and young Coleridge, having married sisters at Bristol, were planning a "Pantisocracy," or ideal community, on the banks of the Susquehannah, and denouncing the British government for going to war with the French Republic. This group of poets, who had met one another first in the south of England, came afterward to be called the Lake Poets, from their residence in the mountainous lake country of Westmoreland and Cumberland, with which their names, and that of Wordsworth, especially, are forever associated. The so-called "Lakers" {227} did not, properly speaking, constitute a school of poetry. They differed greatly from one another in mind and art. But they were connected by social ties and by religious and political sympathies. The excesses of the French Revolution, and the usurpation of Napoleon disappointed them, as it did many other English liberals, and drove them into the ranks of the reactionaries. Advancing years brought conservatism, and they became in time loyal Tories and orthodox Churchmen.

William Wordsworth (1770-1850), the chief of the three, and, perhaps, on the whole, the greatest English poet since Milton, published his *Lyrical Ballads* in 1798. The volume contained a few pieces by his friend Coleridge—among them the *Ancient Mariner*—and its appearance may fairly be said to mark an epoch in the history of English poetry. Wordsworth regarded himself as a reformer of poetry; and in the preface to the second volume of *Lyrical Ballads*, he defended the theory on which they were composed. His innovations were twofold, in subject-matter, and in diction. "The principal object which I proposed to myself in these poems," he said, "was to choose incidents and situations from common life. Low and rustic life was generally chosen, because, in that condition, the essential passions of the heart find a better soil in which they can attain their maturity ... and are incorporated with the beautiful and permanent forms of nature." Wordsworth discarded, in theory, the poetic diction of his predecessors, {228} and professed to use "a selection of the real language of men in a state of vivid sensation." He adopted, he said, the language of men in rustic life, "because such men hourly communicate with the best objects from which the best part of language is originally derived."

In the matter of poetic diction Wordsworth did not, in his practice, adhere to the doctrine of this preface. Many of his most admired poems, such as the *Lines written near Tintern Abbey*, the great *Ode on the Intimations of Immortality*, the *Sonnets*, and many parts of his longest poems, *The Excursion* and *The Prelude*, deal with philosophic thought and highly intellectualized emotions. In all of these and in many others the language is rich, stately, involved, and as remote from the "real language" of Westmoreland shepherds, as is the epic blank verse of Milton. On the other hand, in those of his poems which were consciously written in illustration of his theory, the affectation of simplicity, coupled with a defective sense of humor, sometimes led him to the selection of vulgar and trivial themes, and the use of language which is bald, childish, or even ludicrous. His simplicity is too often the simplicity of Mother Goose rather than of Chaucer. Instances of this occur in such poems as *Peter Bell*, the *Idiot Boy*, *Goody Blake and Harry Gill*, *Simon Lee*, and the *Wagoner*. But there are multitudes of Wordsworth's ballads and lyrics which are simple without being silly, and which, in their homeliness and clear {229} profundity, in their production of the strongest effects by the fewest strokes, are among the choicest modern examples of *pure*, as distinguished from decorated, art. Such are (out of many) *Ruth, Lucy, A Portrait, To a Highland Girl, The Reverie of Poor Susan, To the Cuckoo, The Reaper, We Are Seven, The Pet Lamb, The Fountain, The Two April Mornings, The Leech Gatherer, The Thorn*, and *Yarrow Revisited*.

Wordsworth was something of a Quaker in poetry, and loved the sober drabs and grays of life. Quietism was his literary religion, and the sensational was to him not merely vulgar, but almost wicked. "The human mind," he wrote, "is capable of being excited without the application of gross and violent stimulants." He disliked the far-fetched themes and high-colored style of Scott and Byron. He once told Landor that all of Scott's poetry together was not worth sixpence. From action and passion he turned away to sing the inward life of the soul and the outward life of Nature. He said:

"To me the meanest flower that blows can give
Thoughts that do often lie too deep for tears."

And again:

"Long have I loved what I behold,
The night that calms, the day that cheers;
The common growth of mother earth
Suffices me—her tears, her mirth,
Her humblest mirth and tears."

Wordsworth's life was outwardly uneventful. The companionship of the
mountains and of his {230} own thoughts; the sympathy of his household; the
lives of the dalesmen and cottagers about him furnished him with all the
stimulus that he required.

"Love had he found in huts where poor men lie:
His only teachers had been woods and rills,
The silence that is in the starry sky,
The sleep that is among the lonely hills."

He read little, but reflected much, and made poetry daily, composing, by
preference, out of doors, and dictating his verses to some member of his
family. His favorite amanuensis was his sister Dorothy, a woman of fine gifts,
to whom Wordsworth was indebted for some of his happiest inspirations. She
was the subject of the poem beginning "Her eyes are wild," and her charming
Memorials of a Tour in the Scottish Highlands records the origin of many of
her brother's best poems. Throughout life Wordsworth was remarkably self-
centered. The ridicule of the reviewers, against which he gradually made his
way to public recognition, never disturbed his serene belief in himself, or in
the divine message which he felt himself commissioned to deliver. He was a
slow and serious person, a preacher as well as a poet, with a certain rigidity,
not to say narrowness, of character. That plastic temperament which we
associate with poetic genius Wordsworth either did not possess, or it hardened
early. Whole sides of life were beyond the range of his sympathies. He {231}
touched life at fewer points than Byron and Scott, but touched it more
profoundly. It is to him that we owe the phrase "plain living and high
thinking," as also a most noble illustration of it in his own practice. His was
the wisest and deepest spirit among the English poets of his generation,
though hardly the most poetic. He wrote too much, and, attempting to make
every petty incident or reflection the occasion of a poem, he finally reached
the point of composing verses *On Seeing a Harp in the shape of a Needle
Case*, and on other themes more worthy of Mrs. Sigourney. In parts of his
long blank-verse poems, *The Excursion*, 1814, and *The Prelude*—which was
printed after his death in 1850, though finished as early as 1806—the poetry

wears very thin and its place is taken by prosaic, tedious didacticism. These two poems were designed as portions of a still more extended work, *The Recluse*, which was never completed. *The Excursion* consists mainly of philosophical discussions on nature and human life between a school-master, a solitary, and an itinerant peddler. *The Prelude* describes the development of Wordsworth's own genius. In parts of *The Excursion* the diction is fairly Shaksperian.

"The good die first,
And they whose hearts are dry as summer dust
Burn to the socket."

A passage not only beautiful in itself, but dramatically true, in the mouth of the bereaved mother {232} who utters it, to that human instinct which generalizes a private sorrow into a universal law. Much of *The Prelude* can hardly be called poetry at all, yet some of Wordsworth's loftiest poetry is buried among its dreary wastes, and now and then, in the midst of commonplaces, comes a flash of Miltonic splendor—like

"Golden cities ten months' journey deep
Among Tartarian wilds."

Wordsworth is, above all things, the poet of Nature. In this province he was not without forerunners. To say nothing of Burns and Cowper, there was George Crabbe, who had published his *Village* in 1783—fifteen years before the *Lyrical Ballads*—and whose last poem, *Tales of the Hall*, came out in 1819, five years after *The Excursion*. Byron called Crabbe "Nature's sternest painter, and her best." He was a minutely accurate delineator of the harsher aspects of rural life. He photographs a Gypsy camp; a common, with its geese and donkey; a salt marsh, a shabby village street, or tumble-down manse. But neither Crabbe nor Cowper has the imaginative lift of Wordsworth,

"The light that never was on sea or land
The consecration and the poet's dream."

In a note on a couplet in one of his earliest poems, descriptive of an oak tree standing dark against the sunset, Wordsworth says: "I recollect distinctly the very spot where this struck me. {233} The moment was important in my poetical history, for I date from it my consciousness of the infinite variety of natural appearances which had been unnoticed by the poets of any age or country, and I made a resolution to supply, in some degree, the deficiency." In later life he is said to have been impatient of any thing spoken or written by another about mountains, conceiving himself to have a monopoly of "the power of hills." But Wordsworth did not stop with natural description. Matthew Arnold has said that the office of modern poetry is the "moral interpretation of Nature." Such, at any rate, was Wordsworth's office. To him Nature was alive and divine. He felt, under the veil of phenomena,

"A presence that disturbs me with the joy
Of elevated thought: a sense sublime
Of something far more deeply interfused."

He approached, if he did not actually reach, the view of Pantheism, which identifies God with Nature; and the mysticism of the Idealists, who identify Nature with the soul of man. This tendency was not inspired in Wordsworth by German philosophy. He was no metaphysician. In his rambles with Coleridge about Nether Stowey and Alfoxden, when both were young, they had, indeed, discussed Spinoza. And in the autumn of 1798, after the publication of the *Lyrical Ballads*, the two friends went together to Germany, where Wordsworth spent half a year. But the literature {234} and philosophy of Germany made little direct impression upon Wordsworth. He disliked Goethe, and he quoted with approval the saying of the poet Klopstock, whom he met at Hamburg, that he placed the romanticist Burger above both Goethe and Schiller.

It was through Samuel Taylor Coleridge (1772-1834), who was pre-eminently the *thinker* among the literary men of his generation, that the new German thought found its way into England. During the fourteen months which he spent in Germany—chiefly at Ratzburg and Göttingen—he had familiarized himself with the transcendental philosophy of Immanuel Kant and of his continuators, Fichte and Schelling, as well as with the general literature of Germany. On his return to England, he published, in 1800, a free translation of Schiller's *Wallenstein*, and through his writings, and more especially through his conversations, he became the conductor by which German philosophic ideas reached the English literary class.

Coleridge described himself as being from boyhood a book-worm and a day-dreamer. He remained through life an omnivorous, though unsystematic, reader. He was helpless in practical affairs, and his native indolence and procrastination were increased by his indulgence in the opium habit. On his return to England, in 1800, he went to reside at Keswick, in the Lake Country, with his brother-in-law, Southey, whose industry supported both families. During his last nineteen {235} years Coleridge found an asylum under the roof of Mr. James Gilman, of Highgate, near London, whither many of the best young men in England were accustomed to resort to listen to Coleridge's wonderful talk. Talk, indeed, was the medium through which he mainly influenced his generation. It cost him an effort to put his thoughts on paper. His *Table Talk*—crowded with pregnant paragraphs—was taken down from his lips by his nephew, Henry Coleridge. His criticisms of Shakspere are nothing but notes, made here and there, from a course of lectures delivered before the Royal Institute, and never fully written out. Though only hints and suggestions, they are, perhaps, the most penetrative and helpful Shaksperian criticism in English. He was always forming projects and abandoning them. He projected a great work on Christian philosophy, which was to have been his *magnum opus*, but he never wrote it. He projected an epic poem on the fall of Jerusalem. "I schemed it at twenty-five," he said, "but, alas! *venturum expectat.*" What bade fair to be his best poem, *Christabel*, is a fragment. Another strangely beautiful poem, *Kubla Khan*—which came to him, he said, in sleep—is even more fragmentary. And the most important of his prose remains, his *Biographia Literaria*, 1817, a history of his own opinions, breaks off abruptly.

It was in his suggestiveness that Coleridge's great service to posterity resided. He was what J. S. Mill called a "seminal mind," and his thought {236} had that power of stimulating thought in others, which is the mark and the privilege of original genius. Many a man has owed to some sentence of Coleridge's, if not the awakening in himself of a new intellectual life, at least the starting of fruitful trains of reflection which have modified his whole view of certain great subjects. On every thing that he left is set the stamp of high mental authority. He was not, perhaps, primarily, he certainly was not exclusively, a poet. In theology, in philosophy, in political thought, and literary criticism, he set currents flowing which are flowing yet. The terminology of criticism, for example, is in his debt for many of those convenient distinctions—such as that between genius and talent, between wit and humor, between fancy and imagination—which are familiar enough now, but which he first introduced, or enforced. His definitions and apothegms we meet every-where. Such are, for example, the sayings: "Every man is born an Aristotelian or a Platonist." "Prose is words in their best order; poetry, the best words in the best order." And among the bits of subtle interpretation, that abound in his writings, may be mentioned his estimate of Wordsworth, in the *Biographia Literaria*, and his sketch of Hamlet's character—one with which he was personally in strong sympathy—in the *Lectures on Shakspere*.

The Broad-Church party, in the English Church, among whose most eminent exponents have been Frederic Robertson, Arnold of Rugby, {237} F. D. Maurice, Charles Kingsley, and the late Dean Stanley, traces its intellectual origin to Coleridge's *Aids to Reflection*; to his writings and conversations in general, and particularly to his ideal of a national Clerisy, as set forth in his essay on *Church and State*. In politics, as in religion, Coleridge's conservatism represents the reaction against the destructive spirit of the eighteenth century and the French revolution. To this root-and-branch democracy he opposed the view, that every old belief, or institution, such as the throne or the Church, had served some need, and had a rational idea at the bottom of it, to which it might be again recalled, and made once more a benefit to society, instead of a curse and an anachronism.

As a poet, Coleridge has a sure, though slender, hold upon immortal fame. No English poet has "sung so wildly well" as the singer of *Christabel* and the *Ancient Mariner*. The former of these is, in form, a romance in a variety of meters, and in substance, a tale of supernatural possession, by which a lovely and innocent maiden is brought under the control of a witch. Though unfinished and obscure in intention, it haunts the imagination with a mystic power. Byron had seen *Christabel* in MS., and urged Coleridge to publish it. He hated all the "Lakers," but when, on parting from Lady Byron, he wrote his song,

"Fare thee well, and ifforever,
Still forever fare thee well,"

{238} he prefixed to it the noble lines from Coleridge's poem, beginning

"Alas! they had been friends in youth."

In that weird ballad, the *Ancient Mariner*, the supernatural is handled with even greater subtlety than in *Christabel*. The reader is led to feel that amid the loneliness of the tropic sea, the line between the earthly and the unearthly vanishes, and the poet leaves him to discover for himself whether the spectral shapes that the mariner saw were merely the visions of the calenture, or a glimpse of the world of spirits. Coleridge is one of our most perfect metrists. The poet Swinburne—than whom there can be no higher authority on this point (though he is rather given to exaggeration)—pronounces *Kubla Khan*, "for absolute melody and splendor, the first poem in the language."

Robert Southey, the third member of this group, was a diligent worker and one of the most voluminous of English writers. As a poet, he was lacking in inspiration, and his big Oriental epics, *Thalaba*, 1801, and the *Curse of Kehama*, 1810, are little better than wax-work. Of his numerous works in prose, the *Life of Nelson* is, perhaps, the best, and is an excellent biography.

Several other authors were more or less closely associated with the Lake Poets by residence or social affiliation. John Wilson, the editor of *Blackwood's*, lived for some time, when a young man, at Elleray, on the banks of Windermere. He was an {239} athletic man of out-door habits, an enthusiastic sportsman, and a lover of natural scenery. His admiration of Wordsworth was thought to have led him to imitation of the latter, in his *Isle of Palms*, 1812, and his other poetry.

One of Wilson's companions, in his mountain walks, was Thomas De

Quincey, who had been led by his reverence for Wordsworth and Coleridge to take up his residence, in 1808, at Grasmere, where he occupied for many years the cottage from which Wordsworth had removed to Allan Bank. De Quincey was a shy, bookish little man, of erratic, nocturnal habits, who impresses one, personally, as a child of genius, with a child's helplessness and a child's sharp observation. He was, above all things, a magazinist. All his writings, with one exception, appeared first in the shape of contributions to periodicals; and his essays, literary criticisms, and miscellaneous papers are exceedingly rich and varied. The most famous of them was his *Confessions of an English Opium Eater*, published as a serial in the *London Magazine*, in 1821. He had begun to take opium, as a cure for the toothache, when a student at Oxford, where he resided from 1803 to 1808. By 1816 he had risen to eight thousand drops of laudanum a day. For several years after this he experienced the acutest misery, and his will suffered an entire paralysis. In 1821 he succeeded in reducing his dose to a comparatively small allowance, and in shaking off his torpor so as to become capable of literary work. {240} The most impressive effect of the opium habit was seen in his dreams, in the unnatural expansion of space and time, and the infinite repetition of the same objects. His sleep was filled with dim, vast images; measureless cavalcades deploying to the sound of orchestral music; an endless succession of vaulted halls, with staircases climbing to heaven, up which toiled eternally the same solitary figure. "Then came sudden alarms, hurrying to and fro; trepidations of innumerable fugitives; darkness and light; tempest and human faces." Many of De Quincey's papers were autobiographical, but there is always something baffling in these reminiscences. In the interminable wanderings of his pen—for which, perhaps, opium was responsible—he appears to lose all trace of facts or of any continuous story. Every actual experience of his life seems to have been taken up into a realm of dream, and there distorted till the reader sees not the real figures, but the enormous, grotesque shadows of them, executing wild dances on a screen. An instance of this process is described by himself in his *Vision of Sudden Death*. But his unworldliness and faculty of vision-seeing were not inconsistent with the keenness of judgment and the justness and delicacy of perception displayed in his *Biographical Sketches* of Wordsworth, Coleridge, and other contemporaries: in his critical papers on *Pope, Milton, Lessing, Homer and the Homeridae*: his essay on *Style*; and his *Brief Appraisal of the Greek Literature*. His curious scholarship is seen in his articles on the *Toilet of a {241} Hebrew Lady*, and the *Casuistry of Roman Meals*; his ironical and somewhat elaborate humor in his essay on *Murder Considered as One of the Fine Arts*. Of his narrative pieces the most remarkable is his *Revolt of the Tartars*, describing the flight of a Kalmuck tribe of six hundred thousand souls from Russia to the Chinese frontier: a great hegira or anabasis, which extended for four thousand miles over desert steppes infested with foes; occupied six months' time, and left nearly half of the tribe dead upon the way. The subject was suited to De Quincey's imagination. It was like one of his own opium visions, and he handled it with a dignity and force which make the history not altogether unworthy of comparison with Thucydides's great chapter on the Sicilian Expedition.

An intimate friend of Southey was Walter Savage Landor, a man of kingly nature, of a leonine presence, with a most stormy and unreasonable temper, and yet with the courtliest graces of manner and with—said Emerson—a "wonderful brain, despotic, violent, and inexhaustible." He inherited wealth, and lived a great part of his life at Florence, where he died, in 1864, in his ninetieth year. Dickens, who knew him at Bath, in the latter part of his life, made a kindly caricature of him as Lawrence Boythom, in *Bleak House*, whose "combination of superficial ferocity and inherent tenderness," testifies Henry Crabb Robinson, in his *Diary*, was true to the life. Landor is the most purely classical of English writers. Not merely his themes {242} but his whole way of thinking was pagan and antique. He composed, indifferently, in English or Latin, preferring the latter, if any thing, in obedience to his instinct for compression and exclusiveness. Thus portions of his narrative poem, *Gebir*, 1798, were written originally in Latin, and he added a Latin version, *Gebirius*, to the English edition. In like manner his *Hellenics*, 1847, were mainly translations from his Latin *Idyllia Heroica*, written years before. The Hellenic clearness and repose which were absent from his life, Landor sought in his art. His poems, in their restraint, their objectivity, their aloofness from modern feeling, have something chill and artificial. The verse of poets like Byron and Wordsworth is alive; the blood runs in it. But Landor's polished, clean-cut *intaglios* have been well described as "written in marble." He was a master of fine and solid prose. His *Pericles and Aspasia* consists of a series of letters passing between the great Athenian demagogue, the hetaira, Aspasia, her friend, Cleone of Miletus, Anaxagorus, the philosopher, and Pericles's nephew, Alcibiades. In this masterpiece the intellectual life of Athens, at its period of highest refinement, is brought before the reader with singular vividness, and he is made to breathe an atmosphere of high-bred grace, delicate wit, and thoughtful sentiment, expressed in English "of Attic choice." The *Imaginary Conversations*, 1824-1846, were Platonic dialogues between a great variety of historical characters; between, for example, Dante and Beatrice, Washington {243} and Franklin, Queen Elisabeth and Cecil, Xenophon and Cyrus the Younger, Bonaparte and the President of the Senate. Landor's writings have never been popular; they address an aristocracy of scholars; and Byron—whom Landor disliked and considered vulgar—sneered at the latter as a writer who "cultivated much private renown in the shape of Latin verses." He said of himself that he "never contended with a

120

contemporary, but walked alone on the far eastern uplands, meditating and remembering."

A schoolmate of Coleridge, at Christ's Hospital, and his friend and correspondent through life, was Charles Lamb, one of the most charming of English essayists. He was an old bachelor, who lived alone with his sister Mary a lovable and intellectual woman, but subject to recurring attacks of madness. Lamb was "a notched and cropped scrivener, a votary of the desk," a clerk, that is, in the employ of the East India Company. He was of antiquarian tastes, an ardent play-goer, a lover of whist and of the London streets; and these tastes are reflected in his *Essays of Elia*, contributed to the *London Magazine* and reprinted in book form in 1823. From his mousing among the Elisabethan dramatists and such old humorists as Burton and Fuller, his own style imbibed a peculiar quaintness and pungency. His *Specimens of English Dramatic Poets*, 1808, is admirable for its critical insight. In 1802 he paid a visit to Coleridge at Keswick, in the Lake Country; but he felt or {244} affected a whimsical horror of the mountains, and said, "Fleet Street and the Strand are better places to live in." Among the best of his essays are *Dream Children*, *Poor Relations*, *The Artificial Comedy of the Last Century*, *Old China*, *Roast Pig*, *A Defense of Chimney-sweeps*, *A Complaint of the Decay of Beggars in the Metropolis*, and *The Old Benchers of the Inner Temple*.

The romantic movement, preluded by Gray, Collins, Chatterton, Macpherson, and others, culminated in Walter Scott (1771-1832). His passion for the medieval was first excited by reading Percy's *Reliques*, when he was a boy; and in one of his school themes he maintained that Ariosto was a greater poet than Homer. He began early to collect manuscript ballads, suits of armor, pieces of old plate, border-horns, and similar relics. He learned Italian in order to read the romancers—Ariosto, Tasso, Pulci, and Boiardo, preferring them to Dante. He studied Gothic architecture, heraldry, and the art of fortification, and made drawings of famous ruins and battle-fields. In particular he read eagerly every thing that he could lay hands on relating to the history, legends, and antiquities of the Scottish border—the vale of Tweed, Teviotdale, Ettrick Forest, and the Yarrow, of all which land he became the laureate, as Burns had been of Ayrshire and the "West Country." Scott, like Wordsworth, was an out-door poet. He spent much time in the saddle, and was fond of horses, dogs, hunting, and salmon-fishing. He had a keen {245} eye for the beauties of natural scenery, though "more especially," he admits, "when combined with ancient ruins or remains of our forefathers' piety or splendor." He had the historic imagination, and, in creating the historical novel, he was the first to throw a poetic glamour over European annals. In 1803 Wordsworth visited Scott at Lasswade, near Edinburgh; and Scott afterward returned the visit at Grasmere. Wordsworth noted that his guest was "full of anecdote and averse from disquisition." The Englishman was a moralist and much given to "disquisition," while the Scotchman was, above all things, a *raconteur*, and, perhaps, on the whole, the foremost of British story-tellers. Scott's Toryism, too, was of a different stripe from Wordsworth's, being rather the result of sentiment and imagination than of philosophy and reflection. His mind struck deep root in the past; his local attachments and family pride were intense. Abbotsford was his darling, and the expenses of this domain and of the baronial hospitality which he there extended to all comers were among the causes of his bankruptcy. The enormous toil which he exacted of himself, to pay off the debt of 117,000 pounds, contracted by the failure of his publishers, cost him his life. It is said that he was more gratified when the Prince Regent created him a baronet, in 1820, than by all the public recognition that he acquired as the author of the Waverley Novels.

Scott was attracted by the romantic side of {246} German literature. His first published poem was a translation made in 1796 from Burger's wild ballad, *Leonora*. He followed this up with versions of the same poet's *Wilde Jäger*, of Goethe's violent drama of feudal life, *Götz Van Berlichingen*, and with other translations from the German, of a similar class. On his horseback trips through the border, where he studied the primitive manners of the Liddesdale people, and took down old ballads from the recitation of ancient dames and cottagers, he amassed the materials for his *Minstrelsy of the Scottish Border*, 1802. But the first of his original poems was the *Lay of the Last Minstrel*, published in 1805, and followed, in quick succession, by *Marmion*, the *Lady of the Lake*, *Rokeby*, the *Lord of the Isles*, and a volume of ballads and lyrical pieces, all issued during the years 1806-1814. The popularity won by this series of metrical romances was immediate and wide-spread. Nothing so fresh, or so brilliant, had appeared in English poetry for nearly two centuries. The reader was hurried along through scenes of rapid action, whose effect was heightened by wild landscapes and picturesque manners. The pleasure was a passive one. There was no deep thinking to perplex, no subtler beauties to pause upon; the feelings were stirred pleasantly, but not deeply; the effect was on the surface. The spell employed was novelty—or, at most, wonder— and the chief emotion aroused was breathless interest in the progress of the story. Carlyle said that Scott's genius was *in extenso*, {247} rather than *in intenso*, and that its great praise was its healthiness. This is true of his verse, but not altogether so of his prose, which exhibits deeper qualities. Some of Scott's most perfect poems, too, are his shorter ballads, like *Jock o' Hazeldean*, and *Proud Maisie is in the Wood*, which have a greater intensity and compression than his metrical tales.

From 1814 to 1831 Scott wrote and published the *Waverley* novels, some
thirty in number; if we consider the amount of work done, the speed with
which it was done, and the general average of excellence maintained, perhaps
the most marvelous literary feat on record. The series was issued
anonymously, and takes its name from the first number, *Waverley, or 'Tis
Sixty Years Since*. This was founded upon the rising of the clans, in 1745, in
support of the Young Pretender, Charles Edward Stuart, and it revealed to the
English public that almost foreign country which lay just across their
threshold, the Scottish Highlands. The *Waverley* novels remain, as a whole,
unequaled as historical fiction, although, here and there a single novel, like
George Eliot's *Romola*, or Thackeray's *Henry Esmond*, or Kingsley's
Hypatia, may have attained a place beside the best of them. They were a
novelty when they appeared. English prose fiction had somewhat declined
since the time of Fielding and Goldsmith. There were truthful, though rather
tame, delineations of provincial life, like Jane Austen's *Sense and Sensibility*,
1811, and {248} *Pride and Prejudice*, 1813; or Maria Edgeworth's *Popular
Tales*, 1804. On the other hand, there were Gothic romances, like the *Monk* of
Matthew Gregory Lewis, to whose *Tales of Wonder* some of Scott's
translations from the German had been contributed; or like Anne Radcliffe's
Mysteries of Udolpho. The great original of this school of fiction was Horace
Walpole's *Castle of Otranto*, 1765, an absurd tale of secret trap-doors,
subterranean vaults, apparitions of monstrous mailed figures and colossal
helmets, pictures that descend from their frames, and hollow voices that
proclaim the ruin of ancient families.

Scott used the machinery of romance, but he was not merely a romancer, or a
historical novelist even, and it is not, as Carlyle implies, the buff-belts and
jerkins which principally interest us in his heroes. *Ivanhoe* and *Kenilworth*
and the *Talisman* are, indeed, romances pure and simple, and very good
romances at that. But, in novels such as *Rob Roy*, the *Antiquary*, the *Heart of
Midlothian*, and the *Bride of Lammermoor*, Scott drew from contemporary
life, and from his intimate knowledge of Scotch character. The story is there,
with its entanglement of plot and its exciting adventures, but there are also, as
truly as in Shakspere, though not in the same degree, the observation of life,
the knowledge of men, the power of dramatic creation. No writer awakens in
his readers a warmer personal affection than Walter Scott, the brave, honest,
kindly gentleman, the noblest {249} figure among the literary men of his
generation.

Another Scotch poet was Thomas Campbell, whose *Pleasures of Hope*, 1799,
was written in Pope's couplet, and in the stilted diction of the eighteenth
century. *Gertrude of Wyoming*, 1809, a long narrative poem in Spenserian
stanza, is untrue to the scenery and life of Pennsylvania, where its scene is

laid. But Campbell turned his rhetorical manner and his clanking, martial verse to fine advantage in such pieces as *Hohenlinden, Ye Mariners of England,* and the *Battle of the Baltic.* These have the true lyric fire, and rank among the best English war-songs.

When Scott was asked why he had left off writing poetry, he answered, "Byron *bet* me." George Gordon Byron (1788-1824) was a young man of twenty-four, when, on his return from a two years' sauntering through Portugal, Spain, Albania, Greece, and the Levant, he published, in the first two cantos of *Childe Harold,* 1812, a sort of poetic itinerary of his experiences and impressions. The poem took, rather to its author's surprise, who said that he woke one morning and found himself famous. *Childe Harold* opened a new field to poetry, the romance of travel, the picturesque aspects of foreign scenery, manners, and costumes. It is instructive of the difference between the two ages, in poetic sensibility to such things, to compare Byron's glowing imagery with Addison's tame *Letter from Italy,* written a century before. *Childe {250} Harold* was followed by a series of metrical tales, the *Giaour,* the *Bride of Abydos,* the *Corsair, Lara,* the *Siege of Corinth, Parasina,* and *Prisoner of Chillon,* all written in the years 1813-1816. These poems at once took the place of Scott's in popular interest, dazzling a public that had begun to weary of chivalry romances, with pictures of Eastern life, with incidents as exciting as Scott's, descriptions as highly colored, and a much greater intensity of passion. So far as they depended for this interest upon the novelty of their accessories, the effect was a temporary one. Seraglios, divans, bulbuls, Gulistans, Zuleikas, and other Oriental properties, deluged English poetry for a time, and then subsided; even as the tide of moss-troopers, sorcerers, hermits, and feudal castles had already had its rise and fall.

But there was a deeper reason for the impression made by Byron's poetry upon his contemporaries. He laid his finger right on the sore spot in modern life. He had the disease with which the time was sick, the world-weariness, the desperation which proceeded from "passion incapable of being converted into action." We find this tone in much of the literature which followed the failure of the French Revolution and the Napoleonic wars. From the irritations of that period, the disappointment of high hopes for the future of the race, the growing religious disbelief, and the revolt of democracy and free thought against conservative reaction, sprang what Southey called the "Satanic {251} school," which spoke its loudest word in Byron. Titanic is the better word, for the rebellion was not against God, but Jupiter, that is, against the State, Church, and society of Byron's day; against George III., the Tory cabinet of Lord Castlereigh, the Duke of Wellington, the bench of Bishops, London gossip, the British Constitution, and British cant. In these poems of Byron,

and in his dramatic experiments, *Manfred* and *Cain*, there is a single figure—
the figure of Byron under various masks—and one pervading mood, a restless
and sardonic gloom, a weariness of life, a love of solitude, and a melancholy
exaltation in the presence of the wilderness and the sea. Byron's hero is
always represented as a man originally noble, whom some great wrong, by
others, or some mysterious crime of his own, has blasted and embittered, and
who carries about the world a seared heart and a somber brow. Harold—who
may stand as a type of all his heroes—has run "through sin's labyrinth" and
feeling the "fullness of satiety," is drawn abroad to roam, "the wandering
exile of his own dark mind." The loss of a capacity for pure, unjaded emotion
is the constant burden of Byron's lament.

"No more, no more, O never more on me
The freshness of the heart shall fall like dew."

and again,

"O could I feel as I have felt—or be what I have been,
Or weep as I could once have wept, o'er many a vanished scene;
{252}
As springs in deserts found seem sweet, all brackish tho' they be,
So, midst the withered waste of life, those tears would flow to me."

This mood was sincere in Byron; but by cultivating it, and posing too long in
one attitude, he became self-conscious and theatrical, and much of his serious
poetry has a false ring. His example infected the minor poetry of the time, and
it was quite natural that Thackeray—who represented a generation that had a
very different ideal of the heroic—should be provoked into describing Byron
as "a big, sulky dandy."

Byron was well fitted by birth and temperament to be the spokesman of this
fierce discontent. He inherited from his mother a haughty and violent temper,
and profligate tendencies from his father. He was through life a spoiled child,
whose main characteristic was willfulness. He liked to shock people by
exaggerating his wickedness, or by perversely maintaining the wrong side of
a dispute. But he had traits of bravery and generosity. Women loved him, and
he made strong friends. There was a careless charm about him which
fascinated natures as unlike each other as Shelley and Scott. By the death of
the fifth Lord Byron without issue, Byron came into a title and estates at the
age of ten. Though a liberal in politics he had aristocratic feelings, and was
vain of his rank as he was of his beauty. He was educated at Harrow and at
Trinity College, Cambridge, where he was idle and {253} dissipated, but did
a great deal of miscellaneous reading. He took some of his Cambridge set—
Hobhouse, Matthews, and others—to Newstead Abbey, his ancestral seat,
where they filled the ancient cloisters with eccentric orgies. Byron was

strikingly handsome. His face had a spiritual paleness and a classic regularity, and his dark hair curled closely to his head. A deformity in one of his feet was a mortification to him, though it did not greatly impair his activity, and he prided himself upon his powers as a swimmer.

In 1815, when at the height of his literary and social *éclat* in London, he married. In February of the following year he was separated from Lady Byron, and left England forever, pursued by the execrations of outraged respectability. In this chorus of abuse there was mingled a share of cant; but Byron got, on the whole, what he deserved. From Switzerland, where he spent a summer by Lake Leman, with the Shelleys; from Venice, Ravenna, Pisa, and Rome, scandalous reports of his intrigues and his wild debaucheries were wafted back to England, and with these came poem after poem, full of burning genius, pride, scorn, and anguish, and all hurling defiance at English public opinion. The third and fourth cantos of *Childe Harold*, 1816-1818, were a great advance upon the first two, and contain the best of Byron's serious poetry. He has written his name all over the continent of Europe, and on a hundred memorable spots has made the scenery his own. On the field of Waterloo, on "the castled {254} crag of Drachenfels," "by the blue rushing of the arrowy Rhone," in Venice, on the Bridge of Sighs, in the Coliseum at Rome, and among the "Isles of Greece," the tourist is compelled to see with Byron's eyes and under the associations of his pilgrimage. In his later poems, such as *Beppo*, 1818, and *Don Juan*, 1819-1823, he passed into his second manner, a mocking cynicism gaining ground upon the somewhat stagy gloom of his early poetry—Mephistophiles gradually elbowing out Satan. *Don Juan*, though morally the worst, is intellectually the most vital and representative of Byron's poems. It takes up into itself most fully the life of the time; exhibits most thoroughly the characteristic alternations of Byron's moods and the prodigal resources of wit, passion, and understanding, which—rather than imagination—were his prominent qualities as a poet. The hero, a graceless, amorous, stripling, goes wandering from Spain to the Greek islands and Constantinople, thence to St. Petersburg, and finally to England. Every-where his seductions are successful, and Byron uses him as a means of exposing the weakness of the human heart and the rottenness of society in all countries. In 1823, breaking away from his life of selfish indulgence in Italy, Byron threw himself into the cause of Grecian liberty, which he had sung so gloriously in the *Isles of Greece*. He died at Missolonghi, in the following year, of a fever contracted by exposure and overwork.

Byron was a great poet but not a great literary {255} artist. He wrote negligently and with the ease of assured strength, his mind gathering heat as it moved, and pouring itself forth in reckless profusion. His work is diffuse and imperfect; much of it is melodrama or speech-making rather than true poetry.

But on the other hand, much, very much of it, is unexcelled as the direct, strong, sincere utterance of personal feeling. Such is the quality of his best lyrics, like *When We Two Parted*, the *Elegy on Thyrza, Stanzas to Augusta, She Walks in Beauty*, and of innumerable passages, lyrical and descriptive, in his longer poems. He had not the wisdom of Wordsworth, nor the rich and subtle imagination of Coleridge, Shelley, and Keats when they were at their best. But he had greater body and motive force than any of them. He is the strongest personality among English poets since Milton, though his strength was wasted by want of restraint and self-culture. In Milton the passion was there, but it was held in check by the will and the artistic conscience, made subordinate to good ends, ripened by long reflection, and finally uttered in forms of perfect and harmonious beauty. Byron's love of Nature was quite different in kind from Wordsworth's. Of all English poets he has sung most lyrically of that national theme, the sea, as witness among many other passages, the famous apostrophe to the ocean, which closes *Childe Harold*, and the opening of the third canto in the same poem,

"Once more upon the waters," etc.

{256} He had a passion for night and storm, because they made him forget himself.

"Most glorious night!
Thou wert not sent for slumber! Let me be
A sharer in thy fierce and far delight,
A portion of the tempest and of thee!"

Byron's literary executor and biographer was the Irish poet, Thomas Moore, a born song-writer, whose *Irish Melodies*, set to old native airs, are, like Burns's, genuine, spontaneous, singing, and run naturally to music. Songs such as the *Meeting of the Waters, The Harp of Tara, Those Evening Bells*, the *Light of Other Days, Araby's Daughter*, and the *Last Rose of Summer* were, and still are, popular favorites. Moore's Oriental romance, *Lalla Rookh*, 1817, is overladen with ornament and with a sugary sentiment that clogs the palate. He had the quick Irish wit, sensibility rather than passion, and fancy rather than imagination.

Byron's friend, Percy Bysshe Shelley (1792-1822), was also in fiery revolt against all conventions and institutions, though his revolt proceeded not, as in Byron's case, from the turbulence of passions which brooked no restraint, but rather from an intellectual impatience of any kind of control. He was not, like Byron, a sensual man, but temperate and chaste. He was, indeed, in his life and in his poetry, as nearly a disembodied spirit as a human creature can be. The German poet, Heine, said that liberty was the religion of this century, {257} and of this religion Shelley was a worshiper. His rebellion against authority began early. He refused to fag at Eton, and was expelled from Oxford for publishing a tract on the *Necessity of Atheism*. At nineteen, he ran away with Harriet Westbrook, and was married to her in Scotland. Three years later he deserted her for Mary Godwin, with whom he eloped to Switzerland. Two years after this his first wife drowned herself in the Serpentine, and Shelley was then formally wedded to Mary Godwin. All this is rather startling, in the bare statement of it, yet it is not inconsistent with the many testimonies that exist, to Shelley's singular purity and beauty of character, testimonies borne out by the evidence of his own writings. Impulse with him took the place of conscience. Moral law, accompanied by the sanction of power, and imposed by outside authority, he rejected as a form of tyranny. His nature lacked robustness and ballast. Byron, who was at bottom intensely practical, said that Shelley's philosophy was too spiritual and romantic. Hazlitt, himself a Radical, wrote of Shelley: "He has a fire in his eye, a fever in his blood, a maggot in his brain, a hectic flutter in his speech, which mark out the philosophic fanatic. He is sanguine complexioned and shrill voiced." It was, perhaps, with some recollection of this last-mentioned trait of Shelley the man, that Carlyle wrote of Shelley the poet, that "the sound of him was shrieky," and that he had "filled the earth with an inarticulate wailing."

His career as a poet began characteristically enough, with the publication, while at Oxford, of a volume of political rimes, entitled *Margaret Nicholson's Remains*, Margaret Nicholson being the crazy woman who tried to stab George III. His boyish poem, *Queen Mab*, was published in 1813; *Alastor* in 1816, and the *Revolt of Islam*—his longest—in 1818, all before he was twenty-one. These were filled with splendid, though unsubstantial, imagery, but they were abstract in subject, and had the faults of incoherence and formlessness which make Shelley's longer poems wearisome and confusing. They sought to embody his social creed of Perfectionism, as well as a certain vague Pantheistic system of belief in a spirit of love in nature and man, whose presence is a constant source of obscurity in Shelley's verse. In 1818 he went to Italy, where the last four years of his life were passed, and where, under the influences of Italian art and poetry, his writing became deeper and stronger. He was fond of yachting, and spent much of his time upon the Mediterranean. In the summer of 1822, his boat was swamped in a squall off the Gulf of Spezzia, and Shelley's drowned body was washed ashore, and burned in the presence of Byron and Leigh Hunt. The ashes were entombed in the Protestant cemetery at Rome, with the epitaph, *Cor cordium*.

Shelley's best and maturest work, nearly all of which was done in Italy, includes his tragedy, *The Cenci*, 1819, and his lyrical drama, *Prometheus {259} Unbound*, 1821. The first of these has a unity, and a definiteness of contour unusual with Shelley, and is, with the exception of some of Robert Browning's, the best English tragedy since Otway. *Prometheus* represented to Shelley's mind the human spirit fighting against divine oppression, and in his portrayal of this figure, he kept in mind not only the *Prometheus* of Aeschylus, but the Satan of *Paradise Lost*. Indeed, in this poem, Shelley came nearer to the sublime than any English poet since Milton. Yet it is in lyrical, rather than in dramatic, quality that *Prometheus Unbound* is great. If Shelley be not, as his latest editor, Mr. Forman, claims him to be, the foremost of English lyrical poets, he is at least the most lyrical of them. He had, in a supreme degree, the "lyric cry." His vibrant nature trembled to every breath of emotion, and his nerves craved ever newer shocks; to pant, to quiver, to thrill, to grow faint in the spasm of intense sensation. The feminine cast observable in Shelley's portrait is borne out by this tremulous sensibility in his verse. It is curious how often he uses the metaphor of wings: of the winged spirit, soaring, like his skylark, till lost in music, rapture, light, and then falling back to earth. Three successive moods—longing, ecstasy, and the revulsion of despair—are expressed in many of his lyrics; as in the *Hymn to the Spirit of Nature*, in *Prometheus*, in the ode *To a Skylark*, and in the *Lines to an Indian Air*—Edgar Poe's favorite. His passionate desire to lose {260} himself in

Nature, to become one with that spirit of love and beauty in the universe, which was to him in place of God, is expressed in the *Ode to the West Wind*, his most perfect poem:

"Make me thy lyre, even as the forest is;
What if my leaves are falling like its own!
The tumult of thy mighty harmonies
Will take from both a deep autumnal tone.
Sweet, though in sadness, be thou, Spirit fierce,
My spirit! be thou me, impetuous one!"

In the lyrical pieces already mentioned, together with *Adonais*, the lines *Written in the Euganean Hills*, *Epipsychidion*, *Stanzas Written in Dejection near Naples*, *A Dream of the Unknown*, and many others, Shelley's lyrical genius reaches a rarer loveliness and a more faultless art than Byron's ever attained, though it lacks the directness and momentum of Byron.

In Shelley's longer poems, intoxicated with the music of his own singing, he abandons himself wholly to the guidance of his imagination, and the verse seems to go on of itself, like the enchanted boat in *Alastor*, with no one at the helm. Vision succeeds vision in glorious but bewildering profusion; ideal landscapes and cities of cloud "pinnacled dim in the intense inane." These poems are like the water-falls in the Yosemite, which, tumbling from a height of several thousand feet, are shattered into foam by the air, and waved about over the valley. Very beautiful is this descending spray, and the rainbow dwells in its {261} bosom; but there is no longer any stream, nothing but an irridescent mist. The word *etherial*, best expresses the quality of Shelley's genius. His poetry is full of atmospheric effects; of the tricks which light plays with the fluid elements of water and air; of stars, clouds, rain, dew, mist, frost, wind, the foam of seas, the phases of the moon, the green shadows of waves, the shapes of flames, the "golden lightning of the setting sun." Nature, in Shelley, wants homeliness and relief. While poets like Wordsworth and Burns let in an ideal light upon the rough fields of earth, Shelley escapes into a "moonlight-colored" realm of shadows and dreams, among whose abstractions the heart turns cold. One bit of Wordsworth's mountain turf is worth them all.

By the death of John Keats (1796-1821), whose elegy Shelley sang in *Adonais*, English poetry suffered an irreparable loss. His *Endymion*, 1818, though disfigured by mawkishness and by some affectations of manner, was rich in promise. Its faults were those of youth, the faults of exuberance and of a tremulous sensibility, which time corrects. *Hyperion*, 1820, promised to be his masterpiece, but he left it unfinished—"a Titanic torso"—because, as he said, "there were too many Miltonic inversions in it." The subject was the

130

displacement, by Phoebus Apollo, of the ancient sun-god, Hyperion, the last of the Titans who retained his dominion. It was a theme of great capabilities, and the poem was begun by Keats, {262} with a strength of conception which leads to the belief that here was once more a really epic genius, had fate suffered it to mature. The fragment, as it stands—"that inlet to severe magnificence"—proves how rapidly Keats's diction was clarifying. He had learned to string up his looser chords. There is nothing maudlin in *Hyperion*; all there is in whole tones and in the grand manner, "as sublime as Aeschylus," said Byron, with the grave, antique simplicity, and something of modern sweetness interfused.

Keats's father was a groom in a London livery-stable. The poet was apprenticed at fifteen to a surgeon. At school he had studied Latin, but not Greek. He, who of all English poets had the most purely Hellenic spirit, made acquaintance with Greek literature and art only through the medium of classical dictionaries, translations, and popular mythologies; and later through the marbles and casts in the British Museum. His friend, the artist Haydon, lent him a copy of Chapman's Homer, and the impression that it made upon him he recorded in his sonnet, *On First Looking into Chapman's Homer*. Other poems of the same inspiration are his three sonnets, *To Homer, On Seeing the Elgin Marbles, On a Picture of Leander, Lamia*, and the beautiful *Ode on a Grecian Urn*. But Keats's art was retrospective and eclectic, the blossom of a double root; and "golden-tongued Romance with serene lute" had her part in him, as well as the classics. In his seventeenth year he {263} had read the *Faery Queene*, and from Spenser he went on to a study of Chaucer, Shakspere, and Milton. Then he took up Italian and read *Ariosto*. The influence of these studies is seen in his poem, *Isabella, or the Pot of Basil*, taken from a story of Boccaccio; in his wild ballad, *La Belle Dame sans Merci*; and in his love tale, the *Eve of Saint Agnes*, with its wealth of medieval adornment. In the *Ode to Autumn*, and *Ode to a Nightingale*, the Hellenic choiceness is found touched with the warmer hues of romance.

There is something deeply tragic in the short story of Keats's life. The seeds of consumption were in him; he felt the stirrings of a potent genius, but knew that he could not wait for it to unfold, but must die

"Before high-piled books, in charactry
Hold like rich garners the full-ripened grain."

His disease was aggravated, possibly, by the stupid brutality with which the reviewers had treated *Endymion*; and certainly by the hopeless love which devoured him. "The very thing which I want to live most for," he wrote, "will be a great occasion of my death. If I had any chance of recovery, this passion would kill me." In the autumn of 1820, his disease gaining apace, he went on a sailing vessel to Italy, accompanied by a single friend, a young artist named Severn. The change was of no avail, and he died at Rome a few weeks after, in his twenty-sixth year.

{264}

Keats was, above all things, the *artist*, with that love of the beautiful and that instinct for its reproduction which are the artist's divinest gifts. He cared little about the politics and philosophy of his day, and he did not make his poetry the vehicle of ideas. It was sensuous poetry, the poetry of youth and gladness. But if he had lived, and if, with wider knowledge of men and deeper experience of life, he had attained to Wordsworth's spiritual insight and to Byron's power of passion and understanding, he would have become a greater poet than either. For he had a style—a "natural magic"—which only needed the chastening touch of a finer culture to make it superior to any thing in modern English poetry and to force us back to Milton or Shakspere for a comparison. His tombstone, not far from Shelley's, bears the inscription of his own choosing: "Here lies one whose name was writ in water." But it would be within the limits of truth to say that it is written in large characters on most of our contemporary poetry. "Wordsworth," says Lowell, "has influenced most the ideas of succeeding poets; Keats their forms." And he has influenced these out of all proportion to the amount which he left, or to his intellectual range, by virtue of the exquisite quality of his technique.

1. Wordsworth's Poems. Chosen and edited by Matthew Arnold. London, 1879.

2. Poetry of Byron. Chosen and arranged by Matthew Arnold. London, 1881.

{265}

3. Shelley. Julian and Maddalo, Prometheus Unbound, The Cenci, Lyrical Pieces.

4. Landor. Pericles and Aspasia.

5. Coleridge. Table Talk, Notes on Shakspere, The Ancient Mariner, Christabel, Love, Ode to France, Ode to the Departing Year, Kubla Khan, Hymn before Sunrise in the Vale of Chamouni, Youth and Age, Frost at Midnight.

6. De Quincey. Confessions of an English Opium Eater, Flight of a Tartar Tribe, Biographical Sketches.

7. Scott. Waverley, Heart of Midlothian, Bride of Lammermoor, Rob Roy, Antiquary, Marmion, Lady of the Lake.

8. Keats. Hyperion, Eve of St. Agnes, Lyrical Pieces.

9. Mrs. Oliphant's Literary History of England, 18th-19th Centuries.
{266}

CHAPTER VIII

FROM THE DEATH OF SCOTT TO THE PRESENT TIME.

1832-1886.

The literature of the past fifty years is too close to our eyes to enable the critic to pronounce a final judgment, or the literary historian to get a true perspective. Many of the principal writers of the time are still living, and many others have been dead but a few years. This concluding chapter, therefore, will be devoted to the consideration of the few who stand forth, incontestably, as the leaders of literary thought, and who seem likely, under all future changes of fashion and taste, to remain representative of their generation. As regards *form*, the most striking fact in the history of the period under review is the immense preponderance in its imaginative literature of prose fiction, of the novel of real life. The novel has become to the solitary reader of to-day what the stage play was to the audiences of Elisabeth's reign, or the periodical essay, like the *Tatlers* and *Spectators*, to the clubs and breakfast-tables of Queen Anne's. And, if its criticism of life is less concentrated and brilliant than the drama gives, it is far {267} more searching and minute. No period has ever left in its literary records so complete a picture of its whole society as the period which is just closing. At any other time than the present, the names of authors like Charlotte Bronté, Charles Kingsley, and Charles Reade—names which are here merely mentioned in passing—besides many others which want of space forbids us even to mention—would be of capital importance. As it is, we must limit our review to the three acknowledged masters of modern English fiction, Charles Dickens (1812-1870), William Makepeace Thackeray (1811-1863), and "George Eliot" (Mary Ann Evans, 1819-1880).

It is sometimes helpful to reduce a great writer to his lowest term, in order to see what the prevailing bent of his genius is. This lowest term may often be found in his early work, before experience of the world has overlaid his original impulse with foreign accretions. Dickens was much more than a humorist, Thackeray than a satirist, and George Eliot than a moralist; but they had their starting-points respectively in humor, in burlesque, and in strong ethical and religious feeling. Dickens began with a broadly comic series of papers, contributed to the *Old Magazine* and the *Evening Chronicle*, and reprinted in book form, in 1836, as *Sketches by Boz*. The success of these suggested to a firm of publishers the preparation of a number of similar sketches of the misadventures of cockney sportsmen, to accompany plates by the {268} comic draughtsman, Mr. R. Seymour. This suggestion resulted in the *Pickwick Papers*, published in monthly installments, in 1836-1837. The series grew, under Dickens's hand, into a continuous, though rather loosely strung narrative of the doings of a set of characters, conceived with such exuberant and novel humor that it took the public by storm, and raised its author at once to fame. *Pickwick* is by no means Dickens's best, but it is his most characteristic, and most popular, book. At the time that he wrote these early sketches he was a reporter for the *Morning Chronicle*. His naturally acute powers of observation had been trained in this pursuit to the utmost efficiency, and there always continued to be about his descriptive writing a reportorial and newspaper air. He had the eye for effect, the sharp fidelity to detail, the instinct for rapidly seizing upon and exaggerating the salient point, which are developed by the requirements of modern journalism. Dickens knew London as no one else has ever known it, and, in particular, he knew its hideous and grotesque recesses, with the strange developments of human nature that abide there; slums like Tom-all-Alone's, in *Bleak House*; the riverside haunts of Rogue Riderhood, in *Our Mutual Friend*; as well as the old inns, like the "White Hart," and the "dusky purlieus of the law." As a man, his favorite occupation was walking the streets, where, as a child, he had picked up the most valuable part of his education. His tramps about London—often after {269} nightfall—sometimes extended to fifteen miles in a day. He knew, too, the shifts of poverty. His father—some traits of whom are preserved in Mr. Micawber—was imprisoned for debt in the Marshalsea prison, where his wife took lodging with him, while Charles, then a boy of ten, was employed at six shillings a week to cover blacking-pots in Warner's blacking warehouse. The hardships and loneliness of this part of his life are told under a thin disguise in Dickens's masterpiece, *David Copperfield*, the most autobiographical of his novels. From these young experiences he gained that insight into the lives of the lower classes, and that sympathy with children and with the poor which shine out in his pathetic sketches of Little Nell, in *The Old Curiosity Shop*, of Paul Dombey, of Poor Jo, in *Bleak House*, of "the Marchioness," and a hundred other figures.

In *Oliver Twist*, contributed, during 1837-1838, to *Bentley's Miscellany*, a monthly magazine of which Dickens was editor, he produced his first regular novel. In this story of the criminal classes the author showed a tragic power which he had not hitherto exhibited. Thenceforward his career was a series of dazzling successes. It is impossible here to particularize his numerous novels, sketches, short tales, and "Christmas Stories"—the latter a fashion which he inaugurated, and which has produced a whole literature in itself. In *Nicholas Nickleby*, 1839; *Master Humphrey's Clock*, 1840; *Martin Chuzzlewit*, 1844;

Dombey and Son, 1848; {270} *David Copperfield*, 1850; and *Bleak House*, 1853, there is no falling off in strength. The last named was, in some respects, and especially in the skillful construction of the plot, his best novel. In some of his latest books, as *Great Expectations*, 1861, and *Our Mutual Friend*, 1865, there are signs of a decline. This showed itself in an unnatural exaggeration of characters and motives, and a painful straining after humorous effects; faults, indeed, from which Dickens was never wholly free. There was a histrionic side to him, which came out in his fondness for private theatricals, in which he exhibited remarkable talent, and in the dramatic action which he introduced into the delightful public readings from his works that he gave before vast audiences all over the United Kingdom, and in his two visits to America. It is not surprising, either, to learn that upon the stage his preference was for melodrama and farce. His own serious writing was always dangerously close to the melodramatic, and his humor to the farcical. There is much false art, bad taste, and even vulgarity in Dickens. He was never quite a gentleman, and never succeeded well in drawing gentlemen or ladies. In the region of low comedy he is easily the most original, the most inexhaustible, the most wonderful of modern humorists. Creations such as Mrs. Nickleby, Mr. Micawber, Sam Weller, Sairy Gamp, take rank with Falstaff and Dogberry; while many others, like Dick Swiveller, Stiggins, Chadband, Mrs. Jellyby, and Julia Mills are almost {271} equally good. In the innumerable swarm of minor characters with which he has enriched our comic literature, there is no indistinctness. Indeed, the objection that has been made to him is that his characters are too distinct—that he puts labels on them; that they are often mere personifications of a single trick of speech or manner, which becomes tedious and unnatural by repetition; thus, Grandfather Smallweed is always settling down into his cushion, and having to be shaken up; Mr. Jellyby is always sitting with his head against the wall; Peggotty is always bursting her buttons off, etc., etc. As Dickens's humorous characters tend perpetually to run into caricatures and grotesques, so his sentiment, from the same excess, slops over too frequently into "gush," and into a too deliberate and protracted attack upon the pity. A favorite humorous device in his style is a stately and roundabout way of telling a trivial incident as where, for example, Mr. Roker "muttered certain unpleasant invocations concerning his own eyes, limbs, and circulating fluids;" or where the drunken man who is singing comic songs in the Fleet received from Mr. Smangle "a gentle intimation, through the medium of the water-jug, that his audience were not musically disposed." This manner was original with Dickens, though he may have taken a hint of it from the mock heroic language of *Jonathan Wild*; but as practiced by a thousand imitators, ever since, it has gradually become a burden.

It would not be the whole truth to say that the {272} difference between the humor of Thackeray and Dickens is the same as between that of Shakspere and Ben Jonson. Yet it is true that the "humors" of Ben Jonson have an analogy with the extremer instances of Dickens's character sketches in this respect, namely: that they are both studies of the eccentric, the abnormal, the whimsical, rather than of the typical and universal—studies of manners, rather than of whole characters. And it is easily conceivable that, at no distant day, the oddities of Captain Cuttle, Deportment Turveydrop, Mark Tapley, and Newman Noggs will seem as far-fetched and impossible as those of Captain Otter, Fastidious Brisk, and Sir Amorous La-Foole.

When Dickens was looking about for some one to take Seymour's place as illustrator of Pickwick, Thackeray applied for the job, but without success. He was then a young man of twenty-five, and still hesitating between art and literature. He had begun to draw caricatures with his pencil when a schoolboy at the Charter House, and to scribble them with his pen when a student at Cambridge, editing *The Snob*, a weekly under-graduate paper, and parodying the prize poem *Timbuctoo* of his contemporary at the university, Alfred Tennyson. Then he went abroad to study art, passing a season at Weimar, where he met Goethe and filled the albums of the young Saxon ladies with caricatures; afterward living, in the Latin Quarter at Paris, a Bohemian existence, studying art in a desultory way, and seeing men and cities; {273} accumulating portfolios full of sketches, but laying up stores of material to be used afterward to greater advantage when he should settle upon his true medium of expression. By 1837, having lost his fortune of 500 pounds a year in speculation and gambling, he began to contribute to *Fraser's*, and thereafter to the *New Monthly*, *Cruikshank's Comic Almanac*, *Punch*, and other periodicals, clever burlesques, art criticisms by "Michael Angelo Titmarsh," *Yellow Plush Papers*, and all manner of skits, satirical character sketches, and humorous tales, like the *Great Hoggarty Diamond* and the *Luck of Barry Lyndon*. Some of these were collected in the *Paris Sketch-Book*, 1840, and the *Irish Sketch-Book*, 1843; but Thackeray was slow in winning recognition, and it was not until the publication of his first great novel, *Vanity Fair*, in monthly parts, during 1846-1848, that he achieved any thing like the general reputation which Dickens had reached at a bound. *Vanity Fair* described itself, on its title-page, as "a novel without a hero." It was also a novel without a plot—in the sense in which *Bleak House* or *Nicholas Nickleby* had a plot—and in that respect it set the fashion for the latest school of realistic fiction, being a transcript of life, without necessary beginning or end. Indeed, one of the pleasantest things to a reader of Thackeray is the way which his characters have of re-appearing, as old acquaintances, in his different books; just as, in real life, people drop out of mind and then turn

{274} up again in other years and places. *Vanity Fair* is Thackeray's masterpiece, but it is not the best introduction to his writings. There are no illusions in it, and, to a young reader fresh from Scott's romances or Dickens's sympathetic extravagances, it will seem hard and repellant. But men who, like Thackeray, have seen life and tasted its bitterness and felt its hollowness, know how to prize it. Thackeray does not merely expose the cant, the emptiness, the self-seeking, the false pretenses, flunkeyism, and snobbery —the "mean admiration of mean things"—in the great world of London society: his keen, unsparing vision detects the base alloy in the purest natures. There are no "heroes" in his books, no perfect characters. Even his good women, such as Helen and Laura Pendennis, are capable of cruel injustice toward less fortunate sisters, like little Fanny; and Amelia Sedley is led, by blind feminine instinct, to snub and tyrannize over poor Dobbin. The shabby miseries of life, the numbing and belittling influences of failure and poverty upon the most generous natures, are the tragic themes which Thackeray handles by preference. He has been called a cynic, but the boyish playfulness of his humor and his kindly spirit are incompatible with cynicism. Charlotte Brontë said that Fielding was the vulture and Thackeray the eagle. The comparison would have been truer if made between Swift and Thackeray. Swift was a cynic; his pen was driven by hate, but Thackeray's by love, and it was not {275} in bitterness but in sadness that the latter laid bare the wickedness of the world. He was himself a thorough man of the world, and he had that dislike for a display of feeling which characterizes the modern Englishman. But behind his satiric mask he concealed the manliest tenderness, and a reverence for every thing in human nature that is good and true. Thackeray's other great novels are *Pendennis*, 1849; *Henry Esmond*, 1852; and *The Newcomes*, 1855—the last of which contains his most lovable character, the pathetic and immortal figure of Colonel Newcome, a creation worthy to stand, in its dignity and its sublime weakness, by the side of Don Quixote. It was alleged against Thackeray that he made all his good characters, like Major Dobbin and Amelia Sedley and Colonel Newcome, intellectually feeble, and his brilliant characters, like Becky Sharp and Lord Steyne and Blanche Amory, morally bad. This is not entirely true, but the other complaint—that his women are inferior to his men—is true in a general way. Somewhat inferior to his other novels were *The Virginians*, 1858, and *The Adventures of Philip*, 1862. All of these were stories of contemporary life, except *Henry Esmond* and its sequel, *The Virginians*, which, though not precisely historical fictions, introduced historical figures, such as Washington and the Earl of Peterborough. Their period of action was the 18th century, and the dialogue was a cunning imitation of the language of that time. Thackeray was strongly {276} attracted by the 18th century. His literary teachers were Addison, Swift, Steele, Gay, Johnson, Richardson, Goldsmith, Fielding,

Smollett, and Sterne, and his special master and model was Fielding. He projected a history of the century, and his studies in this kind took shape in his two charming series of lectures on *The English Humorists* and *The Four Georges*. These he delivered in England and in America, to which country he, like Dickens, made two several visits.

Thackeray's genius was, perhaps, less astonishing than Dickens's, less fertile, spontaneous, and inventive; but his art is sounder, and his delineation of character more truthful. After one has formed a taste for his books, Dickens's sentiment will seem overdone, and much of his humor will have the air of buffoonery. Thackeray had the advantage in another particular: he described the life of the upper classes, and Dickens of the lower. It may be true that the latter offers richer material to the novelist, in the play of elementary passions and in strong, native developments of character. It is true, also, that Thackeray approached "society" rather to satirize it than to set forth its agreeableness. Yet, after all, it is "the great world" which he describes, that world upon which the broadening and refining processes of a high civilization have done their utmost, and which, consequently, must possess an intellectual interest superior to any thing in the life of London thieves, traveling showmen, and coachees. Thackeray is {277} the equal of Swift as a satirist, of Dickens as a humorist, and of Scott as a novelist. The one element lacking in him—and which Scott had in a high degree—is the poetic imagination. "I have no brains above my eyes," he said; "I describe what I see." Hence there is wanting in his creations that final charm which Shakspere's have. For what the eyes see is not all.

The great woman who wrote under the pen-name of George Eliot was a humorist, too. She had a rich, deep humor of her own, and a wit that crystallized into sayings which are not epigrams, only because their wisdom strikes more than their smartness. But humor was not, as with Thackeray and Dickens, her point of view. A country girl, the daughter of a land agent and surveyor at Nuneaton, in Warwickshire, her early letters and journals exhibit a Calvinistic gravity and moral severity. Later, when her truth to her convictions led her to renounce the Christian belief, she carried into Positivism the same religious earnestness, and wrote the one English hymn of the religion of humanity:

"O, let me join the choir invisible," etc.

Her first published work was a translation of Strauss's *Leben Jesu*, 1846. In 1851 she went to London and became one of the editors of the Radical organ, the *Westminster Review*. Here she formed a connection—a marriage in all but the name—with George Henry Lewes, who was, like {278} herself, a freethinker, and who published, among other things, a *Biographical History of Philosophy.* Lewes had also written fiction, and it was at his suggestion that his wife undertook story writing. Her *Scenes of Clerical Life* were contributed to *Blackwood's Magazine* for 1857, and published in book form in the following year. *Adam Bede* followed in 1859, the *Mill on the Floss* in 1860, *Silas Marner* in 1861, *Romola* in 1863, *Felix Holt* in 1866, and *Middlemarch* in 1872. All of these, except *Romola*, are tales of provincial, and largely of domestic, life in the midland counties. *Romola* is a historical novel, the scene of which is Florence, in the 15th century, the Florence of Macchiavelli and of Savonarola. George Eliot's method was very different from that of Thackeray or Dickens. She did not crowd her canvas with the swarming life of cities. Her figures are comparatively few, and they are selected from the middle-class families of rural parishes or small towns, amid that atmosphere of "fine old leisure," whose disappearance she lamented. Her drama is a still life drama, intensely and profoundly inward. Character is the stuff that she works in, and she deals with it more subtly than Thackeray. With him the tragedy is produced by the pressure of society and its false standards upon the individual; with her, by the malign influence of individuals upon one another. She watches "the stealthy convergence of human fates," the intersection at various angles of the planes of character, the power {279} that the lower nature has to thwart, stupefy, or corrupt the higher, which has become entangled with it in the mesh of destiny. At the bottom of every one of her stories, there is a problem of the conscience or the intellect. In this respect she resembles Hawthorne, though she is not, like him, a romancer, but a realist.

There is a melancholy philosophy in her books, most of which are tales of failure or frustration. The *Mill on the Floss* contains a large element of autobiography, and its heroine, Maggie Tulliver, is, perhaps, her idealized self. Her aspirations after a fuller and nobler existence are condemned to struggle against the resistance of a narrow, provincial environment, and the pressure of untoward fates. She is tempted to seek an escape even through a desperate throwing off of moral obligations, and is driven back to her duty only to die by a sudden stroke of destiny. "Life is a bad business," wrote George Eliot, in a letter to a friend, "and we must make the most of it." *Adam Bede* is, in construction, the most perfect of her novels, and Silas Marner of her shorter stories. Her analytic habit gained more and more upon her as she wrote. *Middlemarch*, in some respects her greatest book, lacks the unity of her earlier novels, and the story tends to become subordinate to the working out of character stories and social problems. The philosophic speculations, which she shared with her husband, were seemingly unfavorable to her artistic growth, a circumstance which {280} comes apparent in her last novel, *Daniel Deronda*, 1877. Finally in the *Impressions of Theophrastus Such*, 1879, she abandoned narrative altogether, and recurred to that type of "character" books which we have met, as a flourishing department of literature in the 17th century, represented by such works as Earle's *Microcosmographie* and Fuller's *Holy and Profane State*. The moral of George Eliot's writings is not obtruded. She never made the artistic mistake of writing a novel of purpose, or what the Germans call a *tendenz-roman*; as Dickens did, for example, when he attacked imprisonment for debt, in *Pickwick*; the poor laws, in *Oliver Twist*; the Court of Chancery, in *Bleak House*; and the Circumlocution office, in *Little Dorrit*.

Next to the novel, the essay has been the most overflowing literary form used by the writers of this generation—a form, characteristic, it may be, of an age which "lectures, not creates." It is not the essay of Bacon, nor yet of Addison, nor of Lamb, but attempts a complete treatment. Indeed, many longish books, like Carlyle's *Heroes and Hero Worship* and Ruskin's *Modern Painters*, are, in spirit, rather literary essays than formal treatises. The most popular essayist and historian of his time was Thomas Babington Macaulay, (1800-1859), an active and versatile man, who won splendid success in many fields of labor. He was prominent in public life as one of the leading orators and writers of the Whig party. He sat many times in the House of Commons, as member for Calne, for Leeds, and {281} for Edinburgh, and took a distinguished part in the debates on the Reform bill of 1832. He held office in several Whig governments, and during his four years' service in British India, as member of the Supreme Council of Calcutta, he did valuable work in promoting education in that province, and in codifying the Indian penal law. After his return to England, and especially after the publication of his *History of England from The Accession of James II.*, honors and appointments of all kinds were showered upon him. In 1857 he was raised to the peerage as Baron Macaulay of Rothley.

Macaulay's equipment, as a writer on historical and biographical subjects, was, in some points, unique. His reading was prodigious, and his memory so tenacious, that it was said, with but little exaggeration, that he never forgot any thing that he had read. He could repeat the whole of *Paradise Lost* by heart, and thought it probable that he could rewrite *Sir Charles Grandison* from memory. In his books, in his speeches in the House of Commons, and in private conversation—for he was an eager and fluent talker, running on often for hours at a stretch—he was never at a loss to fortify and illustrate his positions by citation after citation of dates, names, facts of all kinds, and passages quoted *verbatim* from his multifarious reading. The first of Macaulay's writings to attract general notice was his article on *Milton*, printed in the August number of the *Edinburgh Review*, for 1825. The editor, Lord Jeffrey, in {282} acknowledging the receipt of the MS., wrote to his new contributor, "The more I think, the less I can conceive where you picked up that style." That celebrated style—about which so much has since been written—was an index to the mental character of its owner. Macaulay was of a confident, sanguine, impetuous nature. He had great common sense, and he saw what he saw quickly and clearly, but he did not see very far below the surface. He wrote with the conviction of an advocate, and the easy omniscience of a man whose learning is really nothing more than "general information," raised to a very high power, rather than with the subtle penetration of an original or truly philosophic intellect, like Coleridge's or De Quincey's. He always had at hand explanations of events or of characters, which were admirably easy and simple—too simple, indeed, for the complicated phenomena which they professed to explain. His style was clear, animated, showy, and even its faults were of an exciting kind. It was his habit to give piquancy to his writing by putting things concretely. Thus, instead of saying, in general terms—as Hume or Gibbon might have done—that the Normans and Saxons began to mingle about 1200, he says: "The great grandsons of those who had fought under William and the great grandsons of those who had fought under Harold began to draw near to each other." Macaulay was a great scene painter, who neglected delicate truths of detail for exaggerated distemper effects. He used the {283} rhetorical machinery of climax and hyperbole for all that it was worth, and he "made points"—as in his essay on *Bacon*—by creating antithesis. In his *History of England*, he inaugurated the picturesque method of historical writing. The book was as fascinating as any novel. Macaulay, like Scott, had the historic imagination, though his method of turning history into romance was very different from Scott's. Among his essays, the best are those which, like the ones on *Lord Clive*, *Warren Hastings*, and *Frederick the Great*, deal with historical subjects; or those which deal with literary subjects under their public historic relations, such as the essays on *Addison*, *Bunyan*, and *The Comic Dramatists of the Restoration*. "I have never written a page of criticism on poetry, or the fine arts," wrote Macaulay, "which I would not burn if I had the power." Nevertheless his own *Lays of Ancient Rome*, 1842, are good, stirring verse of the emphatic and declamatory kind, though their quality may be rather rhetorical than poetic.

Our critical time has not forborne to criticize itself, and perhaps the writer who impressed himself most strongly upon his generation was the one who railed most desperately against the "spirit of the age." Thomas Carlyle (1795-1881) was occupied between 1822 and 1830 chiefly in imparting to the British public a knowledge of German literature. He published, among other things, a *Life of Schiller*, a translation of Goethe's *Wilhelm Meister*, and two volumes of translations from the German {284} romancers—Tieck, Hoffmann, Richter, and Fouque, and contributed to the *Edinburgh* and

Foreign Review, articles on Goethe, Werner, Novalis, Richter, German playwrights, the *Nibelungen Lied*, etc. His own diction became more and more tinctured with Germanisms. There was something Gothic in his taste, which was attracted by the lawless, the grotesque, and the whimsical in the writings of Jean Paul Richter. His favorite among English humorists was Sterne, who has a share of these same qualities. He spoke disparagingly of "the sensuous literature of the Greeks," and preferred the Norse to the Hellenic mythology. Even in his admirable critical essays on Burns, on Richter, on Scott, Diderot, and Voltaire, which are free from his later mannerism—written in English, and not in Carlylese—his sense of spirit is always more lively than his sense of form. He finally became so impatient of art as to maintain—half-seriously—the paradox that Shakspere would have done better to write in prose. In three of these early essays—on the *Signs of the Times*, 1829; on *History*, 1830; and on *Characteristics*, 1831—are to be found the germs of all his later writings. The first of these was an arraignment of the mechanical spirit of the age. In every province of thought he discovered too great a reliance upon systems, institutions, machinery, instead of upon men. Thus, in religion, we have Bible Societies, "machines for converting the heathen." "In defect of Raphaels and Angelos and Mozarts, we have royal {285} academies of painting, sculpture, music." In like manner, he complains, government is a machine. "Its duties and faults are not those of a father, but of an active parish-constable." Against the "police theory," as distinguished from the "paternal" theory of government, Carlyle protested with ever-shriller iteration. In *Chartism*, 1839; *Past and Present*, 1843; and *Latter-day Pamphlets*, 1850, he denounced this *laissez faire* idea. The business of government, he repeated, is to govern; but this view makes it its business to refrain from governing. He fought most fiercely against the conclusions of political economy, "the dismal science," which, he said, affirmed that men were guided exclusively by their stomachs. He protested, too, against the Utilitarians, followers of Bentham and Mill, with their "greatest happiness principle," which reduced virtue to a profit-and-loss account. Carlyle took issue with modern liberalism; he ridiculed the self-gratulation of the time, all the talk about progress of the species, unexampled prosperity, etc. But he was reactionary without being conservative. He had studied the French Revolution, and he saw the fateful, irresistible approach of democracy. He had no faith in government "by counting noses," and he hated talking parliaments; but neither did he put trust in an aristocracy that spent its time in "preserving the game." What he wanted was a great individual ruler, a real king or hero; and this doctrine he set forth afterward most fully in *Hero Worship*, 1841, and {286} illustrated in his lives of representative heroes, such as his *Cromwell's Letters and Speeches*, 1845, and his great *History of Frederick the Great*, 1858-1865. Cromwell and Frederick were well enough;

but as Carlyle grew older, his admiration for mere force grew, and his latest hero was none other than that infamous Dr. Francia, the South American dictator, whose career of bloody and crafty crime horrified the civilized world.

The essay on *History* was a protest against the scientific view of history which attempts to explain away and account for the wonderful. "Wonder," he wrote in *Sartor Resartus*, "is the basis of all worship." He defined history as "the essence of innumerable biographies." "Mr. Carlyle," said the Italian patriot, Mazzini, "comprehends only the individual. The nationality of Italy is, in his eyes, the glory of having produced Dante and Christopher Columbus." This trait comes out in his greatest book, *The French Revolution*, 1837, which is a mighty tragedy, enacted by a few leading characters, Mirabeau, Danton, Napoleon. He loved to emphasize the superiority of history over fiction as dramatic material. The third of the three essays mentioned was a Jeremiad on the morbid self-consciousness of the age, which shows itself in religion and philosophy, as skepticism and introspective metaphysics; and in literature, as sentimentalism, and "view-hunting."

But Carlyle's epoch-making book was *Sartor Resartus* (The Tailor Retailored), published in *Fraser's {287} Magazine* for 1833-1834, and first reprinted in book form in America. This was a satire upon shams, conventions, the disguises which overlie the most spiritual realities of the soul. It purported to be the life and "clothes-philosophy" of a certain Diogenes Teufelsdröckh, Professor der Allerlei Wissenschaft—of things in general—in the University of Weissnichtwo. "Society," said Carlyle, "is founded upon cloth," following the suggestions of Lear's speech to the naked bedlam beggar: "Thou art the thing itself: unaccommodated man is no more but such a poor, bare, forked animal as thou art;" and borrowing also, perhaps, an ironical hint from a paragraph in Swift's *Tale of a Tub*: "A sect was established who held the universe to be a large suit of clothes... . If certain ermines or furs be placed in a certain position, we style them a judge; and so an apt conjunction of lawn and black satin we entitle a bishop." In *Sartor Resartus* Carlyle let himself go. It was willful, uncouth, amorphous, titanic. There was something monstrous in the combination, the hot heart of the Scot married to the transcendental dream of Germany. It was not English, said the reviewers; it was not sense; it was disfigured by obscurity and "mysticism." Nevertheless even the thin-witted and the dry-witted had to acknowledge the powerful beauty of many chapters and passages, rich with humor, eloquence, poetry, deep-hearted tenderness, or passionate scorn.

Carlyle was a voracious reader, and the plunder {288} of whole literatures is strewn over his pages. He flung about the resources of the language with a giant's strength, and made new words at every turn. The concreteness and the swarming fertility of his mind are evidenced by his enormous vocabulary, computed greatly to exceed Shakspere's, or any other single writer's in the English tongue. His style lacks the crowning grace of simplicity and repose. It astonishes, but it also fatigues.

Carlyle's influence has consisted more in his attitude than in any special truth which he has preached. It has been the influence of a moralist, of a practical, rather than a speculative, philosopher. "The end of man," he wrote, "is an action, not a thought." He has not been able to persuade the time that it is going wrong, but his criticisms have been wholesomely corrective of its self-conceit. In a democratic age he has insisted upon the undemocratic virtues of obedience, silence, and reverence. *Ehrfurcht*—reverence—the text of his address to the students of Edinburgh University, in 1866, is the last word of his philosophy.

In 1830 Alfred Tennyson (1809- ——), a young graduate of Cambridge, published a thin duodecimo of 154 pages, entitled *Poems, Chiefly Lyrical*. The pieces in this little volume, like the *Sleeping Beauty, Ode to Memory*, and *Recollections of the Arabian Nights*, were full of color, fragrance, melody; but they had a dream-like character, and were without definite theme, resembling an artist's studies, or {289} exercises in music—a few touches of the brush, a few sweet chords, but no aria. A number of them—*Claribel, Lilian, Adeline, Isabel, Mariana, Madeline*—were sketches of women; not character portraits, like Browning's *Men and Women*, but impressions of temperament, of delicately, differentiated types of feminine beauty. In *Mariana*, expanded from a hint of the forsaken maid, in Shakspere's *Measure for Measure*, "Mariana at the moated grange," the poet showed an art then peculiar, but since grown familiar, of heightening the central feeling by landscape accessories. The level waste, the stagnant sluices, the neglected garden, the wind in the single poplar, re-enforce, by their monotonous sympathy, the loneliness, the hopeless waiting and weariness of life in the one human figure of the poem. In *Mariana*, the *Ode to Memory*, and the *Dying Swan*, it was the fens of Cambridge and of his native Lincolnshire that furnished Tennyson's scenery.

> "Stretched wide and wild, the waste enormous marsh,
> Where from the frequent bridge,
> Like emblems of infinity,
> The trenched waters run from sky to sky."

A second collection, published in 1833, exhibited a greater scope and variety, but was still in his earlier manner. The studies of feminine types were continued in *Margaret, Fatima, Eleanore, Mariana in the South*, and *A Dream of Fair Women*, suggested by Chaucer's *Legend of Good {290} Women*. In the *Lady of Shalott*, the poet first touched the Arthurian legends. The subject is the same as that of *Elaine*, in the *Idylls of the King*, but the treatment is shadowy, and even allegorical. In *Oenone* and the *Lotus Eaters*, he handled Homeric subjects, but in a romantic fashion, which contrasts markedly with the style of his later pieces, *Ulysses* and *Tithonus*. These last have the true classic severity, and are among the noblest specimens of weighty and sonorous blank verse in modern poetry. In general, Tennyson's art is unclassical. It is rich, ornate, composite, not statuesque, so much as picturesque. He is a great painter, and the critics complain that in passages calling for movement and action—a battle, a tournament, or the like—his figures stand still as in a tableau; and they contrast such passages unfavorably with scenes of the same kind in Scott, and with Browning's spirited ballad, *How we brought the Good News from Ghent to Aix*. In the *Palace of Art*, these elaborate pictorial effects were combined with allegory; in the *Lotus Eaters*, with that expressive treatment of landscape, noted in *Mariana*; the lotus land, "in which it seemed always afternoon," reflecting and promoting the enchanted indolence of the heroes. Two of the pieces in this 1833 volume, the *May Queen* and the *Miller's Daughter*, were Tennyson's first poems of the affections, and as ballads of simple, rustic life, they anticipated his more perfect idyls in blank verse, such as *Dora*, the *Brook, Edwin Morris*, and {291} the *Gardener's Daughter*. The songs in the *Miller's Daughter* had a more spontaneous, lyrical movement than any thing that he had yet published, and foretokened the lovely songs which interlude the divisions of the *Princess*, the famous *Bugle Song*, the no-less famous *Cradle Song*, and the rest. In 1833 Tennyson's friend, Arthur Hallam, died, and the effect of this great sorrow upon the poet was to deepen and strengthen the character of his genius. It turned his mind in upon itself, and set it brooding over questions which his poetry had so far left untouched; the meaning of life and death, the uses of adversity, the future of the race, the immortality of the soul, and the dealings of God with mankind.

"Thou madest Death; and, lo, thy foot
Is on the skull which thou hast made."

His elegy on Hallam, *In Memoriam*, was not published till 1850. He kept it by him all those years, adding section after section, gathering up into it whatever reflections crystallized about its central theme. It is his most intellectual and most individual work, a great song of sorrow and consolation. In 1842 he published a third collection of poems, among which were *Locksley Hall*, displaying a new strength of passion; *Ulysses*, suggested by a passage in Dante: pieces of a speculative cast, like the *Two Voices* and the *Vision of Sin*; the song *Break, Break, Break*, which preluded *In Memoriam*; and, lastly, some additional {292} gropings toward the subject of the Arthurian romance, such as *Sir Galahad, Sir Launcelot and Queen Guinevere* and *Morte d'Arthur*. The last was in blank verse, and, as afterward incorporated in the *Passing of Arthur*, forms one of the best passages in the *Idylls of the King*. The *Princess, a Medley,* published in 1849, represents the eclectic character of Tennyson's art; a medieval tale with an admixture of modern sentiment, and with the very modern problem of woman's sphere for its theme. The first four *Idylls of the King,* 1859, with those since added, constitute, when taken together, an epic poem on the old story of King Arthur. Tennyson went to Malory's *Morte d'Arthur* for his material, but the outline of the first idyl, *Enid,* was taken from Lady Charlotte Guest's translation of the Welsh *Mabinogion.* In the idyl of *Guinevere* Tennyson's genius reached its high-water mark. The interview between Arthur and his fallen queen is marked by a moral sublimity and a tragic intensity which move the soul as nobly as any scene in modern literature. Here, at least, the art is pure and not "decorated;" the effect is produced by the simplest means, and all is just, natural, and grand. *Maud*—a love novel in verse—published in 1855, and considerably enlarged in 1856, had great sweetness and beauty, particularly in its lyrical portions, but it was uneven in execution, imperfect in design, and marred by lapses into mawkishness and excesses in language. Since 1860 Tennyson has added little of permanent {293} value to his work. His dramatic experiments, like *Queen Mary,* are not, on the whole, successful, though it would be unjust to deny dramatic power to the poet who has written, upon one hand, *Guinevere* and the *Passing of Arthur,* and upon the other the homely, dialectic monologue of the *Northern Farmer.*

When we tire of Tennyson's smooth perfection, of an art that is over exquisite, and a beauty that is well-nigh too beautiful, and crave a rougher touch, and a meaning that will not yield itself too readily, we turn to the thorny pages of his great contemporary, Robert Browning (1812-———). Dr. Holmes says that Tennyson is white meat and Browning is dark meat. A masculine taste, it is inferred, is shown in a preference for the gamier flavor. Browning makes us think; his poems are puzzles, and furnish business for "Browning Societies." There are no Tennyson societies, because Tennyson is his own interpreter. Intellect in a poet may display itself quite as properly in the construction of his poem as in its content; we value a building for its architecture, and not entirely for the amount of timber in it. Browning's thought never wears so thin as Tennyson's sometimes does in his latest verse, where the trick of his style goes on of itself with nothing behind it. Tennyson, at his worst, is weak. Browning, when not at his best, is hoarse. Hoarseness, in itself, is no sign of strength. In Browning, however, the failure is in art, not in thought.

He chooses his subjects from abnormal character types, such as are presented, for example, in *Caliban upon Setebos*, the *Grammarian's Funeral, My Last Duchess*, and *Mr. Sludge, the Medium*. These are all psychological studies, in which the poet gets into the inner consciousness of a monster, a pedant, a criminal, and a quack, and gives their point of view. They are dramatic soliloquies; but the poet's self-identification with each of his creations, in turn, remains incomplete. His curious, analytic observation, his way of looking at the soul from outside, gives a doubleness to the monologues in his *Dramatic Lyrics*, 1845, *Men and Women*, 1855, *Dramatis Personae*, 1864, and other collections of the kind. The words are the words of Caliban or Mr. Sludge; but the voice is the voice of Robert Browning. His first complete poem, *Paracelsus*, 1835, aimed to give the true inwardness of the career of the famous 16th century doctor, whose name became a synonym with charlatan. His second, *Sordello*, 1840, traced the struggles of an Italian poet who lived before Dante, and could not reconcile his life with his art. *Paracelsus* was hard, but *Sordello* was incomprehensible. Mr. Browning has denied that he is ever perversely crabbed or obscure. Every great artist must be allowed to say things in his own way, and obscurity has its artistic uses, as the Gothic builders knew. But there are two kinds of obscurity in literature. One is inseparable from the subtlety and difficulty of the thought or the compression {295} and pregnant indirectness of the phrase. Instances of this occur in the clear deeps of Dante, Shakspere, and Goethe. The other comes from a vice of style, a willfully enigmatic and unnatural way of expressing thought. Both kinds of obscurity exist in Browning. He is a deep and subtle thinker; but he is also a very eccentric writer, abrupt, harsh, disjointed. It has been well said that the reader of Browning learns a new dialect. But one need not grudge the labor that is rewarded with an intellectual pleasure so peculiar and so stimulating. The odd, grotesque impression made by his poetry arises, in part, from his desire to use the artistic values of ugliness, as well as of obscurity; to avoid the shallow prettiness that comes from blinking the disagreeable truth: not to leave the saltness out of the sea. Whenever he emerges into clearness, as he does in hundreds of places, he is a poet of great qualities. There are a fire and a swing in his *Cavalier Tunes*, and in pieces like the *Glove and the Lost Leader*; and humor in such ballads as the *Pied Piper of Hamelin* and the *Soliloquy of the Spanish Cloister*, which appeal to the most conservative reader. He seldom deals directly in the pathetic, but now and then, as in *Evelyn Hope*, the *Last Ride Together*, or the *Incident of the French Camp*, a tenderness comes over the strong verse

"as sheathes
A film the mother eagle's eye,

When her bruised eaglet breathes."

{296} Perhaps the most astonishing example of Browning's mental vigor is the huge composition, entitled *The Ring and the Book*, 1868, a narrative poem in twenty-one thousand lines, in which the same story is repeated eleven times in eleven different ways. It is the story of a criminal trial which occurred at Rome about 1700, the trial of one Count Guido for the murder of his young wife. First the poet tells the tale himself; then he tells what one-half of the world says and what the other; then he gives the deposition of the dying girl, the testimony of witnesses, the speech made by the count in his own defense, the arguments of counsel, etc., and, finally, the judgment of the pope. So wonderful are Browning's resources in casuistry, and so cunningly does he ravel the intricate motives at play in this tragedy and lay bare the secrets of the heart, that the interest increases at each repetition of the tale. He studied the Middle Age carefully, not for its picturesque externals, its feudalisms, chivalries, and the like; but because he found it a rich quarry of spiritual monstrosities, strange outcroppings of fanaticism, superstition, and moral and mental distortion of all shapes. It furnished him especially with a great variety of ecclesiastical types, such as are painted in *Fra Lippo Lippi, Bishop Blougram's Apology*, and *The Bishop Orders his Tomb in St.Praxed's Church.*

Browning's dramatic instinct has always attracted him to the stage. His tragedy, *Stratford* (1837), {297} was written for Macready, and put on at Covent Garden Theater, but without pronounced success. He has written many fine dramatic poems, like *Pippa Passes, Colombo's Birthday*, and *In a Balcony*; and at least two good acting plays, *Luria* and *A Blot in the Scutcheon*. The last named has recently been given to the American public, with Lawrence Barrett's careful and intelligent presentation of the leading rôle. The motive of the tragedy is somewhat strained and fantastic, but it is, notwithstanding, very effective on the stage. It gives one an unwonted thrill to listen to a play, by a living English writer, which is really literature. One gets a faint idea of what it must have been to assist at the first night of *Hamlet*.

1. Dickens. Pickwick Papers, Nicholas Nickleby, David Copperfield, Bleak House, Tale of Two Cities.

2. Thackeray. Vanity Fair, Pendennis, Henry Esmond, The Newcomes, The Four Georges.

3. George Eliot. Scenes of Clerical Life, Mill on the Floss, Silas Marner, Romola, Adam Bede, Middlemarch.

4. Macaulay. Essays, Lays of Ancient Rome.

5. Carlyle. Sartor Resartus, French Revolution, Essays on History, Signs of the Times, Characteristics, Burns, Scott, Voltaire, and Goethe.

6. The Works of Alfred Tennyson (6 vols.). London: Strahan & Co., 1872. {298}

7. Selections from the Poetical Works of Robert Browning. (2 vols.) London: Smith, Elder, & Co., 1880.

8. E. C. Stedman's Victorian Poets.

9. Henry Morley's English Literature in the Reign of Victoria. (Tauchnitz Series.) {299}

CHAPTER IX.

THEOLOGICAL AND RELIGIOUS LITERATURE IN GREAT BRITAIN.

BY JOHN FLETCHER HURST.

Miracle plays, rude dramatic representations of the chief events in Scripture history, were used for popular instruction before the invention of printing. In England they began as early as the twelfth century. Moral plays, or moralities, were of the same origin, though dating from the fifteenth century. These were somewhat more refined than the miracle plays, and usually set forth the excellence of the virtues, such as truth, mercy, and the like. Both miracle and moral plays were under the conduct of the clergy.

John Bale (1495-1563) was Bishop of Ossory, and wrote much for popular reform. He was the author of nineteen miracle plays. Lord Edward Herbert, of Cherbury (1581-1648), wrote a deistical work, *De Religione Gentilium*, the first of that school of writers which later appeared in Bolingbroke. John Spotiswood (1565-1639), Archbishop of St. Andrews and afterward Chancellor of Scotland, wrote a voluminous *History of the Church of Scotland*. George Sandys (1577-1643), {300} distinguished also as one of the earliest literary characters in America, wrote metrical versions of several of the poetical books of the Bible, and also a tragedy called *Christ's Passion*.

John Knox (1505-1572), the great Scotch reformer and polemic, while more prominent as the preacher and spokesman of the Scotch Reformation, wrote *First Blast of the Trumpet against the Monstrous Regimen of Women* (1558), and the *Historie of the Reformation of Religion within the Realme of Scotland*, published after his death. John Jewel (1522-1571) wrote in Latin his *Apologia Ecclesiae Anglicanae*. William Whittingham (1524-1589), who succeeded Knox as pastor of the English Church at Geneva, aided in making the Genevan Version of the Bible and also co-operated in the Sternhold and

Hopkins translation of the Psalms.

John Fox (1517-1587) was the author of the *Book of Martyrs*, whose full title was *Acts and Monuments of these Latter and Perilous Days, Touching Matters of the Church*. An abridgment of the work has had a very wide circulation. John Aylmer (1521-1594) replied to Knox's *First Blast of the Trumpet* in a work called *An Harbor for Faithful and True Subjects*. Nicholas Sanders (1527-1580), a Roman Catholic professor of Oxford, wrote *The Rock of the Church*, a defense of the primacy of Peter and the Bishops of Rome. Robert Parsons (1546-1610), a Jesuit, wrote several works in advocacy of Roman Catholicism and some political tracts.

{301}

John Rainolds (1549-1607), a learned Hebraist of Oxford, wrote many ecclesiastical works in Latin and English. He was a chief promoter of King James's Version of the Bible. Miles Smith, (died 1624), Thomas Bilson (1536-1616), John Boys (1560-1643), and George Abbot (1562-1633), Archbishop of Canterbury, were all co-workers on the King James translation of the Scriptures.

Next in importance to the English Bible in its effect upon literature stands the English Prayer Book, which is the rich mosaic of many minds. It came through *The Prymer* of the fourteenth century, and contained the more fundamental and familiar portions of the *Book of Common Prayer*, such as the Ten Commandments, the Lord's Prayer, the Litany, and the Apostles' Creed. This compilation differed in form and somewhat in content in the different dioceses in England, and was partly in Latin and partly in English. In 1542 an attempt was made to produce a common form for all England and to have it entirely in English. The Committee of Convocation, who had the work in charge, were prevented from making it complete through the refusal of Henry VIII to continue the approval which he had given to the appointment of the committee. However, under Edward VI a commission, headed by Archbishop Cranmer, carried their work through, and it was accepted and its use made compulsory by Parliament. It was published in 1549 as the *First Prayer Book of Edward VI*. Three years later the *Second Prayer {302} Book of Edward VI* was issued, it being a revision of the First, also under the shaping hand of Cranmer. The *Prayer Book* received its final revision and substantially its present form in the reign of Elizabeth, in 1559, although in 1662 there was added to the Morning and Evening Prayer a Collection of Prayers and Thanksgivings upon Several Occasions. Gathering thus through three centuries the choice treasures of confession and devotion of the strong and reverent English nation, it has been a large element in the literary training, not only of communicants in the Anglican, the Episcopal, and the Methodist

Churches, but, in a measure, also of those who have received their religious instruction and have worshiped in other branches of the Protestant Church.

The work of the Assembly of Divines at Westminster (1643-1649), particularly the *Confession of Faith*, and the *Shorter Catechism*, became, as specimens of strong and pure English, potent factors in the intellectual and literary discipline of the Presbyterians in all parts of the world.

The modern psalms and hymns, or the simplified and popularized forms of the earlier and mediaeval worship, have had vastly to do with the daily thought and education of the people into whose life they have brought not only increase of lofty devotion but also a positive and stimulative culture.

Foremost of these collections was that made by Thomas Sternhold, John Hopkins, and others, and {303} known as the *Psalter of Sternhold and Hopkins*, published in 1562. Francis Rouse made a version in 1645, which, after revision, was adopted in 1649, and largely used by the Scotch Church. A new version was that by Nahum Tate and Nicholas Brady, which appeared in 1696, and has since been called the *Psalter of Tate and Brady*. The first English hymn book adapted for public worship was that of Isaac Watts, appearing about 1709, although several minor collections and individual productions had preceded Watts, among which should be mentioned those of Joseph Stennett, John Mason, and the fine hymns of Bishop Ken and Joseph Addison.

A little later the prolific and spiritual Charles Wesley, aided by the somewhat stricter taste of his more celebrated brother, John, began (1739) his wonderful series of published hymns, which, together with those of Watts, have since formed the larger portion of the Protestant hymnody of the world. Others of the eighteenth century who have made contributions to the sacred lyrics of the Church are John Byrom (1691-1763), Philip Doddridge (1702-1751), Joseph Hart (1712-1768), Anne Steele (1716-1778), Benjamin Beddome (1717-1795), John Cennick (1717-1755), Thomas Olivers (1725-1799), Joseph Grigg (1728-1768), Augustus M. Toplady (1740-1778), and Edward Perronet (died 1792).

Approaching our own time, the ranks of our hymn writers include James Montgomery {304} (1771-1854), whose *Christian Psalmist* was published in 1825, Thomas Kelly, of Dublin (1769-1855); Harriet Auber (1773-1832), Reginald Heber (1783-1826), Sir Robert Grant (1785-1838), Josiah Conder (1789-1855), Charlotte Elliott (1789-1871), Sir John Bowring (1792-1872), Henry Francis Lyte (1793-1847), John Keble (1792-1866), whose *Christian Year* came out in 1827; John H. Newman (1801-1890), Sarah Flower Adams (1805-1849), and Horatius Bonar (1808-1869).

Richard Mant (1776-1848), Henry Alford (1810-1871), F. W. Faber (1815-1863), John Mason Neale (1818-1866), Miss Catherine Winkworth (born 1829), and some others, have given many beautiful and stirring translations from the Latin and German hymns of the ancient and mediaeval periods.

Theological writers of the middle of the seventeenth century are numerous. Chief of those belonging to the Anglican Church may be named Joseph Hall, Bishop of Norwich (1574-1656), whose *Episcopacy by Divine Right* was replied to in *Smectymnus*, the joint production of five dissenting divines: Stephen Marshal, Edward Calamy, Thomas Young, Matthew Newcomer, and William Spurston; James Ussher (1580-1656), a man of vast literary learning and most known by his *Sacred Chronology*, published after his death; Thomas Fuller and Jeremy Taylor, mentioned in a previous chapter; John Cosin (1594-1672), who wrote chiefly devotional treatises; William Chillingworth {305} (1602-1664), whose *Religion of Protestants* has had a wide circulation; John Pearson (1612-1686), whose *Exposition of the Creed* became a standard; Ralph Cudworth (1617-1688), whose *Intellectual System of the Universe* dealt a stunning blow to the atheism of his day, and Isaac Barrow (1630-1677), the learned vice-chancellor of Cambridge, wit, mathematician, and theologian all in one, who left a rich legacy in his *Sermons*.

Of the Non-conforming authors deserving notice Richard Baxter (1615-1691) is the most voluminous, if not also the most luminous. Controversy engaged his pen almost constantly, but his most permanent works were his *Call to the Unconverted* and *The Saints' Everlasting Rest*. John Owen (1616-1683) was a leading Puritan writer, and under Cromwell was vice-chancellor of Oxford University. His *Commentary on the Epistle to the Hebrews* and his book on *The Holy Spirit* are still in use and highly prized. His pen was strong rather than elegant. John Bunyan's immortal allegory throws a halo on universal literature. John Howe (1630-1705), the chief author among the Puritans, wrote many strong works, among which of special note are *The Living Temple* and *The Office and Work of the Holy Spirit*. He was Cromwell's chaplain.

The spiritual writings of Samuel Rutherford (1600-1661), the Scotch divine; the *Annotations on the Psalms* by Henry Ainsworth (died 1662), an Independent, who was an exile in Holland for {306} conscience' sake; the expository writings of Thomas Manton (1620-1677); the *Synopsis* of Matthew Poole (1624-1679), later abridged into his celebrated *Annotations upon the Bible*; the sermons of Stephen Charnock (1628-1680), particularly the one on "The Divine Attributes;" and *An Alarm to Unconverted Sinners*, by Joseph Alleine (1633-1688), which has had an immense circulation, form a galaxy in the theological firmament of the time of Milton.

A later group of theological writers in the latter part of the seventeenth century contains the commanding figures of Symon Patrick (1626-1707), bishop and author of a *Commentary on the Old Testament*; John Flavel (1627-1691) and his works on practical piety; John Tillotson (1630-1694), the Anglican archbishop, whose eloquent sermons are still held in high repute; Robert South (1633-1716), the great pulpit orator, whose discourses are an ornament to the English tongue; Edward Stillingfleet (1635-1699), from whose prolific pen came several valuable treatises, one of which was *The Antiquities of the British Churches*; and William Beveridge (1637-1708), whose *Private Thoughts upon Religion* is still in much esteem. To these we may add Thomas Ken (1637-1710), the good bishop now best known as the author of *Praise God, from Whom all Blessings Flow*; Benjamin Keach (1640-1704), a Baptist preacher of much note and author of *Gospel Mysteries Opened*, which, like his other writings, is marred by an {307} excessive use of figures; Gilbert Burnet (1643-1709), the writer and bishop, who mingled freely in the political affairs of the day and wrote much on a variety of subjects, one being a *History of the Reformation of the Church of England*; William Wall (1646-1728), the prominent defender of infant baptism; Humphrey Prideaux (1648-1724), who wrote the *Connection of the Old and New Testaments*; and Matthew Henry (1662-1714), still valued for his quaint and suggestive *Commentary on the Scriptures*.

Here, too, belong George Fox (1624-1690) and Robert Barclay (1648-1690), the heroic founder and the learned champion of the Society of Friends, the former's *Journal* and the latter's *Apology for the True Christian Divinity* being worthy of special note. William Penn (1644-1718), more eminent as the chief colonizer of Pennsylvania, also wrote many powerful works in advocacy of Quaker teachings; and William Sewel's (1650-1726) *History of the Quakers* is a notable contribution to the literature of that much-misunderstood and persecuted people.

Among those who graced the first half of the eighteenth century we find the Irish man of letters, Charles Leslie (1650-1722), who gave among others a celebrated treatise on *A Short and Easy Method with the Deists*; Francis Atterbury (1662-1732), Bishop of Rochester, whose *Sermons* still survive; William Wollaston (1659-1724), known as the author of *The Religion of Nature*, a plea for truth; Samuel Clarke (1675-1729), the {308} philosophical writer of *The Demonstration of the Being and Attributes of God*; Matthew Tindal (1657-1733), the leading deist of his day, whose chief work was *Christianity as Old as Creation*; Robert Wodrow (1679-1734), a Scotch preacher who wrote a *History of the Sufferings of the Church of Scotland*; and Thomas Wilson (1663-1755), Bishop of Sodor and Man for fifty-seven years and the author of many useful works on the Scriptures and Christianity. Bishop Joseph Butler (1692-1752) appeared as the champion of Christianity and successfully answered the deistical tendency of Tindal and others by his *Analogy of Religion, Natural and Revealed, to the Constitution and Course of Nature*, which, though obscure in style, is still in high repute for its massive thought and mighty logic.

Thomas Stackhouse (1680-1752) and his *History of the Bible*; John Bampton (1689-1751), whose estate still speaks at Oxford in defense of Christianity in the annual lectures on Divinity; Daniel Waterland (1683-1740), in his defense of the divinity of Christ; and Joseph Bingham (1668-1723), in his learned treatise on *The Antiquities of the Christian Church*, are also in the front rank of this period. Daniel Neal (1678-1743), in his *History of the Puritans*; John Leland (1691-1766), the Dublin preacher, in his *View of the Deistical Writers*; and Philip Doddridge (1702-1751), in his *Family Expositor* and his briefer and more famous *Rise and Progress of Religion in the Soul*, furnished valuable contributions to theological literature.

{309}

The latter half of the eighteenth century was prolific of letters. Noteworthy among those who wrote on religious themes are the following: Nathaniel Lardner (1684-1768), who wrote *The Credibility of the Gospel History*; William Law (1687-1761), whose *Serious Call to a Holy Life* and *Christian Perfection* are still powerful works; Richard Challoner (1691-1781), a Roman Catholic author of many practical and devotional works and of a *Version of the Bible*, much prized in his own Church; Alban Butler (1700-1773), who compiled *The Lives of the Saints*; William Warburton (1698-1779), in his *Divine Legation of Moses*; Alexander Cruden (1701-1770), the Scotch author of the famous *Concordance to the Holy Scriptures*; and Lord George Lyttleton (1708-1773), the author of *Observations on the Conversion and Apostleship of St. Paul*.

In the same category belong: Robert Lowth (1710-1787), whose book on *Hebrew Poetry* is still consulted; James Hervey (1713-1758), whose *Meditations* became very popular; Hugh Blair (1718-1800), the Scotchman whose *Sermons* for many years rivaled his *Lectures on Rhetoric* in popularity; Joseph Priestley (1733-1804), illustrious in the annals of chemical discovery, who wrote *Institutes of Natural and Revealed Religion*, and is one of the most distinguished Socinian writers; and William Paley (1743-1805), whose *Natural Theology* and *Horae Paulinae* are still standard works.

During this period also came the great impulse {310} to the literature of the common people through the tireless pen of John Wesley (1703-1791), whose *Sermons and Notes on the New Testament* have had a powerful influence wherever the Wesleyan revival has spread. James McKnight (1721-1800), the scholarly commentator and harmonist; John Fletcher (1729-1785), the sweet-souled defender of Methodism and author of *Checks to Antinomianism*; Bishop Richard Watson (1737-1816), the learned apologist; Augustus M. Toplady (1740-1778); the hymnist and polemic; Joseph Milner (1744-1797), the Church historian; Thomas Coke (1747-1814), in his *Commentary on the Old and New Testaments*; and Andrew Fuller (1754-1815) were authors of marked force and ability.

Belonging to the first quarter of the nineteenth century the leading theological productions are *The Immateriality and Immortality of the Soul*, by Samuel Drew (1765-1833); the *Translation of the Book of Job*, by John Mason Good (1764-1827); the popular *Commentaries on the Bible* by Thomas Scott (1747-1821), Adam Clarke (1762-1832), and Joseph Benson (1748-1821); the *Sermons* of Robert Hall (1764-1831), the great Baptist preacher; the *Introduction to the Literary History of the Bible*, by James Townley (died 1833); the missionary narratives of Henry Martyn (1781-1812), William Ward (1769-1822) and John Williams (1796-1839); and the pathetic story of *The Dairyman's Daughter*, by Legh Richmond (1772-1827). A little later in this century the first ranks {311} of theological scholarship include the Wordsworths—Christopher (1774-1846), the brother of the poet, and his two sons, Charles (1806-1892) and Christopher, Jr. (1809-1885).

Tracts for the Times, written by a group of men styling themselves Anglo-Catholics, whose leaders were Edward B. Pusey (1800-1882), John H. Newman (1801-1890), John Keble (1792-1866), Richard H. Froude and others, began in 1833, and for several years continued to be published, reaching ninety in number. Their main purpose was a discussion and defense of the character and work of the Established Church, but a large result was that several of the leading spirits, with about two hundred clergymen and the same number of prominent laymen, became Roman Catholics. This High-

Church series of writings was followed in 1860 by *Essays and Reviews*, a volume containing seven articles, whose authors were Frederick Temple (born 1821), Rowland Williams (1817-1870), Baden Powell (1796-1860), Henry B. Wilson (born 1804), C. W. Goodwin, Mark Pattison (1813-1884), and Benjamin Jowett (1817-1893). The purpose of these men was to liberalize the thought of the Church. They accomplished this result, and with it the overthrow of the faith of some.

Thomas Chalmers (1780-1847), the great Scotch preacher, left much fruit of his pen, the most celebrated being *Astronomical Discourses*. Other distinguished books are: *A Practical View of {312} Christianity*, by William Wilberforce (1759-1833); *Horae Homileticae*, by Charles Simeon (1759-1836); *The Lives of Knox and Melville*, by Thomas McCrie (1772-1835); *Horae Mosaicae*, by George Stanley Faber (1773-1854); *The Scripture Testimony to the Messiah*, by John Pye Smith (1774-1851); *Theological Institutes*, by the Wesleyan theologian, Richard Watson (1781-1833); the *Histories of the Jews* and *of Christianity*, by Henry Hart Milman (1791-1868); the *Cyclopaedia of Biblical Literature*, by John Kitto (1804-1854); *Mammon*, by John Harris (1804-1856); the *Theological Essays* of John Frederick Denison Maurice (1805-1872); *Missions the Chief End of the Christian Church*, by Alexander Duff (1806-1878); the *Sermons* of Frederick William Robertson (1816-1853); and *The Life and Epistles of Paul*, by William J. Conybeare (1815-1857) and John S. Howson (1816-1885).

The latter half of the present century has been marked by many strong and profound theological publications, of which we may name as worthy of particular notice: *The Introduction to the Study of the Holy Scriptures*, by Thomas Hartwell Horne (1780-1862); *Historic Doubts Relative to Napoleon Bonaparte*, by Richard Whately (1787-1863); *Apologia pro Vita Sua* of John H. Newman (1801-1890); *The Typology of Scripture*, by Patrick Fairbairn (1805-1892); *The Eclipse of Faith*, by Henry Rogers (1806-1877); the *Notes on the Parables and Miracles*, by Richard Chenevix Trench (1807-1886); {313} *The Temporal Mission of the Holy Ghost*, by Henry Edward Manning (1808-1892); the series of lectures on the Scriptures, by John Gumming (1810-1881); the *Greek New Testament*, edited by Henry Alford (1810-1871); and the same by Samuel Prideaux Tregelles (1813-1875); the historical works of Arthur Penrhyn Stanley (1815-1881); *Hypatia, or Old Foes with a New Face*, by Charles Kingsley (1819-1875); *Ecce Homo*, by John Robert Seeley (1834-1895); the *Sermons* of Charles Haddon Spurgeon (1834-1892); and *Natural Law in the Spiritual World*, the brilliant venture of the beloved and lamented Henry Drummond (1851-1897), whose *Greatest Thing in the World* bids fair to become a Christian classic.

{317}

PREFACE.

This little volume is intended as a companion to the *Outline Sketch of English Literature*, published last year for the Chautauqua Circle. In writing it I have followed the same plan, aiming to present the subject in a sort of continuous essay rather than in the form of a "primer" or elementary manual. I have not undertaken to describe or even to mention every American author or book of importance, but only those which seemed to me of most significance. Nevertheless I believe that the sketch contains enough detail to make it of some use as a guide-book to our literature. Though meant to be mainly a history of American *belles-lettres* it makes some mention of historical and political writings, {318} but hardly any of philosophical, scientific, and technical works.

A chronological rather than a topical order has been followed, although the fact that our best literature is of recent growth has made it impossible to adhere as closely to a chronological plan as in the English sketch. In the reading courses appended to the different chapters I have named a few of the most important authorities in American literary history, such as Duyckinck, Tyler, Stedman, and Richardson.

HENRY A. BEERS.

{319}

CONTENTS.

CHAPTER PAGE

I. THE COLONIAL PERIOD, 1607-1765 ... ... 321 II. THE REVOLUTIONARY PERIOD, 1765-1815 ... ... 365 III. THE ERA OF NATIONAL EXPANSION, 1815-1837 ... . 400 IV. THE CONCORD WRITERS, 1837-1861 ... ... 434 V. THE CAMBRIDGE SCHOLARS, 1837-1861 ... . 472 VI. LITERATURE IN THE CITIES, 1837-1861 ... ... 511 VII. LITERATURE SINCE 1861 ... ... 554 VIII. THEOLOGICAL AND RELIGIOUS LITERATURE IN AMERICA ... ... 594 INDEX 609

{321}

CHAPTER I.

THE COLONIAL PERIOD.

1607-1765.

The writings of our colonial era have a much greater importance as history than as literature. It would be unfair to judge of the intellectual vigor of the English colonists in America by the books that they wrote; those "stern men with empires in their brains" had more pressing work to do than the making of books. The first settlers, indeed, were brought face to face with strange and exciting conditions—the sea, the wilderness, the Indians, the flora and fauna of a new world—things which seem stimulating to the imagination, and incidents and experiences which might have lent themselves easily to poetry or romance. Of all these they wrote back to England reports which were faithful and sometimes vivid, but which, upon the whole, hardly rise into the region of literature. "New England," said Hawthorne, "was then in a {322} state incomparably more picturesque than at present." But to a contemporary that old New England of the seventeenth century doubtless seemed any thing but picturesque, filled with grim, hard, worky-day realities. The planters both of Virginia and Massachusetts were decimated by sickness and starvation, constantly threatened by Indian wars, and troubled by quarrels among themselves and fears of disturbance from England. The wrangles between the royal governors and the House of Burgesses in the Old Dominion, and the theological squabbles in New England, which fill our colonial records, are petty and wearisome to read of. At least, they would be so did we not bear in mind to what imperial destinies these conflicts were slowly educating the little communities which had hardly as yet secured a foothold on the edge of the raw continent.

Even a century and a half after the Jamestown and Plymouth settlements, when the American plantations had grown strong and flourishing, and commerce was building up large towns, and there were wealth and generous living and fine society, the "good old colony days when we lived under the king," had yielded little in the way of literature that is of any permanent interest. There would seem to be something in the relation of a colony to the mother country which dooms the thought and art of the former to a hopeless provincialism. Canada and Australia are great provinces, wealthier and more populous than the {323} thirteen colonies at the time of their separation from England. They have cities whose inhabitants number hundreds of thousands, well equipped universities, libraries, cathedrals, costly public buildings, all the outward appliances of an advanced civilization; and yet what have Canada and Australia contributed to British literature?

American literature had no infancy. That engaging *naïveté* and that heroic rudeness which give a charm to the early popular tales and songs of Europe find, of course, no counterpart on our soil. Instead of emerging from the twilight of the past, the first American writings were produced under the garish noon of a modern and learned age. Decrepitude rather than youthfulness is the mark of a colonial literature. The poets, in particular, instead of finding a challenge to their imagination in the new life about them, are apt to go on imitating the cast off literary fashions of the mother country. America was settled by Englishmen who were contemporary with the greatest names in English literature. Jamestown was planted in 1607, nine years before Shakspeare's death, and the hero of that enterprize, Captain John Smith, may not improbably have been a personal acquaintance of the great dramatist. "They have acted my fatal tragedies on the stage," wrote Smith. Many circumstances in *The Tempest* were doubtless suggested by the wreck of the *Sea Venture* on "the still vext Bermoothes," as described by William Strachey in his *True Repertory of the Wrack and {324} Redemption of Sir Thomas Gates*, written at Jamestown, and published at London in 1510. Shakspere's contemporary, Michael Drayton, the poet of the *Polyolbion*, addressed a spirited valedictory ode to the three shiploads of "brave, heroic minds" who sailed from London in 1606 to colonize Virginia; an ode which ended with the prophecy of a future American literature:

"And as there plenty grows
Of laurel every-where,—
Apollo's sacred tree—
You it may see
A poet's brows
To crown, that may sing there."

Another English poet, Samuel Daniel, the author of the *Civil Wars*, had also prophesied in a similar strain:

"And who in time knows whither we may vent
The treasure of our tongue, to what strange shores~.~.~.
What worlds in the yet unformed Occident
May come refined with accents that are ours."

It needed but a slight movement in the balances of fate, and Walter Raleigh might have been reckoned among the poets of America. He was one of the original promoters of the Virginia colony, and he made voyages in person to Newfoundland and Guiana. And more unlikely things have happened than that when John Milton left Cambridge in 1632, he should have been tempted to follow Winthrop and the colonists of Massachusetts Bay, {325} who had sailed two years before. Sir Henry Vane, the younger, who was afterward Milton's friend—

"Vane, young in years, but in sage counsel old"—

came over in 1635, and was for a short time Governor of Massachusetts. These are idle speculations, and yet, when we reflect that Oliver Cromwell was on the point of embarking for America when he was prevented by the king's officers, we may, for the nonce, "let our frail thoughts dally with false surmise," and fancy by how narrow a chance *Paradise Lost* missed being written in Boston. But, as a rule, the members of the literary guild are not quick to emigrate. They like the feeling of an old and rich civilization about them, a state of society which America has only begun to reach during the present century.

Virginia and New England, says Lowell, were the "two great distributing centers of the English race." The men who colonized the country between the Capes of Virginia were not drawn, to any large extent, from the literary or bookish classes in the Old Country. Many of the first settlers were gentlemen —too many, Captain Smith thought, for the good of the plantation. Some among these were men of worth and spirit, "of good means and great parentage." Such was, for example, George Percy, a younger brother of the Earl of Northumberland, who was one of the original adventurers, and the author of *A Discourse of the Plantation of the Southern Colony of Virginia*, {326} which contains a graphic narrative of the fever and famine summer of 1607 at Jamestown. But many of these gentlemen were idlers, "unruly gallants, packed thither by their friends to escape ill destinies;" dissipated younger sons, soldiers of fortune, who came over after the gold which was supposed to abound in the new country, and who spent their time in playing bowls and drinking at the tavern as soon as there was any tavern. With these was a sprinkling of mechanics and farmers, indented servants, and the off-scourings of the London streets, fruit of press gangs and jail deliveries, sent over to "work in the plantations."

Nor were the conditions of life afterward in Virginia very favorable to literary growth. The planters lived isolated on great estates, which had water fronts on the rivers that flow into the Chesapeake. There the tobacco, the chief staple of the country, was loaded directly upon the trading vessels that tied up to the long, narrow wharves of the plantations. Surrounded by his slaves, and visited occasionally by a distant neighbor, the Virginia country gentleman lived a free and careless life. He was fond of fox-hunting, horse-racing, and cock-fighting. There were no large towns, and the planters met each other mainly on occasion of a county court or the assembling of the Burgesses. The court-house was the nucleus of social and political life in Virginia as the town-meeting was in New England. In such a state of society schools were necessarily few, and popular education did {327} not exist. Sir William Berkeley, who was the royal governor of the colony from 1641 to 1677, said, in 1670, "I thank God there are no free schools nor printing, and I hope we shall not have these hundred years." In the matter of printing, this pious wish was well-nigh realized. The first press set up in the colony, about 1681, was soon suppressed, and found no successor until the year 1729. From that date until some ten years before the Revolution one printing-press answered the needs of Virginia, and this was under official control. The earliest newspaper in the colony was the *Virginia Gazette*, established in 1736.

In the absence of schools the higher education naturally languished. Some of the planters were taught at home by tutors, and others went to England and entered the universities. But these were few in number, and there was no college in the colony until more than half a century after the foundation of Harvard in the younger province of Massachusetts. The college of William and Mary was established at Williamsburg chiefly by the exertions of the Rev. James Blair, a Scotch divine, who was sent by the Bishop of London as "commissary" to the Church in Virginia. The college received its charter in 1693, and held its first commencement in 1700. It is perhaps significant of the difference between the Puritans of New England and the so-called "Cavaliers" of Virginia, that while the former founded and supported Harvard College in 1636, and Yale in 1701, of {328} their own motion, and at their own expense, William and Mary received its endowment from the crown, being provided for in part by a deed of lands and in part by a tax of a penny a pound on all tobacco exported from the colony. In return for this royal grant the college was to present yearly to the king two copies of Latin verse. It is reported of the young Virginian gentlemen who resorted to the new college that they brought their plantation manners with them, and were accustomed to "keep race-horses at the college, and bet at the billiard or other gaming tables." William and Mary College did a good work for the colony, and educated some of the great Virginians of the Revolutionary era, but it has never been a large or flourishing institution, and has held no such relation to the intellectual development of its section as Harvard and Yale have held in the colonies of Massachusetts and Connecticut. Even after the foundation of the University of Virginia, in which Jefferson took a conspicuous part, southern youths were commonly sent to the North for their education, and at the time of the outbreak of the civil war there was a large contingent of southern students in several northern colleges, notably in Princeton and Yale.

Naturally, the first books written in America were descriptions of the country and narratives of the vicissitudes of the infant settlements, which were sent home to be printed for the information of the English public and the encouragement of {329} further immigration. Among books of this kind produced in Virginia the earliest and most noteworthy were the writings of that famous soldier of fortune, Captain John Smith. The first of these was his *True Relation*, namely, "of such occurrences and accidents of note as hath happened in Virginia since the first planting of that colony," printed at London in 1608. Among Smith's other books, the most important is perhaps his *General History of Virginia* (London, 1624), a compilation of various narratives by different hands, but passing under his name. Smith was a man of a restless and daring spirit, full of resource, impatient of contradiction, and of a somewhat vainglorious nature, with an appetite for the marvelous and a disposition to draw the long bow. He had seen service in many parts of the world, and his wonderful adventures lost nothing in the telling. It was alleged against him that the evidence of his prowess rested almost entirely on his own testimony. His truthfulness in essentials has not, perhaps, been successfully impugned, but his narratives have suffered by the embellishments with which he has colored them, and, in particular, the charming story of Pocohontas saving his life at the risk of her own—the one romance of early Virginian history—has passed into the realm of legend.

Captain Smith's writings have small literary value apart from the interest of the events which they describe, and the diverting but forcible {330} personality which they unconsciously display. They are the rough-hewn records of a busy man of action, whose sword was mightier than his pen. As Smith returned to England after two years in Virginia, and did not permanently cast in his lot with the settlement of which he had been for a time the leading spirit, he can hardly be claimed as an American author. No more can Mr. George Sandys, who came to Virginia in the train of Governor Wyat, in 1621, and completed his excellent metrical translation of Ovid on the banks of the James, in the midst of the Indian massacre of 1622, "limned" as he writes "by that imperfect light which was snatched from the hours of night and repose, having wars and tumults to bring it to light instead of the muses." Sandys went back to England for good, probably as early as 1625, and can, therefore, no more be reckoned as the first American poet, on the strength of his paraphrase of the *Metamorphoses*, than he can be reckoned the earliest Yankee inventor, because he "introduced the first water-mill into America."

The literature of colonial Virginia, and of the southern colonies which took their point of departure from Virginia, is almost wholly of this historical and descriptive kind. A great part of it is concerned with the internal affairs of the province, such as "Bacon's Rebellion," in 1676, one of the most striking episodes in our ante-revolutionary annals, and of which there exist a number of narratives, some of them anonymous, and only rescued {331} from a manuscript condition a hundred years after the event. Another part is concerned with the explorations of new territory. Such were the "Westover Manuscripts," left by Colonel William Byrd, who was appointed in 1729 one of the commissioners to fix the boundary between Virginia and North Carolina, and gave an account of the survey in his *History of the Dividing Line*, which was only printed in 1841. Colonel Byrd is one of the most brilliant figures of colonial Virginia, and a type of the Old Virginia gentleman. He had been sent to England for his education, where he was admitted to the bar of the Middle Temple, elected a Fellow of the Royal Society, and formed an intimate friendship with Charles Boyle, the Earl of Orrery. He held many offices in the government of the colony, and founded the cities of Richmond and Petersburg. His estates were large, and at Westover—where he had one of the finest private libraries in America—he exercised a baronial hospitality, blending the usual profusion of plantation life with the elegance of a traveled scholar and "picked man of countries." Colonel Byrd was rather an amateur in literature. His *History of the Dividing Line* is written with a jocularity which rises occasionally into real humor, and which gives to the painful journey through the wilderness the air of a holiday expedition. Similar in tone were his diaries of *A Progress to the Mines* and *A Journey to the Land of Eden* in North Carolina.

{332} The first formal historian of Virginia was Robert Beverley, "a native and inhabitant of the place," whose History of Virginia was printed at London in 1705. Beverley was a rich planter and large slave owner, who, being in London in 1703, was shown by his bookseller the manuscript of a forthcoming work, Oldmixon's *British Empire in America*. Beverley was set upon writing his history by the inaccuracies in this, and likewise because the province "has been so misrepresented to the common people of England as to make them believe that the servants in Virginia are made to draw in cart and plow, and that the country turns all people black," an impression which lingers still in parts of Europe. The most original portions of the book are those in which the author puts down his personal observations of the plants and animals of the New World, and particularly the account of the Indians, to which his third book is devoted, and which is accompanied by valuable plates. Beverley's knowledge of these matters was evidently at first hand, and his descriptions here are very fresh and interesting. The more strictly historical part of his work is not free from prejudice and inaccuracy. A more critical, detailed, and impartial, but much less readable, work was William Stith's *History of the First Discovery and Settlement of Virginia*, 1747, which brought the subject down only to the year 1624. Stith was a clergyman, and at one time a professor in William and Mary College.

The Virginians were stanch royalists and churchmen. The Church of England was established by law, and non-conformity was persecuted in various ways. Three missionaries were sent to the colony in 1642 by the Puritans of New England, two from Braintree, Massachusetts, and one from New Haven. They were not suffered to preach, but many resorted to them in private houses, until, being finally driven out by fines and imprisonments, they took refuge in Catholic Maryland. The Virginia clergy were not, as a body, very much of a force in education or literature. Many of them, by reason of the scattering and dispersed condition of their parishes, lived as domestic chaplains with the wealthier planters, and partook of their illiteracy and their passion for gaming and hunting. Few of them inherited the zeal of Alexander Whitaker, the "Apostle of Virginia," who came over in 1611 to preach to the colonists and convert the Indians, and who published in furtherance of those ends *Good News from Virginia*, in 1613, three years before his death by drowning in James River.

The conditions were much more favorable for the production of a literature in New England than in the southern colonies. The free and genial existence of the "Old Dominion" had no counterpart among the settlers of Plymouth and Massachusetts Bay, and the Puritans must have been rather unpleasant people to live with for persons of a different way of thinking. But their {334} intensity of character, their respect for learning, and the heroic mood which sustained them through the hardships and dangers of their great enterprise are amply reflected in their own writings. If these are not so much literature as the raw materials of literature, they have at least been fortunate in finding interpreters among their descendants, and no modern Virginian has done for the memory of the Jamestown planters what Hawthorne, Whittier, Longfellow, and others have done in casting the glamour of poetry and romance over the lives of the founders of New England.

Cotton Mather, in his *Magnalia*, quotes the following passage from one of those election sermons, delivered before the General Court of Massachusetts, which formed for many years the great annual intellectual event of the colony: "The question was often put unto our predecessors, *What went ye out into the wilderness to see?* And the answer to it is not only too excellent but too notorious to be dissembled.~.~.~. We came hither because we would have our posterity settled under the pure and full dispensations of the gospel, defended by rulers that should be of ourselves." The New England colonies were, in fact, theocracies. Their leaders were clergymen or laymen, whose zeal for the faith was no whit inferior to that of the ministers themselves. Church and State were one. The freeman's oath was only administered to

Church members, and there was no place in the social system for unbelievers or {335} dissenters. The Pilgrim fathers regarded their transplantation to the New World as an exile, and nothing is more touching in their written records than the repeated expressions of love and longing toward the old home which they had left, and even toward that Church of England from which they had sorrowfully separated themselves. It was not in any light or adventurous spirit that they faced the perils of the sea and the wilderness. "This howling wilderness," "these ends of the earth," "these goings down of the sun," are some of the epithets which they constantly applied to the land of their exile. Nevertheless they had come to stay, and, unlike Smith and Percy and Sandys, the early historians and writers of New England cast in their lots permanently with the new settlements. A few, indeed, went back after 1640—Mather says some ten or twelve of the ministers of the first "classis" or immigration were among them—when the victory of the Puritanic party in Parliament opened a career for them in England, and made their presence there seem in some cases a duty. The celebrated Hugh Peters, for example, who was afterward Oliver Cromwell's chaplain, and was beheaded after the Restoration, went back in 1641, and in 1647 Nathaniel Ward, the minister of Ipswich, Massachusetts, and author of a quaint book against toleration, entitled *The Simple Cobbler of Agawam*, written in America and published shortly after its author's arrival in England. The Civil War, too, put a stop to {336} further emigration from England until after the Restoration in 1660.

The mass of the Puritan immigration consisted of men of the middle class, artisans and husbandmen, the most useful members of a new colony. But their leaders were clergymen educated at the universities, and especially at Emanuel College, Cambridge, the great Puritan college; their civil magistrates were also in great part gentlemen of education and substance, like the elder Winthrop, who was learned in the law, and Theophilus Eaton, first governor of New Haven, who was a London merchant of good estate. It is computed that there were in New England during the first generation as many university graduates as in any community of equal population in the old country. Almost the first care of the settlers was to establish schools. Every town of fifty families was required by law to maintain a common school, and every town of a hundred families a grammar or Latin school. In 1636, only sixteen years after the landing of the Pilgrims on Plymouth Rock, Harvard College was founded at Newtown, whose name was thereupon changed to Cambridge, the General Court held at Boston on September 8, 1680, having already advanced 400 pounds "by way of essay towards the building of something to begin a college." "An university," says Mather, "which hath been to these plantations, for the good literature there cultivated, *sal Gentium~.~.~.* and a river, without the streams whereof these regions would {337} have been mere unwatered places for the devil." By 1701 Harvard had put forth a vigorous offshoot, Yale College, at New Haven, the settlers of New Haven and Connecticut plantations having increased sufficiently to need a college at their own doors. A printing press was set up at Cambridge in 1639, which was under the oversight of the university authorities, and afterwards of licensers appointed by the civil power. The press was no more free in Massachusetts than in Virginia, and that "liberty of unlicensed printing," for which the Puritan Milton had pleaded in his *Areopagitica*, in 1644, was unknown in Puritan New England until some twenty years before the outbreak of the Revolutionary War. "The Freeman's Oath" and an almanac were issued from the Cambridge press in 1639, and in 1640 the first English book printed in America, a collection of the psalms in meter, made by various ministers, and known as the *Bay Psalm Book*. The poetry of this version was worse, if possible, than that of Sternhold and Hopkins's famous rendering; but it is noteworthy that one of the principal translators was that devoted "Apostle to the Indians," the Rev. John Eliot, who, in 1661-63, translated the Bible into the Algonkin tongue. Eliot hoped and toiled a lifetime for the conversion of those "salvages," "tawnies," "devil-worshipers," for whom our early writers have usually nothing but bad words. They have been destroyed instead of converted; but his (so entitled) *Mamusse Wunneetupanatamwe {338} Up-Biblum God naneeswe Nukkone Testament kah wonk Wusku Testament*—the first Bible printed in America—remains a monument of missionary zeal and a work of great value to students of the Indian languages.

A modern writer has said that, to one looking back on the history of old New England, it seems as though the sun shone but dimly there, and the landscape was always dark and wintry. Such is the impression which one carries away from the perusal of books like Bradford's and Winthrop's *Journals*, or Mather's *Wonders of the Invisible World*: an impression of gloom, of night and cold, of mysterious fears besieging the infant settlements, scattered in a narrow fringe "between the groaning forest and the shore." The Indian terror hung over New England for more than half a century, or until the issue of King Philip's War, in 1676, relieved the colonists of any danger of a general massacre. Added to this were the perplexities caused by the earnest resolve of the settlers to keep their New English Eden free from the intrusion of the serpent in the shape of heretical sects in religion. The Puritanism of Massachusetts was an orthodox and conservative Puritanism. The later and more grotesque out-crops of the movement in the old England found no toleration in the new. But these refugees for conscience' sake were compelled in turn to persecute Antinomians, Separatists, Familists, Libertines, Anti-pedobaptists, and later, Quakers, and still {339} later, Enthusiasts, who swarmed into their precincts and troubled the Churches with "prophesyings" and novel opinions. Some of these were banished, others were flogged or imprisoned, and a few were put to death. Of the exiles the most noteworthy was Roger Williams, an impetuous, warm-hearted man, who was so far in advance of his age as to deny the power of the civil magistrate in cases of conscience, or who, in other words, maintained the modern doctrine of the separation of Church and State. Williams was driven away from the Massachusetts colony—where he had been minister of the Church at Salem—and with a few followers fled into the southern wilderness, and settled at Providence. There and in the neighboring plantation of Rhode Island, for which he obtained a charter, he established his patriarchal rule, and gave freedom of worship to all comers. Williams was a prolific writer on theological subjects, the most important of his writings being, perhaps, his *Bloody Tenent of Persecution*, 1644, and a supplement to the same called out by a reply to the former work from the pen of Mr. John Cotton, minister of the First Church at Boston, entitled *The Bloody Tenent Washed and made White in the Blood of the Lamb*. Williams was also a friend to the Indians, whose lands, he thought, should not be taken from them without payment, and he anticipated Eliot by writing, in 1643, a *Key into the Language of America*. Although at odds with the theology of {340} Massachusetts Bay, Williams remained in correspondence with Winthrop and others in Boston, by whom he was highly esteemed. He visited England in 1643 and 1652, and made the acquaintance of John Milton.

Besides the threat of an Indian war and their anxious concern for the purity of the Gospel in their Churches, the colonists were haunted by superstitious forebodings of the darkest kind. It seemed to them that Satan, angered by the setting up of the kingdom of the saints in America, had "come down in great wrath," and was present among them, sometimes even in visible shape, to terrify and tempt. Special providences and unusual phenomena, like earthquakes, mirages, and the northern lights, are gravely recorded by Winthrop and Mather and others as portents of supernatural persecutions. Thus Mrs. Anne Hutchinson, the celebrated leader of the Familists, having, according to rumor, been delivered of a monstrous birth, the Rev. John Cotton, in open assembly, at Boston, upon a lecture day, "thereupon gathered that it might signify her error in denying inherent righteousness." "There will be an unusual range of the devil among us," wrote Mather, "a little before the second coming of our Lord. The evening wolves will be much abroad when we are near the evening of the world." This belief culminated in the horrible witchcraft delusion at Salem in 1692, that "spectral puppet play," which, beginning with the malicious pranks of a few children who {341} accused certain uncanny old women and other persons of mean condition and suspected lives of having tormented them with magic, gradually drew into its vortex victims of the highest character, and resulted in the judicial murder of over nineteen people. Many of the possessed pretended to have been visited by the apparition of a little black man, who urged them to inscribe their names in a red book which he carried—a sort of muster-roll of those who had forsworn God's service for the devil's. Others testified to having been present at meetings of witches in the forest. It is difficult now to read without contempt the "evidence" which grave justices and learned divines considered sufficient to condemn to death men and women of unblemished lives. It is true that the belief in witchcraft was general at that time all over the civilized world, and that sporadic cases of witch-burnings had occurred in different parts of America and Europe. Sir Thomas Browne, in his *Religio Medici*, 1635, affirmed his belief in witches, and pronounced those who doubted of them "a sort of atheist." But the superstition came to a head in the Salem trials and executions, and was the more shocking from the general high level of intelligence in the community in which these were held. It would be well if those who lament the decay of "faith" would remember what things were done in New England in the name of faith less than two hundred years ago. It is not wonderful that, to the Massachusetts Puritans of {342} the seventeenth century, the mysterious forest held no beautiful suggestion; to them it was simply a grim and hideous wilderness, whose dark aisles were the ambush of prowling savages and the rendezvous of those other "devil-worshipers" who celebrated there a kind of vulgar Walpurgis night.

The most important of original sources for the history of the settlement of New England are the journals of William Bradford, first governor of Plymouth, and John Winthrop, the second governor of Massachusetts, which hold a place corresponding to the writings of Captain John Smith in the Virginia colony, but are much more sober and trustworthy. Bradford's *History of Plymouth Plantation* covers the period from 1620 to 1646. The manuscript was used by later annalists, but remained unpublished, as a whole, until 1855, having been lost during the war of the revolution and recovered long afterward in England. Winthrop's Journal, or *History of New England*, begun on shipboard in 1630, and extending to 1649, was not published entire until 1826. It is of equal authority with Bradford's, and perhaps, on the whole, the more important of the two, as the colony of Massachusetts Bay, whose history it narrates, greatly outwent Plymouth in wealth and population, though not in priority of settlement. The interest of Winthrop's Journal lies in the events that it records rather than in any charm in the historian's manner of recording them. His style is pragmatic, {343} and some of the incidents which he gravely notes are trivial to the modern mind, though instructive as to our forefathers' way of thinking. For instance, of the year 1632: "At Watertown there was (in the view of divers witnesses) a great combat between a mouse and a snake, and after a long fight the mouse prevailed and killed the snake. The pastor of Boston, Mr. Wilson, a very sincere, holy man, hearing of it, gave this interpretation: that the snake was the devil, the mouse was a poor, contemptible people, which God had brought hither, which should overcome Satan here and dispossess him of his kingdom." The reader of Winthrop's *Journal* comes every-where upon hints which the imagination has since shaped into poetry and romance. The germs of many of Longfellow's *New England Tragedies*, of Hawthorne's *Maypole of Merrymount*, of *Endicott's Red Cross*, and of Whittier's *John Underhill* and *The Familists' Hymn* are all to be found in some dry, brief entry of the old Puritan diarist. "Robert Cole, having been oft punished for drunkenness, was now ordered to wear a red D about his neck for a year" to wit, the year 1633, and thereby gave occasion to the greatest American romance, *The Scarlet Letter*. The famous apparition of the phantom ship in New Haven harbor, "upon the top of the poop a man standing with one hand akimbo under his left side, and in his right hand a sword stretched out toward the sea," was first chronicled by Winthrop under the year 1648. This meterological {344} phenomenon took on the dimensions of a full-grown myth some forty years later, as related, with many embellishments, by Rev. James Pierpont, of New Haven, in a letter to Cotton Mather. Winthrop put great faith in special providences, and among other instances narrates, not without a certain grim satisfaction, how "the *Mary Rose*, a ship of Bristol, of about 200 tons," lying before Charleston, was blown in pieces with her own powder, being twenty-one barrels, wherein the judgment of God appeared, "for the master and company were many of them profane scoffers at us and at the ordinances of religion here." Without any effort at dramatic portraiture or character sketching, Winthrop managed in all simplicity, and by the plain relation of facts, to leave a clear impression of many of the prominent figures in the first Massachusetts immigration. In particular there gradually arises from the entries in his diary a very distinct and diverting outline of Captain John Underhill, celebrated in Whittier's poem. He was one of the few professional soldiers who came over with the Puritan fathers, such as John Mason, the hero of the Pequot War, and Miles Standish, whose *Courtship* Longfellow sang. He had seen service in the Low Countries, and in pleading the privilege of his profession "he insisted much upon the liberty which all States do allow to military officers for free speech, etc., and that himself had spoken sometimes as freely to Count Nassau." Captain Underhill gave the colony no end of {345} trouble, both by his scandalous living and his heresies in religion. Having been seduced into Familistical opinions by Mrs. Anne Hutchinson, who was banished for her beliefs, he was had up before the General Court and questioned, among other points, as to his own report of the manner of his conversion. "He had lain under a spirit of bondage and a legal way for years, and could get no assurance, till, at length, as he was taking a pipe of tobacco, the Spirit set home an absolute promise of free grace with such assurance and joy as he never since doubted of his good estate, neither should he, though he should fall into sin.~.~.~. The Lord's day following he made a speech in the assembly, showing that as the Lord was pleased to convert Paul as he was in persecuting, etc., so he might manifest himself to him as he was taking the moderate use of the creature called tobacco." The gallant captain, being banished the colony, betook himself to the falls of the Piscataquack (Exeter, N. H.), where the Rev. John Wheelwright, another adherent of Mrs. Hutchinson, had gathered a congregation. Being made governor of this plantation, Underhill sent letters to the Massachusetts magistrates, breathing reproaches and imprecations of vengeance. But meanwhile it was discovered that he had been living in adultery at Boston with a young woman whom he had seduced, the wife of a cooper, and the captain was forced to make public confession, which he did with great unction and in a manner highly dramatic. "He came {346} in his worst clothes (being accustomed to take great pride in his bravery and neatness), without a band, in a foul linen cap, and pulled close to his eyes, and standing upon a form, he did, with many deep sighs and abundance of tears, lay open his wicked course." There is a lurking humor in the grave Winthrop's detailed account of Underhill's doings. Winthrop's own personality comes out well in his *Journal*. He was a born leader of men, a *conditor imperii*, just, moderate, patient, wise, and his narrative gives, upon the whole, a favorable impression of the general prudence and fair-mindedness of the Massachusetts settlers in their dealings with one another, with the Indians, and with the neighboring plantations.

Considering our forefathers' errand and calling into this wilderness, it is not strange that their chief literary staples were sermons and tracts in controversial theology. Multitudes of these were written and published by the divines of the first generation, such as John Cotton, Thomas Shepard, John Norton, Peter Bulkley, and Thomas Hooker, the founder of Hartford, of whom it was finely said that "when he was doing his Master's business he would put a king into his pocket." Nor were their successors in the second or the third generation any less industrious and prolific. They rest from their labors and their works do follow them. Their sermons and theological treatises are not literature, they are for the most part dry, heavy, and dogmatic, but they exhibit great learning, {347} logical acuteness, and an earnestness which sometimes rises into eloquence. The pulpit ruled New England, and the sermon was the great intellectual engine of the time. The serious thinking of the Puritans was given almost exclusively to religion; the other world was all their art. The daily secular events of life, the aspects of nature, the vicissitude of the seasons, were important enough to find record in print only in so far as they manifested God's dealings with his people. So much was the sermon depended upon to furnish literary food that it was the general custom of serious minded laymen to take down the words of the discourse in their note-books. Franklin, in his *Autobiography*, describes this as the constant habit of his grandfather, Peter Folger; and Mather, in his life of the elder Winthrop, says that "tho' he wrote not after the preacher, yet such was his *attention* and such his *retention* in hearing, that he repeated unto his family the sermons which he had heard in the congregation." These discourses were commonly of great length; twice, or sometimes thrice, the pulpit hour-glass was silently inverted while the orator pursued his theme even unto n'thly.

The book which best sums up the life and thought of this old New England of the seventeenth century is Cotton Mather's *Magnalia Christi Americana.* Mather was by birth a member of that clerical aristocracy which developed later into Dr. Holmes's "Brahmin Caste of New England." His maternal grandfather was John Cotton. His {348} father was Increase Mather, the most learned divine of his generation in New England, minister of the North Church of Boston, President of Harvard College, and author, *inter alia*, of that characteristically Puritan book, *An Essay for the Recording of Illustrious Providences.* Cotton Mather himself was a monster of erudition and a prodigy of diligence. He was graduated from Harvard at fifteen. He ordered his daily life and conversation by a system of minute observances. He was a book-worm, whose life was spent between his library and his pulpit, and his published works number upward of three hundred and eighty. Of these the most important is the *Magnalia*, 1702, an ecclesiastical history of New England from 1620 to 1698, divided into seven parts: I. Antiquities; II. Lives of the Governors; III. Lives of Sixty Famous Divines; IV. A History of Harvard College, with biographies of its eminent graduates; V. Acts and Monuments of the Faith; VI. Wonderful Providences; VII. The Wars of the Lord, that is, an account of the Afflictions and Disturbances of the Churches and the Conflicts with the Indians. The plan of the work thus united that of Fuller's *Worthies of England* and *Church History* with that of Wood's *Athenae Oxonienses* and Fox's *Book of Martyrs.*

Mather's prose was of the kind which the English Commonwealth writers used. He was younger by a generation than Dryden; but as literary fashions are slower to change in a colony than in the {349} mother country, that nimble English which Dryden and the Restoration essayists introduced had not yet displaced in New England the older manner. Mather wrote in the full and pregnant style of Taylor, Milton, Browne, Fuller, and Burton, a style ponderous with learning and stiff with allusions, digressions, conceits, anecdotes, and quotations from the Greek and the Latin. A page of the *Magnalia* is almost as richly mottled with italics as one from the *Anatomy of*

Melancholy, and the quaintness which Mather caught from his favorite Fuller disports itself in textual pun and marginal anagram and the fantastic sub-titles of his books and chapters. He speaks of Thomas Hooker as having "*angled* many scores of souls into the kingdom of heaven," anagrammatizes Mrs. Hutchinson's surname into "the non-such;" and having occasion to speak of Mr. Urian Oaks's election to the presidency of Harvard College, enlarges upon the circumstance as follows:

"We all know that Britain knew nothing more famous than their ancient sect of DRUIDS; the philosophers, whose order, they say, was instituted by one *Samothes*, which is in English as much as to say, *an heavenly man*. The *Celtic* name *Deru*, for an *Oak* was that from whence they received their denomination; as at this very day the *Welch* call this tree *Drew*, and this order of men *Derwyddon*. But there are no small antiquaries who derive this *oaken religion* and *philosophy* from the *Oaks of Mamre*, where the Patriarch *Abraham* {350} had as well a dwelling as an *altar*. That *Oaken-Plain* and the eminent OAK under which *Abraham* lodged was extant in the days of *Constantine*, as *Isidore, Jerom*, and *Sozomen* have assured us. Yea, there are shrewd probabilities that *Noah* himself had lived in this very *Oak-plain* before him; for this very place was called *Oyye*, which was the name of *Noah*, so styled from the *Oggyan* (*subcineritiis panibus*) sacrifices, which he did use to offer in this renowned *Grove*. And it was from this example that the ancients and particularly that the Druids of the nations, chose *oaken* retirements for their studies. Reader, let us now, upon another account, behold the students of *Harvard College*, as a rendezvous of happy *Druids*, under the influences of so rare a president. But, alas! our joy must be short-lived, for on *July* 25, 1681, the stroke of a sudden death felled the *tree*,

"Qui tantum inter caput extulit omnes
Quantum lenta solent inter viberna cypressi.

"Mr. *Oakes* thus being transplanted into the better world, the presidentship was immediately tendered unto *Mr. Increase Mather*."

This will suffice as an example of the bad taste and laborious pedantry which disfigured Mather's writing. In its substance the book is a perfect thesaurus; and inasmuch as nothing is unimportant in the history of the beginnings of such a nation as this is and is destined to be, the *Magnalia* will always remain a valuable and interesting work. {351} Cotton Mather, born in 1663, was of the second generation of Americans, his grandfather being of the immigration, but his father a native of Dorchester, Mass. A comparison of his writings and of the writings of his contemporaries with the works of Bradford, Winthrop, Hooker, and others of the original colonists, shows that the simple and heroic faith of the Pilgrims had hardened into formalism and doctrinal rigidity. The leaders of the Puritan exodus, notwithstanding their intolerance of errors in belief, were comparatively broad-minded men. They were sharers in a great national movement, and they came over when their cause was warm with the glow of martyrdom and on the eve of its coming triumph at home. After the Restoration, in 1660, the currents of national feeling no longer circulated so freely through this distant member of the body politic, and thought in America became more provincial. The English dissenters, though socially at a disadvantage as compared with the Church of England, had the great benefit of living at the center of national life, and of feeling about them the pressure of vast bodies of people who did not think as they did. In New England, for many generations, the dominant sect had things all its own way, a condition of things which is not healthy for any sect or party. Hence Mather and the divines of his time appear in their writings very much like so many Puritan bishops, jealous of their prerogatives, magnifying their apostolate, and careful to maintain their {352} authority over the laity. Mather had an appetite for the marvelous, and took a leading part in the witchcraft trials, of which he gave an account in his *Wonders of the Invisible World*, 1693. To the quaint pages of the Magnalia our modern authors have resorted as to a collection of romances or fairy tales. Whittier, for example, took from thence the subject of his poem *The Garrison of Cape Anne*; and Hawthorne embodied in *Grandfather's Chair* the most elaborate of Mather's biographies. This was the life of Sir William Phipps, who, from being a poor shepherd boy in his native province of Maine, rose to be the royal governor of Massachusetts, and the story of whose wonderful adventures in raising the freight of a Spanish treasure ship, sunk on a reef near Port de la Plata, reads less like sober fact than like some ancient fable, with talk of the Spanish main, bullion, and plate and jewels and "pieces of eight."

Of Mather's generation was Samuel Sewall, Chief Justice of Massachusetts, a singularly gracious and venerable figure, who is intimately known through his Diary kept from 1673 to 1729. This has been compared with the more famous diary of Samuel Pepys, which it resembles in its confidential character and the completeness of its self-revelation, but to which it is as much inferior in historic interest as "the petty province here" was inferior in political and social importance to "Britain far away." For the most part it is a chronicle of small beer, the diarist jotting down the minutiae {353} of his domestic life and private affairs, even to the recording of such haps as this: "March 23, I had my hair cut by G. Barret." But it also affords instructive glimpses of public events, such as King Philip's War, the Quaker troubles, the English Revolution of 1688, etc. It bears about the same relation to New England history at the close of the seventeenth century as Bradford's and Winthrop's journals bear to that of the first generation. Sewall was one of the justices who

presided at the trial of the Salem witches; but for the part which he took in
that wretched affair he made such atonement as was possible, by open
confession of his mistake and his remorse in the presence of the Church.
Sewall was one of the first writers against African slavery, in his brief tract,
The Selling of Joseph, printed at Boston in 1700. His *Phenomena Quaedam
Apocalyptica*, a mystical interpretation of prophecies concerning the New
Jerusalem, which he identifies with America, is remembered only because
Whittier, in his *Prophecy of Samuel Sewall*, has paraphrased one poetic
passage, which shows a loving observation of nature very rare in our colonial
writers.

Of poetry, indeed, or, in fact, of pure literature, in the narrower sense—that is,
of the imaginative representation of life—there was little or none in the
colonial period. There were no novels, no plays, no satires, and—until the
example of the *Spectator* had begun to work on this side the water—no
experiments even at the lighter forms {354} of essay writing, character
sketches, and literary criticism. There was verse of a certain kind, but the
most generous stretch of the term would hardly allow it to be called poetry.
Many of the early divines of New England relieved their pens, in the intervals
of sermon writing, of epigrams, elegies, eulogistic verses, and similar grave
trifles distinguished by the crabbed wit of the so-called "metaphysical poets,"
whose manner was in fashion when the Puritans left England; the manner of
Donne and Cowley, and those darlings of the New English muse, the
Emblems of Quarles and the *Divine Week* of Du Bartas, as translated by
Sylvester. The *Magnalia* contains a number of these things in Latin and
English, and is itself well bolstered with complimentary introductions in
meter by the author's friends. For example:

COTTONIUS MATHERUS.

ANAGRAM.

Tuos Tecum Ornasti.

"While thus the dead in thy rare pages rise
Thine, with thyself, thou dost immortalise,
To view the odds thy learned lives invite
'Twixt Eleutherian and Edomite.
But all succeeding ages shall despair
A fitting monument for thee to *rear.*
Thy own rich pen (peace, silly Momus, peace!)
Hath given them a lasting *writ of ease.*"

The epitaphs and mortuary verses were especially ingenious in the matter of puns, anagrams, {355} and similar conceits. The death of the Rev. Samuel Stone, of Hartford, afforded an opportunity of this sort not to be missed, and his threnodist accordingly celebrated him as a "whetstone," a "loadstone," an "Ebenezer"—

"A stone for kingly David's use so fit
As would not fail Goliah's front to hit," etc.

The most characteristic, popular, and widely circulated poem of colonial New England was Michael Wigglesworth's *Day of Doom* (1662), a kind of doggerel *Inferno*, which went through nine editions, and "was the solace," says Lowell, "of every fireside, the flicker of the pine-knots by which it was conned perhaps adding a livelier relish to its premonitions of eternal combustion." Wigglesworth had not the technical equipment of a poet. His verse is sing-song, his language rude and monotonous, and the lurid horrors of his material hell are more likely to move mirth than fear in a modern reader. But there are an unmistakable vigor of imagination and a sincerity of belief in his gloomy poem which hold it far above contempt, and easily account for its universal currency among a people like the Puritans. One stanza has been often quoted for its grim concession to unregenerate infants of "the easiest room in hell"—a *limbus infantum* which even Origen need not have scrupled at.

The most authoritative expounder of New England Calvinism was Jonathan Edwards {356} (1703-1758), a native of Connecticut, and a graduate of Yale, who was minister for more than twenty years over the Church in Northampton, Mass., afterward missionary to the Stockbridge Indians, and at the time of his death had just been inaugurated president of Princeton College. By virtue of his *Inquiry into the Freedom of the Will*, 1754, Edwards holds rank as the subtlest metaphysician of his age. This treatise was composed to justify, on philosophical grounds, the Calvinistic doctrines of foreordination and election by grace, though its arguments are curiously coincident with those of the scientific necessitarians, whose conclusions are as far asunder from Edwards's "as from the center thrice to the utmost pole." His writings belong to theology rather than to literature, but there is an intensity and a spiritual elevation about them, apart from the profundity and acuteness of the thought, which lift them here and there into the finer ether of purely emotional or imaginative art. He dwelt rather upon the terrors than the comfort of the word, and his chosen themes were the dogmas of predestination, original sin, total depravity, and eternal punishment. The titles of his sermons are significant: *Men Naturally God's Enemies, Wrath upon the Wicked to the Uttermost, The Final Judgment*, etc. "A natural man," he wrote in the first of these discourses, "has a heart like the heart of a devil.~.~.~. The heart of a natural man is as destitute of love to God as a dead, stiff, cold corpse is of vital heat." Perhaps the most {357} famous of Edwards's sermons was *Sinners in the Hands of an Angry God*, preached at Enfield, Conn., July 8, 1741, "at a time of great awakenings," and upon the ominous text, *Their foot shall slide in due time.* "The God that holds you over the pit of hell" runs an oft-quoted passage from this powerful denunciation of the wrath to come, "much as one holds a spider or some loathsome insect over the fire, abhors you, and is dreadfully provoked.~.~.~. You are ten thousand times more abominable in his eyes than the most hateful venomous serpent is in ours.~.~.~. You hang by a slender thread, with the flames of divine wrath flashing about it.~.~.~. If you cry to God to pity you, he will be so far from pitying you in your doleful case that he will only tread you under foot.~.~.~. He will crush out your blood and make it fly, and it shall be sprinkled on his garments so as to stain all his raiment." But Edwards was a rapt soul, possessed with the love as well as the fear of the God, and there are passages of sweet and exalted feeling in his *Treatise Concerning Religious Affections*, 1746. Such is his portrait of Sarah Pierpont, "a young lady in New Haven," who afterward became his wife, and who "will sometimes go about from place to place singing sweetly, and no one knows for what. She loves to be alone, walking in the fields and groves, and seems to have some one invisible always conversing with her." Edwards's printed works number thirty-six titles. A complete edition of them in ten volumes was published in 1829 by his {358} great-grandson, Sereno Dwight. The memoranda from Edwards's note-books, quoted by his editor and biographer, exhibit a remarkable precocity. Even as a school-boy and a college student he had made deep guesses in physics as well as metaphysics, and, as might have been predicted of a youth of his philosophical insight and ideal cast of mind, he had early anticipated Berkeley in denying the existence of matter. In passing from Mather to Edwards, we step from the seventeenth to the eighteenth century. There is the same difference between them in style and turn of thought as between Milton and Locke, or between Fuller and Dryden. The learned digressions, the witty conceits, the perpetual interlarding of the text with scraps of Latin, have fallen off, even as the full-bottomed wig and the clerical gown and bands have been laid aside for the undistinguishing dress of the modern minister. In Edwards's English all is simple, precise, direct, and business-like.

Benjamin Franklin (1706-1790), who was strictly contemporary with Edwards, was a contrast to him in every respect. As Edwards represents the spirituality and other-worldliness of Puritanism, Franklin stands for the worldly and secular side of American character, and he illustrates the development of the New England Englishman into the modern Yankee. Clear rather than subtle, without ideality or romance or fineness of emotion or poetic lift, intensely practical and utilitarian, broad-minded, inventive, shrewd, versatile, Franklin's sturdy figure {359} became typical of his time and his people. He was the first and the only man of letters in colonial America who acquired a cosmopolitan fame, and impressed his characteristic Americanism upon the mind of Europe. He was the embodiment of common sense and of the useful virtues; with the enterprise but without the nervousness of his modern compatriots, uniting the philosopher's openness of mind with the sagacity and quickness of resource of the self-made business man. He was representative also of his age, an age of *aufklärung, eclaircissement,* or "clearing up." By the middle of the eighteenth century a change had taken place in American society. Trade had increased between the different colonies; Boston, New York, and Philadelphia were considerable towns; democratic feeling was spreading; over forty newspapers were published in America at the outbreak of the Revolution; politics claimed more attention than formerly, and theology less. With all this intercourse and mutual reaction of the various colonies upon one another, the isolated theocracy of New England naturally relaxed somewhat of its grip on the minds of the laity. When Franklin was a printer's apprentice in Boston, setting type on his brother's *New England Courant,* the fourth American newspaper, he got hold of an odd volume of the *Spectator,* and formed his style upon Addison, whose manner he afterward imitated in his *Busy-Body* papers in the Philadelphia *Weekly Mercury.* He also read Locke and the English deistical {360} writers, Collins and Shaftesbury, and became himself a deist and free-thinker; and subsequently when practicing his trade in London, in 1724-26, he made the acquaintance of Dr. Mandeville, author of the *Fable of the Bees,* at a pale-ale house in Cheapside, called "The Horns," where the famous free-thinker presided over a club of wits and boon companions. Though a native of Boston, Franklin is identified with Philadelphia, whither he arrived in 1723, a runaway 'prentice boy, "whose stock of cash consisted of a Dutch dollar and about a shilling in copper." The description in his *Autobiography* of his walking up Market Street munching a loaf of bread, and passing his future wife, standing on her father's doorstep, has become almost as familiar as the anecdote about Whittington and his cat.

It was in the practical sphere that Franklin was greatest, as an originator and executor of projects for the general welfare. The list of his public services is almost endless. He organized the Philadelphia fire department and street cleaning service, and the colonial postal system which grew into the United States Post Office Department. He started the Philadelphia public library, the American Philosophical Society, the University of Pennsylvania, and the first American magazine, *The General Magazine and Historical Chronicle*; so that he was almost singly the father of whatever intellectual life the Pennsylvania colony could boast of. In 1754, when commissioners from the colonies met at Albany, Franklin proposed a plan, which was {361} adopted, for the union of all the colonies under one government. But all these things, as well as his mission to England in 1757, on behalf of the Pennsylvania Assembly in its dispute with the proprietaries; his share in the Declaration of Independence—of which he was one of the signers—and his residence in France as Embassador of the United Colonies, belong to the political history of the country; to the history of American science belong his celebrated experiments in electricity, and his benefits to mankind in both of these departments were aptly summed up in the famous epigram of the French statesman Turgot:

"Eripuit coelo fulmen sceptrumque tyrannis."

Franklin's success in Europe was such as no American had yet achieved, as few Americans since him have achieved. Hume and Voltaire were among his acquaintances and his professed admirers. In France he was fairly idolized, and when he died Mirabeau announced, "The genius which has freed America and poured a flood of light over Europe has returned to the bosom of the Divinity."

Franklin was a great man, but hardly a great writer, though as a writer, too, he had many admirable and some great qualities. Among these were the crystal clearness and simplicity of his style. His more strictly literary performances, such as his essays after the *Spectator*, hardly rise above mediocrity, and are neither better nor worse than other {362} imitations of Addison. But in some of his lighter bagatelles there are a homely wisdom and a charming playfulness which have won them enduring favor. Such are his famous story of the *Whistle*, his *Dialogue between Franklin and the Gout*, his letters to Madame Helvetius, and his verses entitled *Paper*. The greater portion of his writings consists of papers on general politics, commerce, and political economy, contributions to the public questions of his day. These are of the nature of journalism rather than of literature, and many of them were published in his newspaper, the *Pennsylvania Gazette*, the medium through which for many years he most strongly influenced American opinion. The most popular of his writings were his *Autobiography* and *Poor Richard's Almanac*. The former of these was begun in 1771, resumed in 1788, but never completed. It has remained the most widely current book in our colonial literature. *Poor Richard's Almanac*, begun in 1732 and continued for about twenty-five years, had an annual circulation of ten thousand copies. It was filled with proverbial sayings in prose and verse, inculcating the virtues of industry, honesty, and frugality.[1] Some of these were original with Franklin, others were selected from the proverbial wisdom of the ages, but a new force was given {363} them by pungent turns of expression. Poor Richard's saws were such as these: "Little strokes fell great oaks;" "Three removes are as bad as a fire;" "Early to bed and early to rise makes a man healthy, wealthy, and wise;" "Never leave that till to-morrow which you can do to-day;" "What maintains one vice would bring up two children;" "It is hard for an empty bag to stand upright."

Now and then there are truths of a higher kind than these in Franklin, and Sainte Beuve, the great French critic, quotes, as an example of his occasional finer moods, the saying, "Truth and sincerity have a certain distinguishing native luster about them which cannot be counterfeited; they are like fire and flame that cannot be painted." But the sage who invented the Franklin stove had no disdain of small utilities; and in general the last word of his philosophy is well expressed in a passage of his *Autobiography*: "Human felicity is produced not so much by great pieces of good fortune, that seldom happen, as by little advantages that occur every day; thus, if you teach a poor young man to shave himself and keep his razor in order, you may contribute more to the happiness of his life than in giving him a thousand guineas."

1. Captain John Smith. A True Relation of Virginia. Deane's edition. Boston: 1866.

2. Cotton Mather. Magnalia Christi Americana. Hartford: 1820.

{364}

3. Samuel Sewall. Diary. Massachusetts Historical Collections. Fifth Series. Vols. v, vi, and vii. Boston: 1878.

4. Jonathan Edwards. Eight Sermons on Various Occasions. Vol. vii. of Edwards's Words. Edited by Sereno Dwight. New York: 1829.

5. Benjamin Franklin. Autobiography. Edited by John Bigelow. Philadelphia: 1869. [J. B. Lippincott & Co.]

6. Essays and Bagatelles. Vol. ii. of Franklin's Works. Edited by David Sparks. Boston: 1836.

7. Moses Coit Tyler. A History of American Literature. 1607-1765. New York: 1878. [G. P. Putnam's Sons.]

[1] *The Way to Wealth, Plan for Saving One Hundred Thousand Pounds, Rules of Health, Advice to a Young Tradesman, The Way to Make Money Plenty in Every Man's Pocket, etc.*

{365}

CHAPTER II.

1765-1815.

It will be convenient to treat the fifty years which elapsed between the meeting at New York, in 1765, of a Congress of delegates from nine colonies, to protest against the Stamp Act, and the close of the second war with England, in 1815, as, for literary purposes, a single period. This half century was the formative era of the American nation. Historically it is divisible into the years of revolution and the years of construction. But the men who led the movement for independence were also, in great part, the same who guided in shaping the Constitution of the new republic, and the intellectual impress of the whole period is one and the same. The character of the age was as distinctly political as that of the colonial era—in New England at least—was theological; and literature must still continue to borrow its interest from history. Pure literature, or what, for want of a better term we call *belles lettres*, was not born in America until the nineteenth century was well under way. It is true that the Revolution had its humor, its poetry, and even its fiction; but these {366} were strictly for the home market. They hardly penetrated the consciousness of Europe at all, and are not to be compared with the contemporary work of English authors like Cowper and Sheridan and Burke. Their importance for us to-day is rather antiquarian than literary, though the most noteworthy of them will be mentioned in due course in the present chapter. It is also true that one or two of Irving's early books fall within the last years of the period now under consideration. But literary epochs overlap one another at the edges, and these writings may best be postponed to a subsequent chapter.

Among the most characteristic products of the intellectual stir that preceded and accompanied the revolutionary movement, were the speeches of political orators like Samuel Adams, James Otis, and Josiah Quincy in Massachusetts, and Patrick Henry in Virginia. Oratory is the art of a free people, and as in the forensic assemblies of Greece and Rome, and in the Parliament of Great Britain, so in the conventions and congresses of revolutionary America it sprang up and flourished naturally. The age, moreover, was an eloquent, not to say a rhetorical age; and the influence of Johnson's orotund prose, of the declamatory *Letters of Junius*, and of the speeches of Burke, Fox, Sheridan, and the elder Pitt is perceptible in the debates of our early congresses. The fame of a great orator, like that of a great actor, is largely traditionary. The spoken word transferred to the printed page loses {367} the glow which resided in the man and the moment. A speech is good if it attains its aim, if it moves the hearers to the end which is sought. But the fact that this end is often temporary and occasional, rather than universal and permanent explains why so few speeches are really literature.

If this is true, even where the words of an orator are preserved exactly as they were spoken, it is doubly true when we have only the testimony of contemporaries as to the effect which the oration produced. The fiery utterances of Adams, Otis, and Quincy were either not reported at all or very imperfectly reported, so that posterity can judge of them only at second hand. Patrick Henry has fared better, many of his orations being preserved in substance, if not in the letter, in Wirt's biography. Of these the most famous was the defiant speech in the Convention of Delegates, March 28, 1775, throwing down the gauge of battle to the British ministry. The ringing sentences of this challenge are still declaimed by school boys, and many of them remain as familiar as household words. "I have but one lamp by which my feet are guided, and that is the lamp of experience. I know of no way of judging of the future but by the past.~.~.~. Gentlemen may cry peace, peace, but there is no peace.~.~.~. Is life so dear, or peace so sweet, as to be purchased at the price of chains and slavery! Forbid it, Almighty God! I know not what course others may take, but as for me, give me liberty, or give me death!" The {368} eloquence of Patrick Henry was fervid rather than weighty or rich. But if such specimens of the oratory of the American patriots as have come down to us fail to account for the wonderful impression that their words are said to have produced upon their fellow-countrymen, we should remember that they are at a disadvantage when read instead of heard. The imagination should supply all those accessories which gave them vitality when first pronounced: the living presence and voice of the speaker; the listening Senate; the grave excitement of the hour and of the impending conflict. The wordiness and exaggeration; the highly latinized diction; the rhapsodies about freedom which hundreds of Fourth-of-July addresses have since turned into platitudes—all these coming hot from the lips of men whose actions in the field confirmed the earnestness of their speech—were effective enough in the crisis and for the purpose to which they were addressed.

The press was an agent in the cause of liberty no less potent than the platform, and patriots such as Adams, Otis, Quincy, Warren, and Hancock wrote constantly for the newspapers essays and letters on the public questions of the time signed "Vindex," "Hyperion," "Independent," "Brutus," "Cassius," and the like, and couched in language which to the taste of to-day seems rather over rhetorical. Among the most important of these political essays were the *Circular Letter to each Colonial Legislature*, published by Adams {369} and Otis in 1768; Quincy's *Observations on the Boston Port Bill*, 1774, and Otis's *Rights of the British Colonies*, a pamphlet of one hundred and twenty pages, printed in 1764. No collection of Otis's writings has ever been made. The life of Quincy, published by his son, preserves for posterity his journals and correspondence, his newspaper essays, and his speeches at the bar, taken from the Massachusetts law reports.

Among the political literature which is of perennial interest to the American people are such State documents as the Declaration of Independence, the Constitution of the United States, and the messages, inaugural addresses, and other writings of our early presidents. Thomas Jefferson, the third president of the United States, and the father of the Democratic party, was the author of the Declaration of Independence, whose opening sentences have become commonplaces in the memory of all readers. One sentence in particular has been as a shibboleth, or war-cry, or declaration of faith among Democrats of all shades of opinion: "We hold these truths to be self-evident: that all men are created equal; that they are endowed by their Creator with certain unalienable rights; that among these are life, liberty, and the pursuit of happiness." Not so familiar to modern readers is the following, which an English historian of our literature calls "the most eloquent clause of that great document," and "the most interesting suppressed passage in American literature." Jefferson {370} was a southerner, but even at that early day the South had grown sensitive on the subject of slavery, and Jefferson's arraignment of King George for promoting the "peculiar institution" was left out from the final draft of the Declaration in deference to southern members.

"He has waged cruel war against human nature itself, violating its most sacred rights of life and liberty, in the persons of a distant people who never offended him, captivating and carrying them into slavery in another hemisphere, or to incur miserable death in their transportation thither. This piratical warfare, the opprobrium of infidel powers, is the warfare of the Christian king of Great Britain. Determined to keep open a market where men should be bought and sold, he has prostituted his negative by suppressing every legislative attempt to restrain this execrable commerce. And, that this assemblage of horrors might want no fact of distinguished dye, he is now exciting those very people to rise in arms against us, and purchase that liberty of which he deprived them by murdering the people upon whom he obtruded them, and thus paying off former crimes committed against the liberties of one people by crimes which he urges them to commit against the lives of another."

The tone of apology or defense which Calhoun and other southern statesmen afterward adopted on the subject of slavery was not taken by the men of Jefferson's generation. Another famous {371} Virginian, John Randolph of Roanoke, himself a slaveholder, in his speech on the militia bill in the House of Representatives, December 10, 1811, said: "I speak from facts when I say that the night-bell never tolls for fire in Richmond that the mother does not hug her infant more closely to her bosom." This was said *apropos* of the danger of a servile insurrection in the event of a war with England—a war which actually broke out in the year following, but was not attended with the slave rising which Randolph predicted. Randolph was a thorough-going "States rights" man, and though opposed to slavery on principle, he cried hands off to any interference by the General Government with the domestic institutions of the States. His speeches *read* better than most of his contemporaries. They are interesting in their exhibit of a bitter and eccentric individuality, witty, incisive, and expressed in a pungent and familiar style which contrasts refreshingly with the diplomatic language and glittering generalities of most congressional oratory, whose verbiage seems to keep its subject always at arm's length.

Another noteworthy writing of Jefferson's was his Inaugural Address of March 4, 1801, with its programme of "equal and exact justice to all men, of whatever state or persuasion, religious or political; peace, commerce, and honest friendship with all nations, entangling alliances with none; the support of the State governments in all their rights;~.~.~. absolute acquiescence in the decisions {372} of the majority;~.~.~. the supremacy of the civil over the military authority; economy in the public expense; freedom of religion, freedom of the press, and freedom of person under the protection of the *habeas corpus*, and trial by juries impartially selected."

During his six years' residence in France, as American Minister, Jefferson had become indoctrinated with the principles of French democracy. His main service and that of his party—the Democratic or, as it was then called, the Republican party—to the young republic was in its insistence upon toleration of all beliefs and upon the freedom of the individual from all forms of governmental restraint. Jefferson has some claims, to rank as an author in general literature. Educated at William and Mary College in the old Virginia capital, Williamsburg, he became the founder of the University of Virginia, in which he made special provision for the study of Anglo-Saxon, and in which the liberal scheme of instruction and discipline was conformed, in theory at least, to the "university idea." His *Notes on Virginia* are not without literary quality, and one description, in particular, has been often quoted—the passage of the Potomac through the Blue Ridge—in which is this poetically imaginative touch: "The mountain being cloven asunder, she presents to your eye, through the cleft, a small catch of smooth blue horizon, at an infinite distance in the plain country, inviting you, as it were, from the riot and {373} tumult roaring around, to pass through the breach and participate of the calm below."

After the conclusion of peace with England, in 1783, political discussion centered about the Constitution, which in 1788 took the place of the looser Articles of Confederation adopted in 1778. The Constitution as finally ratified was a compromise between two parties—the Federalists, who wanted a strong central government, and the Anti-Federals (afterward called Republicans, or Democrats), who wished to preserve State sovereignty. The debates on the adoption of the Constitution, both in the General Convention of the States, which met at Philadelphia in 1787, and in the separate State Conventions called to ratify its action, form a valuable body of comment and illustration upon the instrument itself. One of the most notable of the speeches in opposition was Patrick Henry's address before the Virginia Convention. "That this is a consolidated government," he said, "is demonstrably clear; and the danger of such a government is, to my mind, very striking." The leader of the Federal party was Alexander Hamilton, the ablest constructive intellect among the statesmen of our revolutionary era, of whom Talleyrand said that he "had never known his equal;" whom Guizot classed with "the men who have best known the vital principles and fundamental conditions of a government worthy of its name and mission." Hamilton's speech *On the Expediency of Adopting the Federal Constitution*, delivered in {374} the Convention of New York, June 24, 1788, was a masterly statement of the necessity and advantages of the Union. But the most complete exposition of the constitutional philosophy of the Federal party was the series of eighty-five papers entitled the *Federalist*, printed during the years 1787-88, and mostly in the *Independent Journal* of New York, over the signature "*Publius*." These were the work of Hamilton, of John Jay, afterward Chief Justice, and of James Madison, afterward President of the United States. The *Federalist* papers, though written in a somewhat ponderous diction, are among the great landmarks of American history, and were in themselves a political education to the generation that read them. Hamilton was a brilliant and versatile figure, a persuasive orator, a forcible writer, and as Secretary of the Treasury under Washington the foremost of American financiers. He was killed, in a duel, by Aaron Burr, at Hoboken, in 1804.

The Federalists were victorious, and under the provisions of the new

Constitution George Washington was inaugurated first President of the United States, on March 4, 1789. Washington's writings have been collected by Jared Sparks. They consist of journals, letters, messages, addresses, and public documents, for the most part plain and business-like in manner, and without any literary pretensions. The most elaborate and the best known of them is his *Farewell Address*, issued on his retirement from the presidency in 1796. In {375} the composition of this he was assisted by Madison, Hamilton, and Jay. It is wise in substance and dignified, though somewhat stilted in expression. The correspondence of John Adams, second President of the United States, and his diary, kept from 1755-85, should also be mentioned as important sources for a full knowledge of this period.

In the long life-and-death struggle of Great Britain against the French Republic and its successor, Napoleon Bonaparte, the Federalist party in this country naturally sympathized with England, and the Jeffersonian Democracy with France. The Federalists, who distrusted the sweeping abstractions of the French Revolution, and clung to the conservative notions of a checked and balanced freedom, inherited from English precedent, were accused of monarchical and aristocratic leanings. On their side they were not slow to accuse their adversaries of French atheism and French Jacobinism. By a singular reversal of the natural order of things the strength of the Federalist party was in New England, which was socially democratic, while the strength of the Jeffersonians was in the South, whose social structure—owing to the system of slavery—was intensely aristocratic. The war of 1812 with England was so unpopular in New England, by reason of the injury which it threatened to inflict on its commerce, that the Hartford Convention of 1814 was more than suspected of a design to bring about the secession of New England from the Union. A good deal of oratory was called {376} out by the debates on the commercial treaty with Great Britain, negotiated by Jay in 1795, by the Alien and Sedition Law of 1798, and by other pieces of Federalist legislation, previous to the downfall of that party and the election of Jefferson to the presidency in 1800. The best of the Federalist orators during those years was Fisher Ames, of Massachusetts, and the best of his orations was, perhaps, his speech on the British treaty in the House of Representatives, April 18, 1796. The speech was, in great measure, a protest against American chauvinism and the violation of international obligations. "It has been said the world ought to rejoice if Britain was sunk in the sea; if where there are now men and wealth and laws and liberty, there was no more than a sand bank for sea-monsters to fatten on; space for the storms of the ocean to mingle in conflict.~.~.~. What is patriotism? Is it a narrow affection for the spot where a man was born? Are the very clods where we tread entitled to this ardent preference because they are greener?~.~.~. I see no exception to the respect that is paid among nations to the law of good faith.~.~.~. It is observed by barbarians—a whiff of tobacco smoke or a string of beads gives not merely binding force but sanctity to treaties. Even in Algiers a truce may be bought for money, but, when ratified, even Algiers is too wise or too just to disown and annul its obligation." Ames was a scholar, and his speeches are more finished and thoughtful, more *literary*, in a way, than those {377} of his contemporaries. His eulogiums on Washington and Hamilton are elaborate tributes, rather excessive, perhaps, in laudation and in classical allusions. In all the oratory of the revolutionary period there is nothing equal in deep and condensed energy of feeling to the single clause in Lincoln's Gettysburg Address, "that we here highly resolve that these dead shall not have died in vain."

A prominent figure during and after the War of the Revolution was Thomas Paine, or, as he was somewhat disrespectfully called, "Tom Paine." He was a dissenting minister who, conceiving himself ill treated by the British Government, came to Philadelphia in 1774 and threw himself heart and soul into the colonial cause. His pamphlet, *Common Sense*, issued in 1776, began with the famous words: "These are the times that try men's souls." This was followed by the *Crisis*, a series of political essays advocating independence and the establishment of a republic, published in periodical form, though at irregular intervals. Paine's rough and vigorous advocacy was of great service to the American patriots. His writings were popular and his arguments were of a kind easily understood by plain people, addressing themselves to the common sense, the prejudices and passions of unlettered readers. He afterward went to France and took an active part in the popular movement there, crossing swords with Burke in his *Rights of Man*, 1791-92, written in defense of the French Revolution. He {378} was one of the two foreigners who sat in the Convention; but falling under suspicion during the days of the terror, he was committed to the prison of the Luxembourg and only released upon the fall of Robespierre July 27, 1794. While in prison he wrote a portion of his best known work, the *Age of Reason*. This appeared in two parts in 1794 and 1795, the manuscript of the first part having been intrusted to Joel Barlow, the American poet, who happened to be in Paris when Paine was sent to prison.

The *Age of Reason* damaged Paine's reputation in America, where the name of "Tom Paine" became a stench in the nostrils of the godly and a synonym for atheism and blasphemy. His book was denounced from a hundred pulpits, and copies of it were carefully locked away from the sight of "the young," whose religious beliefs it might undermine. It was, in effect, a crude and popular statement of the Deistic argument against Christianity. What the cutting logic and persiflage—the *sourire hideux*—of Voltaire had done in France, Paine, with coarser materials, essayed to do for the English-speaking populations. Deism was in the air of the time; Franklin, Jefferson, Ethan Alien, Joel Barlow, and other prominent Americans were openly or unavowedly deistic. Free thought, somehow, went along with democratic opinions, and was a part of the liberal movement of the age. Paine was a man without reverence, imagination, or religious feeling. He was no scholar, and he was {379} not troubled by any perception of the deeper and subtler aspects of the questions which he touched. In his examination of the Old and New Testaments, he insisted that the Bible was an imposition and a forgery, full of lies, absurdities, and obscenities. Supernatural Christianity, with all its mysteries and miracles, was a fraud practiced by priests upon the people, and churches were instruments of oppression in the hands of tyrants. This way of accounting for Christianity would not now be accepted by even the most "advanced" thinkers. The contest between skepticism and revelation has long since shifted to other grounds. Both the philosophy and the temper of the *Age of Reason* belong to the eighteenth century. But Paine's downright pugnacious method of attack was effective with shrewd, half-educated doubters, and in America well-thumbed copies of his book passed from hand to hand in many a rural tavern or store, where the village atheist wrestled in debate with the deacon or the school-master. Paine rested his argument against Christianity upon the familiar grounds of the incredibility of miracles, the falsity of prophecy, the cruelty or immorality of Moses and David and other Old Testament worthies, the disagreement of the evangelists in their gospels, etc. The spirit of his book and his competence as a critic are illustrated by his saying of the New Testament: "Any person who could tell a story of an apparition, or of a man's walking, could have made such books, for the story is most wretchedly told. {380} The sum total of a parson's learning is a b, ab, and hic, haec, hoc, and this is more than sufficient to have enabled them, had they lived at the time, to have written all the books of the New Testament."

When we turn from the political and controversial writings of the Revolution to such lighter literature as existed, we find little that would deserve mention in a more crowded period. The few things in this kind that have kept afloat on the current of time—*rari nantes in gurgite vasto*—attract attention rather by reason of their fewness than of any special excellence that they have. During the eighteenth century American literature continued to accommodate itself to changes of caste in the old country. The so-called classical or Augustan writers of the reign of Queen Anne replaced other models of style: the *Spectator* set the fashion of almost all of our lighter prose, from Franklin's *Busybody* down to the time of Irving, who perpetuated the Addisonian tradition later than any English writer. The influence of Locke, of Dr. Johnson, and of the Parliamentary orators has already been mentioned. In poetry the example of Pope was dominant, so that we find, for example,

William Livingston, who became governor of New Jersey and a member of the Continental Congress, writing in 1747 a poem on *Philosophic Solitude* which reproduces the trick of Pope's antitheses and climaxes with the imagery of the *Rape of the Lock*, and the didactic morality of the *Imitations* from Horace and the *Moral Essays*:

{381}

"Let ardent heroes seek renown in arms,
Pant after fame and rush to war's alarms;
To shining palaces let fools resort
And dunces cringe to be esteemed at court.
Mine be the pleasure of a rural life,
From noise remote and ignorant of strife,
Far from the painted belle and white-gloved beau,
The lawless masquerade and midnight show;
From ladies, lap-dogs, courtiers, garters, stars,
Fops, fiddlers, tyrants, emperors, and czars."

The most popular poem of the Revolutionary period was John Trumbull's *McFingal*, published in part at Philadelphia in 1775, and in complete shape at Hartford in 1782. It went through more than thirty editions in America, and was several times reprinted in England. *McFingal* was a satire in four cantos, directed against the American Loyalists, and modeled quite closely upon Butler's mock heroic poem, *Hudibras*. As Butler's hero sallies forth to put down May games and bear-baitings, so the tory McFingal goes out against the liberty-poles and bon-fires of the patriots, but is tarred and feathered, and otherwise ill entreated, and finally takes refuge in the camp of General Gage at Boston. The poem is written with smartness and vivacity, attains often to drollery and sometimes to genuine humor. It remains one of the best of American political satires, and unquestionably the most successful of the many imitations of *Hudibras*, whose manner it follows so closely that some of its lines, which {382} have passed into currency as proverbs, are generally attributed to Butler. For example:

"No man e'er felt the halter draw
With good opinion of the law."

Or this:

"For any man with half an eye
What stands before him may espy;
But optics sharp it needs, I ween,
To see what is not to be seen."

Trumbull's wit did not spare the vulnerable points of his own countrymen, as in his sharp skit at slavery in the couplet about the newly adopted flag of the Confederation:

"Inscribed with inconsistent types
Of Liberty and thirteen stripes."

Trumbull was one of a group of Connecticut literati, who made much noise in their time as the "Hartford Wits." The other members of the group were Lemuel Hopkins, David Humphreys, Joel Barlow, Elihu Smith, Theodore Dwight, and Richard Alsop. Trumbull, Humphreys, and Barlow had formed a friendship and a kind of literary partnership at Yale, where they were contemporaries of each other and of Timothy Dwight. During the war they served in the army in various capacities, and at its close they found themselves again together for a few years at Hartford, where they formed a club that met weekly for social and literary purposes. Their presence lent a sort of {383} *éclat* to the little provincial capital, and their writings made it for a time an intellectual center quite as important as Boston or Philadelphia or New York. The Hartford Wits were staunch Federalists, and used their pens freely in support of the administrations of Washington and Adams, and in ridicule of Jefferson and the Democrats. In 1786-87 Trumbull, Hopkins, Barlow, and Humphreys published in the *New Haven Gazette* a series of satirical papers entitled the *Anarchiad,* suggested by the English *Rolliad,* and purporting to be extracts from an ancient epic on "the Restoration of Chaos and Substantial Night." These papers were an effort to correct, by ridicule, the anarchic condition of things which preceded the adoption of the Federal Constitution in 1789. It was a time of great confusion and discontent, when, in parts of the country, Democratic mobs were protesting against the vote of five years' pay by the Continental Congress to the officers of the American army. The *Anarchiad* was followed by the *Echo* and the *Political Green House,* written mostly by Alsop and Theodore Dwight, and similar in character and tendency to the earlier series. Time has greatly blunted the edge of these satires, but they were influential in their day, and are an important part of the literature of the old Federalist party.

Humphreys became afterward distinguished in the diplomatic service, and was, successively, embassador to Portugal and to Spain, whence he {384} introduced into America the breed of merino sheep. He had been on Washington's staff during the war, and was several times an inmate of his house at Mount Vernon, where he produced, in 1785, the best known of his writings, *Mount Vernon,* an ode of a rather mild description, which once had admirers. Joel Barlow cuts a larger figure in contemporary letters. After leaving Hartford, in 1788, he went to France, where he resided for seventeen years, made a fortune in speculations, and became imbued with French principles, writing a song in praise of the Guillotine, which gave great scandal to his old friends at home. In 1805 he returned to America, and built a fine residence near Washington, which he called Kalorama. Barlow's literary fame, in his own generation, rested upon his prodigious epic, the *Columbiad.* The first form of this was the *Vision of Columbus*, published at Hartford in 1787. This he afterward recast and enlarged into the *Columbiad*, issued in Philadelphia in 1807, and dedicated to Robert Fulton, the inventor of the steamboat. This was by far the most sumptuous piece of book-making that had then been published in America, and was embellished with plates executed by the best London engravers.

The *Columbiad* was a grandiose performance, and has been the theme of much ridicule by later writers. Hawthorne suggested its being dramatized, and put on to the accompaniment of artillery {385} and thunder and lightning; and E. P. Whipple declared that "no critic in the last fifty years had read more than a hundred lines of it." In its ambitiousness and its length it was symptomatic of the spirit of the age which was patriotically determined to create, by *tour de force*, a national literature of a size commensurate with the scale of American nature and the destinies of the republic. As America was bigger than Argos and Troy, we ought to have a bigger epic than the *Iliad.* Accordingly, Barlow makes Hesper fetch Columbus from his prison to a "hill of vision," where he unrolls before his eye a panorama of the history of America, or, as our bards then preferred to call it, Columbia. He shows him the conquest of Mexico by Cortez; the rise and fall of the kingdom of the Incas in Peru; the settlements of the English Colonies in North America; the old French and Indian Wars; the Revolution, ending with a prophecy of the future greatness of the new-born nation. The machinery of the *Vision* was borrowed from the 11th and 12th books of *Paradise Lost.* Barlow's verse was the ten-syllabled rhyming couplet of Pope, and his poetic style was distinguished by the vague, glittering imagery and the false sublimity which marked the epic attempts of the Queen Anne poets. Though Barlow was but a masquerader in true heroic, he showed himself a true poet in mock heroic. His *Hasty Pudding*, written in Savoy in 1793, and dedicated to Mrs. Washington, was thoroughly American, in subject at least, and its humor, though {386} over-elaborate, is good. One couplet in particular has prevailed against oblivion:

"E'en in thy native regions how I blush
To hear the Pennsylvanians call thee *Mush!*"

Another Connecticut poet—one of the seven who were fondly named "The Pleiads of Connecticut"—was Timothy Dwight, whose *Conquest of Canaan*, written shortly after his graduation from college, but not published till 1785, was, like the *Columbiad*, an experiment toward the domestication of the epic muse in America. It was written like Barlow's poem, in rhymed couplets, and the patriotic impulse of the time shows oddly in the introduction of our Revolutionary War, by way of episode, among the wars of Israel. *Greenfield Hill*, 1794, was an idyllic and moralizing poem, descriptive of a rural parish in Connecticut of which the author was for a time the pastor. It is not quite without merit; shows plainly the influence of Goldsmith, Thomson, and Beattie, but as a whole is tedious and tame. Byron was amused that there should have been an American poet christened Timothy, and it is to be feared that amusement would have been the chief emotion kindled in the breast of the wicked Voltaire had he ever chanced to see the stern dedication to himself of the same poet's *Triumph of Infidelity*, 1788. Much more important than Dwight's poetry was his able *Theology Explained and Defended*, 1794, a restatement, with modifications, of the Calvinism of Jonathan {387} Edwards, which was accepted by the Congregational churches of New England as an authoritative exponent of the orthodoxy of the time. His *Travels in New England and New York*, including descriptions of Niagara, the White Mountains, Lake George, the Catskills, and other passages of natural scenery, not so familiar then as now, was published posthumously in 1821, was praised by Southey, and is still readable. As President of Yale College from 1795 to 1817, Dwight, by his learning and ability, his sympathy with young men, and the force and dignity of his character, exerted a great influence in the community.

The strong political bias of the time drew into its vortex most of the miscellaneous literature that was produced. A number of ballads, serious and comic, Whig and Tory, dealing with the battles and other incidents of the long war, enjoyed a wide circulation in the newspapers, or were hawked about in printed broadsides. Most of these have no literary merit, and are now mere antiquarian curiosities. A favorite piece on the Tory side was the *Cow Chase*, a cleverish parody on *Chevy Chase*, written by the gallant and unfortunate Major Andre, at the expense of "Mad" Anthony Wayne. The national song *Yankee Doodle* was evolved during the Revolution, and, as is the case with *John Brown's Body* and many other popular melodies, some obscurity hangs about its origin. The air was an old one, and the words of the chorus seem to have been adapted or {388} corrupted from a Dutch song, and applied in derision to the Provincials by the soldiers of the British army as early as 1755. Like many another nickname, the term Yankee Doodle was taken up by the nicknamed and proudly made their own. The stanza,

"Yankee Doodle came to town," etc.,

antedates the war; but the first complete set of words to the tune was the

Yankee's Return from Camp, which is apparently of the year 1775. The most popular humorous ballad on the Whig side was the *Battle of the Kegs*, founded on a laughable incident of the campaign at Philadelphia. This was written by Francis Hopkinson, a Philadelphian, and one of the signers of the Declaration of Independence. Hopkinson has some title to rank as one of the earliest American humorists. Without the keen wit of *McFingal* some of his *Miscellaneous Essays and Occasional Writings*, published in 1792, have more geniality and heartiness than Trumbull's satire. His *Letter on Whitewashing* is a bit of domestic humor that foretokens the *Danbury News* man, and his *Modern Learning*, 1784, a burlesque on college examinations, in which a salt-box is described from the point of view of metaphysics, logic, natural philosophy, mathematics, anatomy, surgery and chemistry, long kept its place in school-readers and other collections. His son, Joseph Hopkinson, wrote the song of *Hail Columbia*, which is saved from insignificance only by the music to which it was married, {389} the then popular air of "The President's March." The words were written in 1798, on the eve of a threatened war with France, and at a time when party spirit ran high. It was sung nightly by crowds in the streets, and for a whole season by a favorite singer at the theater; for by this time there were theaters in Philadelphia, in New York, and even in Puritanic Boston. Much better than *Hail Columbia* was the *Star Spangled Banner*, the words of which were composed by Francis Scott Key, a Marylander, during the bombardment by the British of Fort McHenry, near Baltimore, in 1812. More pretentious than these was the once celebrated ode of Robert Treat Paine, Jr., *Adams and Liberty*, recited at an anniversary of the Massachusetts Charitable Fire Society. The sale of this is said to have netted its author over $750, but it is, notwithstanding, a very wooden performance. Paine was a young Harvard graduate, who had married an actress playing at the old Federal Street Theater, the first play-house opened in Boston, in 1794. His name was originally Thomas, but this was changed for him by the Massachusetts Legislature, because he did not wish to be confounded with the author of the *Age of Reason*. "Dim are those names erstwhile in battle loud," and many an old Revolutionary worthy who fought for liberty with sword and pen is now utterly forgotten, or consigned to the limbo of Duyckinck's *Cyclopedia* and Griswold's *Poets of America*. Here and there a line has, by accident, survived to do {390} duty as a motto or inscription, while all its context is buried in oblivion. Few have read any thing more of Jonathan M. Sewall's, for example, than the couplet,

"No pent-up Utica contracts your powers,
But the whole boundless continent is yours,"

taken from his *Epilogue to Cato*, written in 1778.

Another Revolutionary poet was Philip Freneau; "that rascal Freneau," as Washington called him, when annoyed by the attacks upon his administration in Freneau's *National Gazette*. He was of Huguenot descent, was a classmate of Madison at Princeton College, was taken prisoner by the British during the war, and when the war was over, engaged in journalism, as an ardent supporter of Jefferson and the Democrats. Freneau's patriotic verses and political lampoons are now unreadable; but he deserves to rank as the first real American poet, by virtue of his *Wild Honeysuckle, Indian Burying Ground, Indian Student*, and a few other little pieces, which exhibit a grace and delicacy inherited, perhaps, with his French blood.

Indeed, to speak strictly, all of the "poets" hitherto mentioned were nothing but rhymers but in Freneau we meet with something of beauty and artistic feeling; something which still keeps his verses fresh. In his treatment of Indian themes, in particular, appear for the first time a sense of the picturesque and poetic {391} elements in the character and wild life of the red man, and that pensive sentiment which the fading away of the tribes toward the sunset has left in the wake of their retreating footsteps. In this Freneau anticipates Cooper and Longfellow, though his work is slight compared with the *Leatherstocking Tales* or *Hiawatha*. At the time when the Revolutionary War broke out the population of the colonies was over three millions; Philadelphia had thirty thousand inhabitants, and the frontier had retired to a comfortable distance from the sea-board. The Indian had already grown legendary to town dwellers, and Freneau fetches his *Indian Student* not from the outskirts of the settlement, but from the remote backwoods of the State:

"From Susquehanna's farthest springs,
 Where savage tribes pursue their game
 (His blanket tied with yellow strings),
 A shepherd of the forest came."

Campbell "lifted"—in his poem *O'Conor's Child*—the last line of the following stanza from Freneau's *Indian Burying Ground*:

"By midnight moons, o'er moistening dews,
 In vestments for the chase arrayed,
 The hunter still the deer pursues—
 The hunter and the deer a shade."

And Walter Scott did Freneau the honor to borrow, in *Marmion*, the final line of one of the {392} stanzas of his poem on the battle of Eutaw Springs:

"They saw their injured country's woe,
 The flaming town, the wasted field;
 Then rushed to meet the insulting foe;

They took the spear, but left the shield."

Scott inquired of an American gentleman who wished him the authorship of this poem, which he had by heart, and pronounced it as fine a thing of the kind as there was in the language.

The American drama and American prose fiction had their beginnings during the period now under review. A company of English players came to this country in 1752 and made the tour of many of the principal towns. The first play acted here by professionals on a public stage was the *Merchant of Venice*, which was given by the English company at Williamsburg, Va., in 1752. The first regular theater building was at Annapolis, Md., where in the same year this troupe performed, among other pieces, Farquhar's *Beaux' Stratagem*. In 1753 a theater was built in New York, and one in 1759 in Philadelphia. The Quakers of Philadelphia and the Puritans of Boston were strenuously opposed to the acting of plays, and in the latter city the players were several times arrested during the performances, under a Massachusetts law forbidding dramatic performances. At Newport, R. I., on the other hand, which was a health resort for planters from the Southern States and the West Indies. {393} and the largest slave-market in the North, the actors were hospitably received. The first play known to have been written by an American was the *Prince of Parthia*, 1765, a closet drama, by Thomas Godfrey, of Philadelphia. The first play by an American writer, acted by professionals in a public theater, was Royal Tyler's *Contrast*, performed in New York in 1786. The former of these was very high tragedy, and the latter very low comedy; and neither of them is otherwise remarkable than as being the first of a long line of indifferent dramas. There is, in fact, no American dramatic literature worth speaking of; not a single American play of even the second rank, unless we except a few graceful parlor comedies, like Mr. Howell's *Elevator* and *Sleeping-Car*. Royal Tyler, the author of the *Contrast*, cut quite a figure in his day as a wit and journalist, and eventually became Chief Justice of Vermont. His comedy, the *Georgia Spec*, 1797, had a great run in Boston, and his *Algerine Captive*, published in the same year, was one of the earliest American novels. It was a rambling tale of adventure, constructed somewhat upon the plan of Smollett's novels and dealing with the piracies which led to the war between the United States and Algiers in 1815.

Charles Brockden Brown, the first American novelist of any note, was also the first professional man of letters in this country who supported himself entirely by his pen. He was born in {394} Philadelphia in 1771, lived a part of his life in New York and part in his native city, where he started, in 1803, the *Literary Magazine and American Register*. During the years 1798-1801 he published in rapid succession six romances, *Wieland, Ormond, Arthur*

Mervyn, *Edgar Huntley*, *Clara Howard*, and *Jane Talbot*. Brown was an invalid and something of a recluse, with a relish for the ghastly in incident and the morbid in character. He was in some points a prophecy of Poe and Hawthorne, though his art was greatly inferior to Poe's, and almost infinitely so to Hawthorne's. His books belong more properly to the contemporary school of fiction in England which preceded the "Waverley Novels"—to the class that includes Beckford's *Vathek*, Godwin's *Caleb Williams* and *St. Leon*, Mrs. Shelley's *Frankenstein*, and such "Gothic" romances as Lewis's *Monk*, Walpole's *Castle of Otranto*, and Mrs. Radcliffe's *Mysteries of Udolpho*. A distinguishing characteristic of this whole school is what we may call the clumsy-horrible. Brown's romances are not wanting in inventive power, in occasional situations that are intensely thrilling, and in subtle analysis of character; but they are fatally defective in art. The narrative is by turns abrupt and tiresomely prolix, proceeding not so much by dialogue as by elaborate dissection and discussion of motives and states of mind, interspersed with the author's reflections. The wild improbabilities of plot and the unnatural and even monstrous developments of character {395} are in startling contrast with the old-fashioned preciseness of the language; the conversations, when there are any, being conducted in that insipid dialect in which a fine woman was called an "elegant female." The following is a sample description of one of Brown's heroines, and is taken from his novel of *Ormond*, the leading character in which—a combination of unearthly intellect with fiendish wickedness—is thought to have been suggested by Aaron Burr: "Helena Cleves was endowed with every feminine and fascinating quality. Her features were modified by the most transient sentiments and were the seat of a softness at all times blushful and bewitching. All those graces of symmetry, smoothness and lustre, which assemble in the imagination of the painter when he calls from the bosom of her natal deep the Paphian divinity, blended their perfections in the shade, complexion, and hair of this lady." But, alas! "Helena's intellectual deficiencies could not be concealed. She was proficient in the elements of no science. The doctrine of lines and surfaces was as disproportionate with her intellects as with those of the mock-bird. She had not reasoned on the principles of human action, nor examined the structure of society.~.~.~. She could not commune in their native dialect with the sages of Rome and Athens.~.~.~. The constitution of nature, the attributes of its Author, the arrangement of the parts of the external universe, and the substance, modes of operation, and ultimate destiny of human {396} intelligence were enigmas unsolved and insoluble by her."

Brown frequently raises a superstructure of mystery on a basis ludicrously weak. Thus the hero of his first novel, *Wieland* (whose father anticipates "Old Krook," in Dickens's *Bleak House*, by dying of spontaneous combustion), is led on by what he mistakes for spiritual voices to kill his wife and children; and the voices turn out to be produced by the ventriloquism of one Carwin, the villain of the story. Similarly in *Edgar Huntley*, the plot turns upon the phenomena of sleep-walking. Brown had the good sense to place the scene of his romances in his own country, and the only passages in them which have now a living interest are his descriptions of wilderness scenery in *Edgar Huntley*, and his graphic account in *Arthur Mervyn* of the yellow-fever epidemic in Philadelphia in 1793. Shelley was an admirer of Brown, and his experiments in prose fiction, such as *Zastrozzi* and *St. Irvyne the Rosicrucian*, are of the same abnormal and speculative type.

Another book which falls within this period was the *Journal*, 1774, of John Woolman, a New Jersey Quaker, which has received the highest praise from Channing, Charles Lamb, and many others. "Get the writings of John Woolman by heart," wrote Lamb, "and love the early Quakers." The charm of this journal resides in its singular sweetness and innocence cf feeling, the "deep inward stillness" peculiar to the people called Quakers. {397} Apart from his constant use of certain phrases peculiar to the Friends, Woolman's English is also remarkably graceful and pure, the transparent medium of a soul absolutely sincere, and tender and humble in its sincerity. When not working at his trade as a tailor, Woolman spent his time in visiting and ministering to the monthly, quarterly, and yearly meetings of Friends, traveling on horseback to their scattered communities in the backwoods of Virginia and North Carolina, and northward along the coast as far as Boston and Nantucket. He was under a "concern" and a "heavy exercise" touching the keeping of slaves, and by his writing and speaking did much to influence the Quakers against slavery. His love went out, indeed, to all the wretched and oppressed; to sailors, and to the Indians in particular. One of his most perilous journeys was made to the settlements of Moravian Indians in the wilderness of Western Pennsylvania, at Bethlehem, and at Wehaloosing, on the Susquehanna. Some of the scruples which Woolman felt, and the quaint *naïveté* with which he expresses them, may make the modern reader smile— but it is a smile which is very close to a tear. Thus, when in England—where he died in 1772—he would not ride nor send a letter by mail-coach, because the poor post-boys were compelled to ride long stages in winter nights, and were sometimes frozen to death. "So great is the hurry in the spirit of this world, that in aiming to do business quickly and to gain wealth, {398} the creation at this day doth loudly groan." Again, having reflected that war was caused by luxury in dress, etc., the use of dyed garments grew uneasy to him, and he got and wore a hat of the natural color of the fur. "In attending meetings, this singularity was a trial to me~.~.~. and some Friends, who knew not from what motives I wore it, grew shy of me.~.~.~. Those who spoke with me I generally informed, in a few words, that I believed my wearing it was not in my own will."

1. Representative American Orations. Edited by Alexander Johnston. New York; G. P. Putnam's Sons. 1884.

2. The Federalist. New York: Charles Scribner. 1863.

3. Notes on Virginia. By Thomas Jefferson. Boston. 1829.

4. Travels in New England and New York. By Timothy Dwight. New Haven. 1821.

5. McFingal: in Trumbull's Poetical Works. Hartford: 1820.

6. Joel Barlow's *Hasty Pudding*. Francis Hopkinson's *Modern Learning*. Philip Freneau's *Indian Student, Indian Burying Ground*, and *White Honeysuckle*: in Vol. I. of Duyckinck's Cyclopedia of American Literature. New York: Charles Scribner. 1866.

7. Arthur Mervyn. By Charles Brockden Brown. Boston: S. G. Goodrich. 1827.

8. The Journal of John Woolman. With an {399} Introduction by John G. Whittier. Boston: James R. Osgood & Co. 1871.

9. American Literature. By Charles F. Richardson. New York: G.P. Putnam's Sons. 1887.

10. American Literature. By John Nichol. Edinburgh: Adam & Charles Black. 1882.

{400}

CHAPTER III.

THE ERA OF NATIONAL EXPANSION.

1815-1837.

The attempt to preserve a strictly chronological order must here be abandoned. About all the American literature in existence, that is of any value *as literature*, is the product of the past three quarters of a century, and the men who produced it, though older or younger, were still contemporaries. Irving's *Knickerbocker's History of New York*, 1809, was published within the recollection of some yet living, and the venerable poet, Richard H. Dana— Irving's junior by only four years—survived to 1879, when the youngest of the generation of writers that now occupy public attention had already won their spurs. Bryant, whose *Thanatopsis* was printed in 1816, lived down to

1878. He saw the beginnings of our national literature, and he saw almost as much of the latest phase of it as we see to-day in this year 1887. Still, even within the limits of a single life-time, there have been progress and change. And so, while it will happen that the consideration of writers a part of whose work falls between the dates at the head of this chapter may be postponed {401} to subsequent chapters, we may in a general way follow the sequence of time.

The period between the close of the second war with England, in 1815, and the great financial crash of 1837, has been called, in language attributed to President Monroe, "the era of good feeling." It was a time of peace and prosperity, of rapid growth in population and rapid extension of territory. The new nation was entering upon its vast estates and beginning to realize its manifest destiny. The peace with Great Britain, by calling off the Canadian Indians and the other tribes in alliance with England, had opened up the North-west to settlement. Ohio had been admitted as a State in 1802; but at the time of President Monroe's tour, in 1817, Cincinnati had only seven thousand inhabitants, and half of the State was unsettled. The Ohio River flowed for most of its course through an unbroken wilderness. Chicago was merely a fort. Hitherto the emigration to the West had been sporadic; now it took on the dimensions of a general and almost a concerted exodus. This movement was stimulated in New England by the cold summer of 1816 and the late spring of 1817, which produced a scarcity of food that amounted in parts of the interior to a veritable famine. All through this period sounded the axe of the pioneer clearing the forest about his log cabin, and the rumble of the canvas-covered emigrant wagon over the primitive highways which crossed the Alleghanies {402} or followed the valley of the Mohawk. S. G. Goodrich, known in letters as "Peter Parley," in his *Recollections of a Lifetime*, 1856, describes the part of the movement which he had witnessed as a boy in Fairfield County, Conn.: "I remember very well the tide of emigration through Connecticut, on its way to the West, during the summer of 1817. Some persons went in covered wagons—frequently a family consisting of father, mother, and nine small children, with one at the breast—some on foot, and some crowded together under the cover, with kettles, gridirons, feather beds, crockery, and the family Bible, Watts's Psalms and Hymns, and Webster's Spelling-book—the lares and penates of the household. Others started in ox-carts, and trudged on at the rate of ten miles a day.... Many of these persons were in a state of poverty, and begged their way as they went. Some died before they reached the expected Canaan; many perished after their arrival from fatigue and privation; and others from the fever and ague, which was then certain to attack the new settlers. It was, I think, in 1818 that I published a small tract entitled *'Tother Side of Oldo*—that is, the other view, in contrast to the popular notion that it was the paradise of the world. It was written by Dr. Hand—a talented young physician of Berlin—who had made a visit to the West about these days. It consisted mainly of vivid but painful pictures of the accidents and incidents attending this wholesale migration. The roads over the Alleghanies, {403} between Philadelphia and Pittsburg, were then rude, steep, and dangerous, and some of the more precipitous slopes were consequently strewn with the carcases of wagons, carts, horses, oxen, which had made shipwreck in their perilous descents."

But in spite of the hardships of the settler's life, the spirit of that time, as reflected in its writings, was a hopeful and a light-hearted one.

"Westward the course of empire takes its way,"

runs the famous line from Berkeley's poem on America. The New Englanders who removed to the Western Reserve went there to better themelves; and their children found themselves the owners of broad acres of virgin soil, in place of the stony hill pastures of Berkshire and Litchfield. There was an attraction, too, about the wild, free life of the frontiersman, with all its perils and discomforts. The life of Daniel Boone, the pioneer of Kentucky—that "dark and bloody ground"—is a genuine romance. Hardly less picturesque was the old river life of the Ohio boatmen, before the coming of steam banished their queer craft from the water. Between 1810 and 1840 the center of population in the United States had moved from the Potomac to the neighborhood of Clarksburg, in West Virginia, and the population itself had increased from seven to seventeen millions. The gain was made partly in the East and South, but the general drift was westward. During the years now under review, {404} the following new States were admitted, in the order named: Indiana, Mississippi, Illinois, Alabama, Maine, Missouri, Arkansas, Michigan. Kentucky and Tennessee had been made States in the last years of the eighteenth century, and Louisiana—acquired by purchase from France—in 1812.

The settlers, in their westward march, left large tracts of wilderness behind them. They took up first the rich bottom lands along the river courses, the Ohio and Miami and Licking, and later the valleys of the Mississippi and Missouri, and the shores of the great lakes. But there still remained back woods in New York and Pennsylvania, though the cities of New York and Philadelphia had each a population of more than one hundred thousand in 1815. When the Erie Canal was opened, in 1825, it ran through a primitive forest. N. P. Willis, who went by canal to Buffalo and Niagara in 1827, describes the houses and stores at Rochester as standing among the burnt stumps left by the first settlers. In the same year that saw the opening of this great water way, the Indian tribes, numbering now about one hundred and thirty thousand souls, were moved across the Mississippi. Their power had been broken by General Harrison's victory over Tecumseh at the battle of Tippecanoe, in 1811, and they were in fact mere remnants and fragments of the race which had hung upon the skirts of civilization, and disputed the advance of the white man for two centuries. It was not until some years later than this that railroads began {405} to take an important share in opening up new country.

The restless energy, the love of adventure, the sanguine anticipation which characterized American thought at this time, the picturesque contrasts to be seen in each mushroom town where civilization was encroaching on the raw edge of the wilderness—all these found expression, not only in such well-known books as Copper's *Pioneers*, 1823, and Irving's *Tour on the Prairies*, 1835, but in the minor literature which is read to-day, if at all, not for its own sake, but for the light that it throws on the history of national development: in such books as Paulding's story of *Westward Ho!* and his poem, *The Backwoodsman*, 1818; or as Timothy Flint's *Recollections*, 1826, and his *Geography and History of the Mississippi Valley*, 1827. It was not an age of great books, but it was an age of large ideas and expanding prospects. The new consciousness of empire uttered itself hastily, crudely, ran into buncombe, "spread-eagleism," and other noisy forms of patriotic exultation; but it was thoroughly democratic and American. Though literature—or at least the best literature of the time—was not yet emancipated from English models, thought and life, at any rate, were no longer in bondage—no longer provincial. And it is significant that the party in office during these years was the Democratic, the party which had broken most completely with conservative traditions. The famous "Monroe doctrine" was {406} a pronunciamento of this aggressive democracy, and though the Federalists returned to power for a single term, under John Quincy Adams (1825-1829,) Andrew Jackson received the largest number of electoral votes, and Adams was only chosen by the House of Representatives in the absence of a majority vote for any one candidate. At the close of his term "Old Hickory," the hero of the people, the most characteristically democratic of our Presidents, and the first backwoodsman who entered the White House, was borne into office on a wave of popular enthusiasm. We have now arrived at the time when American literature, in the higher and stricter sense of the term, really began to have an existence. S. G. Goodrich, who settled at Hartford as a bookseller and publisher in 1818, says, in his *Recollections*: "About this time I began to think of trying to bring out original American works.... . The general impression was that we had not, and could not have, a literature. It was the precise point at which Sidney Smith had uttered that bitter taunt in the *Edinburgh Review*, 'Who reads an American book?' ... It was positively injurious to the commercial credit of a bookseller to undertake American works." Washington Irving (1783-1859) was the first American author whose books, as *books*, obtained recognition abroad; whose name was thought worthy of mention beside the names of English contemporary authors, like Byron, Scott, and Coleridge. He was also the first American writer whose writings are still read {407} for their own sake. We read Mather's *Magnalia*, and Franklin's *Autobiography*, and Trumbull's *McFingal*—if we read them at all—as history, and to learn about the times or the men. But we read the *Sketch Book*, and *Knickerbocker's History of New York*, and the *Conquest of Granada* for themselves, and for the pleasure that they give as pieces of literary art.

We have arrived, too, at a time when we may apply a more cosmopolitan standard to the works of American writers, and may disregard many a minor author whose productions would have cut some figure had they come to light amid the poverty of our colonial age. Hundreds of these forgotten names, with specimens of their unread writings, are consigned to a limbo of immortality in the pages of Duyckinck's *Cyclopedia*, and of Griswold's *Poets of America* and *Prose Writers of America*. We may select here for special mention, and as most representative of the thought of their time, the names of Irving, Cooper, Webster, and Channing.

A generation was now coming upon the stage who could recall no other government in this country than the government of the United States, and to whom the Revolutionary War was but a tradition. Born in the very year of the peace, it was a part of Irving's mission, by the sympathetic charm of his writings and by the cordial recognition which he won in both countries, to allay the soreness which the second war, of 1812-15, had left between England and America. He was {408} well fitted for the task of mediator. Conservative by nature, early drawn to the venerable worship of the Episcopal Church, retrospective in his tastes, with a preference for the past and its historic associations which, even in young America, led him to invest the Hudson and the region about New York with a legendary interest, he wrote of American themes in an English fashion, and interpreted to an American public the mellow attractiveness that he found in the life and scenery of Old England. He lived in both countries, and loved them both; and it is hard to say whether Irving is more of an English or of an American writer. His first visit to Europe, in 1804-6, occupied nearly two years. From 1815 to 1832 he was abroad continuously, and his "domicile," as the lawyers say, during these seventeen years was really in England, though a portion of his time was spent upon the continent, and several successive years in Spain, where he engaged upon the *Life of Columbus*, the *Conquest of Granada*, the *Companions of Columbus*, and the *Alhambra*, all published between 1828-32. From 1842 to 1846 he was again in Spain as American Minister at Madrid.

Irving was the last and greatest of the Addisonians. His boyish letters, signed "Jonathan Oldstyle," contributed in 1802 to his brother's newspaper, the *Morning Chronicle*, were, like Franklin's *Busybody*, close imitations of the *Spectator*. To the same family belonged his *Salmagundi* papers, 1807, a series of town-satires on New York society, written {409} in conjunction with his brother William and with James K. Paulding. The little tales, essays, and sketches which compose the *Sketch Book* were written in England, and published in America, in periodical numbers, in 1819-20. In this, which is in some respects his best book, he still maintained that attitude of observation and spectatorship taught him by Addison. The volume had a motto taken from Burton, "I have no wife nor children, good or bad, to provide for—a mere spectator of other men's fortunes," etc.; and "The Author's Account of Himself" began in true Addisonian fashion: "I was always fond of visiting new scenes and observing strange characters and manners."

But though never violently "American," like some later writers who have consciously sought to throw off the trammels of English tradition, Irving was in a real way original. His most distinct addition to our national literature was in his creation of what has been called "the Knickerbocker legend." He was the first to make use, for literary purposes, of the old Dutch traditions which clustered about the romantic scenery of the Hudson. Col. T. W. Higginson, in his *History of the United States*, tells how "Mrs. Josiah Quincy, sailing up that river in 1786, when Irving was a child three years old, records that the captain of the sloop had a legend, either supernatural or traditional, for every scene, and not a mountain reared its head unconnected with some marvelous {410} story.'" The material thus at hand Irving shaped into his *Knickerbocker's History of New York*, into the immortal story of *Rip Van Winkle*, and the *Legend of Sleepy Hollow* (both published in the *Sketch Book*), and in later additions to the same realm of fiction, such as Dolph Heyliger in *Bracebridge Hall*, the *Money Diggers*, *Wolfert Webber*, and *Kidd the Pirate*, in the *Tales of a Traveler*, and in some of the miscellanies from the *Knickerbocker Magazine*, collected into a volume, in 1855, under the title of *Wolfert's Roost*.

The book which made Irving's reputation was his *Knickerbocker's History of New York*, 1809, a burlesque chronicle, making fun of the old Dutch settlers of New Amsterdam, and attributed, by a familiar and now somewhat threadbare device,[1] to a little old gentleman named Diedrich Knickerbocker, whose manuscript had come into the editor's hands. The book was gravely dedicated to the New York Historical Society, and it is said to have been quoted, as authentic history, by a certain German scholar named Goeller, in a note on a passage in Thucydides. This story, though well vouched, is hard of belief: for *Knickerbocker*, though excellent fooling, has nothing of the grave irony of Swift in his *Modest Proposal* or of Defoe in his *Short Way with*

Dissenters. Its mock-heroic intention is as transparent as in Fielding's parodies of Homer, which it somewhat resembles, {411} particularly in the delightfully absurd description of the mustering of the clans under Peter Stuyvesant and the attack on the Swedish Fort Christina. *Knickerbocker's History of New York* was a real addition to the comic literature of the world; a work of genuine humor, original and vital. Walter Scott said that it reminded him closely of Swift, and had touches resembling Sterne. It is not necessary to claim for Irving's little masterpiece a place beside *Gulliver's Travels* and *Tristram Shandy.* But it was, at least, the first American book in the lighter departments of literature which needed no apology and stood squarely on its own legs. It was written, too, at just the right time. Although New Amsterdam had become New York as early as 1664, the impress of its first settlers, with their quaint conservative ways, was still upon it when Irving was a boy. The descendants of the Dutch families formed a definite element not only in Manhattan, but all up along the kills of the Hudson, at Albany, at Schenectady, in Westchester County, at Hoboken, and Communipaw, localities made familiar to him in many a ramble and excursion. He lived to see the little provincial town of his birth grow into a great metropolis, in which all national characteristics were blended together, and a tide of immigration from Europe and New England flowed over the old landmarks and obliterated them utterly.

Although Irving was the first to reveal to his countrymen the literary possibilities of their early {412} history, it must be acknowledged that with modern American life he had little sympathy. He hated politics, and in the restless democratic movement of the time, as we have described it, he found no inspiration. This moderate and placid gentleman, with his distrust of all kinds of fanaticism, had no liking for the Puritans or for their descendants, the New England Yankees, if we may judge from his sketch of Ichabod Crane, in the *Legend of Sleepy Hollow.* His genius was reminiscent, and his imagination, like Scott's, was the historic imagination. In crude America his fancy took refuge in the picturesque aspects of the past, in "survivals" like the Knickerbocker Dutch and the Acadian peasants, whose isolated communities on the lower Mississippi he visited and described. He turned naturally to the ripe civilization of the Old World. He was our first picturesque tourist, the first "American in Europe." He rediscovered England, whose ancient churches, quiet landscapes, memory-haunted cities, Christmas celebrations, and rural festivals had for him an unfailing attraction. With pictures of these, for the most part, he filled the pages of the *Sketch Book* and *Bracebridge Hall,* 1822. Delightful as are these English sketches, in which the author conducts his readers to Windsor Castle, or Stratford-on-Avon, or the Boar's Head Tavern, or sits beside him on the box of the old English stage-coach, or shares with him the Yuletide cheer at the ancient English country house, their interest has somewhat faded. {413} The pathos of the *Broken Heart* and the *Pride of the Village*, the mild satire of the *Art of Book Making*, the rather obvious reflections in *Westminster Abbey* are not exactly to the taste of this generation. They are the literature of leisure and retrospection; and already Irving's gentle elaboration, the refined and slightly artificial beauty of his style, and his persistently genial and sympathetic attitude have begun to pall upon readers who demand a more nervous and accented kind of writing. It is felt that a little roughness, a little harshness, even, would give relief to his pictures of life. There is, for instance, something a little irritating in the old-fashioned courtliness of his manner toward women; and one reads with a certain impatience smoothly punctuated passages like the following: "As the vine, which has long twined its graceful foliage about the oak, and been lifted by it into sunshine, will, when the hardy plant is rifted by the thunderbolt, cling round it with its caressing tendrils, and bind up its shattered boughs, so is it beautifully ordered by Providence that woman, who is the mere dependent and ornament of man in his happier hours, should be his stay and solace when smitten with sudden calamity; winding herself into the rugged recesses of his nature, tenderly supporting the drooping head, and binding up the broken heart."

Irving's gifts were sentiment and humor, with an imagination sufficiently fertile, and an observation sufficiently acute to support those two main {414} qualities, but inadequate to the service of strong passion or subtle thinking, though his pathos, indeed, sometimes reached intensity. His humor was always delicate and kindly; his sentiment never degenerated into sentimentality. His diction was graceful and elegant—too elegant, perhaps; and in his modesty he attributed the success of his books in England to the astonishment of Englishmen that an American could write good English.

In Spanish history and legend Irving found a still newer and richer field for his fancy to work upon. He had not the analytic and philosophical mind of a great historian, and the merits of his *Conquest of Granada* and *Life of Columbus* are rather *belletristisch* than scientific. But he brought to these undertakings the same eager love of the romantic past which had determined the character of his writings in America and England, and the result—whether we call it history or romance—is at all events charming as literature. His *Life of Washington*—completed in 1859—was his *magnum opus*, and is accepted as standard authority. *Mahomet and His Successors*, 1850, was comparatively a failure. But of all Irving's biographies, his *Life of Oliver Goldsmith*, 1849, was the most spontaneous and perhaps the best. He did not impose it upon himself as a task, but wrote it from a native and loving sympathy with his subject, and it is, therefore, one of the choicest literary memoirs in the language.

{415}

When Irving returned to America, in 1832, he was the recipient of almost national honors. He had received the medal of the Royal Society of Literature and the degree of D.C.L. from Oxford University, and had made American literature known and respected abroad. In his modest home at Sunnyside, on the banks of the river over which he had been the first to throw the witchery of poetry and romance, he was attended to the last by the admiring affection of his countrymen. He had the love and praises of the foremost English writers of his own generation and the generation which followed—of Scott, Byron, Coleridge, Thackeray, and Dickens, some of whom had been among his personal friends. He is not the greatest of American authors, but the influence of his writings is sweet and wholesome, and it is in many ways fortunate that the first American man of letters who made himself heard in Europe should have been in all particulars a gentleman.

Connected with Irving, at least by name and locality, were a number of authors who resided in the city of New York and who are known as the Knickerbocker writers, perhaps because they were contributors to the *Knickerbocker Magazine*. One of these was James K. Paulding, a connection of Irving by marriage, and his partner in the *Salmagundi Papers*. Paulding became Secretary of the Navy under Van Buren, and lived down to the year 1860. He was a {416} voluminous author, but his writings had no power of continuance, and are already obsolete, with the possible exception of his novel, the *Dutchman's Fireside*, 1831.

A finer spirit than Paulding was Joseph Rodman Drake, a young poet of great promise, who died in 1820, at the age of twenty-five. Drake's patriotic lyric, the *American Flag*, is certainly the most spirited thing of the kind in our poetic literature, and greatly superior to such national anthems as *Hail Columbia* and the *Star Spangled Banner*. His *Culprit Fay*, published in 1819, was the best poem that had yet appeared in America, if we except Bryant's *Thanatopsis*, which was three years the elder. The *Culprit Fay* was a fairy story, in which, following Irving's lead, Drake undertook to throw the glamour of poetry about the Highlands of the Hudson. Edgar Poe said that the poem was fanciful rather than imaginative; but it is prettily and even brilliantly fanciful, and has maintained its popularity to the present time. Such verse as the following—which seems to show that Drake had been reading Coleridge's *Christabel*, published three years before—was something new in American poetry:

"The winds are whist and the owl is still,
The bat in the shelvy rock is hid,

And naught is heard on the lonely hill,
But the cricket's chirp and the answer shrill,
   Of the gauze-winged katydid,
And the plaint of the wailing whip-poor-will
{417}
   Who moans unseen, and ceaseless sings
Ever a note of wail and woe,
   Till morning spreads her rosy wings,
And earth and sky in her glances glow."

Here we have, at last, the whip-poor-will, an American bird, and not the conventional lark or nightingale, although the elves of the Old World seem scarcely at home on the banks of the Hudson. Drake's memory has been kept fresh not only by his own poetry, but by the beautiful elegy written by his friend Fitz-Greene Halleck, the first stanza of which is universally known:

"Green be the turf above thee,
   Friend of my better days;
None knew thee but to love thee,
   Nor named thee but to praise."

Halleck was born in Guilford, Connecticut, whither he retired in 1849, and resided there till his death in 1867. But his literary career is identified with New York. He was associated with Drake in writing the *Croaker Papers*, a series of humorous and satirical verses contributed in 1814 to the *Evening Post*. These were of a merely local and temporary interest; but Halleck's fine ode, *Marco Bozzaris*—though declaimed until it has become hackneyed—gives him a sure title to a remembrance; and his *Alnwick Castle*, a monody, half serious and half playful on the contrasts between feudal associations and modern life, has {418} much of that pensive lightness which characterizes Praed's best *vers de societé*.

A friend of Drake and Halleck was James Fenimore Cooper (1789-1851), the first American novelist of distinction, and, if a popularity which has endured for nearly three quarters of a century is any test, still the most successful of all American novelists. Cooper was far more intensely American than Irving, and his books reached an even wider public. "They are published as soon as he produces them," said Morse, the electrician, in 1833, "in thirty-four different places in Europe. They have been seen by American travelers in the languages of Turkey and Persia, in Constantinople, in Egypt, at Jerusalem, at Ispahan." Cooper wrote altogether too much; he published, besides his fictions, a *Naval History of the United States*, a series of naval biographies, works of travel, and a great deal of controversial matter. He wrote over thirty novels, the greater part of which are little better than trash, and tedious trash at that. This is especially true of his *tendenz* novels and his novels of society. He was a man of strongly marked individuality, fiery, pugnacious, sensitive to criticism, and abounding in prejudices. He was embittered by the scurrilous attacks made upon him by a portion of the American press, and spent a great deal of time and energy in conducting libel suits against the newspapers. In the same spirit he used fiction as a vehicle for attack upon the abuses and follies of American life. Nearly all of {419} his novels, written with this design, are worthless. Nor was Cooper well equipped by nature and temperament for depicting character and passion in social life. Even in his best romances his heroines and his "leading juveniles"—to borrow a term from the amateur stage—are insipid and conventional. He was no satirist, and his humor was not of a high order. He was a rapid and uneven writer, and, unlike Irving, he had no style.

Where Cooper was great was in the story, in the invention of incidents and plots, in a power of narrative and description in tales of wild adventure which keeps the reader in breathless excitement to the end of the book. He originated the novel of the sea and the novel of the wilderness. He created the Indian of literature; and in this, his peculiar field, although he has had countless imitators, he has had no equals. Cooper's experiences had prepared him well for the kingship of this new realm in the world of fiction. His childhood was passed on the borders of Otsego Lake, when central New York was still a wilderness, with boundless forests stretching westward, broken only here and there by the clearings of the pioneers. He was taken from college (Yale) when still a lad, and sent to sea in a merchant vessel, before the mast. Afterward he entered the navy and did duty on the high seas and upon Lake Ontario, then surrounded by virgin forests. He married and resigned his commission in 1811, just before the outbreak of the war with England, so {420} that he missed the opportunity of seeing active service in any of those engagements on the ocean and our great lakes which were so glorious to American arms. But he always retained an active interest in naval affairs.

His first successful novel was *The Spy*, 1821, a tale of the Revolutionary War, the scene of which was laid in Westchester County, N. Y., where the author was then residing. The hero of this story, Harvey Birch, was one of the most skillfully drawn figures on his canvas. In 1823 he published the *Pioneers*, a work somewhat overladen with description, in which he drew for material upon his boyish recollections of frontier life at Cooperstown. This was the first of the series of five romances known as the *Leatherstocking Tales*. The others were the *Last of the Mohicans*, 1826; the *Prairie*, 1827; the *Pathfinder*, 1840; and the *Deerslayer*, 1841. The hero of this series, Natty Bumpo, or "Leatherstocking," was Cooper's one great creation in the sphere of character, his most original addition to the literature of the world in the way of a new human type. This backwoods philosopher—to the conception of whom the historic exploits of Daniel Boone perhaps supplied some hints; unschooled, but moved by noble impulses and a natural sense of piety and justice; passionately attached to the wilderness, and following its westering edge even unto the prairies—this man of the woods was the first real American in fiction. Hardly less individual and vital {421} were the various types of Indian character, in Chingachgook, Uncas, Hist, and the Huron warriors. Inferior to these, but still vigorously though somewhat roughly drawn, were the waifs and strays of civilization, whom duty, or the hope of gain, or the love of adventure, or the outlawry of crime had driven to the wilderness—the solitary trapper, the reckless young frontiersman, the officers and men of out-post garrisons. Whether Cooper's Indian was the real being, or an idealized and rather melo-dramatic version of the truth, has been a subject of dispute. However this be, he has taken his place in the domain of art, and it is safe to say that his standing there is secure. No boy will ever give him up.

Equally good with the *Leatherstocking* novels, and especially national, were Cooper's tales of the sea, or at least the two best of them—the *Pilot*, 1823, founded upon the daring exploits of John Paul Jones, and the *Red Rover*, 1828. But here, though Cooper still holds the sea, he has had to admit competitors; and Britannia, who rules the waves in song, has put in some claim to a share in the domain of nautical fiction in the persons of Mr. W. Clarke Russell and others. Though Cooper's novels do not meet the deeper needs of the heart and the imagination, their appeal to the universal love of a story is perennial. We devour them when we are boys, and if we do not often return to them when we are men, that is perhaps only because we have read them before, and "know the {422} ending." They are good yarns for the forecastle and the camp-fire; and the scholar in his study, though he may put the *Deerslayer* or the *Last of the Mohicans* away on the top-shelf, will take it down now and again, and sit up half the night over it.

Before dismissing the *belles-lettres* writings of this period, mention should be made of a few poems of the fugitive kind which seem to have taken a permanent place in popular regard. John Howard Payne, a native of Long Island, a wandering actor and playwright, who died American Consul at Tunis in 1852, wrote about 1820 for Covent Garden Theater an opera, entitled *Clari*, the libretto of which included the now famous song of *Home, Sweet Home*. Its literary pretensions were of the humblest kind, but it spoke a true word which touched the Anglo-Saxon heart in its tenderest spot, and being happily married to a plaintive air was sold by the hundred thousand, and is evidently destined to be sung forever. A like success has attended the *Old Oaken Bucket*, composed by Samuel Woodworth, a printer and journalist from Massachusetts, whose other poems, of which two collections were issued in 1818 and 1826, were soon forgotten. Richard Henry Wilde, an Irishman by birth, a gentleman of scholarly tastes and accomplishments, who wrote a great deal on Italian literature, and sat for several terms in Congress as Representative of the State of Georgia, was the author of the favorite song, *My Life is Like the Summer Rose*. Another {423} Southerner, and a member of a distinguished Southern family, was Edward Coate Pinkney, who served nine years in the navy, and died in 1828, at the age of twenty-six, having published in 1825 a small volume of lyrical poems which had a fire and a grace uncommon at that time in American verse. One of these, *A Health*, beginning

"I fill this cup to one made up of loveliness alone,"

though perhaps somewhat overpraised by Edgar Poe, has rare beauty of thought and expression. John Quincy Adams, sixth President of the United States (1825-29), was a man of culture and of literary tastes. He published his lectures on rhetoric delivered during his tenure of the Boylston Professorship at Harvard in 1806-09; he left a voluminous diary, which has been edited since his death in 1848; and among his experiments in poetry is one of considerable merit, entitled the *Wants of Man*, an ironical sermon on Goldsmith's text:

"Man wants but little here below
Nor wants that little long."

As this poem is a curiously close anticipation of Dr. Holmes's *Contentment*, so the very popular ballad, *Old Grimes*, written about 1818, by Albert Gorton Greene, an undergraduate of Brown University in Rhode Island, is in some respects an anticipation of Holmes's quaintly pathetic *Last Leaf*.

The political literature and public oratory of {424} the United States during this period, although not absolutely of less importance than that which preceded and followed the Declaration of Independence and the adoption of the Constitution, demands less relative attention in a history of literature by reason of the growth of other departments of thought. The age was a political one, but no longer exclusively political. The debates of the time centered about the question of "State Rights," and the main forum of discussion was the old Senate chamber, then made illustrious by the presence of Clay, Webster, and Calhoun. The slavery question, which had threatened trouble, was put off for awhile by the Missouri Compromise of 1820, only to break out more fiercely in the debates on the Wilmot Proviso, and the Kansas and Nebraska Bill. Meanwhile the Abolition movement had been transferred to the press and the platform. Garrison started his *Liberator* in 1830, and the Antislavery Society was founded in 1833. The Whig party, which had inherited the constitutional principles of the old Federal party, advocated internal improvements at national expense and a high protective tariff. The State Rights party, which was strongest at the South, opposed these views, and in 1832 South Carolina claimed the right to "nullify" the tariff imposed by the general government. The leader of this party was John Caldwell Calhoun, a South Carolinian, who in his speech in the United States Senate, on February 13, 1832, on Nullification and the {425} Force Bill, set forth most authoritatively the "Carolina doctrine." Calhoun was a great debater, but hardly a great orator. His speeches are the arguments of a lawyer and a strict constitutionalist, severely logical, and with a sincere conviction in the soundness of his case. Their language is free from bad rhetoric; the reasoning is cogent, but there is an absence of emotion and imagination; they contain few quotable things, and no passages of commanding eloquence, such as strew the orations of Webster and Burke. They are not, in short, literature. Again, the speeches of Henry Clay, of Kentucky, the leader of the Whigs, whose persuasive oratory is a matter of tradition, disappoint in the reading. The fire has gone out of them.

Not so with Daniel Webster, the greatest of American forensic orators, if, indeed, he be not the greatest of all orators who have used the English tongue. Webster's speeches are of the kind that have power to move after the voice of the speaker is still. The thought and the passion in them lay hold on feelings of patriotism more lasting than the issues of the moment. It is, indeed, true of Webster's speeches, as of all speeches, that they are known to posterity more by single brilliant passages than as wholes. In oratory the occasion is of the essence of the thing, and only those parts of an address which are permanent and universal in their appeal take their place in literature. But of such detachable passages there are happily {426} many in Webster's orations. One great thought underlay all his public life, the thought of the Union; of American nationality. What in Hamilton had been a principle of political philosophy had become in Webster a passionate conviction. The Union was his idol, and he was intolerant of any faction which threatened it from any quarter, whether the Nullifiers of South Carolina or the Abolitionists of the North. It is this thought which gives grandeur and elevation to all his utterances, and especially to the wonderful peroration of his reply to Hayne, on Mr. Foot's resolution touching the sale of the public lands, delivered in the Senate on January 26, 1830, whose closing words, "liberty and union, now and forever, one and inseparable," became the rallying cry of a great cause. Similar in sentiment was his famous speech of March 7, 1850, *On the Constitution and the Union*, which gave so much offense to the extreme Antislavery party, who held with Garrison that a Constitution which protected slavery was "a league with death and a covenant with hell." It is not claiming too much for Webster to assert that the sentences of these and other speeches, memorized and declaimed by thousands of school-boys throughout the North, did as much as any single influence to train up a generation in hatred of secession, and to send into the fields of the civil war armies of men animated with the stern resolution to fight till the last drop of blood was shed, rather than allow the Union to be dissolved.

{427}

The figure of this great senator is one of the most imposing in American annals. The masculine force of his personality impressed itself upon men of a very different stamp—upon the unworldly Emerson, and upon the captious Carlyle, whose respect was not willingly accorded to any contemporary, much less to a representative of American democracy. Webster's looks and manner were characteristic. His form was massive, his skull and jaw solid, the underlip projecting, and the mouth firmly and grimly shut; his complexion was swarthy, and his black, deep set eyes, under shaggy brows, glowed with a smoldering fire. He was rather silent in society; his delivery in debate was grave and weighty, rather than fervid. His oratory was massive and sometimes even ponderous. It may be questioned whether an American orator of to-day, with intellectual abilities equal to Webster's—if such a one there were—would permit himself the use of sonorous and elaborate pictures like the famous period which follows: "On this question of principle, while actual suffering was yet afar off, they raised their flag against a power, to which, for purposes of foreign conquest and subjugation, Rome, in the height of her glory, is not to be compared; a power which has dotted over the surface of the whole globe with her possessions and military posts, whose morning drum-beat, following the sun and keeping company with the hours, circles the earth with one continuous and unbroken strain of the {428} martial airs of England." The secret of this kind of oratory has been lost. The present generation distrusts rhetorical ornament, and likes something swifter, simpler, and more familiar in its speakers. But every thing, in declamation of this sort, depends on the way in which it is done. Webster did it supremely well; a smaller man would merely have made buncombe of it.

Among the legal orators of the time the foremost was Rufus Choate, an eloquent pleader, and, like Webster, a United States Senator from Massachusetts. Some of his speeches, though excessively rhetorical, have literary quality, and are nearly as effective in print as Webster's own. Another Massachusetts orator, Edward Everett, who in his time was successively professor in Harvard College, Unitarian minister in Boston, editor of the *North American Review*, member of both houses of Congress, Minister to England, Governor of his State, and President of Harvard, was a speaker of great finish and elegance. His addresses were mainly of the memorial and anniversary kind, and were rather lectures and Ph. B. K. prolusions than speeches. Everett was an instance of careful culture bestowed on a soil of no very great natural richness. It is doubtful whether his classical orations on Washington, the Republic, Bunker Hill Monument, and kindred themes, have enough of the breath of life in them to preserve them much longer in recollection.

New England, during these years, did not take {429} that leading part in the purely literary development of the country which it afterward assumed. It had no names to match against those of Irving and Cooper. Drake and Halleck—slender as was their performance in point of quantity—were better poets than the Boston bards, Charles Sprague, whose *Shakespere Ode*, delivered at the Boston theater in 1823, was locally famous; and Richard Henry Dana, whose longish narrative poem, the *Buccaneer*, 1827, once had admirers. But Boston has at no time been without a serious intellectual life of its own, nor without a circle of highly educated men of literary pursuits, even in default of great geniuses. The *North American Review*, established in 1815, though it has been wittily described as "ponderously revolving through space" for a few years after its foundation, did not exist in an absolute vacuum, but was scholarly, if somewhat heavy. Webster, to be sure, was a Massachusetts man —as were Everett and Choate—but his triumphs were won in the wider field of national politics. There was, however, a movement at this time in the intellectual life of Boston and Eastern Massachusetts, which, though not immediately contributory to the finer kinds of literature, prepared the way, by its clarifying and stimulating influences, for the eminent writers of the next generation. This was the Unitarian revolt against Puritan orthodoxy, in which William Ellery Channing was the principal leader. In a community so intensely theological as New England it was natural that any {430} new movement in thought should find its point of departure in the churches. Accordingly, the progressive and democratic spirit of the age, which in other parts of the country took other shapes, assumed in Massachusetts the form of "liberal Christianity." Arminianism, Socinianism, and other phases of anti-Trinitarian doctrine, had been latent in some of the Congregational churches of Massachusetts for a number of years. But about 1812 the heresy broke out openly, and within a few years from that date most of the oldest and wealthiest church societies of Boston and its vicinity had gone over to Unitarianism, and Harvard College had been captured, too. In the controversy that ensued, and which was carried on in numerous books, pamphlets, sermons, and periodicals, there were eminent disputants on both sides. So far as this controversy was concerned with the theological doctrine of the Trinity, it has no place in a history of literature. But the issue went far beyond that. Channing asserted the dignity of human nature against the Calvinistic doctrine of innate depravity, and affirmed the rights of human reason and man's capacity to judge of God. "We must start in religion from our own souls," he said. And in his *Moral Argument against Calvinism*, 1820, he wrote: "Nothing is gained to piety by degrading human nature, for in the competency of this nature to know and judge of God all piety has its foundation." In opposition to Edwards's doctrine of necessity, he emphasized {431} the freedom of the will. He maintained that the Calvinistic dogmas of original sin, foreordination, election by grace, and eternal punishment were inconsistent with the divine perfection, and made God a monster. In Channing's view the great sanction of religious truth is the moral sanction, is its agreement with the laws of conscience. He was a passionate vindicator of the liberty of the individual not only as against political oppression but against the tyranny of public opinion over thought and conscience: "We were made for free action. This alone is life, and enters into all that is good and great." This jealous love of freedom inspired all that he did and wrote. It led him to join the Antislavery party. It expressed itself in his elaborate arraignment of Napoleon in the Unitarian organ, the *Christian Examiner*, for 1827-28; in his *Remarks on Associations*, and his paper *On the Character and Writings of John Milton*, 1826. This was his most considerable contribution to literary criticism. It took for a text Milton's recently discovered *Treatise on Christian Doctrine*—the tendency of which was anti-Trinitarian—but it began with a general defense of poetry against "those who are accustomed to speak of poetry as light reading." This would now seem a somewhat superfluous introduction to an article in any American review. But it shows the nature of the milieu through which the liberal movement in Boston had to make its way. To re-assert the dignity and usefulness of the beautiful arts was, {432} perhaps, the chief service which the Massachusetts Unitarians rendered to humanism. The traditional prejudice of the Puritans against the ornamental side of life had to be softened before polite literature could find a congenial atmosphere in New England. In Channing's *Remarks on National Literature*, reviewing a work published in 1823, he asks the question, "Do we possess what may be called a national literature?" and answers it, by implication at least, in the negative. That we do now possess a national literature is in great part due to the influence of Channing and his associates, although his own writings, being in the main controversial and, therefore, of temporary interest, may not themselves take rank among the permanent treasures of that literature.

1. Washington Irving. Knickerbocker's History of New York. The Sketch Book. Bracebridge Hall. Tales of a Traveler. The Alhambra. Life of Oliver Goldsmith.

2. James Fenimore Cooper. The Spy. The Pilot. The Red Rover. The Leather-Stocking Tales.

3. Daniel Webster. Great Speeches and Orations. Boston: Little, Brown, & Co. 1879.

4. William Ellery Channing. The Character and Writings of John Milton. The Life and Character of Napoleon Bonaparte. Slavery. [Vols. I. and II. of the Works of William E. Channing. Boston: James Munroe & Co. 1841.]

{433}

5. Joseph Rodman Drake. The Culprit Fay. The American Flag. [Selected Poems. New York. 1835.]

6. Fitz-Greene Halleck. Marco Bozzaris. Alnwick Castle. On the Death of Drake. [Poems. New York. 1827.]

[1] Compare Carlyle's Herr Diogenes Teufelsdröckh, in *Sartor Resartus,* the

author of the famous "Clothes Philosophy."

{434}

CHAPTER IV.

THE CONCORD WRITERS.

1837-1861.

There has been but one movement in the history of the American mind which has given to literature a group of writers having coherence enough to merit the name of a school. This was the great humanitarian movement, or series of movements, in New England, which, beginning in the Unitarianism of Channing, ran through its later phase in Transcendentalism, and spent its last strength in the antislavery agitation and the enthusiasms of the Civil War. The second stage of this intellectual and social revolt was Transcendentalism, of which Emerson wrote, in 1842: "The history of genius and of religion in these times will be the history of this tendency." It culminated about 1840-41 in the establishment of the *Dial* and the Brook Farm Community, although Emerson had given the signal a few years before in his little volume entitled *Nature*, 1836, his Phi-Beta Kappa address at Harvard on the *American Scholar*, 1837, and his address in 1838 before the Divinity School at Cambridge. Ralph Waldo Emerson (1803-1882) was the prophet of the sect, and {435} Concord was its Mecca; but the influence of the new ideas was not confined to the little group of professed Transcendentalists; it extended to all the young writers within reach, who struck their roots deeper into the soil that it had loosened and freshened. We owe to it, in great measure, not merely Emerson, Alcott, Margaret Fuller, and Thoreau, but Hawthorne, Lowell, Whittier, and Holmes.

In its strictest sense Transcendentalism was a restatement of the idealistic philosophy, and an application of its beliefs to religion, nature, and life. But in a looser sense, and as including the more outward manifestations which drew popular attention most strongly, it was the name given to that spirit of dissent and protest, of universal inquiry and experiment, which marked the third and fourth decades of this century in America, and especially in New England. The movement was contemporary with political revolutions in Europe and with the preaching of many novel gospels in religion, in sociology, in science, education, medicine, and hygiene. New sects were formed, like the Swedenborgians, Universalists, Spiritualists, Millerites, Second Adventists, Shakers, Mormons, and Come-outers, some of whom believed in trances, miracles, and direct revelations from the divine Spirit; others in the quick coming of Christ, as deduced from the opening of the seals and the number of the beast in the Apocalypse; and still others in the reorganization of society and {436} of the family on a different basis. New systems of education were tried, suggested by the writings of the Swiss reformer, Pestalozzi, and others. The pseudo-sciences of mesmerism and of phrenology, as taught by Gall and Spurzheim, had numerous followers. In medicine, homeopathy, hydropathy, and what Dr. Holmes calls "kindred delusions," made many disciples. Numbers of persons, influenced by the doctrines of Graham and other vegetarians, abjured the use of animal food, as injurious not only to health but to a finer spirituality. Not a few refused to vote or pay taxes. The writings of Fourier and St. Simon were translated, and societies were established where co-operation and a community of goods should take the place of selfish competition.

About the year 1840 there were some thirty of these "phalansteries" in America, many of which had their organs in the shape of weekly or monthly journals, which advocated the principle of Association. The best known of these was probably the *Harbinger*, the mouth-piece of the famous Brook Farm Community, which was founded at West Roxbury, Mass., in 1841, and lasted till 1847. The head man of Brook Farm was George Ripley, a Unitarian clergyman, who had resigned his pulpit in Boston to go into the movement, and who after its failure became and remained for many years literary editor of the *New York Tribune*. Among his associates were Charles A. Dana—now the editor of the *Sun*—Margaret Fuller, Nathaniel {437} Hawthorne and others not unknown to fame. The *Harbinger*, which ran from 1845 to 1849— two years after the break up of the community—had among its contributors many who were not Brook Farmers, but who sympathized more or less with the experiment. Of the number were Horace Greeley, Dr. F. H. Hedge—who did so much to introduce American readers to German literature—J. S. Dwight, the musical critic, C. P. Cranch, the poet, and younger men, like G. W. Curtis, and T. W. Higginson. A reader of to-day, looking into an odd volume of the *Harbinger*, will find in it some stimulating writing, together with a great deal of unintelligible talk about "Harmonic Unity," "Love Germination," and other matters now fallen silent. The most important literary result of this experiment at "plain living and high thinking," with its queer mixture of culture and agriculture, was Hawthorne's *Blithedale Romance*, which has for its background an idealized picture of the community life, whose heroine, Zenobia, has touches of Margaret Fuller; and whose hero, with his hobby of prison reform, was a type of the one-idead philanthropists that abounded in such an environment. Hawthorne's attitude was always in part one of reserve and criticism, an attitude which is apparent in the reminiscences of Brook Farm in his *American Note Books*, wherein he speaks with a certain resentment of "Miss Fuller's transcendental heifer," which hooked the other cows, and was evidently to Hawthorne's {438} mind not unsymbolic in this respect of Miss Fuller herself.

It was the day of seers and "Orphic" utterances; the air was full of the enthusiasm of humanity and thick with philanthropic projects and plans for the regeneration of the universe. The figure of the wild-eyed, long-haired reformer—the man with a panacea—the "crank" of our later terminology—became a familiar one. He abounded at non-resistance conventions and meetings of universal peace societies and of woman's rights associations. The movement had its grotesque aspects, which Lowell has described in his essay on Thoreau. "Bran had its apostles and the pre-sartorial simplicity of Adam its martyrs, tailored impromptu from the tar-pot... . Not a few impecunious zealots abjured the use of money (unless earned by other people), professing to live on the internal revenues of the spirit... . Communities were established where every thing was to be common but common sense."

This ferment has long since subsided and much of what was then seething has gone off in vapor or other volatile products. But some very solid matters also have been precipitated, some crystals of poetry translucent, symmetrical, enduring. The immediate practical outcome was disappointing, and the external history of the agitation is a record of failed experiments, spurious sciences, Utopian philosophies, and sects founded only to dwindle away or be reabsorbed into some form of {439} orthodoxy. In the eyes of the conservative, or the worldly-minded, or of the plain people who could not understand the enigmatic utterances of the reformers, the dangerous or ludicrous sides of transcendentalism were naturally uppermost. Nevertheless the movement was but a new avatar of the old Puritan spirit; its moral earnestness, its spirituality, its tenderness for the individual conscience. Puritanism, too, in its day had run into grotesque extremes. Emerson bore about the same relation to the absurder outcroppings of transcendentalism that Milton bore to the New Lights, Ranters, Fifth Monarchy Men, etc., of his time. There is in him that mingling of idealism with an abiding sanity, and even a Yankee shrewdness, which characterizes the race. The practical, inventive, calculating, money-getting side of the Yankee has been made sufficiently obvious. But the deep heart of New England is full of dreams, mysticism, romance:

"And in the day of sacrifice,
When heroes piled the pyre,
The dismal Massachusetts ice
Burned more than others' fire."

The one element which the odd and eccentric developments of this movement shared in common with the real philosophy of transcendentalism was the rejection of authority and the appeal to the private consciousness as the sole standard of truth and right. This principle certainly lay in the ethical {440} systems of Kant and Fichte, the great transcendentalists of Germany. It had been strongly asserted by Channing. Nay, it was the starting point of Puritanism itself, which had drawn away from the ceremonial religion of the English Church and by its Congregational system had made each church society independent in doctrine and worship. And although Puritan orthodoxy in New England had grown rigid and dogmatic, it had never used the weapons of obscurantism. By encouraging education to the utmost it had shown its willingness to submit its beliefs to the fullest discussion and had put into the hands of dissent the means with which to attack them.

In its theological aspect transcendentalism was a departure from conservative Unitarianism, as that had been from Calvinism. From Edwards to Channing, from Channing to Emerson and Theodore Parker, there was a natural and logical unfolding. Not logical in the sense that Channing accepted Edwards' premises and pushed them out to their conclusions, or that Parker accepted all of Channing's premises, but in the sense that the rigid pushing out of Edwards' premises into their conclusions by himself and his followers had brought about a moral *reductio ad absurdum* and a state of opinion against which Channing rebelled; and that Channing, as it seemed to Parker, stopped short in the carrying out of his own principles. Thus the "Channing Unitarians," while denying that Christ was God, had held that he was of {441} divine nature, was the Son of God, and had existed before he came into the world. While rejecting the doctrine of the "Vicarious sacrifice" they maintained that Christ was a mediator and intercessor, and that his supernatural nature was testified by miracles. For Parker and Emerson it was easy to take the step to the assertion that Christ was a good and great man, divine only in the sense that God possessed him more fully than any other man known in history; that it was his preaching and example that brought salvation to men, and not any special mediation or intercession, and that his own words and acts, and not miracles, are the only and the sufficient witness to his mission. In the view of the transcendentalists Christ was as human as Buddha, Socrates or Confucius, and the Bible was but one among the "Ethnical Scriptures" or sacred writings of the peoples, passages from which were published in the transcendental organ, the *Dial*. As against these new views Channing Unitarianism occupied already a conservative position. The Unitarians as a body had never been very numerous outside of Eastern Massachusets. They had a few churches in New York and in the larger cities and towns elsewhere, but the sect, as such, was a local one. Orthodoxy made a sturdy fight against the heresy, under leaders like Leonard Woods and Moses Stuart, of Andover, and Lyman Beecher, of Connecticut. In the neighboring State of Connecticut, for example, there was until lately, for

{442} a period of several years, no distinctly Unitarian congregation worshiping in a church edifice of its own. On the other hand, the Unitarians claimed, with justice, that their opinions had to a great extent modified the theology of the orthodox churches. The writings of Horace Bushnell, of Hartford, one of the most eminent Congregational divines, approach Unitarianism in their interpretation of the doctrine of the Atonement; and the "progressive orthodoxy" of Andover is certainly not the Calvinism of Thomas Hooker or of Jonathan Edwards. But it seemed to the transcendentalists that conservative Unitarianism was too negative and "cultured," and Margaret Fuller complained of the coldness of the Boston pulpits. While contrariwise the central thought of transcendentalism, that the soul has an immediate connection with God, was pronounced by Dr. Channing a "crude speculation." This was the thought of Emerson's address in 1838 before the Cambridge Divinity School, and it was at once made the object of attack by conservative Unitarians like Henry Ware and Andrews Norton. The latter in an address before the same audience, on the *Latest Form of Infidelity*, said: "Nothing is left that can be called Christianity if its miraculous character be denied.... . There can be no intuition, no direct perception of the truth of Christianity." And in a pamphlet supporting the same side of the question he added: "It is not an intelligible error but a mere absurdity to maintain {443} that we are conscious, or have an intuitive knowledge, of the being of God, of our own immortality ... or of any other fact of religion." Ripley and Parker replied in Emerson's defense; but Emerson himself would never be drawn into controversy. He said that he could not argue. He announced truths; his method was that of the seer, not of the disputant. In 1832 Emerson, who was a Unitarian clergyman, and descended from eight generations of clergymen, had resigned the pastorate of the Second Church of Boston because he could not conscientiously administer the sacrament of the communion—which he regarded as a mere act of commemoration—in the sense in which it was understood by his parishioners. Thenceforth, though he sometimes occupied Unitarian pulpits, and was, indeed, all his life a kind of "lay preacher," he never assumed the pastorate of a church. The representative of transcendentalism in the pulpit was Theodore Parker, an eloquent preacher, an eager debater and a prolific writer on many subjects, whose collected works fill fourteen volumes. Parker was a man of strongly human traits, passionate, independent, intensely religious, but intensely radical, who made for himself a large personal following. The more advanced wing of the Unitarians were called, after him, "Parkerites." Many of the Unitarian churches refused to "fellowship" with him; and the large congregation, or audience, which assembled in Music Hall to hear his sermons was {444} stigmatized as a "boisterous assembly" which came to hear Parker preach irreligion.

It has been said that, on its philosophical side, New England transcendentalism was a restatement of idealism. The impulse came from Germany, from the philosophical writings of Kant, Fichte, Jacobi, and Schelling, and from the works of Coleridge and Carlyle, who had domesticated German thought in England. In Channing's *Remarks on a National Literature*, quoted in our last chapter, the essayist urged that our scholars should study the authors of France and Germany as one means of emancipating American letters from a slavish dependence on British literature. And in fact German literature began, not long after, to be eagerly studied in New England. Emerson published an American edition of Carlyle's *Miscellanies*, including his essays on German writers that had appeared in England between 1822 and 1830. In 1838 Ripley began to publish *Specimens of Foreign Standard Literature*, which extended to fourteen volumes. In his work of translating and supplying introductions to the matter selected he was helped by Ripley, Margaret Fuller, John S. Dwight and others who had more or less connection with the transcendental movement.

The definition of the new faith given by Emerson in his lecture on the *Transcendentalist*, 1842, is as follows: "What is popularly called transcendentalism among us is idealism.... . The idealism of the present day acquired the name of transcendental {445} from the use of that term by Immanuel Kant, who replied to the skeptical philosophy of Locke, which insisted that there was nothing in the intellect which was not previously in the experience of the senses, by showing that there was a very important class of ideas, or imperative forms, which did not come by experience, but through which experience was acquired; that these were intuitions of the mind itself, and he denominated them *transcendental* forms." Idealism denies the independent existence of matter. Transcendentalism claims for the innate ideas of God and the soul a higher assurance of reality than for the knowledge of the outside world derived through the senses. Emerson shares the "noble doubt" of idealism. He calls the universe a shade, a dream, "this great apparition." "It is a sufficient account of that appearance we call the world," he wrote in *Nature*, "that God will teach a human mind, and so makes it the receiver of a certain number of congruent sensations which we call sun and moon, man and woman, house and trade. In my utter impotence to test the authenticity of the report of my senses, to know whether the impressions on me correspond with outlying objects, what difference does it make whether Orion is up there in heaven or some god paints the image in the firmament of the soul?" On the other hand our evidence of the existence of God and of our own souls, and our knowledge of right and wrong, are immediate, and are independent of the senses. {446} We are in direct communication with the "Oversoul," the infinite Spirit. "The soul in man is the background of our being—an immensity not possessed, that cannot be possessed." "From within or from behind a light shines through us upon things, and makes us aware that we are nothing, but the light is all." Revelation is "an influx of the Divine mind into our mind. It is an ebb of the individual rivulet before the flowing surges of the sea of life." In moods of exaltation, and especially in the presence of nature, this contact of the individual soul with the absolute is felt. "All mean egotism vanishes. I become a transparent eyeball; I am nothing; I see all; the currents of the Universal Being circulate through me; I am part and particle of God." The existence and attributes of God are not deducible from history or from natural theology, but are thus directly given us in consciousness. In his essay on the *Transcendentalist*, Emerson says: "His experience inclines him to behold the procession of facts you call the world as flowing perpetually outward from an invisible, unsounded center in himself; center alike of him and of them and necessitating him to regard all things as having a subjective or relative existence—relative to that aforesaid Unknown Center of him. There is no bar or wall in the soul where man, the effect, ceases, and God, the cause, begins. We lie open on one side to the deeps of spiritual nature, to the attributes of God."

{447}

Emerson's point of view, though familiar to students of philosophy, is strange to the popular understanding, and hence has arisen the complaint of his obscurity. Moreover, he apprehended and expressed these ideas as a poet, in figurative and emotional language, and not as a metaphysician, in a formulated statement. His own position in relation to systematic philosophers is described in what he says of Plato, in his series of sketches entitled *Representative Men*, 1850: "He has not a system. The dearest disciples and defenders are at fault. He attempted a theory of the universe, and his theory is not complete or self-evident. One man thinks he means this, and another that; he has said one thing in one place, and the reverse of it in another place." It happens, therefore, that, to many students of more formal philosophies Emerson's meaning seems elusive, and he appears to write from temporary moods and to contradict himself. Had he attempted a reasoned exposition of the transcendental philosophy, instead of writing essays and poems, he might have added one more to the number of system-mongers; but he would not have taken that significant place which he occupies in the general literature of the time, nor exerted that wide influence upon younger writers which has been one of the stimulating forces in American thought. It was because Emerson was a poet that he is our Emerson. And yet it would be impossible to disentangle his peculiar philosophical ideas from the body of his {448} writings and to leave the latter to stand upon their merits as literature merely. He is the poet of certain high abstractions, and his religion is central to all his work—excepting, perhaps, his *English Traits*, 1856, an acute study of national characteristics, and a few of his essays and verses, which are independent of any particular philosophical standpoint.

When Emerson resigned his parish in 1832 he made a short trip to Europe, where he visited Carlyle at Craigenputtoch, and Landor at Florence. On his return he retired to his birthplace, the village of Concord, Massachusetts, and settled down among his books and his fields, becoming a sort of "glorified farmer," but issuing frequently from his retirement to instruct and delight audiences of thoughtful people at Boston and at other points all through the country. Emerson was the perfection of a lyceum lecturer. His manner was quiet but forcible; his voice of charming quality, and his enunciation clean cut and refined. The sentence was his unit in composition. His lectures seemed to begin anywhere and to end anywhere, and to resemble strings of exquisitely polished sayings rather than continuous discourses. His printed essays, with unimportant exceptions, were first written and delivered as lectures. In 1836 he published his first book, *Nature*, which remains the most systematic statement of his philosophy. It opened a fresh spring-head in American thought, and the words of its introduction announced that its author had broken with {449} the past. "Why should not we also enjoy an original relation to the universe? Why should not we have a poetry and philosophy of insight and not of tradition, and a religion by revelation to us and not the history of theirs?"

It took eleven years to sell five hundred copies of this little book. But the year following its publication the remarkable Phi Beta Kappa address at Cambridge, on the *American Scholar*, electrified the little public of the university. This is described by Lowell as "an event without any former parallel in our literary annals, a scene to be always treasured in the memory for its picturesqueness and its inspiration. What crowded and breathless aisles, what windows clustering with eager heads, what grim silence of foregone dissent!" To Concord came many kindred spirits, drawn by Emerson's magnetic attraction. Thither came, from Connecticut, Amos Bronson Alcott, born a few years before Emerson, whom he outlived; a quaint and benignant figure, a visionary and a mystic even among the transcendentalists themselves, and one who lived in unworldly simplicity the life of the soul. Alcott had taught school at Cheshire, Conn., and afterward at Boston on an original plan—compelling his scholars, for example, to flog *him*, when they did wrong, instead of taking a flogging themselves. The experiment was successful until his *Conversations on the Gospels*, in Boston, and his insistence upon admitting colored children to his benches, offended conservative opinion and {450} broke up his school. Alcott renounced the eating of animal food in 1835. He believed in the union of thought and manual labor, and supported himself for some years by the work of his hands, gardening, cutting wood, etc. He traveled into the West and elsewhere, holding conversations on philosophy, education, and religion. He set up a little community at the village of Harvard, which was rather less successful than Brook Farm, and he contributed *Orphic Sayings* to the *Dial*, which were harder for the exoteric to understand than even Emerson's *Brahma* or the *Over-soul*.

Thither came, also, Sarah Margaret Fuller, the most intellectual woman of her time in America, an eager student of Greek and German literature and an ardent seeker after the True, the Good, and the Beautiful. She threw herself into many causes—temperance, antislavery, and the higher education of women. Her brilliant conversation classes in Boston attracted many "minds" of her own sex. Subsequently, as literary editor of the *New York Tribune*, she furnished a wider public with reviews and book-notices of great ability. She took part in the Brook Farm experiment, and she edited the *Dial* for a time, contributing to it the papers afterward expanded into her most considerable book, *Woman in the Nineteenth Century*. In 1846 she went abroad, and at Rome took part in the revolutionary movement of Mazzini, having charge of one of the hospitals during the siege of the city by the {451} French. In 1847 she married an impecunious Italian nobleman, the Marquis Ossoli. In 1850 the ship on which she was returning to America, with her husband and child, was wrecked on Fire Island beach and all three were lost. Margaret Fuller's collected writings are somewhat disappointing, being mainly of temporary interest. She lives less through her books than through the memoirs of her friends, Emerson, James Freeman Clarke, T. W. Higginson, and others who knew her as a personal influence. Her strenuous and rather overbearing individuality made an impression not altogether agreeable upon many of her contemporaries. Lowell introduced a caricature of her as "Miranda" into his *Fable for Critics*, and Hawthorne's caustic sketch of her, preserved in the biography written by his son, has given great offense to her admirers. "Such a determination to *eat* this huge universe!" was Carlyle's characteristic comment on her appetite for knowledge and aspirations after perfection.

To Concord also came Nathaniel Hawthorne, who took up his residence there first at the "Old Manse," and afterward at "The Wayside." Though naturally an idealist, he said that he came too late to Concord to fall decidedly under Emerson's influence. Of that he would have stood in little danger even had he come earlier. He appreciated the deep and subtle quality of Emerson's imagination, but his own shy genius always jealously guarded its independence and {452} resented the too close approaches of an alien mind. Among the native disciples of Emerson at Concord the most noteworthy were Henry Thoreau, and his friend and biographer, William Ellery Channing, Jr., a nephew of the great Channing. Channing was a contributor to the *Dial*, and he published a volume of poems which elicited a fiercely contemptuous review from Edgar Poe. Though disfigured by affectation and obscurity, many of Channing's verses were distinguished by true poetic feeling, and the last line of his little piece, *A Poet's Hope*,

"If my bark sink 'tis to another sea,"

has taken a permanent place in the literature of transcendentalism.

The private organ of the transcendentalists was the *Dial*, a quarterly magazine, published from 1840 to 1844, and edited by Emerson and Margaret Fuller. Among its contributors, besides those already mentioned, were Ripley, Thoreau, Parker, James Freeman Clarke, Charles A. Dana, John S. Dwight, C. P. Cranch, Charles Emerson and William H. Channing, another nephew of Dr. Channing. It contained, along with a good deal of rubbish, some of the best poetry and prose that have been published in America. The most lasting part of its contents were the contributions of Emerson and Thoreau. But even as a whole, it is so unique a way-mark in the history of our literature that all its four volumes—copies of which {453} had become scarce—have been recently reprinted in answer to a demand certainly very unusual in the case of an extinct periodical.

From time to time Emerson collected and published his lectures under various titles. A first series of *Essays* came out in 1841, and a second in 1844; the *Conduct of Life* in 1860, *Society and Solitude* in 1870, *Letters and Social Aims*, in 1876, and the *Fortune of the Republic* in 1878. In 1847 he issued a volume of *Poems*, and 1865 *Mayday and Other Poems*. These writings, as a whole, were variations on a single theme, expansions and illustrations of the philosophy set forth in *Nature*, and his early addresses. They were strikingly original, rich in thought, filled with wisdom, with lofty morality and spiritual religion. Emerson, said Lowell, first "cut the cable that bound us to English thought and gave us a chance at the dangers and glories of blue water." Nevertheless, as it used to be the fashion to find an English analogue for every American writer, so that Cooper was called the American Scott, and Mrs. Sigourney was described as the Hemans of America, a well-worn critical tradition has coupled Emerson with Carlyle. That his mind received a nudge from Carlyle's early essays and from *Sartor Resartus* is beyond a doubt. They were life-long friends and correspondents, and Emerson's *Representative Men* is, in some sort, a counterpart of Carlyle's *Hero Worship*. But in temper and style the two writers were widely different. Carlyle's pessimism and {454} dissatisfaction with the general drift of things gained upon him more and more, while Emerson was a consistent optimist to the end. The last of his writings published during his life-time, the *Fortune of the Republic*, contrasts strangely in its hopefulness with the desperation of Carlyle's later utterances. Even in presence of the doubt as to man's personal immortality he takes refuge in a high and stoical faith. "I think all sound minds rest on a certain preliminary conviction, namely: that if it be best that conscious personal life shall continue it will continue, and if not best, then it will not; and we, if we saw the whole, should of course see that it was better so." It is this conviction that gives to Emerson's writings their serenity and their tonic quality at the same time that it narrows the range of his dealings with life. As the idealist declines to cross-examine those facts which he regards as merely phenomenal, and looks upon this outward face of things as upon a mask not worthy to dismay the fixed soul, so the optimist turns away his eyes from the evil which he disposes of as merely negative, as the shadow of the good. Hawthorne's interest in the problem of sin finds little place in Emerson's philosophy. Passion comes not nigh him and *Faust* disturbs him with its disagreeableness. Pessimism is to him "the only skepticism."

The greatest literature is that which is most broadly human, or, in other words, that which will square best with all philosophies. But Emerson's {455} genius was interpretive rather than constructive. The poet dwells in the cheerful world of phenomena. He is most the poet who realizes most intensely the good and the bad of human life. But Idealism makes experience shadowy and subordinates action to contemplation. To it the cities of men, with their "frivolous populations,"

"… are but sailing foam-bells Along thought's causing stream."

Shakespere does not forget that the world will one day vanish "like the baseless fabric of a vision," and that we ourselves are "such stuff as dreams are made on;" but this is not the mood in which he dwells. Again: while it is for the philosopher to reduce variety to unity, it is the poet's task to detect the manifold under uniformity. In the great creative poets, in Shakespere and Dante and Goethe, how infinite the swarm of persons, the multitude of forms! But with Emerson the type is important, the common element. "In youth we are mad for persons. But the larger experience of man discovers the identical nature appearing through them all." "The same—the same!" he exclaims in his essay on *Plato*. "Friend and foe are of one stuff; the plowman, the plow and the furrow are of one stuff." And this is the thought in *Brahma*:

"They reckon ill who leave me out;
　When me they fly I am the wings:
I am the doubter and the doubt,
　And I the hymn the Brahmin sings."

{456} It is not easy to fancy a writer who holds this altitude toward "persons" descending to the composition of a novel or a play. Emerson showed, indeed, a fine power of character analysis in his *English Traits* and *Representative Men* and in his memoirs of Thoreau and Margaret Fuller. There is even a sort of dramatic humor in his portrait of Socrates. But upon the whole he stands midway between constructive artists, whose instinct it is to tell a story or sing a song, ami philosophers, like Schelling, who give poetic expression to a system of thought. He belongs to the class of minds of which Sir Thomas Browne is the best English example. He set a high value upon Browne, to whose style his own, though far more sententious, bears aresemblance. Browne's saying, for example, "All things are artificial, for nature is the art of God," sounds like Emerson, whose workmanship, for the rest, in his prose essays was exceedingly fine and close. He was not afraid to be homely and racy in expressing thought of the highest spirituality. "Hitch your wagon to a star" is a good instance of his favorite manner.

Emerson's verse often seems careless in technique. Most of his pieces are scrappy and have the air of runic rimes, or little oracular "voicings"—as they say in Concord—in rhythmic shape, of single thoughts on "Worship," "Character," "Heroism," "Art," "Politics," "Culture," etc. The content is the important thing, and the form is too frequently awkward or bald. Sometimes, indeed, in the {457} clear-obscure of Emerson's poetry the deep wisdom of the thought finds its most natural expression in the imaginative simplicity of the language. But though this artlessness in him became too frequently in his imitators, like Thoreau and Ellery Channing, an obtruded simplicity, among his own poems are many that leave nothing to be desired in point of wording and of verse. His *Hymn Sung at the Completion of the Concord Monument*, in 1836, is the perfect model of an occasional poem. Its lines were on every one's lips at the time of the centennial celebrations in 1876, and "the shot heard round the world" has hardly echoed farther than the song which chronicled it. Equally current is the stanza from *Voluntaries*:

> "So nigh is grandeur to our dust,
> So near is God to man,
> When Duty whispers low, 'Thou must,'
> The youth replies, 'I can.'"

So, too, the famous lines from the *Problem*:

> "The hand that rounded Peter's dome,
> And groined the aisles of Christian Rome,
> Wrought in a sad sincerity.
> Himself from God he could not free;
> He builded better than he knew;
> The conscious stone to beauty grew."

The most noteworthy of Emerson's pupils was Henry David Thoreau, "the poet-naturalist." After his graduation from Harvard College, in 1837, Thoreau engaged in school teaching and in {458} the manufacture of lead-pencils, but soon gave up all regular business and devoted himself to walking, reading, and the study of nature. He was at one time private tutor in a family on Staten Island, and he supported himself for a season by doing odd jobs in land surveying for the farmers about Concord. In 1845 he built, with his own hands, a small cabin on the banks of Walden Pond, near Concord, and lived there in seclusion for two years. His expenses during these years were nine cents a day, and he gave an account of his experiment in his most characteristic book, *Walden*, published in 1854. His *Week on the Concord and Merrimac Rivers* appeared in 1849. From time to time he went farther afield, and his journeys were reported in *Cape Cod*, the *Maine Woods*, *Excursions*, and a *Yankee in Canada*, all of which, as well as a volume of *Letters* and *Early Spring in Massachusetts*, have been given to the public since his death, which happened in 1862. No one has lived so close to nature, and written of it so intimately, as Thoreau. His life was a lesson in economy and a sermon on Emerson's text, "Lessen your denominator." He wished to reduce existence to the simplest terms—to

"live all alone
Close to the bone,
And where life is sweet
Constantly eat."

He had a passion for the wild, and seems like an Anglo-Saxon reversion to the type of the Red {459} Indian. The most distinctive note in Thoreau is his inhumanity. Emerson spoke of him as a "perfect piece of stoicism." "Man," said Thoreau, "is only the point on which I stand." He strove to realize the objective life of nature—nature in its aloofness from man; to identify himself, with the moose and the mountain. He listened, with his ear close to the ground, for the voice of the earth. "What are the trees saying?" he exclaimed. Following upon the trail of the lumberman he asked the primeval wilderness for its secret, and

"saw beneath dim aisles, in odorous beds,
The slight linnaea hang its twin-born heads."

He tried to interpret the thought of Ktaadn and to fathom the meaning of the billows on the back of Cape Cod, in their indifference to the shipwrecked bodies that they rolled ashore. "After sitting in my chamber many days, reading the poets, I have been out early on a foggy morning and heard the cry of an owl in a neighboring wood as from a nature behind the common, unexplored by science or by literature. None of the feathered race has yet realized my youthful conceptions of the woodland depths. I had seen the red

227

election-birds brought from their recesses on my comrade's string, and fancied that their plumage would assume stranger and more dazzling colors, like the tints of evening, in proportion as I advanced farther into the darkness and solitude of the forest. Still less have I seen such strong and wild tints on any poet's string."

{460}

It was on the mystical side that Thoreau apprehended transcendentalism. Mysticism has been defined as the soul's recognition of its identity with nature. This thought lies plainly in Schelling's philosophy, and he illustrated it by his famous figure of the magnet. Mind and nature are one; they are the positive and negative poles of the magnet. In man, the Absolute—that is, God—becomes conscious of himself; makes of himself, as nature, an object to himself as mind. "The souls of men," said Schelling, "are but the innumerable individual eyes with which our infinite World-Spirit beholds himself." This thought is also clearly present in Emerson's view of nature, and has caused him to be accused of pantheism. But if by pantheism is meant the doctrine that the underlying principle of the universe is matter or force, none of the transcendentalists was a pantheist. In their view nature was divine. Their poetry is always haunted by the sense of a spiritual reality which abides beyond the phenomena. Thus in Emerson's *Two Rivers*:

"Thy summer voice, Musketaquit,[1]
  Repeats the music of the rain,
But sweeter rivers pulsing flit
  Through thee as thou through Concord plain.

"Thou in thy narrow banks art pent:
  The stream I love unbounded goes;
Through flood and sea and firmament,
  Through light, through life, it forward flows.

{461}

"I see the inundation sweet,
  I hear the spending of the stream,
Through years, through men, through nature fleet,
  Through passion, thought, through power and dream."

This mood occurs frequently in Thoreau. The hard world of matter becomes suddenly all fluent and spiritual, and he sees himself in it—sees God. "This earth," he cries, "which is spread out like a map around me, is but the lining of my inmost soul exposed." "In *me* is the sucker that I see;" and, of Walden Pond,

"I am its stony shore,
And the breeze that passes o'er."

"Suddenly old Time winked at me—ah, you know me, you rogue—and news
had come that IT was well. That ancient universe is in such capital health, I
think, undoubtedly, it will never die.... I see, smell, taste, hear, feel that
everlasting something to which we are allied, at once our maker, our abode,
our destiny, our very selves." It was something ulterior that Thoreau sought in
nature. "The other world," he wrote, "is all my art: my pencils will draw no
other: my jackknife will cut nothing else." Thoreau did not scorn, however,
like Emerson, to "examine too microscopically the universal tablet." He was a
close observer and accurate reporter of the ways of birds and plants and the
minuter aspects of nature. He has had many followers, who have produced
much pleasant literature on out-door {462} life. But in none of them is there
that unique combination of the poet, the naturalist and the mystic which gives
his page its wild original flavor. He had the woodcraft of a hunter and the eye
of a botanist, but his imagination did not stop short with the fact. The sound
of a tree falling in the Maine woods was to him "as though a door had shut
somewhere in the damp and shaggy wilderness." He saw small things in
cosmic relations. His trip down the tame Concord has for the reader the
excitement of a voyage of exploration into far and unknown regions. The
river just above Sherman's Bridge, in time of flood "when the wind blows
freshly on a raw March day, heaving up the surface into dark and sober
billows," was like Lake Huron, "and you may run aground on Cranberry
Island," and "get as good a freezing there as anywhere on the North-west
coast." He said that most of the phenomena described in Kane's voyages
could be observed in Concord.

The literature of transcendentalism was like the light of the stars in a winter
night, keen and cold and high. It had the pale cast of thought, and was almost
too spiritual and remote to "hit the sense of mortal sight." But it was at least
indigenous. If not an American literature—not national and not inclusive of
all sides of American life—it was, at all events, a genuine New England
literature and true to the spirit of its section. The tough Puritan stock had at
last put forth a {463} blossom which compared with the warm, robust
growths of English soil even as the delicate wind flower of the northern
spring compares with the cowslips and daisies of old England.

In 1842 Nathaniel Hawthorne (1804-1864) the greatest American romancer,
came to Concord. He had recently left Brook Farm, had just been married,
and with his bride he settled down in the "Old Manse" for three paradisaical
years. A picture of this protracted honeymoon and this sequestered life, as
tranquil as the slow stream on whose banks it was passed, is given in the

introductory chapter to his *Mosses from an Old Manse*, 1846, and in the more personal and confidential records of his *American Note Books*, posthumously published. Hawthorne was thirty-eight when he took his place among the Concord literati. His childhood and youth had been spent partly at his birthplace, the old and already somewhat decayed sea-port town of Salem, and partly at his grandfather's farm on Sebago Lake, in Maine, then on the edge of the primitive forest. Maine did not become a State, indeed, until 1820, the year before Hawthorne entered Bowdoin College, whence he was graduated in 1825, in the same class with Henry W. Longfellow and one year behind Franklin Pierce, afterward President of the United States. After leaving college Hawthorne buried himself for years in the seclusion of his home at Salem. His mother, who was early widowed, had withdrawn entirely from the world. For months {464} at a time Hawthorne kept his room, seeing no other society than that of his mother and sisters, reading all sorts of books and writing wild tales, most of which he destroyed as soon as he had written them. At twilight he would emerge from the house for a solitary ramble through the streets of the town or along the sea-side. Old Salem had much that was picturesque in its associations. It had been the scene of the witch trials in the seventeenth century, and it abounded in ancient mansions, the homes of retired whalers and India merchants. Hawthorne's father had been a ship captain, and many of his ancestors had followed the sea. One of his forefathers, moreover, had been a certain Judge Hawthorne, who in 1691 had sentenced several of the witches to death. The thought of this affected Hawthorne's imagination with a pleasing horror and he utilized it afterward in his *House of the Seven Gables*. Many of the old Salem houses, too, had their family histories, with now and then the hint of some obscure crime or dark misfortune which haunted posterity with its curse till all the stock died out, or fell into poverty and evil ways, as in the Pyncheon family of Hawthorne's romance. In the preface to the *Marble Faun* Hawthorne wrote: "No author without a trial can conceive of the difficulty of writing a romance about a country where there is no shadow, no antiquity, no mystery, no picturesque and gloomy wrong, nor any thing but a commonplace prosperity in broad and simple daylight." And yet it may {465} be doubted whether any environment could have been found more fitted to his peculiar genius than this of his native town, or any preparation better calculated to ripen the faculty that was in him than these long, lonely years of waiting and brooding thought. From time to time he contributed a story or a sketch to some periodical, such as S. G. Goodrich's Annual, the *Token*, or the *Knickerbocker Magazine*. Some of these attracted the attention of the judicious; but they were anonymous and signed by various *noms de plume*, and their author was at this time—to use his own words—"the obscurest man of letters in America." In 1828 he had issued anonymously and at his own expense a short romance, entitled

Fanshawe. It had little success, and copies of the first edition are now exceedingly rare. In 1837 he published a collection of his magazine pieces under the title, *Twice Told Tales*. The book was generously praised in the *North American Review* by his former classmate, Longfellow; and Edgar Poe showed his keen critical perception by predicting that the writer would easily put himself at the head of imaginative literature in America if he would discard allegory, drop short stories and compose a genuine romance. Poe compared Hawthorne's work with that of the German romancer, Tieck, and it is interesting to find confirmation of this dictum in passages of the *American Note Books*, in which Hawthorne speaks of laboring over Tieck with a German dictionary. The {466} *Twice Told Tales* are the work of a recluse, who makes guesses at life from a knowledge of his own heart, acquired by a habit of introspection, but who has had little contact with men. Many of them were shadowy and others were morbid and unwholesome. But their gloom was of an interior kind, never the physically horrible of Poe. It arose from weird psychological situations like that of *Ethan Brand* in his search for the unpardonable sin. Hawthorne was true to the inherited instinct of Puritanism; he took the conscience for his theme, and in these early tales he was already absorbed in the problem of evil, the subtle ways in which sin works out its retribution, and the species of fate or necessity that the wrong-doer makes for himself in the inevitable sequences of his crime. Hawthorne was strongly drawn toward symbols and types, and never quite followed Poe's advice to abandon allegory. The *Scarlet Letter* and his other romances are not, indeed, strictly allegories, since the characters are men and women and not mere personifications of abstract qualities. Still they all have a certain allegorical tinge. In the *Marble Faun*, for example, Hilda, Kenyon, Miriam and Donatello have been ingeniously explained as personifications respectively of the conscience, the reason, the imagination and the senses. Without going so far as this, it is possible to see in these and in Hawthorne's other creations something typical and representative. He uses his characters like algebraic symbols to work {467} out certain problems with: they are rather more and yet rather less than flesh and blood individuals. The stories in *Twice Told Tales* and in the second collection, *Mosses from an Old Manse*, 1846, are more openly allegorical than his later work. Thus the *Minister's Black Veil* is a sort of anticipation of Arthur Dimmesdale in the *Scarlet Letter*. From 1846 to 1849 Hawthorne held the position of Surveyor of the Custom House of Salem. In the preface to the *Scarlet Letter* he sketched some of the government officials with whom this office had brought him into contact in a way that gave some offense to the friends of the victims and a great deal of amusement to the public. Hawthorne's humor was quiet and fine, like Irving's, but less genial and with a more satiric edge to it. The book last named was written at Salem and published in 1850, just before its author's removal to Lenox, now a sort of inland Newport, but then an unfashionable resort among the Berkshire hills. Whatever obscurity may have hung over Hawthorne hitherto was effectually dissolved by this powerful tale, which was as vivid in coloring as the implication of its title. Hawthorne chose for his background the somber life of the early settlers in New England. He had always been drawn toward this part of American history, and in *Twice Told Tales* had given some illustrations of it in *Endicott's Red Cross* and *Legends of the Province House*. Against this dark foil moved in strong relief the figures of Hester {468} Prynne, the woman taken in adultery, her paramour, the Rev. Arthur Dimmesdale, her husband, old Roger Chillingworth, and her illegitimate child. In tragic power, in its grasp of the elementary passions of human nature and its deep and subtle insight into the inmost secrets of the heart, this is Hawthorne's greatest book. He never crowded his canvas with figures. In the *Blithedale Romance* and the *Marble Faun* there is the same *parti carré* or group of four characters. In the *House of the Seven Gables* there are five. The last mentioned of these, published in 1852, was of a more subdued intensity than the *Scarlet Letter*, but equally original and, upon the whole, perhaps equally good. The *Blithedale Romance*, published in the same year, though not strikingly inferior to the others, adhered more to conventional patterns in its plot and in the sensational nature of its ending. The suicide of the heroine by drowning, and the terrible scene of the recovery of her body, were suggested to the author by an experience of his own on Concord River, the account of which, in his own words, may be read in Julian Hawthorne's *Nathaniel Hawthorne and His Wife*. In 1852 Hawthorne returned to Concord and bought the "Wayside" property, which he retained until his death. But in the following year his old college friend Pierce, now become President, appointed him Consul to Liverpool, and he went abroad for seven years. The most valuable fruit of his foreign residence was the {469} romance of the *Marble Faun*, 1860; the longest of his fictions and the richest in descriptive beauty. The theme of this was the development of the soul through the experience of sin. There is a haunting mystery thrown about the story, like a soft veil of mist, veiling the beginning and the end. There is even a delicate teasing suggestion of the preternatural in Donatello, the Faun, a creation as original as Shakspere's Caliban, or Fouqué's Undine, and yet quite on this side the border-line of the human. *Our Old Home*, a book of charming papers on England, was published in 1863. Manifold experience of life and contact with men, affording scope for his always keen observation, had added range, fullness, warmth to the imaginative subtlety which had manifested itself even in his earliest tales. Two admirable books for children, the *Wonder Book* and *Tanglewood Tales*, in which the classical mythologies were retold; should also be mentioned in the list of Hawthorne's writings, as well as the *American, English*, and *Italian Note Books*, the first of which contains the seed thoughts of some of his finished works, together with hundreds of hints for plots, episodes, descriptions, etc., which he never found time to work out. Hawthorne's style, in his first sketches and stories a little stilted and "bookish," gradually acquired an exquisite perfection, and is as well worth study as that of any prose classic in the English tongue.

Hawthorne was no transcendentalist. He dwelt {470} much in a world of ideas, and he sometimes doubted whether the tree on the bank or its image in the stream were the more real. But this had little in common with the philosophical idealism of his neighbors. He reverenced Emerson, and he held kindly intercourse—albeit a silent man and easily bored—with Thoreau and Ellery Channing, and even with Margaret Fuller. But his sharp eyes saw whatever was whimsical or weak in the apostles of the new faith. He had little enthusiasm for causes or reforms, and among so many Abolitionists he remained a Democrat, and even wrote a campaign life of his friend Pierce.

The village of Concord has perhaps done more for American literature than the city of New York. Certainly there are few places where associations, both patriotic and poetic, cluster so thickly. At one side of the grounds of the Old Manse—which has the river at its back—runs down a shaded lane to the Concord monument and the figure of the Minute Man and the successor of "the rude bridge that arched the flood." Scarce two miles away, among the woods, is little Walden—"God's drop." The men who made Concord famous are asleep in Sleepy Hollow, yet still their memory prevails to draw seekers after truth to the Concord Summer School of Philosophy, which meets every year, to reason high of "God, Freedom, and Immortality," next-door to the "Wayside," and under the hill on whose ridge Hawthorne wore a path, as he paced up and down beneath the hemlocks.

{471}

1. Ralph Waldo Emerson. Nature. The American Scholar. Literary Ethics. The Transcendentalist. The Over-soul. Address before the Cambridge Divinity School. English Traits. Representative Men. Poems.

2. Henry David Thoreau. Excursions. Walden. A Week on the Concord and Merrimac Rivers. Cape Cod. The Maine Woods.

3. Nathaniel Hawthorne. Mosses from an Old Manse. The Scarlet Letter. The House of the Seven Gables. The Blithedale Romance. The Marble Faun. Our Old Home.

4. Transcendentalism in New England. By O. B. Frothingham. New York: G. P. Putnam's Sons. 1875.

[1] The Indian name of Concord River.

{472}

CHAPTER V.

THE CAMBRIDGE SCHOLARS.

1837-1861.

With few exceptions, the men who have made American literature what it is have been college graduates. And yet our colleges have not commonly been, in themselves, literary centers. Most of them have been small and poor, and situated in little towns or provincial cities. Their alumni scatter far and wide immediately after graduation, and even those of them who may feel drawn to a life of scholarship or letters find little to attract them at the home of their alma mater, and seek, by preference, the large cities where periodicals and publishing houses offer some hope of support in a literary career. Even in the older and better equipped universities the faculty is usually a corps of working scholars, each man intent upon his specialty and rather inclined to undervalue merely "literary" performance. In many cases the fastidious and hypercritical turn of mind which besets the scholar, the timid conservatism which naturally characterizes an ancient seat of learning and the spirit of theological conformity which suppresses free discussion have exerted their {473} benumbing influence upon the originality and creative impulse of their inmates. Hence it happens that, while the contributions of American college teachers to the exact sciences, to theology and philology, metaphysics, political philosophy and the severer branches of learning have been honorable and important, they have as a class made little mark upon the general literature of the country. The professors of literature in our colleges are usually persons who have made no additions to literature, and the professors of rhetoric seem ordinarily to have been selected to teach students how to write, for the reason that they themselves have never written any thing that any one has ever read.

To these remarks the Harvard College of some fifty years ago offers a striking exception. It was not the large and fashionable university that it has lately grown to be, with its multiplied elective courses, its numerous faculty and its somewhat motley collection of undergraduates; but a small school of the classics and mathematics, with something of ethics, natural science and the modern languages added to its old-fashioned, scholastic curriculum, and with a very homogeneous *clientèle*, drawn mainly from the Unitarian families of Eastern Massachusetts. Nevertheless a finer intellectual life, in many respects, was lived at old Cambridge within the years covered by this chapter than nowadays at the same place, or at any date in any other American university town. The {474} neighborhood of Boston, where the commercial life has never so entirely overlain the intellectual as in New York and Philadelphia, has been a standing advantage to Harvard College. The recent upheaval in religious thought had secured toleration, and made possible that free and even audacious interchange of ideas without which a literary atmosphere is impossible. From these, or from whatever causes, it happened that the old Harvard scholarship had an elegant and tasteful side to it, so that the dry erudition of the schools blossomed into a generous culture, and there were men in the professors' chairs who were no less efficient as teachers because they were also poets, orators, wits and men of the world. In the seventeen years from 1821 to 1839 there were graduated from Harvard College Emerson, Holmes, Sumner, Phillips, Motley, Thoreau, Lowell, and Edward Everett Hale, some of whom took up their residence at Cambridge, others at Boston and others at Concord, which was quite as much a spiritual suburb of Boston as Cambridge was. In 1836, when Longfellow became Professor of Modern Languages at Harvard, Sumner was lecturing in the Law School. The following year—in which Thoreau took his bachelor's degree—witnessed the delivery of Emerson's Phi Beta Kappa lecture on the *American Scholar* in the college chapel and Wendell Phillips's speech on the *Murder of Lovejoy* in Faneuil Hall. Lowell, whose description of the impression produced by {475} the former of these famous addresses has been quoted in a previous chapter, was an undergraduate at the time. He took his degree in 1838 and in 1855 succeeded Longfellow in the chair of Modern Languages. Holmes had been chosen in 1847 Professor of Anatomy and Physiology in the Medical School —a position which he held until 1882. The historians, Prescott and Bancroft, had been graduated in 1814 and 1817 respectively. The former's first important publication, *Ferdinand and Isabella*, appeared in 1837. Bancroft had been a tutor in the college in 1822-23 and the initial volume of his *History of the United States* was issued in 1835. Another of the Massachusetts school of historical writers, Francis Parkman, took his first degree at Harvard in 1844. Cambridge was still hardly more than a village, a rural outskirt of Boston, such as Lowell described it in his article, *Cambridge Thirty Years Ago*, originally contributed to *Putnam's Monthly* in 1853, and afterward reprinted in his *Fireside Travels*, 1864. The situation of a university scholar in old Cambridge was thus an almost ideal one. Within easy reach of a great city, with its literary and social clubs, its theaters, lecture courses, public meetings, dinner parties, etc., he yet lived withdrawn in an academic retirement among elm-shaded avenues and leafy gardens, the dome of the Boston State-house looming distantly across the meadows where the Charles laid its "steel blue sickle" upon the variegated, plush-like ground of the wide marsh. There was {476} thus, at all times during the quarter of a century embraced between 1837 and 1861, a group of brilliant men resident in or about Cambridge and

Boston, meeting frequently and intimately, and exerting upon one another a most stimulating influence. Some of the closer circles—all concentric to the university—of which this group was loosely composed were laughed at by outsiders as "Mutual Admiration Societies." Such was, for instance, the "Five of Clubs," whose members were Longfellow, Sumner, C. C. Tellon, Professor of Greek at Harvard, and afterward president of the college; G. S. Hillard, a graceful lecturer, essayist and poet, of a somewhat amateurish kind; and Henry R. Cleveland, of Jamaica Plain, a lover of books and a writer of them.

Henry Wadsworth Longfellow (1807-1882) the most widely read and loved of American poets—or indeed, of all contemporary poets in England and America—though identified with Cambridge for nearly fifty years was a native of Portland, Maine, and a graduate of Bowdoin College, in the same class with Hawthorne. Since leaving college, in 1825, he had studied and traveled for some years in Europe, and had held the professorship of modern languages at Bowdoin. He had published several text books, a number of articles on the Romance languages and literatures in the *North American Review*, a thin volume of metrical translations from the Spanish, a few original poems in various periodicals, and the pleasant sketches of European {477} travel entitled *Outre Mer*. But Longfellow's fame began with the appearance in 1839 of his *Voices of the Night*. Excepting an earlier collection by Bryant this was the first volume of real poetry published in New England, and it had more warmth and sweetness, a greater richness and variety than Bryant's work ever possessed. Longfellow's genius was almost feminine in its flexibility and its sympathetic quality. It readily took the color of its surroundings and opened itself eagerly to impressions of the beautiful from every quarter, but especially from books. This first volume contained a few things written during his student days at Bowdoin, one of which, a blank verse piece on *Autumn*, clearly shows the influence of Bryant's *Thanatopsis*. Most of these *juvenilia* had nature for their theme, but they were not so sternly true to the New England landscape as Thoreau or Bryant. The skylark and the ivy appear among their scenic properties, and in the best of them, *Woods in Winter*, it is the English "hawthorn" and not any American tree, through which the gale is made to blow, just as later Longfellow uses "rooks" instead of crows. The young poet's fancy was instinctively putting out feelers toward the storied lands of the Old World, and in his *Hymn of the Moravian Nuns of Bethlehem* he transformed the rude church of the Moravian sisters to a cathedral with "glimmering tapers," swinging censers, chancel, altar, cowls and "dim mysterious aisle." After his visit to Europe, {478} Longfellow returned deeply imbued with the spirit of romance. It was his mission to refine our national taste by opening to American readers, in their own vernacular, new springs of beauty in the literatures of foreign tongues. The fact that this mission was interpretative, rather than creative, hardly detracts from Longfellow's true originality. It merely indicates that his inspiration came to him in the first instance from other sources than the common life about him. He naturally began as a translator, and this first volume contained, among other things, exquisite renderings from the German of Uhland, Salis, and Müller, from the Danish, French, Spanish and Anglo-Saxon, and a few passages from Dante. Longfellow remained all his life a translator, and in subtler ways than by direct translation he infused the fine essence of European poetry into his own. He loved—

"Tales that have the rime of age
And chronicles of eld."

The golden light of romance is shed upon his page, and it is his habit to borrow mediaeval and Catholic imagery from his favorite middle ages, even when writing of American subjects. To him the clouds are hooded friars, that "tell their beads in drops of rain;" the midnight winds blowing through woods and mountain passes are chanting solemn masses for the repose of the dying year, and the strain ends with the prayer—

"Kyrie, eleyson,
Christe, eleyson."

{479} In his journal he wrote characteristically: "The black shadows lie upon the grass like engravings in a book. Autumn has written his rubric on the illuminated leaves, the wind turns them over and chants like a friar." This in Cambridge, of a moonshiny night, on the first day of the American October. But several of the pieces in *Voices of the Night* sprang more immediately from the poet's own inner experience. The *Hymn to the Night*, the *Psalm of Life*, the *Reaper and the Flowers*, *Footsteps of Angels*, the *Light of Stars*, and the *Beleaguered City* spoke of love, bereavement, comfort, patience and faith. In these lovely songs and in many others of the same kind which he afterward wrote, Longfellow touched the hearts of all his countrymen. America is a country of homes, and Longfellow, as the poet of sentiment and of the domestic affections, became and remains far more general in his appeal than such a "cosmic" singer as Whitman, who is still practically unknown to the "fierce democracy" to which he has addressed himself. It would be hard to over-estimate the influence for good exerted by the tender feeling and the pure and sweet morality which the hundreds of thousands of copies of Longfellow's writings, that have been circulated among readers of all classes in America and England, have brought with them.

Three later collections, *Ballads and Other Poems*, 1842; the *Belfry of Bruges*, 1846; and the *Seaside and the Fireside*, 1850, comprise most of what is {480} noteworthy in Longfellow's minor poetry. The first of these embraced, together with some renderings from the German and the Scandinavian languages, specimens of stronger original work than the author had yet put forth; namely, the two powerful ballads of the *Skeleton in Armor* and the *Wreck of the Hesperus*. The former of these, written in the swift leaping meter of Drayton's *Ode to the Cambro Britons on their Harp*, was suggested by the digging up of a mail-clad skeleton at Fall River—a circumstance which the poet linked with the traditions about the Round Tower at Newport and gave to the whole the spirit of a Norse viking song of war and of the sea. The *Wreck of the Hesperus* was occasioned by the news of shipwrecks on the coast near

Gloucester and by the name of a reef—"Norman's Woe"—where many of them took place. It was written one night between twelve and three, and cost the poet, he said, "hardly an effort." Indeed, it is the spontaneous ease and grace, the unfailing taste of Longfellow's lines, which are their best technical quality. There is nothing obscure or esoteric about his poetry. If there is little passion or intellectual depth, there is always genuine poetic feeling, often a very high order of imagination and almost invariably the choice of the right word. In this volume were also included the *Village Blacksmith* and *Excelsior*. The latter, and the *Psalm of Life*, have had a "damnable iteration" which causes them to figure as Longfellow's most popular {481} pieces. They are by no means, however, among his best. They are vigorously expressed commonplaces of that hortatory kind which passes for poetry, but is, in reality, a vague species of preaching.

In the *Belfry of Bruges* and the *Seaside and the Fireside*, the translations were still kept up, and among the original pieces were the *Occultation of Orion*— the most imaginative of all Longfellow's poems; *Seaweed*, which has very noble stanzas, the favorite *Old Clock on the Stairs*, the *Building of the Ship*, with its magnificent closing apostrophe to the Union, and the *Fire of Driftwood*, the subtlest in feeling of any thing that the poet ever wrote. With these were verses of a more familiar quality, such as the *Bridge, Resignation*, and the *Day Is Done*, and many others, all reflecting moods of gentle and pensive sentiment, and drawing from analogies in nature or in legend lessons which, if somewhat obvious, were expressed with perfect art. Like Keats, he apprehended every thing on its beautiful side. Longfellow was all poet. Like Ophelia in *Hamlet*,

> "Thought and affection, passion, hell itself, *He* turns to favor and to prettiness."

He cared very little about the intellectual movement of the age. The transcendental ideas of Emerson passed over his head and left him undisturbed. For politics he had that gentlemanly distaste which the cultivated class in America had {482} already begun to entertain. In 1842 he printed a small volume of *Poems on Slavery*, which drew commendation from his friend Sumner, but had nothing of the fervor of Whittier's or Lowell's utterances on the same subject. It is interesting to compare his journals with Hawthorne's *American Note Books* and to observe in what very different ways the two writers made prey of their daily experiences for literary material. A favorite haunt of Longfellow's was the bridge between Boston and Cambridgeport, the same which he put into verse in his poem, the *Bridge*. "I always stop on the bridge," he writes in his journal; "tide waters are beautiful. From the ocean up into the land they go, like messengers, to ask why the tribute has not been paid. The brooks and rivers answer that there has been little harvest of snow and rain this year. Floating sea-weed and kelp is carried up into the meadows, as returning sailors bring oranges in bandanna handkerchiefs to friends in the country." And again: "We leaned for awhile on the wooden rail and enjoyed the silvery reflection on the sea, making sundry comparisons. Among other thoughts we had this cheering one, that the whole sea was flashing with this heavenly light, though we saw it only in a single track; the dark waves are the dark providences of God; luminous, though not to us; and even to ourselves in another position." "Walk on the bridge, both ends of which are lost in the fog, like human life midway between two eternities; {483} beginning and ending in mist." In Hawthorne an allegoric meaning is usually something deeper and subtler than this, and seldom so openly expressed. Many of Longfellow's poems—the *Beleaguered City*, for example—may be definitely divided into two parts; in the first, a story is told or a natural phenomenon described; in the second, the spiritual application of the parable is formally set forth. This method became with him almost a trick of style, and his readers learned to look for the *haec fabula docet* at the end as a matter of course. As for the prevailing optimism in Longfellow's view of life—of which the above passage is an instance—it seemed to be in him an affair of temperament, and not, as in Emerson, the result of philosophic insight. Perhaps, however, in the last analysis optimism and pessimism are subjective—the expression of temperament or individual experience, since the facts of life are the same, whether seen through Schopenhauer's eyes or through Emerson's. If there is any particular in which Longfellow's inspiration came to him at first hand and not through books, it is in respect to the aspects of the sea. On this theme no American poet has written more beautifully and with a keener sympathy than the author of the *Wreck of the Hesperus* and of *Seaweed*.

In 1847 was published the long poem of *Evangeline*. The story of the Acadian peasant girl, who was separated from her lover in the dispersion of her people by the English troops, and after weary wanderings and a life-long search found him at last, {484} an old man dying in a Philadelphia hospital, was told to Longfellow by the Rev. H. L. Conolly, who had previously suggested it to Hawthorne as a subject for a story. Longfellow, characteristically enough, "got up" the local color for his poem from Haliburton's account of the dispersion of the Grand-Pré Acadians, from Darby's *Geographical Description of Louisiana* and Watson's *Annals of Philadelphia*. He never needed to go much outside of his library for literary impulse and material. Whatever may be held as to Longfellow's inventive powers as a creator of characters or an interpreter of American life, his originality as an artist is manifested by his successful domestication in *Evangeline* of the dactylic hexameter, which no English poet had yet used with effect. The English poet, Arthur Hugh Clough, who lived for a time in Cambridge, followed Longfellow's example in the use of hexameter in his *Bothie of Tober-na-Vuolich*, so that we have now arrived at the time—a proud moment for American letters—when the works of our writers began to react upon the literature of Europe. But the beauty of the descriptions in *Evangeline* and the pathos—somewhat too drawn out—of the story made it dear to a multitude of readers who cared nothing about the technical disputes of Poe and other critics as to whether or not Longfellow's lines were sufficiently "spondaic" to truthfully represent the quantitative hexameters of Homer and Vergil.

In 1855 appeared *Hiawatha*, Longfellow's most {485} aboriginal and "American" book. The tripping trochaic measure he borrowed from the Finnish epic *Kalevala*. The vague, childlike mythology of the Indian tribes, with its anthropomorphic sense of the brotherhood between men, animals, and the forms of inanimate nature, he took from Schoolcraft's *Algic Researches*, 1839. He fixed forever, in a skillfully chosen poetic form, the more inward and imaginative part of Indian character, as Cooper had given permanence to its external and active side. Of Longfellow's dramatic experiments the *Golden Legend*, 1851, alone deserves mention here. This was in his chosen realm; a tale taken from the ecclesiastical annals of the middle ages, precious with martyrs' blood and bathed in the rich twilight of the cloister. It contains some of his best work, but its merit is rather poetic than dramatic; although Ruskin praised it for the closeness with which it entered into the temper of the monk.

Longfellow has pleased the people more than the critics. He gave freely what he had, and the gift was beautiful. Those who have looked in his poetry for something else than poetry, or for poetry of some other kind, have not been slow to assert that he was a lady's poet; one who satisfied callow youths and school-girls by uttering commonplaces in graceful and musical shape, but who offered no strong meat for men. Miss Fuller called his poetry thin and the poet himself a "dandy Pindar." This is not true of his poetry, {486} or of the best of it. But he had a singing and not a talking voice, and in his prose one becomes sensible of a certain weakness. *Hyperion*, for example, published in 1839, a loitering fiction, interspersed with descriptions of European travel, is, upon the whole, a weak book, over flowery in diction and sentimental in tone.

The crown of Longfellow's achievements as a translator was his great version of Dante's *Divina Commedia*, published between 1867 and 1870. It is a severely literal, almost a line for line, rendering. The meter is preserved, but the rhyme sacrificed. If not the best English poem constructed from Dante, it is at all events the most faithful and scholarly paraphrase. The sonnets which accompanied it are among Longfellow's best work. He seems to have been raised by daily communion with the great Tuscan into a habit of deeper and more subtle thought than is elsewhere common in his poetry.

Oliver Wendell Holmes (1809-) is a native of Cambridge and a graduate of Harvard in the class of '29; a class whose anniversary reunions he has celebrated in something like forty distinct poems and songs. For sheer cleverness and versatility Dr. Holmes is, perhaps, unrivaled among American men of letters. He has been poet, wit, humorist, novelist, essayist and a college lecturer and writer on medical topics. In all of these departments he has produced work which ranks high, if not with the highest. His father, {487} Dr. Abiel Holmes, was a graduate of Yale and an orthodox minister of liberal temper, but the son early threw in his lot with the Unitarians; and, as was natural to a man of a satiric turn and with a very human enjoyment of a fight, whose youth was cast in an age of theological controversy, he has always had his fling at Calvinism and has prolonged the slogans of old battles into a later generation; sometimes, perhaps, insisting upon them rather wearisomely and beyond the limits of good taste. He had, even as an undergraduate, a reputation for cleverness at writing comic verses, and many of his good things in this kind, such as the *Dorchester Giant* and the *Height of the Ridiculous*, were contributed to the *Collegian*, a students' paper. But he first drew the attention of a wider public by his spirited ballad of *Old Ironsides*—

"Ay! Tear her tattered ensign down!"—

composed about 1830, when it was proposed by the government to take to pieces the unseaworthy hulk of the famous old man-of-war, "Constitution." Holmes's indignant protest—which has been a favorite subject for school-boy declamation—had the effect of postponing the vessel's fate for a great many years. From 1830-35 the young poet was pursuing his medical studies in Boston and Paris, contributing now and then some verses to the magazines. Of his life as a medical student in Paris there are many pleasant reminiscences in his *Autocrat* and other writings, as where he tells, for {488} instance, of a dinner party of Americans in the French capital, where one of the company brought tears of home-sickness into the eyes of his *sodales* by saying that the tinkle of the ice in the champagne-glasses reminded him of the cowbells in the rocky old pastures of New England. In 1836 he printed his first collection of poems. The volume contained among a number of pieces broadly comic, like the *September Gale*, the *Music Grinders*, and the *Ballad of the Oysterman*—which at once became widely popular—a few poems of a finer and quieter temper, in which there was a quaint blending of the humorous and the pathetic. Such were *My Aunt* and the *Last Leaf*—which Abraham Lincoln found "inexpressibly touching," and which it is difficult to read without the double tribute of a smile and a tear. The volume contained also *Poetry: A Metrical Essay*, read before the Harvard Chapter of the Phi Beta Kappa Society, which was the first of that long line of capital occasional poems which Holmes has been spinning for half a century with no sign of fatigue and with scarcely any falling off in freshness; poems read or spoken or sung at all manner of gatherings, public and private; at Harvard commencements, class days, and other academic anniversaries; at inaugurations, centennials, dedications of cemeteries, meetings of medical associations, mercantile libraries, Burns clubs and New England societies; at rural festivals and city fairs; openings of theaters, layings of corner stones, {489} birthday celebrations, jubilees, funerals, commemoration services, dinners of welcome or farewell to Dickens, Bryant, Everett, Whittier, Longfellow, Grant, Farragut, the Grand Duke Alexis, the Chinese Embassy and what not. Probably no poet of any age or clime has written so much and so well to order. He has been particularly happy in verses of a convivial kind, toasts for big civic feasts, or post-prandial rhymes for the *petit comité*—the snug little dinners of the chosen few. His

"The quaint trick to cram the pithy line
That cracks so crisply over bubbling wine."

And although he could write on occasion a *Song for a Temperance Dinner*, he has preferred to chant the praise of the punch bowl and to

"feel the old convivial glow (unaided) o'er me stealing,
The warm, champagny, old-particular-brandy-punchy feeling."

It would be impossible to enumerate the many good things of this sort which Holmes has written, full of wit and wisdom, and of humor lightly dashed with sentiment and sparkling with droll analogies, sudden puns, and unexpected turns of rhyme and phrase. Among the best of them are *Nux Postcoenatica*, *A Modest Request*, *Ode for a Social Meeting*, *The Boys*, and *Rip Van Winkle, M.D.* Holmes's favorite measure, in his longer poems, is the heroic couplet which Pope's example seems to have consecrated forever to satiric and didactic verse. He writes as easily in this {490} meter as if it were prose, and with much of Pope's epigrammatic neatness. He also manages with facility the anapaestics of Moore and the ballad stanza which Hood had made the vehicle for his drolleries. It cannot be expected that verses manufactured to pop with the corks and fizz with the champagne at academic banquets should much outlive the occasion; or that the habit of producing such verses on demand should foster in the producer that "high seriousness" which Matthew Arnold asserts to be one mark of all great poetry. Holmes's poetry is mostly on the colloquial level, excellent society-verse, but even in its serious moments too smart and too pretty to be taken very gravely; with a certain glitter, knowingness and flippancy about it and an absence of that self-forgetfulness and intense absorption in its theme which characterize the work of the higher imagination. This is rather the product of fancy and wit. Wit, indeed, in the old sense of quickness in the perception of analogies is the staple of his mind. His resources in the way of figure, illustration, allusion and anecdote are wonderful. Age cannot wither him nor custom stale his infinite variety, and there is as much powder in his latest pyrotechnics as in the rockets which he sent up half a century ago. Yet, though the humorist in him rather outweighs the poet, he has written a few things, like the *Chambered Nautilus* and *Homesick in Heaven*, which are as purely and deeply poetic as the *One-Hoss Shay* and the *Prologue* are funny. {491} Dr. Holmes is not of the stuff of which idealists and enthusiasts are made. As a physician and a student of science, the facts of the material universe have counted for much with him. His clear, positive, alert intellect was always impatient of mysticism. He had the sharp eye of the satirist and the man of the world for oddities of dress, dialect and manners. Naturally the transcendental movement struck him on its ludicrous side, and in his *After-Dinner Poem*, read at the Phi Beta Kappa dinner at Cambridge in 1843, he had his laugh at the "Orphic odes" and "runes" of the bedlamite seer and bard of mystery

"Who rides a beetle which he calls a 'sphinx,'
And O what questions asked in club-foot rhyme
Of Earth the tongueless, and the deaf-mute Time!
Here babbling 'Insight' shouts in Nature's ears
His last conundrum on the orbs and spheres;
There Self-inspection sucks its little thumb,
With 'Whence am I?' and 'Wherefore did I come?'"

Curiously enough, the author of these lines lived to write an appreciative life of the poet who wrote the *Sphinx*. There was a good deal of toryism or social conservatism in Holmes. He acknowledged a preference for the man with a pedigree, the man who owned family portraits, had been brought up in familiarity with books, and could pronounce "view" correctly. Readers unhappily not of the "Brahmin caste of New England" have sometimes resented as snobbishness Holmes's harping {492} on "family," and his perpetual application of certain favorite shibboleths to other people's ways of speech. "The woman who calc'lates is lost."

"Learning condemns beyond the reach of hope
The careless lips that speak of soap for soap... .
Do put your accents in the proper spot;
Don't, let me beg you, don't say 'How?' for 'What?'
The things named 'pants' in certain documents,

A word not made for gentlemen, but 'gents.'"

With the rest of "society" he was disposed to ridicule the abolition movement as a crotchet of the eccentric and the long-haired. But when the civil war broke out he lent his pen, his tongue, and his own flesh and blood to the cause of the Union. The individuality of Holmes's writings comes in part from their local and provincial bias. He has been the laureate of Harvard College and the bard of Boston city, an urban poet, with a cockneyish fondness for old Boston ways and things—the Common and the Frog Pond, Faneuil Hall and King's Chapel and the Old South, Bunker Hill, Long Wharf, the Tea Party, and the town crier. It was Holmes who invented the playful saying that "Boston State House is the hub of the solar system."

In 1857 was started the *Atlantic Monthly*, a magazine which has published a good share of the best work done by American writers within the past thirty years. Its immediate success was assured by Dr. Holmes's brilliant series of papers, the {493} *Autocrat of the Breakfast Table*, 1858, followed at once by the *Professor at the Breakfast Table*, 1859, and later by the *Poet at the Breakfast Table*, 1873. The *Autocrat* is its author's masterpiece, and holds the fine quintessence of his humor, his scholarship, his satire, genial observation, and ripe experience of men and cities. The form is as unique and original as the contents, being something between an essay and a drama; a succession of monologues or table-talks at a typical American boarding-house, with a thread of story running through the whole. The variety of mood and thought is so great that these conversations never tire, and the prose is interspersed with some of the author's choicest verse. The *Professor at the Breakfast Table* followed too closely on the heels of the *Autocrat*, and had less freshness. The third number of the series was better, and was pleasantly reminiscent and slightly garrulous, Dr. Holmes being now (1873) sixty-four years old, and entitled to the gossiping privilege of age. The *personnel* of the *Breakfast Table* series, such as the landlady and the landlady's daughter and her son, Benjamin Franklin; the schoolmistress, the young man named John, the Divinity Student, the Kohinoor, the Sculpin, the Scarabaeus and the Old Gentleman who sits opposite, are not fully drawn characters, but outlined figures, lightly sketched—as is the Autocrat's wont—by means of some trick of speech, or dress, or feature, but they are quite life-like enough for their purpose, which is mainly to {494} furnish listeners and foils to the eloquence and wit of the chief talker.

In 1860 and 1867 Holmes entered the field of fiction with two "medicated novels," *Elsie Venner* and the *Guardian Angel*. The first of these was a singular tale, whose heroine united with her very fascinating human attributes something of the nature of a serpent; her mother having been bitten by a rattlesnake a few months before the birth of the girl, and kept alive meanwhile by the use of powerful antidotes. The heroine of the *Guardian Angel* inherited lawless instincts from a vein of Indian blood in her ancestry. These two books were studies of certain medico-psychological problems. They preached Dr. Holmes's favorite doctrines of heredity and of the modified nature of moral responsibility by reason of transmitted tendencies which limit the freedom of the will. In *Elsie Venner*, in particular, the weirdly imaginative and speculative character of the leading motive suggests Hawthorne's method in fiction, but the background and the subsidiary figures have a realism that is in abrupt contrast with this, and gives a kind of doubleness and want of keeping to the whole. The Yankee characters, in particular, and the satirical pictures of New England country life are open to the charge of caricature. In the *Guardian Angel* the figure of Byles Gridley, the old scholar, is drawn with thorough sympathy, and though some of his acts are improbable he is, on the whole, Holmes's most {495} vital conception in the region of dramatic creation.

James Russell Lowell (1819-), the foremost of American critics and of living American poets is, like Holmes, a native of Cambridge, and, like Emerson and Holmes, a clergyman's son. In 1855 he succeeded Longfellow as Professor of Modern Languages in Harvard College. Of late years he has held important diplomatic posts, like Everett, Irving, Bancroft, Motley, and other Americans distinguished in letters, having been United States Minister to Spain, and, under two administrations, to the Court of St. James. Lowell is not so spontaneously and exclusively a poet as Longfellow. His fame has been of slower growth, and his popularity with the average reader has never been so great. His appeal has been to the few rather than the many, to an audience of scholars and of the judicious rather than to the "groundlings" of the general public. Nevertheless his verse, though without the evenness, instinctive grace, and unerring good taste of Longfellow's, has more energy and a stronger intellectual fiber; while in prose he is very greatly the superior. His first volume, *A Year's Life*, 1841, gave little promise. In 1843 he started a magazine, the *Pioneer*, which only reached its third number, though it counted among its contributors Hawthorne, Poe, Whittier, and Miss Barrett (afterward Mrs. Browning). A second volume of poems, printed in 1844, showed a distinct advance, in such {496} pieces as the *Shepherd of King Admetus*, *Rhoecus*, a classical myth, told in excellent blank verse, and the same in subject with one of Landor's polished intaglios; and the *Legend of Britanny*, a narrative poem, which had fine passages, but no firmness in the management of the story. As yet, it was evident, the young poet had not found his theme. This came with the outbreak of the Mexican War, which was unpopular in New England, and which the Free Soil party regarded as a slaveholders' war waged without provocation against a sister republic, and simply for the purpose of extending the area of slavery.

In 1846, accordingly, the *Biglow Papers* began to appear in the *Boston Courier*, and were collected and published in book form in 1848. These were a series of rhymed satires upon the government and the war party, written in the Yankee dialect, and supposed to be the work of Hosea Biglow, a home-spun genius in a down-east country town, whose letters to the editor were indorsed and accompanied by the comments of the Rev. Homer Wilbur, A.M., pastor of the First Church in Jaalam, and (prospective) member of many learned societies. The first paper was a derisive address to a recruiting sergeant, with a denunciation of the "nigger-drivin' States" and the "northern dough-faces," a plain hint that the North would do better to secede than to continue doing dirty work for the South, and an expression of those universal peace doctrines which were then in the air, and to which {497} Longfellow gave serious utterance in his *Occultation of Orion*.

"Ez for war, I call it murder—
  There you hev it plain an' flat:
I don't want to go no furder
  Than my Testyment for that;
God hez said so plump an' fairly,
  It's ez long as it is broad,
An' you've gut to git up airly
  Ef you want to take in God."

The second number was a versified paraphrase of a letter received from Mr. Birdofredom Sawin, "a yung feller of our town that wuz cussed fool enuff to goe atrottin inter Miss Chiff arter a drum and fife," and who finds when he gets to Mexico that

"This kind o' sogerin' aint a mite like our October trainin'."

Of the subsequent papers the best was, perhaps, *What Mr. Robinson Thinks*, an election ballad, which caused universal laughter, and was on every body's tongue.

The *Biglow Papers* remain Lowell's most original contribution to American literature. They are, all in all, the best political satires in the language, and unequaled as portraitures of the Yankee character, with its 'cuteness, its homely wit, and its latent poetry. Under the racy humor of the dialect—which became in Lowell's hands a medium of literary expression almost as effective as {498} Burns's Ayrshire Scotch—burned that moral enthusiasm and that hatred of wrong and deification of duty—"Stern daughter of the voice of God"—which, in the tough New England stock, stands instead of the passion in the blood of southern races. Lowell's serious poems on political questions, such as the *Present Crisis, Ode to Freedom*, and the *Capture of Fugitive Slaves*, have the old Puritan fervor, and such lines as

"They are slaves who dare not be
In the right with two or three,"

and the passage beginning

"Truth forever on the scaffold, Wrong forever on the throne,"

became watchwords in the conflict against slavery and disunion. Some of these were published in his volume of 1848 and the collected edition of his poems, in two volumes, issued in 1850. These also included his most ambitious narrative poem, the *Vision of Sir Launfal*, an allegorical and spiritual treatment of one of the legends of the Holy Grail. Lowell's genius was not epical, but lyric and didactic. The merit of *Sir Launfal* is not in the telling of the story, but in the beautiful descriptive episodes, one of which, commencing,

"And what is so rare as a day in June?
Then if ever come perfect days;"

is as current as any thing that he has written. It is significant of the lack of a natural impulse {499} toward narrative invention in Lowell, that, unlike Longfellow and Holmes, he never tried his hand at a novel. One of the most important parts of a novelist's equipment he certainly possesses; namely, an insight into character, and an ability to delineate it. This gift is seen especially in his sketch of Parson Wilbur, who edited the *Biglow Papers* with a delightfully pedantic introduction, glossary, and notes; in the prose essay *On a Certain Condescension in Foreigners*, and in the uncompleted poem, *Fitz-Adam's Story*. See also the sketch of Captain Underhill in the essay on *New England Two Centuries Ago*.

The *Biglow Papers* when brought out in a volume were prefaced by imaginary notices of the press, including a capital parody of Carlyle, and a reprint from the "Jaalam Independent Blunderbuss," of the first sketch—afterward amplified and enriched—of that perfect Yankee idyl, the *Courtin'*. Between 1862 and 1865 a second series of *Biglow Papers* appeared, called out by the events of the civil war. Some of these, as, for instance, *Jonathan to John*, a remonstrance with England for her unfriendly attitude toward the North, were not inferior to any thing in the earlier series; and others were even superior as poems, equal indeed, in pathos and intensity to any thing that Lowell has written in his professedly serious verse. In such passages the dialect wears rather thin, and there is a certain incongruity between the rustic spelling and the vivid beauty and power {500} and the figurative cast of the phrase in stanzas like the following:

"Wut's words to them whose faith an' truth
On war's red techstone rang true metal,
Who ventered life an' love an' youth
For the gret prize o' death in battle?
To him who, deadly hurt, agen
Flashed on afore the charge's thunder,
Tippin' with fire the bolt of men
That rived the rebel line asunder?"

Charles Sumner, a somewhat heavy person, with little sense of humor, wished that the author of the *Biglow Papers* "could have used good English." In the lines just quoted, indeed, the bad English adds nothing to the effect. In 1848 Lowell wrote *A Fable for Critics*, something after the style of Sir John Suckling's *Session of the Poets*; a piece of rollicking doggerel in which he surveyed the American Parnassus, scattering about headlong fun, sharp satire and sound criticism in equal proportion. Never an industrious workman, like Longfellow, at the poetic craft, but preferring to wait for the mood to seize him, he allowed eighteen years to go by, from 1850 to 1868, before publishing another volume of verse. In the latter year appeared *Under the Willows*, which contains some of his ripest and most perfect work; notably *A Winter Evening Hymn to my Fire*, with its noble and touching close— suggested by, perhaps, at any rate recalling, the dedication of Goethe's *Faust*,

"Ihr naht euch wieder, schwankende Gestalten;"

{501} the subtle *Footpath* and *In the Twilight*, the lovely little poems *Auf Wiedersehen* and *After the Funeral*, and a number of spirited political pieces, such as *Villa Franca*, and the *Washers of the Shroud*. This volume contained also his *Ode Recited at the Harvard Commemoration* in 1865. This, although uneven, is one of the finest occasional poems in the language, and the most important contribution which our civil war has made to song. It was charged with the grave emotion of one who not only shared the patriotic grief and exultation of his *alma mater* in the sacrifice of her sons, but who felt a more personal sorrow in the loss of kindred of his own, fallen in the front of battle. Particularly noteworthy in this memorial ode are the tribute to Abraham Lincoln, the third strophe, beginning, "Many loved Truth:" the exordium—"O Beautiful! my Country! ours once more!" and the close of the eighth strophe, where the poet chants of the youthful heroes who

"Come transfigured back,
Secure from change in their high-hearted ways,
Beautiful evermore and with the rays
Of morn on their white Shields of Expectation."

From 1857 to 1862 Lowell edited the *Atlantic Monthly*, and from 1863 to 1872 the *North American Review*. His prose, beginning with an early volume of *Conversations on Some of the Old Poets*, 1844, has consisted mainly of critical essays on individual writers, such as Dante, Chaucer, Spenser, {502} Emerson, Shakespere, Thoreau, Pope, Carlyle, etc., together with papers of a more miscellaneous kind, like *Witchcraft, New England Two Centuries Ago, My Garden Acquaintance, A Good Word for Winter, Abraham Lincoln*, etc., etc. Two volumes of these were published in 1870 and 1876, under the title *Among My Books*, and another, *My Study Windows*, in 1871. As a literary critic Lowell ranks easily among the first of living writers. His scholarship is thorough, his judgment sure, and he pours out upon his page an unwithholding wealth of knowledge, humor, wit and imagination from the fullness of an overflowing mind. His prose has not the chastened correctness and "low tone" of Matthew Arnold's. It is rich, exuberant, and sometimes over fanciful, running away into excesses of allusion or following the lead of a chance pun so as sometimes to lay itself open to the charge of pedantry and bad taste. Lowell's resources in the way of illustration and comparison are endless, and the readiness of his wit and his delight in using it put many temptations in his way. Purists in style accordingly take offense at his saying that "Milton is the only man who ever got much poetry out of a cataract, and that was a cataract in his eye;" or of his speaking of "a gentleman for whom the bottle before him reversed the wonder of the stereoscope and substituted the Gaston *v* for the *b* in binocular," which is certainly a puzzling and roundabout fashion of telling us that he had drunk so much {503} that he saw double. The critics also find fault with his coining such words as "undisprivacied" and with his writing such lines as the famous one—from the *Cathedral*, 1870—

"Spume-sliding down the baffled decuman."

It must be acknowledged that his style lacks the crowning grace of simplicity, but it is precisely by reason of its allusive quality that scholarly readers take pleasure in it. They like a diction that has stuff in it and is woven thick, and where a thing is said in such a way as to recall many other things.

Mention should be made, in connection with this Cambridge circle, of one writer who touched its circumference briefly. This was Sylvester Judd, a graduate of Yale, who entered the Harvard Divinity School in 1837 and in 1840 became minister of a Unitarian church in Augusta, Maine. Judd published several books, but the only one of them at all rememberable was *Margaret*, 1845, a novel of which Lowell said in *A Fable for Critics* that it was "the first Yankee book with the soul of Down East in it." It was very imperfect in point of art, and its second part—a rhapsodical description of a

sort of Unitarian Utopia—is quite unreadable. But in the delineation of the
few chief characters and of the rude, wild life of an outlying New England
township just after the close of the revolutionary war, as well as in the tragic
power of the catastrophe, there was genius of a high order.

{504}

As the country has grown older and more populous, and works in all
departments of thought have multiplied, it becomes necessary to draw more
strictly the line between the literature of knowledge and the literature of
power. Political history, in and of itself, scarcely falls within the limits of this
sketch, and yet it cannot be altogether dismissed; for the historian's art at its
highest demands imagination, narrative skill, and a sense of unity and
proportion in the selection and arrangement of his facts, all of which are
literary qualities. It is significant that many of our best historians have begun
authorship in the domain of imaginative literature: Bancroft with an early
volume of poems; Motley with his historical romances *Merry Mount* and
Morton's Hope; and Parkman with a novel, *Vassall Morton*. The oldest of that
modern group of writers that have given America an honorable position in the
historical literature of the world was William Hickling Prescott (1796-1859.)
Prescott chose for his theme the history of the Spanish conquests in the New
World, a subject full of romantic incident and susceptible of that glowing and
perhaps slightly over gorgeous coloring which he laid on with a liberal hand.
His completed histories, in their order, are the *Reign of Ferdinand and
Isabella*, 1837; the *Conquest of Mexico*, 1843—a topic which Irving had
relinquished to him; and the *Conquest of Peru*, 1847. Prescott was fortunate
in being born to leisure and fortune, but he had difficulties of {505} another
kind to overcome. He was nearly blind, and had to teach himself Spanish and
look up authorities through the help of others and to write with a noctograph
or by amanuenses.

George Bancroft (1800-) issued the first volume of his great *History of the
United States* in 1834, and exactly half a century later the final volume of the
work, bringing the subject down to 1789. Bancroft had studied at Göttingen
and imbibed from the German historian Heeren the scientific method of
historical study. He had access to original sources, in the nature of collections
and state papers in the governmental archives of Europe, of which no
American had hitherto been able to avail himself. His history in thoroughness
of treatment leaves nothing to be desired, and has become the standard
authority on the subject. As a literary performance merely, it is somewhat
wanting in flavor, Bancroft's manner being heavy and stiff when compared
with Motley's or Parkman's. The historian's services to his country have been
publicly recognized by his successive appointments as Secretary of the Navy,

Minister to England, and Minister to Germany.

The greatest, on the whole, of American historians was John Lothrop Motley (1814-1877), who, like Bancroft, was a student at Göttingen and United States Minister to England. His *Rise of the Dutch Republic*, 1856, and *History of the United Netherlands*, published in installments from 1861 to {506} 1868, equaled Bancroft's work in scientific thoroughness and philosophic grasp, and Prescott's in the picturesque brilliancy of the narrative, while it excelled them both in its masterly analysis of great historic characters, reminding the reader, in this particular, of Macaulay's figure painting. The episodes of the siege of Antwerp and the sack of the cathedral, and of the defeat and wreck of the Spanish Armada, are as graphic as Prescott's famous description of Cortez's capture of the city of Mexico; while the elder historian has nothing to compare with Motley's vivid personal sketches of Queen Elizabeth, Philip the Second, Henry of Navarre, and William the Silent. The *Life of John of Barneveld*, 1874, completed this series of studies upon the history of the Netherlands, a theme to which Motley was attracted because the heroic struggle of the Dutch for liberty offered, in some respects, a parallel to the growth of political independence in Anglo-Saxon communities, and especially in his own America.

The last of these Massachusetts historical writers whom we shall mention is Francis Parkman (1823-), whose subject has the advantage of being thoroughly American. His *Oregon Trail*, 1847, a series of sketches of prairie and Rocky Mountain life, originally contributed to the *Knickerbocker Magazine*, displays his early interest in the American Indians. In 1851 appeared his first historical work, the *Conspiracy of Pontiac*. This has been followed by the series entitled *France and England {507} in North America*, the six successive parts of which are as follows: the *Pioneers of France in the New World*; the *Jesuits in North America*; *La Salle and the Discovery of the Great West*; the *Old Régime in Canada*; *Count Frontenac and New France*; and *Montcalm and Wolfe*. These narratives have a wonderful vividness, and a romantic interest not inferior to Cooper's novels. Parkman made himself personally familiar with the scenes which he described, and some of the best descriptions of American woods and waters are to be found in his histories. If any fault is to be found with his books, indeed, it is that their picturesqueness and "fine writing" are a little in excess.

The political literature of the years from 1837 to 1861 hinged upon the antislavery struggle. In this "irrepressible conflict" Massachusetts led the van. Garrison had written in his *Liberator*, in 1830, "I will be as harsh as truth and as uncompromising as justice. I am in earnest; I will not equivocate; I will not excuse; I will not retreat a single inch; and I will be heard." But the

Garrisonian abolitionists remained for a long time, even in the North, a small and despised faction. It was a great point gained when men of education and social standing like Wendell Phillips (1811-1884), and Charles Sumner (1811-1874), joined themselves to the cause. Both of these were graduates of Harvard and men of scholarly pursuits. They became the representative orators of the antislavery party, Phillips on the platform {508} and Sumner in the Senate. The former first came before the public in his fiery speech, delivered in Faneuil Hall December 8, 1837, before a meeting called to denounce the murder of Lovejoy, who had been killed at Alton, Ill., while defending his press against a pro-slavery mob. Thenceforth Phillips's voice was never idle in behalf of the slave. His eloquence was impassioned and direct, and his English singularly pure, simple, and nervous. He is perhaps nearer to Demosthenes than any other American orator. He was a most fascinating platform speaker on themes outside of politics, and his lecture on the *Lost Arts* was a favorite with audiences of all sorts.

Sumner was a man of intellectual tastes, who entered politics reluctantly, and only in obedience to the resistless leading of his conscience. He was a student of literature and art; a connoisseur of engravings, for example, of which he made a valuable collection. He was fond of books, conversation, and foreign travel, and in Europe, while still a young man, had made a remarkable impression in society. But he left all this for public life, and in 1851 was elected, as Webster's successor, to the Senate of the United States. Thereafter he remained the leader of the Abolitionists in Congress until slavery was abolished. His influence throughout the North was greatly increased by the brutal attack upon him in the Senate chamber in 1856 by "Bully Brooks" of South Carolina. {509} Sumner's oratory was stately and somewhat labored. While speaking he always seemed, as has been wittily said, to be surveying a "broad landscape of his own convictions." His most impressive qualities as a speaker were his intense moral earnestness and his thorough knowledge of his subject. The most telling of his parliamentary speeches are perhaps his speech *On the Kansas-Nebraska Bill*, of February 3, 1854, and *On the Crime against Kansas*, May 19 and 20, 1856; of his platform addresses, the oration on the *True Grandeur of Nations*.

1. Henry Wadsworth Longfellow. Voices of the Night. The Skeleton in Armor. The Wreck of the Hesperus. The Village Blacksmith. The Belfry of Bruges and Other Poems (1846). By the Seaside. Hiawatha. Tales of a Wayside Inn.

2. Oliver Wendell Holmes. Autocrat of the Breakfast Table. Elsie Venner. Old Ironsides. The Last Leaf. My Aunt. The Music-Grinders. On Lending a Punch Bowl. Nux Postcoenatica. A Modest Request. The Living Temple. Meeting of the Alumni of Harvard College. Homesick in

Heaven. Epilogue to the Breakfast Table Series. The Boys. Dorothy. The Iron Gate.

3. James Russell Lowell. The Biglow Papers (two series). Under the Willows and Other Poems. 1868. Rhoecus. The Shepherd of King Admetus. The Vision of Sir Launfal. The {510} Present Crisis. The Dandelion. The Birch Tree. Beaver Brook. Essays on Chaucer: Shakspere Once More: Dryden: Emerson; the Lecturer: Thoreau: My Garden Acquaintance: A Good Word for Winter: A Certain Condescension in Foreigners.

4. William Hickling Prescott. The Conquest of Mexico.

5. John Lothrop Motley. The United Netherlands.

6. Francis Parkman. The Oregon Trail. The Jesuits in North America.

7. Representative American Orations; volume v. Edited by Alexander Johnston. New York: G. P. Putnam's Sons. 1884.

{511}

CHAPTER VI.

LITERATURE IN THE CITIES.

1837-1861.

Literature as a profession has hardly existed in the United States until very recently. Even now the number of those who support themselves by purely literary work is small, although the growth of the reading public and the establishment of great magazines, such as *Harper's*, the *Century*, and the *Atlantic*, have made a market for intellectual wares which forty years ago would have seemed a godsend to poorly paid Bohemians like Poe or obscure men of genius like Hawthorne. About 1840 two Philadelphia magazines—*Godey's Lady's Book* and *Graham's Monthly*—began to pay their contributors twelve dollars a page, a price then thought wildly munificent. But the first magazine of the modern type was *Harper's Monthly*, founded in 1850. American books have always suffered, and still continue to suffer, from the want of an international copyright, which has flooded the country with cheap reprints and translations of foreign works, with which the domestic product has been unable to contend on such uneven terms. With the first ocean steamers there {512} started up a class of large-paged weeklies in New York and elsewhere, such as *Brother Jonathan*, the *New World*, and the *Corsair*, which furnished their readers with the freshest writings of Dickens and Bulwer and other British celebrities within a fortnight after their appearance in London. This still further restricted the profits of native authors and nearly drove them from the field of periodical literature. By special arrangement the novels of Thackeray and other English writers were printed in *Harper's* in installments simultaneously with their issue in English periodicals. The *Atlantic* was the first of our magazines which was founded expressly for the encouragement of home talent, and which had a purely Yankee flavor. Journalism was the profession which naturally attracted men of letters, as having most in common with their chosen work and as giving them a medium, under their own control, through which they could address the public. A few favored scholars, like Prescott, were made independent by the possession of private fortunes. Others, like Holmes, Longfellow, and Lowell, gave to literature such leisure as they could get in the intervals of an active profession or of college work. Still others, like Emerson and Thoreau, by living in the country and making their modest competence—eked out in Emerson's case by lecturing here and there—suffice for their simple needs, secured themselves freedom from the restraints of any regular calling. But in default of some such *pou sto* our men of {513} letters have usually sought the cities and allied themselves with the press. It will be remembered that Lowell started a short-lived magazine on his own account, and that he afterward edited the *Atlantic* and the *North American*. Also that Ripley and Charles A. Dana betook themselves to journalism after the break up of the Brook Farm Community.

In the same way William Cullen Bryant (1794-1878), the earliest American poet of importance, whose impulses drew him to the solitudes of nature, was compelled to gain a livelihood by conducting a daily newspaper; or, as he himself puts it, was

"Forced to drudge for the dregs of men,
And scrawl strange words with the barbarous pen."

Bryant was born at Cummington, in Berkshire, the westernmost county of Massachusetts. After two years in Williams College he studied law, and practiced for nine years as a country lawyer in Plainfield and Great Barrington. Following the line of the Housatonic Valley, the social and theological affiliations of Berkshire have always been closer with Connecticut and New York than with Boston and Eastern Massachusetts. Accordingly, when, in 1825, Bryant yielded to the attractions of a literary career, he betook himself to New York city, where, after a brief experiment in conducting a monthly magazine, the *New York Review and Athenaeum*, he assumed the editorship of the {514} *Evening Post*, a Democratic and Free-trade journal, with which he remained connected till his death. He already had a reputation as a poet when he entered the ranks of metropolitan journalism. In 1816 his

Thanatopsis had been published in the *North American Review*, and had attracted immediate and general admiration. It had been finished, indeed, two years before, when the poet was only in his nineteenth year, and was a wonderful instance of precocity. The thought in this stately hymn was not that of a young man, but of a sage who has reflected long upon the universality, the necessity, and the majesty of death. Bryant's blank verse when at its best, as in *Thanatopsis* and the *Forest Hymn*, is extremely noble. In gravity and dignity it is surpassed by no English blank verse of this century, though in rich and various modulation it falls below Tennyson's *Ulysses* and *Morte d'Arthur*. It was characteristic of Bryant's limitations that he came thus early into possession of his faculty. His range was always a narrow one, and about his poetry, as a whole, there is a certain coldness, rigidity, and solemnity. His fixed position among American poets is described in his own *Hymn to the North Star*:

> "And thou dost see them rise,
>   Star of the pole! and thou dost see them set.
> Alone, in thy cold skies,
>   Thou keep'st thy old, unmoving station yet,
> Nor join'st the dances of that glittering train,
> Nor dipp'st thy virgin orb in the blue western main."

{515}

In 1821 he read the *Ages*, a didactic poem in thirty-five stanzas, before the Phi Beta Kappa Society at Cambridge, and in the same year brought out his first volume of poems. A second collection appeared in 1832, which was printed in London under the auspices of Washington Irving. Bryant was the first American poet who had much of an audience in England, and Wordsworth is said to have learned *Thanatopsis* by heart. Bryant was, indeed, in a measure, a scholar of Wordsworth's school, and his place among American poets corresponds roughly, though not precisely, to Wordsworth's among English poets. With no humor, with somewhat restricted sympathies, with little flexibility or openness to new impressions, but gifted with a high, austere imagination, Bryant became the meditative poet of nature. His best poems are those in which he draws lessons from nature, or sings of its calming, purifying, and bracing influences upon the human soul. His office, in other words, is the same which Matthew Arnold asserts to be the peculiar office of modern poetry, "the moral interpretation of nature." Poems of this class are *Green River*, *To a Waterfowl*, *June*, the *Death of the Flowers*, and the *Evening Wind*. The song, "O fairest of the Rural Maids," which has more fancy than is common in Bryant, and which Poe pronounced his best poem, has an obvious resemblance to Wordsworth's "Three years she grew in sun and shade," and both of these nameless pieces might fitly be {516} entitled—as Wordsworth's is in Mr. Palgrave's *Golden Treasury*—"The Education of Nature."

Although Bryant's career is identified with New York, his poetry is all of New England. His heart was always turning back fondly to the woods and streams of the Berkshire hills. There was nothing of that urban strain in him which appears in Holmes and Willis. He was, in especial, the poet of autumn, of the American October and the New England Indian Summer, that season of "dropping nuts" and "smoky light," to whose subtle analogy with the decay of the young by the New England disease, consumption, he gave such tender expression in the *Death of the Flowers*; and amid whose "bright, late quiet," he wished himself to pass away. Bryant is our poet of "the melancholy days," as Lowell is of June. If, by chance, he touches upon June, it is not with the exultant gladness of Lowell in meadows full of bobolinks, and in the summer day that is

"—simply perfect from its own resource As to the bee the new campanula's Illuminate seclusion swung in air."

Rather, the stir of new life in the clod suggests to Bryant by contrast the thought of death; and there is nowhere in his poetry a passage of deeper feeling than the closing stanzas of *June*, in which he speaks of himself, by anticipation, as of one

"Whose part in all the pomp that fills
The circuit of the summer hills Is—
that his grave is green."

{517} Bryant is, *par excellence*, the poet of New England wild flowers, the yellow violet, the fringed gentian—to each of which he dedicated an entire poem—the orchis and the golden rod, "the aster in the wood and the yellow sunflower by the brook." With these his name will be associated as Wordsworth's with the daffodil and the lesser celandine, and Emerson's with the rhodora.

Except when writing of nature he was apt to be commonplace, and there are not many such energetic lines in his purely reflective verse as these famous ones from the *Battle Field*:

"Truth crushed to earth shall rise again;
The eternal years of God are hers;
But Error, wounded, writhes in pain,
And dies among his worshipers."

He added but slowly to the number of his poems, publishing a new collection in 1840, another in 1844, and *Thirty Poems* in 1864. His work at all ages was remarkably even. *Thanatopsis* was as mature as any thing that he wrote afterward, and among his later pieces, the *Planting of the Apple Tree* and the *Flood of Years* were as fresh as any thing that he had written in the first flush of youth. Bryant's poetic style was always pure and correct, without any tincture of affectation or extravagance. His prose writings are not important, consisting mainly of papers of the *Salmagundi* variety contributed to the *Talisman*, an annual published in 1827-30; some rather sketchy stories, *Tales of the {518} Glauber Spa*, 1832; and impressions of Europe, entitled, *Letters of a Traveler*, issued in two series, in 1849 and 1858. In 1869 and 1871 appeared his blank-verse translations of the *Iliad* and *Odyssey*, a remarkable achievement for a man of his age, and not excelled, upon the whole, by any recent metrical version of Homer in the English tongue. Bryant's half century of service as the editor of a daily paper should not be overlooked. The *Evening Post*, under his management, was always honest, gentlemanly, and courageous, and did much to raise the tone of journalism in New York.

Another Massachusetts poet, who was outside the Boston coterie, like Bryant, and, like him, tried his hand at journalism, was John Greenleaf Whittier (1807-). He was born in a solitary farmhouse near Haverhill, in the valley of the Merrimack, and his life has been passed mostly at his native place and at the neighboring town of Amesbury. The local color, which is very pronounced in his poetry, is that of the Merrimack from the vicinity of Haverhill to its mouth at Newburyport, a region of hillside farms, opening out below into wide marshes—"the low, green prairies of the sea," and the beaches of Hampton and Salisbury. The scenery of the Merrimack is familiar to all readers of Whittier: the cotton-spinning towns along its banks, with their factories and dams, the sloping pastures and orchards of the back country, the sands of Plum Island and the level reaches of water meadow between which glide the broad-sailed "gundalows"—a {519} local corruption of gondola— laden with hay. Whittier was a farmer lad, and had only such education as the district school could supply, supplemented by two years at the Haverhill Academy. In his *School Days* he gives a picture of the little old country school-house as it used to be, the only *alma mater* of so many distinguished Americans, and to which many others who have afterward trodden the pavements of great universities look back so fondly as to their first wicket gate into the land of knowledge.

"Still sits the school-house by the road,
  A ragged beggar sunning;
Around it still the sumachs grow
  And blackberry vines are running.

"Within, the master's desk is seen,

Deep-scarred by raps official;
The warping floor, the battered seats,
The jack-knife's carved initial."

A copy of Burns awoke the slumbering instinct in the young poet, and he began to contribute verses to Garrison's *Free Press*, published at Newburyport, and to the *Haverhill Gazette*. Then he went to Boston, and became editor for a short time of the *Manufacturer*. Next he edited the *Essex Gazette*, at Haverhill, and in 1830 he took charge of George D. Prentice's paper, the *New England Weekly Review*, at Hartford, Conn. Here he fell in with a young Connecticut poet of much promise, J. G. C. Brainard, editor of the {520} *Connecticut Mirror*, whose "Remains" Whittier edited in 1832. At Hartford, too, he published his first book, a volume of prose and verse, entitled *Legends of New England*, 1831, which is not otherwise remarkable than as showing his early interest in Indian colonial traditions—especially those which had a touch of the supernatural—a mine which he afterward worked to good purpose in the *Bridal of Pennacook*, the *Witch's Daughter*, and similar poems. Some of the *Legends* testify to Brainard's influence and to the influence of Whittier's temporary residence at Hartford. One of the prose pieces, for example, deals with the famous "Moodus Noises" at Haddam, on the Connecticut River, and one of the poems is the same in subject with Brainard's *Black Fox of Salmon River*. After a year and a half at Hartford, Whittier returned to Haverhill and to farming.

The antislavery agitation was now beginning, and into this he threw himself with all the ardor of his nature. He became the poet of the reform as Garrison was its apostle, and Sumner and Phillips its speakers. In 1833 he published *Justice and Expediency*, a prose tract against slavery, and in the same year he took part in the formation of the American Antislavery Society at Philadelphia, sitting in the convention as a delegate of the Boston Abolitionists. Whittier was a Quaker, and that denomination, influenced by the preaching of John Woolman and others, had long since quietly abolished slavery within its own communion. The {521} Quakers of Philadelphia and elsewhere took an earnest though peaceful part in the Garrisonian movement. But it was a strange irony of fate that had made the fiery-hearted Whittier a Friend. His poems against slavery and disunion have the martial ring of a Tyrtaeus or a Körner, added to the stern religious zeal of Cromwell's Ironsides. They are like the sound of the trumpet blown before the walls of Jericho, or the Psalms of David denouncing woe upon the enemies of God's chosen people. If there is any purely Puritan strain in American poetry it is in the war-hymns of the Quaker "Hermit of Amesbury." Of these patriotic poems there were three principal collections: *Voices of Freedom*, 1849; the *Panorama and Other Poems*, 1856; and *In War Time*, 1863; Whittier's work as the poet of freedom was done when, on hearing the bells ring for the passage of the constitutional amendment abolishing slavery, he wrote his splendid *Laus Deo*, thrilling with the ancient Hebrew spirit:

"Loud and long
Lift the old exulting song,
  Sing with Miriam by the sea—
He has cast the mighty down,
Horse and rider sink and drown,
  He hath triumphed gloriously."

Of his poems distinctly relating to the events of the civil war, the best, or at all events the most popular, is *Barbara Frietchie*. *Ichabod*, expressing the indignation of the Free Soilers at Daniel Webster's seventh of March speech in defense of the {522} Fugitive Slave Law, is one of Whittier's best political poems, and not altogether unworthy of comparison with Browning's *Lost Leader*. The language of Whittier's warlike lyrics is biblical, and many of his purely devotional pieces are religious poetry of a high order and have been included in numerous collections of hymns. Of his songs of faith and doubt, the best are perhaps *Our Master*, *Chapel of the Hermits*, and *Eternal Goodness*; one stanza from the last of which is familiar:

"I know not where His islands lift
  Their fronded palms in air,
I only know I cannot drift
  Beyond His love and care."

But from politics and war Whittier turned gladly to sing the homely life of the New England country side. His rural ballads and idyls are as genuinely American as any thing that our poets have written, and have been recommended, as such, to English working-men by Whittier's co-religionist, John Bright. The most popular of these is probably *Maud Muller*, whose closing couplet has passed into proverb. *Skipper Ireson's Ride* is also very current. Better than either of them, as poetry, is *Telling the Bees*. But Whittier's masterpiece in work of a descriptive and reminiscent kind is *Snow Bound*, 1866, a New England fireside idyl which in its truthfulness recalls the *Winter Evening* of Cowper's *Task* and Burns's *Cotter's Saturday Night*, but in sweetness and animation is superior to either of them. Although in {523} some things a Puritan of the Puritans, Whittier has never forgotten that he is also a Friend, and several of his ballads and songs have been upon the subject of the early Quaker persecutions in Massachusetts. The most impressive of these is *Cassandra Southwick*. The latest of them, the *King's Missive*, originally contributed to the *Memorial History of Boston* in 1880, and reprinted the next year in a volume with other poems, has been the occasion of a rather lively controversy. The *Bridal of Pennacook*, 1848, and the *Tent on the Beach*, 1867, which contain some of his best work, were series of ballads told by different narrators, after the fashion of Longfellow's *Tales of a Wayside Inn*. As an artist in verse Whittier is strong and fervid, rather than delicate or rich. He uses only a few metrical forms—by preference the eight-syllabled rhyming couplet

—"Maud Muller on a summer's day
Raked the meadow sweet with hay,"etc.—

and the emphatic tramp of this measure becomes very monotonous, as do some of Whittier's mannerisms; which proceed, however, never from affectation, but from a lack of study and variety, and so, no doubt, in part from the want of that academic culture and thorough technical equipment which Lowell and Longfellow enjoyed. Though his poems are not in dialect, like Lowell's *Biglow Papers*, he knows how to make an artistic use of homely provincial words, such as "chore," {524} which give his idyls of the hearth and the barnyard a genuine Doric cast. Whittier's prose is inferior to his verse. The fluency which was a besetting sin of his poetry when released from the fetters of rhyme and meter ran into wordiness. His prose writings were partly contributions to the slavery controversy, partly biographical sketches of English and American reformers, and partly studies of the scenery and folk-lore of the Merrimack Valley. Those of most literary interest were the *Supernaturalism of New England*, 1847, and some of the papers in *Literary Recreations and Miscellanies*, 1854.

While Massachusetts was creating an American literature, other sections of the Union were by no means idle. The West, indeed, was as yet too raw to add any thing of importance to the artistic product of the country. The South was hampered by circumstances which will presently be described. But in and about the seaboard cities of New York, Philadelphia, Baltimore and Richmond, many pens were busy filling the columns of literary weeklies and monthlies; and there was a considerable output, such as it was, of books of poetry, fiction, travel, and miscellaneous light literature. Time has already relegated most of these to the dusty top-shelves. To rehearse the names of the numerous contributors to the old *Knickerbocker Magazine*, to *Godey's*, and *Graham's*, and the *New Mirror*, and the *Southern Literary Messenger*, or to run over the list of authorlings and poetasters in Poe's papers on {525} the *Literati of New York*, would be very much like reading the inscriptions on the head-stones of an old grave-yard. In the columns of these prehistoric magazines and in the book notices and reviews away back in the thirties and forties, one encounters the handiwork and the names of Emerson, Holmes, Longfellow, Hawthorne, and Lowell, embodied in this mass of forgotten literature. It would have required a good deal of critical acumen, at the time, to predict that these and a few others would soon be thrown out into bold relief, as the significant and permanent names in the literature of their generation, while Paulding, Hirst, Fay, Dawes, Mrs. Osgood, and scores of others who figured beside them in the fashionable periodicals, and filled quite as large a space in the public eye, would sink into oblivion in less than thirty years. Some of these latter were clever enough people; they entertained their contemporary public sufficiently, but their work had no vitality or "power of continuance." The great majority of the writings of any period are necessarily ephemeral, and time by a slow process of natural selection is constantly sifting out the few representative books which shall carry on the memory of the period to posterity. Now and then it may be predicted of some undoubted work of genius, even at the moment that it sees the light, that it is destined to endure. But tastes and fashions change, and few things are better calculated to inspire the literary critic with humility than to read {526} the prophecies in old reviews and see how the future, now become the present, has quietly given them the lie.

From among the professional *littérateurs* of his day emerges, with ever sharper distinctness as time goes on, the name of Edgar Allan Poe (1809-1849.) By the irony of fate Poe was born at Boston, and his first volume, *Tamerlane and Other Poems*, 1827, was printed in that city and bore upon its title page the words, "By a Bostonian." But his parentage, so far as it was any thing, was southern. His father was a Marylander who had gone upon the stage and married an actress, herself the daughter of an actress and a native of England. Left an orphan by the early death of both parents, Poe was adopted by a Mr. Allan, a wealthy merchant of Richmond, Va. He was educated partly at an English school, was student for a time in the University of Virginia and afterward a cadet in the Military Academy at West Point. His youth was wild and irregular: he gambled and drank, was proud, bitter and perverse; finally quarreled with his guardian and adopted father—by whom he was disowned —and then betook himself to the life of a literary hack. His brilliant but underpaid work for various periodicals soon brought him into notice, and he was given the editorship of the *Southern Literary Messenger*, published at Richmond, and subsequently of the *Gentlemen's*—afterward *Graham's* —*Magazine* in Philadelphia. These and all other positions Poe forfeited through his {527} dissipated habits and wayward temper, and finally, in 1844, he drifted to New York, where he found employment on the *Evening Mirror* and then on the *Broadway Journal*. He died of delirium tremens at the Marine Hospital in Baltimore. His life was one of the most wretched in literary history. He was an extreme instance of what used to be called the "eccentricity of genius." He had the irritable vanity which is popularly supposed to accompany the poetic temperament, and was so insanely egotistic as to imagine that Longfellow and others were constantly plagiarizing from him. The best side of Poe's character came out in his domestic relations, in which he displayed great tenderness, patience and fidelity. His instincts were gentlemanly, and his manner and conversation were often winning. In the place of moral feeling he had the artistic conscience. In his critical papers, except where warped by passion or prejudice, he showed neither fear nor favor, denouncing bad work by the most illustrious hands and commending obscure merit. The "impudent literary cliques" who puffed each other's books; the feeble chirrupings of the bardlings who manufactured verses for the "Annuals;" and the twaddle of the "genial" incapables who praised them in flabby reviews—all these Poe exposed with ferocious honesty. Nor, though his writings are _un_moral, can they be called in any sense _im_moral. His poetry is as pure in its unearthliness as Bryant's in its austerity.

By 1831 Poe had published three thin books of verse, none of which had attracted notice, although the latest contained the drafts of a few of his most perfect poems, such as *Israfel*, the *Valley of Unrest*, the *City in the Sea*, and one of the two pieces inscribed *To Helen*. It was his habit to touch and retouch his work until it grew under his more practiced hand into a shape that satisfied his fastidious taste. Hence the same poem frequently reappears in different stages of development in successive editions. Poe was a subtle artist in the realm of the weird and the fantastic. In his intellectual nature there was a strange conjunction; an imagination as spiritual as Shelley's, though, unlike Shelley's, haunted perpetually with shapes of fear and the imagery of ruin; with this, an analytic power, a scientific exactness, and a mechanical ingenuity more usual in a chemist or a mathematician than in a poet. He studied carefully the mechanism of his verse and experimented endlessly with verbal and musical effects, such as repetition, and monotone, and the selection of words in which the consonants alliterated and the vowels varied. In his *Philosophy of Composition* he described how his best known poem, the *Raven*, was systematically built up on a preconceived plan in which the number of lines was first determined and the word "nevermore" selected as a starting point. No one who knows the mood in which poetry is composed will believe that this ingenious piece of dissection really describes the way in {529} which the *Raven* was conceived and written, or that any such deliberate and self-conscious process could *originate* the associations from which a true poem springs. But it flattered Poe's pride of intellect to assert that his cooler reason had control not only over the execution of his poetry, but over the very well-head of thought and emotion. Some of his most successful stories, like the *Gold Bug*, the *Mystery of Marie Roget*, the *Purloined Letter*, and the *Murders in the Rue Morgue*, were applications of this analytic faculty to the solution of puzzles, such as the finding of buried treasure or of a lost document, or the ferreting out of a mysterious crime. After the publication of the *Gold Bug* he received from all parts of the country specimens of cipher writing, which he delighted to work out. Others of his tales were clever pieces of mystification, like *Hans Pfaall*, the story of a journey to the moon, or experiments at giving verisimilitude to wild improbabilities by the skillful introduction of scientific details, as in the *Facts in the Case of M. Valdemar* and *Von Kempelen's Discovery*. In his narratives of this kind Poe anticipated the detective novels of Gaboriau and Wilkie Collins, the scientific hoaxes of Jules Verne, and, though in a less degree, the artfully worked up likeness to fact in Edward Everett Hale's *Man Without a Country*, and similar fictions. While Dickens's *Barnaby Rudge* was publishing in parts, Poe showed his skill as a plot hunter by publishing a paper in *Graham's Magazine* in which the very {530} tangled intrigue of the novel was correctly raveled and the *finale* predicted in advance.

In his union of imagination and analytic power Poe resembled Coleridge, who, if any one, was his teacher in poetry and criticism. Poe's verse often reminds one of *Christabel* and the *Ancient Mariner*, still oftener of *Kubla Khan*. Like Coleridge, too, he indulged at times in the opium habit. But in Poe the artist predominated over every thing else. He began not with sentiment or thought, but with technique, with melody and color, tricks of language, and effects of verse. It is curious to study the growth of his style in his successive volumes of poetry. At first these are metrical experiments and vague images, original, and with a fascinating suggestiveness, but with so little meaning that some of his earlier pieces are hardly removed from nonsense. Gradually, like distant music drawing nearer and nearer, his poetry becomes fuller of imagination and of an inward significance, without ever losing, however, its mysterious aloofness from the real world of the senses. It was a part of Poe's literary creed—formed upon his own practice and his own limitations, but set forth with a great display of *a priori* reasoning in his essay on the *Poetic Principle* and elsewhere—that pleasure and not instruction or moral exhortation was the end of poetry; that beauty and not truth or goodness was its means; and, furthermore, that the pleasure which it gave should be *indefinite*. About his own poetry there was always this {531} indefiniteness. His imagination dwelt in a strange country of dream—a "ghoul-haunted region of Weir," "out of space, out of time"—filled with unsubstantial landscapes, and peopled by spectral shapes. And yet there is a wonderful, hidden significance in this uncanny scenery. The reader feels that the wild, fantasmal imagery is in itself a kind of language, and that it in some way expresses a brooding thought or passion, the terror and despair of a lost soul. Sometimes there is an obvious allegory, as in the *Haunted Palace*, which is the parable of a ruined mind, or in the *Raven*, the most popular of all Poe's poems, originally published in the *American Whig Review* for February, 1845. Sometimes the meaning is more obscure, as in *Ulalume*, which, to most people, is quite incomprehensible, and yet to all readers of poetic feeling is among the most characteristic, and, therefore, the most fascinating, of its author's creations.

Now and then, as in the beautiful ballad, *Annabel Lee*, and *To One in Paradise*, the poet emerges into the light of common human feeling and speaks a more intelligible language. But in general his poetry is not the poetry of the heart, and its passion is not the passion of flesh and blood. In Poe the thought of death is always near, and of the shadowy borderland between death and life.

"The play is the tragedy 'Man,'
And its hero the Conqueror Worm,"

{532}

The prose tale, *Ligeia*, in which these verses are inserted, is one of the most powerful of all Poe's writings, and its theme is the power of the will to overcome death. In that singularly impressive poem, the *Sleeper*, the morbid horror which invests the tomb springs from the same source, the materiality of Poe's imagination, which refuses to let the soul go free from the body.

This quality explains why Poe's *Tales of the Grotesque* and *Arabesque*, 1840, are on a lower plane than Hawthorne's romances, to which a few of them, like *William Wilson* and the *Man of the Crowd*, have some resemblance. The former of these, in particular, is in Hawthorne's peculiar province, the allegory of the conscience. But in general the tragedy in Hawthorne is a spiritual one, while Poe calls in the aid of material forces. The passion of physical fear or of superstitious horror is that which his writings most frequently excite. These tales represent various grades of the frightful and the ghastly, from the mere bug-a-boo story like the *Black Cat*, which makes children afraid to go in the dark, up to the breathless terror of the *Cask of Amontillado*, or the *Red Death*. Poe's masterpiece in this kind is the fateful tale of the *Fall of the House of Usher*, with its solemn and magnificent close. His prose, at its best, often recalls, in its richly imaginative cast, the manner of De Quincey in such passages as his *Dream Fugue*, or *Our Ladies of Sorrow*. In {533} descriptive pieces like the *Domain of Arnheim*, and stories of adventure like the *Descent into the Maelstrom*, and his long sea tale, *The Narrative of Arthur Gordon Pym*, 1838, he displayed a realistic inventiveness almost equal to Swift's or De Foe's. He was not without a mocking irony, but he had no constructive humor, and his attempts at the facetious were mostly failures.

Poe's magical creations were rootless flowers. He took no hold upon the life about him, and cared nothing for the public concerns of his country. His poems and tales might have been written *in vacuo* for any thing American in them. Perhaps for this reason, in part, his fame has been so cosmopolitan. In France especially his writings have been favorites. Charles Baudelaire, the author of the *Fleurs du Mal*, translated them into French, and his own impressive but unhealthy poetry shows evidence of Poe's influence. The defect in Poe was in character, a defect which will make itself felt in art as in life. If he had had the sweet home feeling of Longfellow or the moral fervor of Whittier he might have been a greater poet than either.

"If I could dwell
Where Israfel

Hath dwelt, and he where I,
He might not sing so wildly well
A mortal melody,
While a bolder note than this mightswell
From my lyre within the sky!"

{534}

Though Poe was a southerner, if not by birth, at least by race and breeding,
there was nothing distinctly southern about his peculiar genius, and in his
wandering life he was associated as much with Philadelphia and New York as
with Baltimore and Richmond. The conditions which had made the southern
colonies unfruitful in literary and educational works before the Revolution
continued to act down to the time of the civil war. Eli Whitney's invention of
the cotton gin in the closing years of the last century gave extension to
slavery, making it profitable to cultivate the new staple by enormous gangs of
field hands working under the whip of the overseer in large plantations.
Slavery became henceforth a business speculation in the States furthest south,
and not, as in Old Virginia and Kentucky, a comparatively mild domestic
system. The necessity of defending its peculiar institution against the attacks
of a growing faction in the North compelled the South to throw all its
intellectual strength into politics, which, for that matter, is the natural
occupation and excitement of a social aristocracy. Meanwhile immigration
sought the free States, and there was no middle class at the South. The "poor
whites" were ignorant and degraded. There were people of education in the
cities and on some of the plantations, but there was no great educated class
from which a literature could proceed. And the culture of the South, such as it
was, was becoming old-fashioned and local, as the section was isolated {535}
more and more from the rest of the Union and from the enlightened public
opinion of Europe by its reactionary prejudices and its sensitiveness on the
subject of slavery. Nothing can be imagined more ridiculously provincial than
the sophomorical editorials in the southern press just before the outbreak of
the war, or than the backward and ill-informed articles which passed for
reviews in the poorly supported periodicals of the South.

In the general dearth of work of high and permanent value, one or two
southern authors may be mentioned whose writings have at least done
something to illustrate the life and scenery of their section. When in 1833 the
Baltimore *Saturday Visitor* offered a prize of a hundred dollars for the best
prose tale, one of the committee who awarded the prize to Poe's first story,
the MS. *Found in a Bottle*, was John P. Kennedy, a Whig gentleman of
Baltimore, who afterward became Secretary of the Navy in Fillmore's
administration. The year before he had published *Swallow Barn*, a series of

agreeable sketches of country life in Virginia. In 1835 and 1838 he published his two novels, *Horse-Shoe Robinson* and *Rob of the Bowl*, the former a story of the Revolutionary War in South Carolina; the latter an historical tale of colonial Maryland. These had sufficient success to warrant reprinting as late as 1852. But the most popular and voluminous of all Southern writers of fiction was William Gilmore Simms, a South Carolinian, who died in 1870. He wrote over thirty {536} novels, mostly romances of Revolutionary history, southern life and wild adventure, among the best of which were the *Partisan*, 1835, and the *Yemassee*. Simms was an inferior Cooper, with a difference. His novels are good boys' books, but are crude and hasty in composition. He was strongly southern in his sympathies, though his newspaper, the *Charleston City Gazette*, took part against the Nullifiers. His miscellaneous writings include several histories and biographies, political tracts, addresses and critical papers contributed to southern magazines. He also wrote numerous poems, the most ambitious of which was *Atlantis, a Story of the Sea*, 1832. His poems have little value except as here and there illustrating local scenery and manners, as in *Southern Passages and Pictures*, 1839. Mr. John Esten Cooke's pleasant but not very strong *Virginia Comedians* was, perhaps, in literary quality the best southern novel produced before the civil war.

When Poe came to New York, the most conspicuous literary figure of the metropolis, with the possible exception of Bryant and Halleck, was N. P. Willis, one of the editors of the *Evening Mirror*, upon which journal Poe was for a time engaged. Willis had made a literary reputation, when a student at Yale, by his *Scripture Poems*, written in smooth blank verse. Afterward he had edited the *American Monthly* in his native city of Boston, and more recently he had published *Pencillings by the Way*, 1835, a pleasant record of {537} European saunterings; *Inklings of Adventure*, 1836, a collection of dashing stories and sketches of American and foreign life; and *Letters from Under a Bridge*, 1839, a series of charming rural letters from his country place at Owego, on the Susquehanna. Willis's work, always graceful and sparkling, sometimes even brilliant, though light in substance and jaunty in style, had quickly raised him to the summit of popularity. During the years from 1835 to 1850 he was the most successful American magazinist, and even down to the day of his death, in 1867, he retained his hold upon the attention of the fashionable public by his easy paragraphing and correspondence in the *Mirror* and its successor, the *Home Journal*, which catered to the literary wants of the *beau monde*. Much of Willis's work was ephemeral, though clever of its kind, but a few of his best tales and sketches, such as *F. Smith*, *The Ghost Ball at Congress Hall*, *Edith Linsey*, and the *Lunatic's Skate*, together with some of the *Letters from Under a Bridge*, are worthy of preservation, not only as readable stories, but as society studies of life at

American watering places like Nahant and Saratoga and Ballston Spa half a century ago. A number of his simpler poems, like *Unseen Spirits, Spring, To M——from Abroad*, and *Lines on Leaving Europe*, still retain a deserved place in collections and anthologies.

The senior editor of the *Mirror*, George P. Morris, was once a very popular song writer, and {538} his *Woodman, Spare that Tree*, still survives. Other residents of New York City who have written single famous pieces were Clement C. Moore, a professor in the General Theological Seminary, whose *Visit from St. Nicholas*—"'Twas the Night Before Christmas," etc.—is a favorite ballad in every nursery in the land; Charles Fenno Hoffman, a novelist of reputation in his time, but now remembered only as the author of the song, *Sparkling and Bright*, and the patriotic ballad of *Monterey*; Robert H. Messinger, a native of Boston, but long resident in New York, where he was a familiar figure in fashionable society, who wrote *Give Me the Old*, a fine ode with a choice Horatian flavor; and William Allen Butler, a lawyer and occasional writer, whose capital satire of *Nothing to Wear* was published anonymously and had a great run. Of younger poets, like Stoddard and Aldrich, who formerly wrote for the *Mirror* and who are still living and working in the maturity of their powers, it is not within the limits and design of this sketch to speak. But one of their contemporaries, Bayard Taylor, who died, American Minister at Berlin, in 1878, though a Pennsylvanian by birth and rearing, may be reckoned among the "literati of New York." A farmer lad from Chester County, who had learned the printer's trade and printed a little volume of his juvenile verses in 1844, he came to New York shortly after with credentials from Dr. Griswold, the editor of *Graham's*, and obtaining encouragement and aid {539} from Willis, Horace Greeley and others, he set out to make the tour of Europe, walking from town to town in Germany and getting employment now and then at his trade to help pay the expenses of the trip. The story of these *Wanderjahre* he told in his *Views Afoot*, 1846. This was the first of eleven books of travel written during the course of his life. He was an inveterate nomad, and his journeyings carried him to the remotest regions—to California, India, China, Japan and the isles of the sea, to Central Africa and the Soudan, Palestine, Egypt, Iceland and the "by-ways of Europe." His head-quarters at home were in New York, where he did literary work for the *Tribune*. He was a rapid and incessant worker, throwing off many volumes of verse and prose, fiction, essays, sketches, translations and criticism, mainly contributed in the first instance to the magazines. His versatility was very marked, and his poetry ranged from *Rhymes of Travel*, 1848, and *Poems of the Orient*, 1854, to idyls and home ballads of Pennsylvania life, like the *Quaker Widow* and the *Old Pennsylvania Farmer*, and, on the other side, to ambitious and somewhat mystical poems, like the

Masque of the Gods, 1872—written in four days—and dramatic experiments like the *Prophet*, 1874, and *Prince Deukalion*, 1878. He was a man of buoyant and eager nature, with a great appetite for new experience, a remarkable memory, a talent for learning languages, and a too great readiness to take the hue of his favorite books. From {540} his facility, his openness to external impressions of scenery and costume and his habit of turning these at once into the service of his pen, it results that there is something "newspapery" and superficial about most of his prose. It is reporter's work, though reporting of a high order. His poetry, too, though full of glow and picturesqueness, is largely imitative, suggesting Tennyson not unfrequently, but more often Shelley. His spirited *Bedouin Song*, for example, has an echo of Shelley's *Lines to an Indian Air*:

"From the desert I come to thee
On a stallion shod with fire;
And the winds are left behind
In the speed of my desire.
Under thy window I stand
And the midnight hears my cry;
I love thee, I love but thee
With a love that shall not die."

The dangerous quickness with which he caught the manner of other poets made him an admirable parodist and translator. His *Echo Club*, 1876, contains some of the best travesties in the tongue, and his great translation of Goethe's *Faust*, 1870-71—with its wonderfully close reproduction of the original meters—is one of the glories of American literature. All in all, Taylor may unhesitatingly be put first among our poets of the second generation—the generation succeeding that of Longfellow and Lowell—although the lack in him of original genius self-determined to a {541} peculiar sphere, or the want of an inward fixity and concentration to resist the rich tumult of outward impressions, has made him less significant in the history of our literary thought than some other writers less generously endowed.

Taylor's novels had the qualities of his verse. They were profuse, eloquent and faulty. *John Godfrey's Fortune*, 1864, gave a picture of bohemian life in New York. *Hannah Thurston*, 1863, and the *Story of Kennett*, 1866, introduced many incidents and persons from the old Quaker life of rural Pennsylvania, as Taylor remembered it in his boyhood. The former was like Hawthorne's *Blithedale Romance*, a satire on fanatics and reformers, and its heroine is a nobly conceived character, though drawn with some exaggeration. The *Story of Kennett*, which is largely autobiographic, has a greater freshness and reality than the others and is full of personal recollections. In these novels, as in his short stories, Taylor's pictorial skill is greater on the whole than his power of creating characters or inventing plots.

Literature in the West now began to have an existence. Another young poet from Chester County, Pa., namely, Thomas Buchanan Read, went to Cincinnati, and not to New York, to study sculpture and painting, about 1837, and one of his best-known poems, *Pons Maximus*, was written on the occasion of the opening of the suspension bridge across the Ohio. Read came East, to be sure, in 1841, and spent many years in our {542} seaboard cities and in Italy. He was distinctly a minor poet, but some of his Pennsylvania pastorals, like the *Deserted Road*, have a natural sweetness; and his luxurious *Drifting*, which combines the methods of painting and poetry, is justly popular. *Sheridan's Ride*—perhaps his most current piece—is a rather forced production and has been over-praised. The two Ohio sister poets, Alice and Phoebe Cary, were attracted to New York in 1850, as soon as their literary success seemed assured. They made that city their home for the remainder of their lives. Poe praised Alice Cary's *Pictures of Memory*, and Phoebe's *Nearer Home* has become a favorite hymn. There is nothing peculiarly Western about the verse of the Cary sisters. It is the poetry of sentiment, memory, and domestic affection, entirely feminine, rather tame and diffuse as a whole, but tender and sweet, cherished by many good women and dear to simple hearts.

A stronger smack of the soil is in the negro melodies like *Uncle Ned, O Susanna, Old Folks at Home, Way Down South, Nelly was a Lady, My Old Kentucky Home*, etc., which were the work not of any southern poet, but of Stephen C. Foster, a native of Allegheny, Pa., and a resident of Cincinnati and Pittsburg. He composed the words and music of these, and many others of a similar kind, during the years 1847 to 1861. Taken together they form the most original and vital addition which this country has made to the psalmody {543} of the world, and entitle Foster to the first rank among American song writers.

As Foster's plaintive melodies carried the pathos and humor of the plantation all over the land, so Mrs. Harriet Beecher Stowe's *Uncle Tom's Cabin*, 1852, brought home to millions of readers the sufferings of the negroes in the "black belt" of the cotton-growing States. This is the most popular novel ever written in America. Hundreds of thousands of copies were sold in this country and in England, and some forty translations were made into foreign tongues. In its dramatized form it still keeps the stage, and the statistics of circulating libraries show that even now it is in greater demand than any other single book. It did more than any other literary agency to rouse the public conscience to a sense of the shame and horror of slavery; more even than

Garrison's *Liberator*; more than the indignant poems of Whittier and Lowell or the orations of Sumner and Phillips. It presented the thing concretely and dramatically, and in particular it made the odious Fugitive Slave Law forever impossible to enforce. It was useless for the defenders of slavery to protest that the picture was exaggerated and that overseers like Legree were the exception. The system under which such brutalities could happen, and did sometimes happen, was doomed. It is easy now to point out defects of taste and art in this masterpiece, to show that the tone is occasionally melodramatic, that some of the characters are {544} conventional, and that the literary execution is in parts feeble and in others coarse. In spite of all it remains true that *Uncle Tom's Cabin* is a great book, the work of genius seizing instinctively upon its opportunity and uttering the thought of the time with a power that thrilled the heart of the nation and of the world. Mrs. Stowe never repeated her first success. Some of her novels of New England life, such as the *Minister's Wooing*, 1859, and the *Pearl of Orr's Island*, 1862, have a mild kind of interest, and contain truthful portraiture of provincial ways and traits; while later fictions of a domestic type, like *Pink and White Tyranny*, and *My Wife and I*, are really beneath criticism.

There were other Connecticut writers contemporary with Mrs. Stowe: Mrs. L. H. Sigourney, for example, a Hartford poetess, formerly known as "the Hemans of America," but now quite obsolete; and J. G. Percival of New Haven, a shy and eccentric scholar, whose geological work was of value, and whose memory is preserved by one or two of his simpler poems, still in circulation, such as *To Seneca Lake* and the *Coral Grove*. Another Hartford poet, Brainard—already spoken of as an early friend of Whittier—died young, leaving a few pieces which show that his lyrical gift was spontaneous and genuine but had received little cultivation. A much younger writer than either of these, Donald G. Mitchell, of New Haven, has a more lasting place in our literature, by virtue of his charmingly written *Reveries of a Bachelor*, {545} 1850, and *Dream Life*, 1852, stories which sketch themselves out in a series of reminiscences and lightly connected scenes, and which always appeal freshly to young men because they have that dreamy outlook upon life which is characteristic of youth. But, upon the whole, the most important contribution made by Connecticut in that generation to the literary stock of America was the Beecher family. Lyman Beecher had been an influential preacher and theologian, and a sturdy defender of orthodoxy against Boston Unitarianism. Of his numerous sons and daughters, all more or less noted for intellectual vigor and independence, the most eminent were Mrs. Stowe and Henry Ward Beecher, the great pulpit orator of Brooklyn. Mr. Beecher was too busy a man to give more than his spare moments to general literature. His sermons, lectures, and addresses were reported for the daily papers and printed in part in book form; but these lose greatly when divorced from the large, warm, and benignant personality of the man. His volumes made up of articles in the *Independent* and the *Ledger*, such as *Star Papers*, 1855, and *Eyes and Ears*, 1862, contain many delightful *morceaux* upon country life and similar topics, though they are hardly wrought with sufficient closeness and care to take a permanent place in letters. Like Willis's *Ephemerae*, they are excellent literary journalism, but hardly literature.

We may close our retrospect of American {546} literature before 1861 with a brief notice of one of the most striking literary phenomena of the time—the *Leaves of Grass* of Walt Whitman, published at Brooklyn in 1855. The author, born at West Hills, Long Island, in 1819, had been printer, school-teacher, editor, and builder. He had scribbled a good deal of poetry of the ordinary kind, which attracted little attention, but finding conventional rhymes and meters too cramping a vehicle for his need of expression, he discarded them for a kind of rhythmic chant, of which the following is a fair specimen:

> "Press close, bare bosom'd night! Press close, magnetic,
>   nourishing night!
> Night of south winds! night of the few large stars!
> Still, nodding night! mad, naked, summernight!"

The invention was not altogether a new one. The English translation of the Psalms of David and of some of the Prophets, the *Poems of Ossian*, and some of Matthew Arnold's unrhymed pieces, especially the *Strayed Reveller*, have an irregular rhythm of this kind, to say nothing of the old Anglo-Saxon poems, like *Beowulf*, and the Scripture paraphrases attributed to Caedmon. But this species of *oratio soluta*, carried to the lengths to which Whitman carried it, had an air of novelty which was displeasing to some, while to others, weary of familiar measures and jingling rhymes, it was refreshing in its boldness and freedom. There is no consenting estimate of this poet. {547} Many think that his so-called poems are not poems at all, but simply a bad variety of prose; that there is nothing to him beyond a combination of affectation and indecency; and that the Whitman *culte* is a passing "fad" of a few literary men, and especially of a number of English critics like Rossetti, Swinburne, Buchanan, etc., who, being determined to have something unmistakably American—that is, different from any thing else—in writings from this side of the water before they will acknowledge any originality in them, have been misled into discovering in Whitman "the poet of Democracy." Others maintain that he is the greatest of American poets, or, indeed, of all modern poets; that he is "cosmic," or universal, and that he has put an end forever to puling rhymes and lines chopped up into metrical feet. Whether Whitman's poetry is formally poetry at all or merely the raw material of poetry, the chaotic and amorphous impression which it makes on readers of conservative tastes results from his effort to take up into his verse elements which poetry has usually left out—the ugly, the earthy, and even the disgusting; the "under side of things," which he holds not to be prosaic when apprehended with a strong, masculine joy in life and nature seen in all their aspects. The lack of these elements in the conventional poets seems to him and his disciples like leaving out the salt from the ocean, making poetry merely pretty and blinking whole classes of facts. Hence the naturalism and animalism of some of the {548} divisions in *Leaves of Grass*, particularly that entitled *Children of Adam*, which gave great offense by its immodesty, or its outspokenness. Whitman holds that nakedness is chaste; that all the functions of the body in healthy exercise are equally clean; that all, in fact, are divine; and that matter is as divine as spirit. The effort to get every thing into his poetry, to speak out his thought just as it comes to him, accounts, too, for his way of cataloguing objects without selection. His single expressions are often unsurpassed for descriptive beauty and truth. He speaks of "the vitreous pour of the full moon, just tinged with blue," of the "lisp" of the plane, of the prairies, "where herds of buffalo make a crawling spread of the square miles." But if there is any eternal distinction between poetry and prose the most liberal canons of the poetic art will never agree to accept lines like these:

> "And [I] remember putting plasters on the galls of his neck
> and ankles;
> He stayed with me a week before he was recuperated, and
> passed north."

Whitman is the spokesman of Democracy and of the future; full of brotherliness and hope, loving the warm, gregarious pressure of the crowd and the touch of his comrade's elbow in the ranks. He liked the people—multitudes of people; the swarm of life beheld from a Broadway omnibus or a Brooklyn ferry-boat. The rowdy and the Negro {549} truck-driver were closer to his sympathy than the gentleman and the scholar. "I loafe and invite my soul," he writes: "I sound my barbaric yawp over the roofs of the world." His poem *Walt Whitman*, frankly egotistic, simply describes himself as a typical, average man—the same as any other man, and therefore not individual but universal. He has great tenderness and heartiness—"the good gray poet;" and during the civil war he devoted himself unreservedly to the wounded soldiers in the Washington hospitals—an experience which he has related in the *Dresser* and elsewhere. It is characteristic of his rough and ready *camaraderie* to use slang and newspaper English in his poetry, to call himself Walt instead of Walter, and to have his picture taken in a slouch hat and with a flannel shirt open at the throat. His decriers allege that he poses for effect; that he is simply a backward eddy in the tide, and significant only as a temporary reaction against ultra civilization—like Thoreau, though in a different way. But with all his mistakes in art there is a healthy, virile, tumultuous pulse of life in his lyric utterance and a great sweep of imagination in his panoramic view of times and countries. One likes to read him because he feels so good, enjoys so fully the play of his senses, and has such a lusty confidence in his own immortality and in the prospects of the human race. Stripped of verbiage and repetition, his ideas are not many. His indebtedness to Emerson—who wrote an introduction to {550} the *Leaves of Grass*—is manifest. He sings of man and not men, and the individual differences of character, sentiment, and passion, the *dramatic* elements of life, find small place in his system. It is too early to say what will be his final position in literary history. But it is noteworthy that the democratic masses have not accepted him yet as their poet. Whittier and Longfellow, the poets of conscience and feeling, are the darlings of the American people. The admiration, and even the knowledge of Whitman, are mostly esoteric, confined to the literary class. It is also not without significance as to the ultimate reception of his innovations in verse that he has numerous parodists, but no imitators. The tendency among our younger poets is not toward the abandonment of rhyme and meter, but toward the introduction of new stanza forms and an increasing carefulness and finish in the *technique* of their art. It is observable, too, that in his most inspired passages Whitman reverts to the old forms of verse; to blank verse, for example, in the *Man-o'-War-Bird*:

"Thou who hast slept all night upon the storm,
Waking renewed on thy prodigious pinions," etc.,

and elsewhere not infrequently to dactylic hexameters and pentameters:

"Earth of shine and dark, mottling the tide of the river! …
Far-swooping, elbowed earth! rich, apple-blossomed earth."

{551} Indeed, Whitman's most popular poem, *My Captain*, written after the assassination of Abraham Lincoln, differs little in form from ordinary verse, as a stanza of it will show:

"My captain does not answer, his lips are pale and still;
My father does not feel my arm, he has no pulse nor will;
The ship is anchored safe and sound, its voyage closed and done;
From fearful trip the victor ship comes in with object won.
Exult, O shores, and ring, O bells!
But I, with mournful tread,
Walk the deck, my captain lies
Fallen, cold and dead."

This is from *Drum Taps*, a volume of poems of the civil war. Whitman has also written prose having much the same quality as his poetry: *Democratic Vistas*, *Memoranda of the Civil War*, and more recently, *Specimen Days*. His residence of late years has been at Camden, New Jersey, where a centennial edition of his writings was published in 1876.

1. William Cullen Bryant. Thanatopsis. To a Waterfowl. Green River. Hymn to the North Star. A Forest Hymn. "O Fairest of the Rural Maids." June. The Death of the Flowers. The Evening Wind. The Battle Field. The Planting of the Apple-tree. The Flood of Years.

2. John Greenleaf Whittier. Cassandra {552} Southwick. The New Wife and the Old. The Virginia Slave Mother. Randolph of Roanoke. Barclay of Ary. The Witch of Wenham. Skipper Ireson's Ride. Marguerite. Maud Muller. Telling the Bees. My Playmate. Barbara Frietchie. Ichabod. Laus Deo. Snow Bound.

3. Edgar Allan Poe. The Raven. The Bells. Israfel. Ulalume. To Helen. The City in the Sea. Annabel Lee. To One in Paradise. The Sleeper. The Valley of Unrest. The Fall of the House of Usher. Ligeia. William Wilson. The Cask of Amontillado. The Assignation. The Masque of the Red Death. Narrative of A. Gordon Pym.

4. N. P. Willis. Select Prose Writings. New York: Charles Scribner's Sons. 1886.

5. Mrs. H. B. Stowe. Uncle Tom's Cabin. Oldtown Folks.

6. W. G. Simms. The Partisan. The Yemassee.

7. Bayard Taylor. A Bacchic Ode. Hylas. Kubleh. The Soldier and the Pard. Sicilian Wine. Taurus. Serapion. The Metempsychosis of the Pine. The Temptation of Hassan Ben Khaled. Bedouin Song. Euphorion. The Quaker Widow. John Reid. Lars. Views Afoot. By-ways of Europe. The Story of Kennett. The Echo Club.

8. Walt Whitman. My Captain. "When Lilacs Last in the Door-yard Bloomed." "Out of the Cradle Endlessly Rocking." Pioneers, {553} O Pioneers. The Mystic Trumpeter. A Woman at Auction. Sea-shore Memoirs. Passage to India. Mannahatta. The Wound Dresser. Longings for Home.

9. Poets of America. By E. C. Stedman. Boston: Houghton, Mifflin & Co. 1885.

{554}

CHAPTER VII.

LITERATURE SINCE 1861.

A generation has nearly passed since the outbreak of the civil war, and although public affairs are still mainly in the hands of men who had reached manhood before the conflict opened, or who were old enough at that time to remember clearly its stirring events, the younger men who are daily coming forward to take their places know it only by tradition. It makes a definite break in the history of our literature, and a number of new literary schools and tendencies have appeared since its close. As to the literature of the war itself, it was largely the work of writers who had already reached or passed middle age. All of the more important authors described in the last three chapters survived the Rebellion, except Poe, who died in 1849, Prescott, who died in 1859, and Thoreau and Hawthorne, who died in the second and fourth years of the war, respectively. The final and authoritative history of the struggle has not yet been written, and cannot be written for many years to come. Many partial and tentative accounts have, however, appeared, among which may be mentioned, on the northern side, {555} Horace Greeley's *American Conflict*, 1864-66; Vice-president Wilson's *Rise and Fall of the Slave Power in America*, and J. W. Draper's *American Civil War*, 1868-70; on the southern side Alexander H. Stephens's *Confederate States of America*, Jefferson Davis's *Rise and Fall of the Confederate States of America*, and E. A. Pollard's *Lost Cause*. These, with the exception of Dr. Draper's philosophical narrative, have the advantage of being the work of actors in the political or military events which they describe, and the disadvantage of being, therefore, partisan—in some instances passionately partisan. A storehouse of materials for the coming historian is also at hand in Frank Moore's great collection, the *Rebellion Record*; in numerous regimental histories and histories of special armies, departments, and battles, like W. Swinton's *Army of the Potomac*; in the autobiographies and recollections of Grant and Sherman and other military leaders; in the "war papers," now publishing in the *Century* magazine, and in innumerable sketches and reminiscences by officers and privates on both sides.

The war had its poetry, its humors and its general literature, some of which have been mentioned in connection with Whittier, Lowell, Holmes, Whitman, and others; and some of which remain to be mentioned, as the work of new writers, or of writers who had previously made little mark. There were war songs on both sides, few of which had much literary value excepting, perhaps, James {556} R. Randall's southern ballad, *Maryland, My Maryland*, sung to the old college air of *Lauriger Horatius*, and the grand martial chorus of *John Brown's Body*, an old Methodist hymn, to which the northern armies beat time as they went "marching on." Randall's song, though spirited, was marred by its fire-eating absurdities about "vandals" and "minions" and "northern scum," the cheap insults of the southern newspaper press. To furnish the *John*

Brown chorus with words worthy of the music, Mrs. Julia Ward Howe wrote her *Battle Hymn of the Republic*, a noble poem, but rather too fine and literary for a song, and so never fully accepted by the soldiers. Among the many verses which voiced the anguish and the patriotism of that stern time, which told of partings and homecomings, of women waiting by desolate hearths, in country homes, for tidings of husbands and sons who had gone to the war, or which celebrated individual deeds of heroism or sang the thousand private tragedies and heart-breaks of the great conflict, by far the greater number were of too humble a grade to survive the feeling of the hour. Among the best or the most popular of them were Kate Putnam Osgood's *Driving Home the Cows*, Mrs. Ethel Lynn Beers's *All Quiet Along the Potomac*, Forceythe Willson's *Old Sergeant*, and John James Piatt's *Riding to Vote*. Of the poets whom the war brought out, or developed, the most noteworthy were Henry Timrod, of South Carolina, and Henry Howard Brownell, of Connecticut. During the {557} war Timrod was with the Confederate Army of the West, as correspondent for the *Charleston Mercury*, and in 1864 he became assistant editor of the *South Carolinian*, at Columbia. Sherman's "march to the sea" broke up his business, and he returned to Charleston. A complete edition of his poems was published in 1873, six years after his death. The prettiest of all Timrod's poems is *Katie*, but more to our present purpose are *Charleston*—written in the time of blockade—and the *Unknown Dead*, which tells

"Of nameless graves on battleplains,
Wash'd by a single winter's rains,
Where, some beneath Virginian hills,
And some by green Atlantic rills,
Some by the waters of the West,
Amyriad unknown heroes rest."

When the war was over a poet of New York State, F. M. Finch, sang of these and of other graves in his beautiful Decoration Day lyric, *The Blue and the Gray*, which spoke the word of reconciliation and consecration for North and South alike.

Brownell, whose *Lyrics of a Day* and *War Lyrics* were published respectively in 1864 and 1866, was private secretary to Farragut, on whose flag-ship, the *Hartford*, he was present at several great naval engagements, such as the "Passage of the Forts" below New Orleans, and the action off Mobile, described in his poem, the *Bay Fight*. {558} With some roughness and unevenness of execution, Brownell's poetry had a fire which places him next to Whittier as the Körner of the civil war. In him, especially, as in Whittier, is that Puritan sense of the righteousness of his cause which made the battle for the Union a holy war to the crusaders against slavery:

"Full red the furnace fires must glow
That melt the ore of mortal kind:
The mills of God are grinding slow,
But ah, how close they grind!

"To-day the Dahlgren and the drum
Are dread apostles of his name;
His kingdom here can only come
By chrism of blood and flame."

One of the earliest martyrs of the war was Theodore Winthrop, hardly known as a writer until the publication in the *Atlantic Monthly* of his vivid sketches of *Washington as a Camp*, describing the march of his regiment, the famous New York Seventh, and its first quarters in the Capitol at Washington. A tragic interest was given to these papers by Winthrop's gallant death in the action of Big Bethel, June 10, 1861. While this was still fresh in public recollection his manuscript novels were published, together with a collection of his stories and sketches reprinted from the magazines. His novels, though in parts crude and immature, have a dash and buoyancy—an out-door air about them—which give the reader a winning impression {559} of Winthrop's personality. The best of them is, perhaps, *Cecil Dreeme*, a romance that reminds one a little of Hawthorne, and the scene of which is the New York University building on Washington Square, a locality that has been further celebrated in Henry James's novel of *Washington Square*.

Another member of this same Seventh Regiment, Fitz James O'Brien, an Irishman by birth, who died at Baltimore, in 1862, from the effects of a wound received in a cavalry skirmish, had contributed to the magazines a number of poems and of brilliant though fantastic tales, among which the *Diamond Lens* and *What Was It?* had something of Edgar A. Poe's quality. Another Irish-American, Charles G. Halpine, under the pen-name of "Miles O'Reilly," wrote a good many clever ballads of the war, partly serious and partly in comic brogue. Prose writers of note furnished the magazines with narratives of their experience at the seat of war, among papers of which kind may be mentioned Dr. Holmes's *My Search for the Captain*, in the *Atlantic Monthly*, and Colonel T. W. Higginson's *Army Life in a Black Regiment*, collected into a volume in 1870.

Of the public oratory of the war the foremost example is the ever-memorable address of Abraham Lincoln at the dedication of the National Cemetery at Gettysburg. The war had brought the nation to its intellectual majority. In the stress of that terrible fight there was no room for {560} buncombe and verbiage, such as the newspapers and stump-speakers used to dole out in *ante bellum* days. Lincoln's speech is short—a few grave words which he turned aside for a moment to speak in the midst of his task of saving the country. The speech is simple, naked of figures, every sentence impressed with a sense of responsibility for the work yet to be done and with a stern determination to do it. "In a larger sense," it says, "we cannot dedicate, we cannot consecrate, we cannot hallow this ground. The brave men, living and dead, who struggled here have consecrated it far above our poor power to add or detract. The world will little note nor long remember what we say here, but it can never forget what they did here. It is for us, the living, rather to be dedicated here to the unfinished work which they who fought here have thus far so nobly advanced. It is rather for us to be here dedicated to the great task remaining before us; that from these honored dead we take increased devotion to that cause for which they gave the last full measure of devotion; that we here highly resolve that these dead shall not have died in vain: that this nation, under God, shall have a new birth of freedom; and that government of the people, by the people, for the people, shall not perish from the earth." Here was eloquence of a different sort from the sonorous perorations of Webster or the polished climaxes of Everett. As we read the plain, strong language of this brief classic, with its solemnity, its restraint, {561} its "brave old wisdom of sincerity," we seem to see the president's homely features irradiated with the light of coming martyrdom—

"The kindly-earnest, brave, foreseeing man,
Sagacious, patient, dreading praise, not blame,
New birth of our new soil, the first American."

Within the past quarter of a century the popular school of American humor has reached its culmination. Every man of genius who is a humorist at all is so in a way peculiar to himself. There is no lack of individuality in the humor of Irving and Hawthorne and the wit of Holmes and Lowell, but although they are new in subject and application they are not new in kind. Irving, as we have seen, was the literary descendant of Addison. The character sketches in *Bracebridge Hall* are of the same family with Sir Roger de Coverley and the other figures of the Spectator Club. *Knickerbocker's History of New York*, though purely American in its matter, is not distinctly American in its method, which is akin to the mock heroic of Fielding and the irony of Swift in the *Voyage to Lilliput*. Irving's humor, like that of all the great English humorists, had its root in the perception of character—of the characteristic traits of men and classes of men, as ground of amusement. It depended for its effect, therefore, upon its truthfulness, its dramatic insight and sympathy, as did the humor of Shakspere, of Sterne, Lamb, and Thackeray. This perception of the characteristic, {562} when pushed to excess, issues in grotesque and caricature, as in some of Dickens's inferior creations, which are little more than personified single tricks of manner, speech, feature, or dress.

Hawthorne's rare humor differed from Irving's in temper but not in substance, and belonged, like Irving's, to the English variety. Dr. Holmes's more pronouncedly comic verse does not differ specifically from the *facetiae* of Thomas Hood, but his prominent trait is wit, which is the laughter of the head as humor is of the heart. The same is true, with qualifications, of Lowell, whose *Biglow Papers*, though humor of an original sort in their revelation of Yankee character, are essentially satirical. It is the cleverness, the shrewdness of the hits in the *Biglow Papers*, their logical, that is, *witty* character, as distinguished from their drollery, that arrests the attention. They are funny, but they are not so funny as they are smart. In all these writers humor was blent with more serious qualities, which gave fineness and literary value to their humorous writings. Their view of life was not exclusively comic. But there has been a class of jesters, of professional humorists in America, whose product is so indigenous, so different, if not in essence, yet at least in form and expression, from any European humor, that it may be regarded as a unique addition to the comic literature of the world. It has been accepted as such in England, where Artemus Ward and Mark Twain are familiar to multitudes who have never read the *One-Hoss-Shay* or the *Courtin'*. And though it {563} would be ridiculous to maintain that either of these writers takes rank with Lowell and Holmes, or to deny that there is an amount of flatness and coarseness in many of their labored fooleries which puts large portions of their writings below the line where real literature begins, still it will not do to ignore them as mere buffoons, or even to predict that their humors will soon be forgotten. It is true that no literary fashion is more subject to change than the fashion of a jest, and that jokes that make one generation laugh seem insipid to the next. But there is something perennial in the fun of Rabelais, whom Bacon called "the great jester of France;" and though the puns of Shakspere's clowns are detestable the clowns themselves have not lost their power to amuse.

The Americans are not a gay people, but they are fond of a joke. Lincoln's "little stories" were characteristically Western, and it is doubtful whether he was more endeared to the masses by his solid virtues than by the humorous perception which made him one of them. The humor of which we are speaking now is a strictly popular and national possession. Though America has never, or not until lately, had a comic paper ranking with *Punch* or *Charivari* or the *Fliegende Blätter*, every newspaper has had its funny column. Our humorists have been graduated from the journalist's desk and sometimes from the printing-press, and now and then a local or country newspaper has risen into sudden prosperity from the possession of a {564} new humorist, as in the case of G. D. Prentice's *Courier-Journal*, or more recently of the *Cleveland Plain Dealer*, the *Danbury News*, the *Burlington*

Hawkeye, the *Arkansaw Traveller*, the *Texas Siftings* and numerous others. Nowadays there are even syndicates of humorists, who co-operate to supply fun for certain groups of periodicals. Of course the great majority of these manufacturers of jests for newspapers and comic almanacs are doomed to swift oblivion. But it is not so certain that the best of the class, like Clemens and Browne, will not long continue to be read as illustrative of one side of the American mind, or that their best things will not survive as long as the mots of Sydney Smith, which are still as current as ever. One of the earliest of them was Seba Smith, who, under the name of Major Jack Downing, did his best to make Jackson's administration ridiculous. B. P. Shillaber's "Mrs. Partington"—a sort of American Mrs. Malaprop—enjoyed great vogue before the war. Of a somewhat higher kind were the *Phoenixiana*, 1855, and *Squibob Papers*, 1856, of Lieutenant George H. Derby, "John Phoenix," one of the pioneers of literature on the Pacific coast at the time of the California gold fever of '49. Derby's proposal for *A New System of English Grammar*, his satirical account of the topographical survey of the two miles of road between San Francisco and the Mission Dolores, and his picture gallery made out of the conventional houses, steam-boats, rail-cars, runaway negroes {565} and other designs which used to figure in the advertising columns of the newspapers, were all very ingenious and clever. But all these pale before Artemus Ward—"Artemus the delicious," as Charles Reade called him—who first secured for this peculiarly American type of humor a hearing and reception abroad. Ever since the invention of Hosea Biglow, an imaginary personage of some sort, under cover of whom the author might conceal his own identity, has seemed a necessity to our humorists. Artemus Ward was a traveling showman who went about the country exhibiting a collection of wax "figgers" and whose experiences and reflections were reported in grammar and spelling of a most ingeniously eccentric kind. His inventor was Charles F. Browne, originally of Maine, a printer by trade and afterward a newspaper writer and editor at Boston, Toledo and Cleveland, where his comicalities in the *Plaindealer* first began to attract notice. In 1860 he came to New York and joined the staff of *Vanity Fair*, a comic weekly of much brightness, which ran a short career and perished for want of capital. When Browne began to appear as a public lecturer people who had formed an idea of him from his impersonation of the shrewd and vulgar old showman were surprised to find him a gentlemanly-looking young man, who came upon the platform in correct evening dress, and "spoke his piece" in a quiet and somewhat mournful manner, stopping in apparent surprise when any one in the {566} audience laughed at any uncommonly outrageous absurdity. In London, where he delivered his *Lecture on the Mormons*, in 1866, the gravity of his bearing at first imposed upon his hearers, who had come to the hall in search of instructive information and were disappointed at the inadequate nature of the panorama which Browne had had made to illustrate his lecture. Occasionally some hitch would occur in the machinery of this and the lecturer would leave the rostrum for a few moments to "work the moon" that shone upon the Great Salt Lake, apologizing on his return on the ground that he was "a man short" and offering "to pay a good salary to any respectable boy of good parentage and education who is a good moonist." When it gradually dawned upon the British intellect that these and similar devices of the lecturer—such as the soft music which he had the pianist play at pathetic passages—nay, that the panorama and even the lecture itself were of a humorous intention, the joke began to take, and Artemus's success in England became assured. He was employed as one of the editors of *Punch*, but died at Southampton in the year following.

Some of Artemus Ward's effects were produced by cacography or bad spelling, but there was genius in the wildly erratic way in which he handled even this rather low order of humor. It is a curious commentary on the wretchedness of our English orthography that the phonetic spelling of a word, as for example, *wuz* for *was*, should be {567} in itself an occasion of mirth. Other verbal effects of a different kind were among his devices, as in the passage where the seventeen widows of a deceased Mormon offered themselves to Artemus.

"And I said, 'Why is this thus? What is the reason of this thusness?' They hove a sigh—seventeen sighs of different size. They said—

"'O, soon thou will be gonested away.'

"I told them that when I got ready to leave a place I wentested.'

"They said, 'Doth not like us?'

"I said, 'I doth—I doth.'

"I also said, 'I hope your intentions are honorable, as I am a lone child—my parents being far—far away.'

"They then said, 'Wilt not marry us?'

"I said, 'O no, it cannot was.'

"When they cried, 'O cruel man! this is too much!—O! too much,' I told them that it was on account of the muchness that I declined."

It is hard to define the difference between the humor of one writer and another, or of one nation and another. It can be felt and can be illustrated by quoting examples, but scarcely described in general terms. It has been said of that class of American humorists of which Artemus Ward is a representative that their peculiarity consists in extravagance, surprise, audacity and irreverence. But all these qualities have characterized other schools of humor. There is the same element of surprise in De Quincey's {568} anticlimax, "Many a man has dated his ruin from some murder or other which, perhaps, at the time he thought little of," as in Artemus's truism that "a comic paper ought to publish a joke now and then." The violation of logic which makes us laugh at an Irish bull is likewise the source of the humor in Artemus's saying of Jeff Davis, that "it would have been better than ten dollars in his pocket if he had never been born." Or in his advice, "Always live within your income, even if you have to borrow money to do so;" or, again, in his announcement that, "Mr. Ward will pay no debts of his own contracting." A kind of ludicrous confusion, caused by an unusual collocation of words, is also one of his favorite tricks, as when he says of Brigham Young, "He's the most married man I ever saw in my life;" or when, having been drafted at several hundred different places where he had been exhibiting his wax figures, he says that if he went on he should soon become a regiment, and adds, "I never knew that there was so many of me." With this a whimsical under-statement and an affectation of simplicity, as where he expresses his willingness to sacrifice "even his wife's relations" on the altar of patriotism; or, where, in delightful unconsciousness of his own sins against orthography, he pronounces that "Chaucer was a great poet, but he couldn't spell," or where he says of the feast of raw dog, tendered him by the Indian chief, Wocky-bocky, "It don't agree with me. I prefer simple food." On the {569} whole, it may be said of original humor of this kind, as of other forms of originality in literature, that the elements of it are old, but the combinations are novel. Other humorists, like Henry W. Shaw ("Josh Billings"), and David R. Locke, ("Petroleum V. Nasby"), have used bad spelling as a part of their machinery; while Robert H. Newell, ("Orpheus C. Kerr"), Samuel L. Clemens, ("Mark Twain"), and more recently "Bill Nye," though belonging to the same school of low or broad comedy, have discarded cacography. Of these the most eminent, by all odds, is Mark Twain, who has probably made more people laugh than any other living writer. A Missourian by birth (1835), he served the usual apprenticeship at type-setting and editing country newspapers; spent seven years as a pilot on a Mississippi steam-boat, and seven years more mining and journalizing in Nevada, where he conducted the Virginia City *Enterprise*, finally drifted to San Francisco, and was associated with Bret Harte on the *Californian*, and in 1867 published his first book, the *Jumping Frog*. This was succeeded by the *Innocents Abroad*, 1869; *Roughing It*, 1872; *A Tramp Abroad*, 1880, and by others not so good.

Mark Twain's drolleries have frequently the same air of innocence and surprise as Artemus Ward's, and there is a like suddenness in his turns of expression, as where he speaks of "the calm confidence of a Christian with four aces." If he did not originate, he at any rate employed very {570} effectively that now familiar device of the newspaper "funny man," of putting a painful situation euphemistically, as when he says of a man who was hanged that he "received injuries which terminated in his death." He uses to the full extent the American humorist's favorite resources of exaggeration and irreverence. An instance of the former quality may be seen in his famous description of a dog chasing a coyote, in *Roughing It*, or in his interview with the lightning-rod agent in *Mark Twain's Sketches*, 1875. He is a shrewd observer, and his humor has a more satirical side than Artemus Ward's, sometimes passing into downright denunciation. He delights particularly in ridiculing sentimental humbug and moralizing cant. He runs a tilt, as has been said, at "copy-book texts," at the temperance reformer, the tract distributor, the Good Boy of Sunday-school literature, and the women who send bouquets and sympathetic letters to interesting criminals. He gives a ludicrous turn to famous historical anecdotes, such as the story of George Washington and his little hatchet; burlesques the time-honored adventure, in nautical romances, of the starving crew casting lots in the long boat, and spoils the dignity of antiquity by modern trivialities, saying of a discontented sailor on Columbus's ship, "He wanted fresh shad." The fun of *Innocents Abroad* consists in this irreverent application of modern, common sense, utilitarian, democratic standards to the memorable places and historic associations of {571} Europe. Tried by this test the Old Masters in the picture galleries become laughable. Abelard was a precious scoundrel, and the raptures of the guide books are parodied without mercy. The tourist weeps at the grave of Adam. At Genoa he drives the cicerone to despair by pretending never to have heard of Christopher Columbus, and inquiring innocently, "Is he dead?" It is Europe vulgarized and stripped of its illusions—Europe seen by a Western newspaper reporter without any "historic imagination."

The method of this whole class of humorists is the opposite of Addison's or Irving's or Thackeray's. It does not amuse by the perception of the characteristic. It is not founded upon truth, but upon incongruity, distortion, unexpectedness. Everything in life is reversed, as in opera bouffe, and turned topsy turvy, so that paradox takes the place of the natural order of things. Nevertheless they have supplied a wholesome criticism upon sentimental excesses, and the world is in their debt for many a hearty laugh.

In the *Atlantic Monthly* for December, 1863, appeared a tale entitled the *Man Without a Country*, which made a great sensation, and did much to strengthen patriotic feeling in one of the darkest hours of the nation's history. It was the story of one Philip Nolan, an army officer, whose head had been turned by Aaron Burr, and who, having been censured by a court-martial for some minor offense, exclaimed, petulantly, upon {572} mention being made of the

United States Government, "Damn the United States! I wish that I might never hear the United States mentioned again." Thereupon he was sentenced to have his wish, and was kept all his life aboard the vessels of the navy, being sent off on long voyages and transferred from ship to ship, with orders to those in charge that his country and its concerns should never be spoken of in his presence. Such an air of reality, was given to the narrative by incidental references to actual persons and occurrences that many believed it true, and some were found who remembered Philip Nolan, but had heard different versions of his career. The author of this clever hoax—if hoax it may be called—was Edward Everett Hale, a Unitarian clergyman of Boston, who published a collection of stories in 1868, under the fantastic title, *If, Yes, and Perhaps*, indicating thereby that some of the tales were possible, some of them probable, and others might even be regarded as essentially true. A similar collection, *His Level Best and Other Stories* was published in 1873, and in the interval three volumes of a somewhat different kind, the *Ingham Papers* and *Sybaris and Other Homes*, both in 1869, and *Ten Times One Is Ten*, in 1871. The author shelters himself behind the imaginary figure of Captain Frederic Ingham, pastor of the Sandemanian Church at Naguadavick, and the same characters have a way of re-appearing in his successive volumes as old friends of the reader, which is pleasant at first, but in the end a {573} little tiresome. Mr. Hale is one of the most original and ingenious of American story writers. The old device of making wildly improbable inventions appear like fact by a realistic treatment of details—a device employed by Swift and Edgar Poe, and more lately by Jules Verne—became quite fresh and novel in his hands, and was managed with a humor all his own. Some of his best stories are *My Double and How He Undid Me*, describing how a busy clergyman found an Irishman who looked so much like himself that he trained him to pass as his duplicate, and sent him to do duty in his stead at public meetings, dinners, etc., thereby escaping bores and getting time for real work; the *Brick Moon*, a story of a projectile built and launched into space, to revolve in a fixed meridian about the earth and serve mariners as a mark of longitude; the *Rag Man and Rag Woman*, a tale of an impoverished couple who made a competence by saving the pamphlets, advertisements, wedding cards, etc., that came to them through the mail, and developing a paper business on that basis; and the *Skeleton in the Closet*, which shows how the fate of the Southern Confederacy was involved in the adventures of a certain hoop-skirt, "built in the eclipse and rigged with curses dark." Mr. Hale's historical scholarship and his exact habit of mind have aided him in the art of giving *vraisemblance* to absurdities. He is known in philanthropy as well as in letters, and his tales have a cheerful, busy, {574} practical way with them in consonance with his motto, "Look up and not down, look forward and not back, look out and not in, and lend a hand."

It is too soon to sum up the literary history of the last quarter of a century. The writers who have given it shape are still writing, and their work is therefore incomplete. But on the slightest review of it two facts become manifest: first, that New England has lost its long monopoly; and, secondly, that a marked feature of the period is the growth of realistic fiction. The electric tension of the atmosphere for thirty years preceding the civil war, the storm and stress of great public contests, and the intellectual stir produced by transcendentalism seem to have been more favorable to poetry and literary idealism than present conditions are. At all events there are no new poets who rank with Whittier, Longfellow, Lowell, and others of the elder generation, although George H. Boker, in Philadelphia, R. H. Stoddard and E. C. Stedman, in New York, and T. B. Aldrich, first in New York and afterward in Boston, have written creditable verse; not to speak of younger writers, whose work, however, for the most part, has been more distinguished by delicacy of execution than by native impulse. Mention has been made of the establishment of *Harper's Monthly Magazine*, which, under the conduct of its accomplished editor, George W. Curtis, has provided the public with an abundance of good reading. The {575} old *Putnam's Monthly*, which ran from 1853 to 1858, and had a strong corps of contributors, was revived in 1868, and continued by that name till 1870, when it was succeeded by *Scribner's Monthly*, under the editorship of Dr. J. G. Holland, and this in 1881 by the *Century*, an efficient rival of *Harper's* in circulation, in literary excellence, and in the beauty of its wood engraving, the American school of which art these two great periodicals have done much to develop and encourage. Another New York monthly, the *Galaxy*, ran from 1866 to 1878, and was edited by Richard Grant White. During the present year a new *Scribner's Magazine* has also taken the field. The *Atlantic*, in Boston, and *Lippincott's*, in Philadelphia, are no unworthy competitors with these for public favor.

During the forties began a new era of national expansion, somewhat resembling that described in a former chapter, and, like that, bearing fruit eventually in literature. The cession of Florida to the United States in 1845, and the annexation of Texas in the same year, were followed by the purchase of California in 1847, and its admission as a State in 1850. In 1849 came the great rush to the California gold fields. San Francisco, at first a mere collection of tents and board shanties, with a few adobe huts, grew with incredible rapidity into a great city; the wicked and wonderful city apostrophized by Bret Harte in his poem, *San Francisco*:

{576}

"Serene, indifferent of Fate,
Thou sittest at the Western Gate;

Upon thy heights so lately won
Still slant the banners of the sun....
I know thy cunning and thy greed,
Thy hard, high lust and willful deed."

The adventurers of all lands and races who flocked to the Pacific coast found there a motley state of society between civilization and savagery. There were the relics of the old Mexican occupation, the Spanish missions, with their Christianized Indians; the wild tribes of the plains—Apaches, Utes, and Navajoes; the Chinese coolies and washermen, all elements strange to the Atlantic seaboard and the States of the interior. The gold-hunters crossed, in stages or caravans, enormous prairies, alkaline deserts dotted with sage brush and seamed by deep cañons, and passes through gigantic mountain ranges. On the coast itself nature was unfamiliar: the climate was sub-tropical; fruits and vegetables grew to a mammoth size, corresponding to the enormous redwoods in the Mariposa groves and the prodigious scale of the scenery in the valley of the Yo Semite and the snow-capped peaks of the Sierras. At first there were few women, and the men led a wild, lawless existence in the mining camps. Hard upon the heels of the prospector followed the dram-shop, the gambling-hell, and the dance-hall. Every man carried his "Colt," and looked out for his own life and his "claim." Crime went unpunished or was taken in hand, {577} when it got too rampant, by vigilance committees. In the diggings, shaggy frontiersmen and "pikes" from Missouri mingled with the scum of eastern cities and with broken-down business men and young college graduates seeking their fortune. Surveyors and geologists came of necessity, speculators in mining stock and city lots set up their offices in the towns; later came a sprinkling of school-teachers and ministers. Fortunes were made in one day and lost the next at poker or loo. To-day the lucky miner who had struck a good "lead" was drinking champagne out of pails and treating the town; to-morrow he was "busted," and shouldered the pick for a new onslaught upon his luck. This strange, reckless life, was not without fascination, and highly picturesque and dramatic elements were present in it. It was, as Bret Harte says, "an era replete with a certain heroic Greek poetry," and sooner or later it was sure to find its poet. During the war California remained loyal to the Union, but was too far from the seat of conflict to experience any serious disturbance, and went on independently developing its own resources and becoming daily more civilized. By 1868 San Francisco had a literary magazine, the *Overland Monthly*, which ran until 1875. It had a decided local flavor, and the vignette on its title-page was a happily chosen emblem, representing a grizzly bear crossing a railway track. In an early number of the *Overland* was a story entitled the *Luck of Roaring Camp*, by Francis Bret Harte, a {578} native of Albany, N. Y., 1835, who had come to California at the age of seventeen, in time to catch the unique aspects of the life of the Forty-niners, before their vagabond communities had settled down into the law-abiding society of the present day. His first contribution was followed by other stories and sketches of a similar kind, such as the *Outcasts of Poker Flat*, *Miggles*, and *Tennessee's Partner*, and by verses, serious and humorous, of which last, *Plain Language from Truthful James*, better known as the *Heathen Chinee*, made an immediate hit, and carried its author's name into every corner of the English-speaking world. In 1871 he published a collection of his tales, another of his poems, and a volume of very clever parodies, *Condensed Novels*, which rank with Thackeray's *Novels by Eminent Hands*. Bret Harte's California stories were vivid, highly-colored pictures of life in the mining camps and raw towns of the Pacific coast. The pathetic and the grotesque went hand in hand in them, and the author aimed to show how even in the desperate characters gathered together there—the fortune hunters, gamblers, thieves, murderers, drunkards, and prostitutes—the latent nobility of human nature asserted itself in acts of heroism, magnanimity, self-sacrifice, and touching fidelity. The same men who cheated at cards and shot each another down with tipsy curses were capable on occasion of the most romantic generosity and the most delicate chivalry. Critics were not wanting who held that, in the matter of dialect {579} and manners and other details, the narrator was not true to the facts. This was a comparatively unimportant charge; but a more serious question was the doubt whether his characters were essentially true to human nature, whether the wild soil of revenge and greed and dissolute living ever yields such flowers of devotion as blossom in *Tennessee's Partner* and the *Outcasts of Poker Flat*. However this may be, there is no question as to Harte's power as a narrator. His short stories are skillfully constructed and effectively told. They never drag, and are never overladen with description, reflection, or other lumber.

In his poems in dialect we find the same variety of types and nationalities characteristic of the Pacific coast: the little Mexican maiden, Pachita, in the old mission garden; the wicked Bill Nye, who tries to cheat the Heathen Chinee at euchre and to rob Injin Dick of his winning lottery ticket; the geological society on the Stanislaw who settle their scientific debates with chunks of old red sandstone and the skulls of mammoths; the unlucky Mr. Dow, who finally strikes gold while digging a well, and builds a house with a "coopilow;" and Flynn, of Virginia, who saves his "pard's" life, at the sacrifice of his own, by holding up the timbers in the caving tunnel. These poems are mostly in monologue, like Browning's dramatic lyrics, exclamatory and abrupt in style, and with a good deal of indicated action, as in *Jim*, where a miner comes into a bar-room, looking for his old {580} chum, learns that he is dead, and is just turning away to hide his emotion, when he recognizes Jim in his informant:

> "Well, thar—Good-by—
> No more, sir—I—
>   Eh?
> What's that you say?—
> Why, dern it!—sho!—
> No? Yes! By Jo!
>   Sold!
> Sold! Why, you limb;
> You ornery,
>   Derned old
> Long-legged Jim!"

Bret Harte had many imitators, and not only did our newspaper poetry for a number of years abound in the properties of Californian life, such as gulches, placers, divides, etc., but writers further east applied his method to other conditions. Of these by far the most successful was John Hay, a native of Indiana and private secretary to President Lincoln, whose *Little Breeches*, *Jim Bludso*, and *Mystery of Gilgal* have rivaled Bret Harte's own verses in popularity. In the last-named piece the reader is given to feel that there is something rather cheerful and humorous in a bar-room fight which results in "the gals that winter, as a rule," going "alone to the singing school." In the two former we have heroes of the Bret Harte type, the same combination of superficial wickedness with inherent loyalty and tenderness. The profane farmer {581} of the South-west, who "doesn't pan out on the prophets," and who had taught his little son "to chaw terbacker, just to keep his milk-teeth white," but who believes in God and the angels ever since the miraculous recovery of the same little son when lost on the prairie in a blizzard; and the unsaintly and bigamistic captain of the *Prairie Belle*, who died like a hero, holding the nozzle of his burning boat against the bank

"Till the last galoot's ashore."

The manners and dialect of other classes and sections of the country have received abundant illustration of late years. Edward Eggleston's *Hoosier Schoolmaster*, 1871, and his other novels are pictures of rural life in the early days of Indiana. *Western Windows*, a volume of poems by John James Piatt, another native of Indiana, had an unmistakable local coloring. Charles G. Leland, of Philadelphia, in his *Hans Breitmann* ballads, in dialect, gave a humorous presentation of the German-American element in the cities. By the death, in 1881, of Sidney Lanier, a Georgian by birth, the South lost a poet of rare promise, whose original genius was somewhat hampered by his hesitation between two arts of expression, music and verse, and by his effort to co-ordinate them. His *Science of English Verse*, 1880, was a most suggestive, though hardly convincing, statement of that theory of their relation which he was working out in his practice. Some of his pieces, {582} like the *Mocking Bird* and the *Song of the Chattahoochie*, are the most characteristically Southern poetry that has been written in America. Joel Chandler Harris's *Uncle Remus* stories, in Negro dialect, are transcripts from the folk-lore of the plantations, while his collection of stories, *At Teague Poteet's*, together with Miss Murfree's *In the Tennessee Mountains* and her other books have made the Northern public familiar with the wild life of the "moonshiners," who distill illicit whiskey in the mountains of Georgia, North Carolina, and Tennessee. These tales are not only exciting in incident, but strong and fresh in their delineations of character. Their descriptions of mountain scenery are also impressive, though, in the case of the last named writer, frequently too prolonged. George W. Cable's sketches of French Creole life in New Orleans attracted attention by their freshness and quaintness when published in the magazines and re-issued in book form as *Old Creole Days*, in 1879. His first regular novel, the *Grandissimes*, 1880, was likewise a story of Creole life. It had the same winning qualities as his short stories and sketches, but was an advance upon them in dramatic force, especially in the intensely tragic and powerfully told episode of "Bras Coupe." Mr. Cable has continued his studies of Louisiana types and ways in his later books, but the *Grandissimes* still remains his master-piece. All in all, he is, thus far, the most important literary figure of the New South, and the justness and {583} delicacy of his representations of life speak volumes for the sobering and refining agency of the civil war in the States whose "cause" was "lost," but whose true interests gained even more by the loss than did the interests of the victorious North.

The four writers last mentioned have all come to the front within the past eight or ten years, and, in accordance with the plan of this sketch, receive here a mere passing notice. It remains to close our review of the literary history of the period since the war with a somewhat more extended account of the two favorite novelists whose work has done more than any thing else to shape the movement of recent fiction. These are Henry James, Jr., and William Dean Howells. Their writings, though dissimilar in some respects, are alike in this, that they are analytic in method and realistic in spirit. Cooper was a romancer pure and simple; he wrote the romance of adventure and of external incident. Hawthorne went much deeper, and with a finer spiritual insight dealt with the real passions of the heart and with men's inner experiences. This he did with truth and power; but, although himself a keen observer of whatever passed before his eyes, he was not careful to secure a photographic fidelity to the surface facts of speech, dress, manners, etc. Thus the talk of his characters is book talk, and not the actual language of the parlor or the street, with its slang, its colloquial ease and the intonations and shadings of phrase {584} and pronunciation which mark different sections of the country and different grades of society. His attempts at dialect, for example, were of the slenderest kind. His art is ideal, and his romances certainly do not rank as novels of real life. But with the growth of a richer and more complicated society in America fiction has grown more social and more minute in its observation. It would not be fair to classify the novels of James and Howells as the fiction of manners merely; they are also the fiction of character, but they aim to describe people not only as they are, in their inmost natures, but also as they look and talk and dress. They try to express character through manners, which is the way in which it is most often expressed in the daily existence of a conventional society. It is a principle of realism not to select exceptional persons or occurrences, but to take average men and women and their average experiences. The realists protest that the moving incident is not their trade, and that the stories have all been told. They want no plot and no hero. They will tell no rounded tale with a *dénouement*, in which all the parts are distributed, as in the fifth act of an old-fashioned comedy; but they will take a transcript from life and end when they get through, without informing the reader what becomes of the characters. And they will try to interest this reader in "poor real life" with its "foolish face." Their acknowledged masters are Balzac, George Eliot, Turgénieff, and Anthony {585} Trollope, and they regard novels as studies in sociology, honest reports of the writer's impressions, which may not be without a certain scientific value even.

Mr. James's peculiar province is the international novel; a field which he created for himself, but which he has occupied in company with Howells, Mrs. Burnett, and many others. He was born into the best traditions of New England culture, his father being a resident of Cambridge, and a forcible writer on philosophical subjects, and his brother, William James, a professor in Harvard University. The novelist received most of his schooling in Europe, and has lived much abroad, with the result that he has become half denationalized and has engrafted a cosmopolitan indifference upon his Yankee inheritance. This, indeed, has constituted his opportunity. A close observer and a conscientious student of the literary art, he has added to his intellectual equipment the advantage of a curious doubleness in his point of view. He looks at America with the eyes of a foreigner and at Europe with the eyes of an American. He has so far thrown himself out of relation with American life that he describes a Boston horsecar or a New York hotel table with a sort of amused wonder. His starting-point was in criticism, and he has always maintained the critical attitude. He took up story-writing in order to help himself, by practical experiment, in his chosen art of literary criticism, and his volume on {586} *French Poets and Novelists*, 1878, is by no means the least valuable of his books. His short stories in the magazines were collected into a volume in 1875, with the title, *A Passionate Pilgrim and Other Stories*. One or two of these, as the *Last of the Valerii* and the *Madonna of the Future*, suggest Hawthorne, a very unsympathetic study of whom James afterward contributed to the "English Men of Letters" series. But in the name-story of the collection he was already in the line of his future development. This is the story of a middle-aged invalid American, who comes to England in search of health, and finds, too late, in the mellow atmosphere of the mother country, the repose and the congenial surroundings which he has all his life been longing for in his raw America. The pathos of his self-analysis and his confession of failure is subtly imagined. The impressions which he and his far-away English kinsfolk make on one another, their mutual attraction and repulsion, are described with that delicate perception of national differences which makes the humor and sometimes the tragedy of James's later books, like the *American, Daisy Miller*, the *Europeans*, and *An International Episode*. His first novel was *Roderick Hudson*, 1876, not the most characteristic of his fictions, but perhaps the most powerful in its grasp of elementary passion. The analytic method and the critical attitude have their dangers in imaginative literature. In proportion as this writer's faculty of minute observation and his realistic objectivity {587} have increased upon him, the uncomfortable coldness which is felt in his youthful work has become actually disagreeable, and his art—growing constantly finer and surer in matters of detail—has seemed to dwell more and more in the region of mere manners and less in the higher realm of character and passion. In most of his writings the heart, somehow, is left out. We have seen that Irving, from his knowledge of England and America, and his long residence in both countries, became the mediator between the two great branches of the Anglo-Saxon race. This he did by the power of his sympathy with each. Henry James has likewise interpreted the two nations to one another in a subtler but less genial fashion than Irving, and not through sympathy, but through contrast, by bringing into relief the opposing ideals of life and society which have developed under different institutions. In his novel, the *American*, 1877, he has shown the actual misery which may result from the clashing of opposed social systems. In such clever sketches as *Daisy Miller*, 1879, the *Pension Beaurepas*, and *A Bundle of Letters*, he has exhibited types of the American girl, the American business man, the aesthetic feebling from Boston, and the Europeanized or would-be denationalized American campaigners in the Old World, and has set forth the ludicrous incongruities, perplexities, and misunderstandings which result from contradictory standards of conventional morality and behavior. In the *Europeans*, 1879, and an {588} *International Episode*, 1878, he has reversed the process, bringing Old Word [Transcriber's note: World?] standards to the test of American ideas by transferring his *dramatis personae* to republican soil. The last-named of these illustrates how slender a plot realism requires for its purposes. It is nothing more than the history of an English girl of good family who marries an American gentleman and undertakes to live in America, but finds herself so uncomfortable in strange social conditions that she returns to England for life, while, contrariwise, the heroine's sister is so taken with the freedom of these very conditions that she elopes with another American and "goes West." James is a keen observer of the physiognomy of cities as well as of men, and his *Portraits of Places*, 1884, is among the most delightful contributions to the literature of foreign travel.

Mr. Howells's writings are not without "international" touches. In *A Foregone Conclusion* and the *Lady of the Aroostook*, and others of his novels, the contrasted points of view in American and European life are introduced, and especially those variations in feeling, custom, dialect, etc., which make the modern Englishman and the modern American such objects of curiosity to each other, and which have been dwelt upon of late even unto satiety. But in general he finds his subjects at home, and if he does not know his own countrymen and countrywomen more intimately than Mr. James, at least {589} he loves them better. There is a warmer sentiment in his fictions, too; his men are better fellows and his women are more lovable. Howells was born in Ohio. His early life was that of a western country editor. In 1860 he published, jointly with his friend Piatt, a book of verse—*Poems of Two Friends*. In 1861 he was sent as consul to Venice, and the literary results of his sojourn there appeared in his sketches *Venetian Life*, 1865, and *Italian Journeys*, 1867. In 1871 he became editor of the *Atlantic Monthly*, and in the same year published his *Suburban Sketches*. All of these early volumes showed a quick eye for the picturesque, an unusual power of description, and humor of the most delicate quality; but as yet there was little approach to narrative. *Their Wedding Journey* was a revelation to the public of the interest that may lie in an ordinary bridal trip across the State of New York, when a close and sympathetic observation is brought to bear upon the characteristics of American life as it appears at railway stations and hotels, on steam-boats and in the streets of very commonplace towns. *A Chance Acquaintance*, 1873, was Howells's first novel, though even yet the story was set against a background of travel—pictures, a holiday trip on the St. Lawrence and the Saguenay; and descriptions of Quebec and the Falls of Montmorenci, etc., rather predominated over the narrative. Thus, gradually and by a natural process, complete characters and realistic novels, such as *A Modern {590} Instance*, 1882, and *Indian Summer*, evolved themselves from truthful sketches of places and persons seen by the way.

The incompatibility existing between European and American views of life, which makes the comedy or the tragedy of Henry James's international fictions, is replaced in Howells's novels by the repulsion between differing social grades in the same country. The adjustment of these subtle distinctions forms a part of the problem of life in all complicated societies. Thus in *A Chance Acquaintance* the heroine is a bright and pretty Western girl, who becomes engaged during a pleasure tour to an irreproachable but offensively priggish young gentleman from Boston, and the engagement is broken by her in consequence of an unintended slight—the betrayal on the hero's part of a shade of mortification when he and his betrothed are suddenly brought into the presence of some fashionable ladies belonging to his own *monde*. The little comedy, *Out of the Question*, deals with this same adjustment of social scales; and in many of Howells's other novels, such as *Silas Lapham* and the *Lady of the Aroostook*, one of the main motives may be described to be the contact of the man who eats with his fork with the man who eats with his knife, and the shock thereby ensuing. In *Indian Summer* the complications arise from the difference in age between the hero and heroine, and not from a difference in station or social antecedents. In all of these fictions the {591} misunderstandings come from an incompatibility of manner rather than of character, and, if any thing were to be objected to the probability of the story, it is that the climax hinges on delicacies and subtleties which, in real life, when there is opportunity for explanations, are readily brushed aside. But in *A Modern Instance* Howells touched the deeper springs of action. In this, his strongest work, the catastrophe is brought about, as in George Eliot's great novels, by the reaction of characters upon one another, and the story is realistic in a higher sense than any mere study of manners can be. His nearest approach to romance is in the *Undiscovered Country*, 1880, which deals with the Spiritualists and the Shakers, and in its study of problems that hover on the borders of the supernatural, in its out-of-the-way personages and adventures, and in a certain ideal poetic flavor about the whole book, has a strong resemblance to Hawthorne, especially to Hawthorne in the *Blithedale Romance*, where he comes closer to common ground with other romancers. It is interesting to compare *Undiscovered Country* with Henry James's *Bostonians*, the latest and one of the cleverest of his fictions, which is likewise a study of the clairvoyants, mediums, woman's rights' advocates, and all varieties of cranks, reformers, and patrons of "causes," for whom Boston has long been notorious. A most unlovely race of people they become under the cold scrutiny of Mr. James's cosmopolitan eyes, which see more clearly the {592} charlatanism, narrow-mindedness, mistaken fanaticism, morbid self-consciousness, disagreeable nervous intensity, and vulgar or ridiculous outside peculiarities of the humanitarians, than the nobility and moral enthusiasm which underlie the surface.

Howells is almost the only successful American dramatist, and this in the field of parlor comedy. His little farces, the *Elevator*, the *Register*, the *Parlor Car*, etc., have a lightness and grace, with an exquisitely absurd situation, which remind us more of the *Comedies et Proverbes* of Alfred de Musset, or the many agreeable dialogues and monologues of the French domestic stage, than of any work of English or American hands. His softly ironical yet affectionate treatment of feminine ways is especially admirable. In his numerous types of sweetly illogical, inconsistent, and inconsequent womanhood he has perpetuated with a nicer art than Dickens what Thackeray calls "that great discovery," Mrs. Nickleby.

1. Theodore Winthrop. Life in the Open Air. Cecil Dreeme.

2. Thomas Wentworth Higginson. Life in a Black Regiment.

3. Poetry of the Civil War. Edited by Richard Grant White. New York: 1866.

4. Charles Farrar Browne. Artemus Ward—His Book. Lecture on the Mormons. Artemus Ward in London.

{593}

5. Samuel Langhorne Clemens. The Jumping Frog. Roughing It. The Mississippi Pilot.

6. Charles Godfrey Leland. Hans Breitmann's Ballads.

7. Edward Everett Hale. If, Yes, and Perhaps. His Level Best and Other Stories.

8. Francis Bret Harte. Outcasts of Poker Flat and Other Stories. Condensed Novels. Poems in Dialect.

9. Sidney Lanier. Nirvana. Resurrection. The Harlequin of Dreams. Song of the Chattahoochie. The Mocking Bird. The Stirrup-Cup. Tampa Robins. The Bee. The Revenge of Hamish. The Ship of Earth. The Marshes of Glynn. Sunrise.

10. Henry James, Jr. A Passionate Pilgrim. Roderick Hudson. Daisy Miller. Pension Beaurepas. A Bundle of Letters. An International Episode. The Bostonians. Portraits of Places.

11. William Dean Howells. Their Wedding Journey. Suburban Sketches. A Chance Acquaintance. A Foregone Conclusion. The Undiscovered Country. A Modern Instance.

12. George W. Cable. Old Creole Days. Madam Delphine. The Grandissimes.

13. Joel Chandler Harris. Uncle Remus. Mingo and Other Sketches.

14. Charles Egbert Craddock (Miss Murfree). In the Tennessee Mountains.

{594}